# The Gambler
## A Novel

*by*

Katherine Cecil Thurston

# The Gambler
## A Novel
### by Katherine Cecil Thurston

Copyright © 2024

All Rights reserved.

ISBN: 978-93-61156-29-8

Published by

# DOUBLE 9 BOOKS

2/13-B, Ansari Road
Daryaganj, New Delhi – 110002
info@double9books.com
www.double9books.com
Tel. 011-40042856

This book is under public domain

# ABOUT THE AUTHOR

Katherine Cecil Thurston (née Kathleen Annie Josephine Madden) was an Irish novelist best known for two political thrillers. Kathleen Annie Josephine Madden was born at 14 Bridge Street in Cork, Ireland, the only daughter of banker Paul J. Madden (mayor of Cork from 1885 to 1886 and a friend of Charles Stuart Parnell) and Eliza Madden. She received her education privately at her family's home, Wood's Gift on Blackrock Road. By the end of the nineteenth century, she was writing short stories for several British and American journals, including Pall Mall Magazine, Blackwood's Edinburgh Magazine, Harper's Magazine, Windsor Magazine, and others. On February 16, 1901, five weeks following her father's death, she married novelist Ernest Temple Thurston (1879-1933). They separated in 1907 and divorced in 1910 because of his adultery and desertion. The lawsuit went undefended. Thurston, on the other hand, "complained that she was making more money by her books than he was, that her personality dominated his, and had said that he wanted to leave her." Katherine Thurston's novels were successful in both Britain and the United States. Her best-known work was a political thriller titled John Chilcote, M.P. (also known as The Masquerader in the United States), which was released in 1904 and remained on the New York Times bestseller list for two years, placing third in 1904 and seventh in 1905.

# CONTENTS

# PART I

# CHAPTER I

An eight-mile drive over rain-washed Irish roads in the quick-falling dusk of autumn is an experience trying to the patience, even to the temper, of the average Saxon. Yet James Milbanke made neither comment nor objection as mile after mile of roadway spun away like a ribbon behind him, as the mud rose in showers from the wheels of the old-fashioned trap in which he sat, and the half-trained mare between the shafts swerved now to the right, now to the left—her nervous glance caught by the spectral shapes of the blackthorn hedges or the motionless forms of the wayside donkeys, lying asleep in the ditches. Perhaps this stoicism was the outcome of an innate power to endure; perhaps it was a merely negative quality, illustrating the lack of that doubtful blessing, imagination. But whatever its origin, it stood him in good stead as he covered the long stretch of flat country that links the south-eastern seaport of Muskeere with the remote fishing village of Carrigmore and its outlying district of Orristown.

His outlook upon Ireland, like his outlook upon life, was untinged by humour. He had seen no ground for amusement in the fact that he had been the only passenger to alight from the train at the Muskeere terminus, and consequently no ground for loneliness in the sight of the solitary vehicle, dimly silhouetted against the murky sky, that had awaited his coming. The ludicrous points of the scene: the primitive railway station with its insufficient flickering lights, its little knot of inquisitive idlers, its one porter—slovenly, amiable, incorrigibly lazy—all contributing the unconscious background to his own neat, conventional, totally alien personality, had left him untouched.

The only individual to whom the picture had made its appeal had been the solitary porter. As he relieved Milbanke of his valise and rug on the step of the first-class carriage, an undeniable twinkle had gleamed in his eyes.

"Fine, soft night, sir," he had volunteered. "Tim Burke is outside for you."

For a second Milbanke had stared at him in a mixture of doubt and displeasure. A month's pilgrimage to the ancient Celtic landmarks had left him, as it has left many a Saxon before him, unlearned in that most interesting and most inscrutable of all survivals—the Celt himself. He had surveyed the face of the porter cautiously and half distrustfully; then he had made a guarded reply.

"I am certainly expecting a—a conveyance," he had admitted. "But I have never heard of Tim Burke."

"Why, thin Tim has heard of *you!*" the other had replied with unruffled suavity. "Isn't it the English gintlemen that's goin' to stop wid Mr. Asshlin over at Orristown that you are? Sure, Tim told me all about you; an' I knew you the minute I sat eyes on you—let alone there was no wan else in the train."

Without more ado he had hoisted Milbanke's belongings to his shoulder, and lounged out of the station.

"Here you are, Tim, man!" he had exclaimed as he deposited the articles one after another under the seat of the trap with a lofty disregard of their owner. "'Tis a soft night an' a long road you have before you! Is it cold the mare is?" He had paused to eye the impatient young animal before him, with the Irishman's unfailing appreciation of horse-flesh.

Here Milbanke, feeling that some veiled reproof had been suggested, had broken in upon the monologue.

"I hope I haven't injured the horse by the delay," he had said hastily. "The train was exactly twenty-two minutes behind its time."

Then for the first time the old coachman had bent down from his lofty position.

"An', sure, what harm if it was, sir?" he had exclaimed, voicing the hospitality due to his master's guest. "What hurry is there at all—so long as it brought you safe?"

"True for you, Tim!" the porter had interjected softly; and seizing Milbanke's arm, he had swung him into the trap, precisely as he had swung the luggage a few seconds previously.

"Thank you, sir!" he had murmured a moment later. "Good-night to you! Good-night, Tim! Safe road!" And, drawing back, he had looked on with admiration while Burke had gathered up the reins and the mare had plunged forward into the misty, sea-scented night.

That had been Milbanke's first introduction into the district where he proposed to spend a week with a man he had not seen for nearly thirty years.

As the trap moved forward, leaving the straggling town with its scattered lights far behind, his thoughts—temporarily distracted by the incidents of his arrival—reverted to the channel in which they had run during the greater part of the day. Again his mind returned to the period of his college career when, as a quiet student, he had been drawn by the subtle attraction of contrast into a friendship with Denis Asshlin—the young Irishman whose spirit, whose enthusiasms, whose exuberant joy in life had shone in such vivid colours beside his own neutral-tinted personality. His thoughts passed methodically from those eager, early days to the more sober ones that had followed Asshlin's recall to Ireland, and thence onward over the succeeding tale of years. He reviewed his own calm, if somewhat lonely, manhood; his aimless delving first into one branch of learning, then into another; his gradually dawning interest in the study of archaeology—an interest that, fostered by ample leisure and ample means, had become the temperate and well-ordered passion of his life. The retrospect was pleasant. There is always an agreeable sensation to a man of Milbanke's temperament in looking back upon unruffled times. He became oblivious of the ruts in the road and of the mare's erratic movements as he traced the course of events to the point where, two months before, the discovery of a dozen gold platters and as many drinking vessels, embedded in a bog in the County Tyrone, had turned the eyes of the archæological world upon Ireland; and he, with other students of antiquity, had been bitten with the desire to see the unique and priceless objects for himself.

The journey to Tyrone had been a pleasant experience; and it was there, under the mild exaltation of the genuine find, that it had suddenly been suggested to his mind that certain ancient ruins, including a remarkable specimen of the Irish round tower, were to be found on the south-east coast not three miles from the property of his old college friend.

Whether it was the archaeological instinct to resurrect the past, or the merely human wish to re-live his own small portion of it, that had prompted him to write to Asshlin must remain an open question. It is sufficient that the letter was written and dispatched and that the answer came in hot haste.

It had reached him in the form of a telegram running as follows: "Come at once, and stay for a year. Stagnating to death in this isolation. Asshlin." An hour later another, and a more voluminous message, had followed, in which—as if by an after-thought—he had been given the necessary directions as to the means of reaching Orristown.

It was at the point where his musings reached Asshlin's telegrams that he awakened from his reverie and looked about him. For the first time a personal interest in the country through which he was passing stirred him.

He realised that the salt sting of the sea had again begun to mingle with the night mist, and judged thereby that the road had again emerged upon the coast. He noticed that the hedges had become sparser; that wherever a tree loomed out of the dusk it bore the mark of the sea gales in a certain grotesqueness of shape.

This was the isolation of which Asshlin had spoken!

With an impulse extremely uncommon to him, he turned in his seat and addressed the silent old coachman beside him.

"Has your master altered much in thirty years?" he asked.

There was silence for a while. Old Burke, with the deliberation of his class, liked to weigh his words before giving them utterance.

"Is it Mister Dinis changed?" he repeated at last. Then almost immediately he corrected himself. "Sure, 'tis Mister Asshlin I ought to be sayin', sir. But the ould name slips out. Though the poor master is gone these twenty-nine year—the Lord have mercy on him!—I can niver git it into me head that 'tis to Mister Dinis we ought to be lookin'."

More than once during his brief stay in Ireland, Milbanke had been confronted with this annihilation of time in the Irish mind, and Burke's statement aroused no surprise.

"Has he changed?" he asked again in his dry, precise voice.

Burke was silent while the mare pulled hard on the reins. And having regained his mastery over her, he looked down on his companion.

"Is it changed?" he said. "Sure, why wouldn't he be changed? With the father gone—an' the wife gone—an' the children growin' up. Sure 'tis changed we all are, an' goin' down the hill fast—God help us!"

Milbanke glanced up sharply.

"Children?" he said. "Children?"

Burke turned in his seat.

"Sure 'tisn't to have the ould stock die out you'd be wantin'?" he said. "You'd travel the round of the county before you'd see the like of Mister Dinis's children—though 'tis girls they are."

"Girls?" Milbanke's mind was disturbed by the thought of children. Denis Asshlin with children! The idea was incongruous.

"Two of 'em!" said Burke laconically.

"Dear me!—dear me! And yet I suppose it's only natural. How old are they?"

Burke flicked the mare lightly, and the trap lurched forward.

"Miss Clodagh is turned fifteen," he said, "and the youngster is goin' on ten. 'Twas ten year back, come next December, that she was born. Sure I remember it well. An' six weeks after, Mister Dinis was followin' her poor mother to the churchyard beyant in Carrigmore. The Lord keep us all! 'Twas she was the nice, quiet creature, and Miss Nance is the livin' stamp of her. But God bless us, 'tis Miss Clodagh that's her father's child." He added this last remark with a force that at the time conveyed nothing, though it was destined to recur later to Milbanke's mind.

"But your master?" the stranger repeated. The momentary diversion of the children had ceased to hold him. Again the vision of Asshlin—Asshlin the impetuous hero of past days—had risen intangible, mirage-like and yet compelling from his native stretch of rugged country.

But Burke made no reply. All his energies were directed to the guiding of the mare down a steep incline. For a space Milbanke was conscious of a dangerously accelerated pace; then the white piers of a large gate sped past them, and he was aware of the black shadow of overhanging trees.

Something unusual, something faintly prophetic and only vaguely comprehended, touched his prosaic nature at that moment. He was entering on a new phase of life. Without conscious preparation he was to see the world from a new point of view. With a fresh spur of anxious curiosity, he turned again to Burke.

"But your master?" he asked. "Has he changed much? Will I see a great alteration?"

For an added space the old man remained mute, while he piloted the trap up the sweep of avenue, with that irresistible desire for a fine finish that animates every Irish driver. Then, as they spun round the final curve, as the great square house loomed out of the mist, he replied without slackening his vigilance.

"Is it changed?" he repeated half to himself. "Sure, if the Almighty doesn't change a man in thirty year, it stands to rason that the divil must."

# CHAPTER II

To English ears the reply was curious. Yet with all its vagueness, all its racial inclination towards high colour, it held the germ of truth that frequently lies in such utterances. With native acuteness it threw out a suggestion, without betraying a confidence.

An instant after it was spoken, there was a final flourish of the whip, a scrape of wheels on the wet gravel, a straining and creaking of damp leather, and the trap drew up before the big white house. Milbanke caught a fleeting suggestion of a shabby door with pillars on which rested a square balcony of rusty iron, a number of unlighted windows, a general air of grandeur and decay curiously blended. Then the hall door opened, and a voice, whose first note roused a hundred memories, rolled out across the darkness.

"Is that you, James? Come in!—come in! Keep the mare in hand, Burke. Steady, now, James! Let me hold the rug and give you a hand down. She's a little rogue, and might be making a bolt for her stable. Well, you're as welcome as the flowers in May! Come in!—come in!"

It was over in a flash—the arrival, the tempestuous greeting, the hard grip of Asshlin's hand; and the two men were facing each other in the candle-lit hall.

"Well, you're welcome, James!" Asshlin repeated. "You're welcome! Let me have a look at you. I declare it's younger you are!"

He laid his hand heavily on the other's shoulder, and uttered this obvious untruth with all the warmth and conviction that Irish imagination and Irish hospitality could suggest.

"But you're perished after the long drive! Burke!" he called through the open door. "Burke, when you're done with the mare come round and carry up Mr. Milbanke's baggage. Now, James!" He wheeled round again, catching up a silver candlestick from the hall table. "Now, if you come upstairs, I'll show you where we're going to billet you."

With long, hasty steps he crossed the hall, his tall figure casting gaunt shadows on the bare and lofty wall.

"We're a trifle unsophisticated here," he went on with a loud, hard laugh. "But at least we'll give you enough to eat and a bed to lie on. After all, a decent dinner and a warm welcome are the bone and sinew of hospitality the world over. Unless they include a drop of something to put life into a man——"

He paused, turning round upon his guest.

"By Jupiter, that reminds me! Have a small drink before we go another step, just to take the cold out of you?"

Milbanke, who was close behind him, glanced up. He saw his host's face more clearly than he had seen it in the hall. His answer when it came was hurried and a little confused.

"No, Denis. No," he said. "Nothing; nothing, I assure you."

Asshlin laughed again.

"Still the same stickler?" he said. "How virtues cling to a man!"

He turned and began to mount the stairs. Then, reaching the first door on the wide corridor, he paused.

"Here's your habitation," he said. "Burke will bring up your belongings and get you whatever you want. We dine in a quarter of an hour."

He nodded; and was turning away, when a fresh thought struck him.

"You may as well take this candle," he said; "we haven't arrived at the civilisation of gas. You might stumble over something, looking for the matches. This is practically a bachelor establishment, you know—without any bachelor comforts."

Once more he laughed; and, thrusting the candle into his guest's hand, hurried away across the landing.

In silence Milbanke took the candle and, holding it uncertainly, waited until his host had disappeared. Then slowly he turned and entered the large, bare bedroom. For a moment he hesitated, his eyes wandering from the faded window-hangings to the stiff, old-fashioned furniture. Finally, laying aside the candlestick, he sat down upon the side of the forbidding-looking four-post bedstead.

What motive prompted him to the action he could scarcely have defined. He was strangely moved by the scene just gone through—stirred in a manner he could never have anticipated. For the moment the precise, matter-of-fact archaeologist was submerged; and the man—dry, narrow, pedantic perhaps, but nevertheless capable of human sentiments—was uppermost. The sight of Asshlin, the sound of his voice, and the touch of his hand had possessed an alchemy all their own. The past, that years of separation had dimmed and tarnished, had gleamed out from the shadows and taken shape before his eyes. The influence, the fascination that Asshlin had once exercised, had touched him again at the first contact of personalities. But it was an altered fascination. The alloy of doubt and apprehension had tainted the old feeling. The question he had been prompted to ask Burke had answered itself at the first glimpse of his host's face. Indisputably, unmistakably, Asshlin had changed.

And in what lay that change? That was the question he put to himself as he sat on the bed, unconsciously noting the long, wavering flicker of the candle-flame against the faded wall-paper. He had aged; but the change did not lie with age alone. Something more relentless and more corroding than time had drawn the worn, discontented lines about the mouth, kindled the unnatural, restless glitter in the eyes, and changed the note of the voice from spontaneous vitality to recklessness. The change lay deeper; it lay in the heart and the soul of the man himself.

With a sensation of doubt—of puzzled doubt and inexplicable disappointment—he rose, crossed the room, and, drawing the curtains over the windows, shut out the dark, damp night.

# CHAPTER III

It was nearly three-quarters of an hour later that a tremendous bell, clanging through the house, announced that dinner had been served.

A wash, a change of clothes, and a half-hour of solitude had done much for Milbanke. He felt more normal, less alienated by unfamiliar surroundings than he had done in the first confused moments that had followed his arrival. The vague sense of disappointment and apprehension, the vague suspicion that Asshlin had undergone an immense alteration still tormented him— as half-apprehended evils ever torment the minds of those who see and study life as a thing apart from human nature; but the immediate effect of the feeling was less poignant. He unconsciously found himself anticipating the next glimpse of his old friend with a touch of curiosity; and when the announcement of dinner broke in upon his meditations, he was surprised at the readiness with which he obeyed the summons.

His first sight of the dining-room came pleasantly to his senses, numbed by the long drive and the bare coldness of his bedroom. It was large and lofty: three long curtained windows occupied one of its walls, while from the others numerous pictures of the dead-and-gone Asshlins looked out of their canvases from tarnished gold frames; the mahogany furniture, though of an ugly and ungainly type, was massive; and over the whole room, softening its severity and hiding the ravages of time, lay the warm red glow of a huge peat fire and the radiance of a dozen candles set in heavy silver sconces.

He stood for a moment in the doorway, agreeably conscious of the mingled shadow and light; then his attention was attracted to two figures already occupying the room.

Asshlin himself was standing by the hearth, his back to the fire, his feet apart, while by his side, in evident nervous embarrassment; stood a little girl of nine or ten. Instantly he saw his guest, Asshlin put his hand on the child's shoulder and pushed her forward.

"Here's the youngest shoot on the old tree, James!" he cried with a laugh. "Shake hands with him, Nance!"

Somewhat uncertainly and very shyly the child looked up and smiled. She was extremely pretty, with a gipsy-like prettiness new to Milbanke. The only attribute she had inherited from her father's family was the clear olive skin—that distinguished all the Asshlins. Her dark brown hair, her deep blue eyes, her peculiarly winning smile, had all come to her from her dead mother.

With an embarrassment almost equal to her own, Milbanke extended his hand. The average modern child he ignored with comfortable superiority, but this small girl, with her warm smile and her overwhelming shyness, was something infinitely more different to deal with. He shifted his position uneasily.

"How d'you do?" he hazarded. "How d'you do—Nance?"

The little brown fingers stirred nervously in his clasp, and the child, still smiling, made some totally unintelligible reply.

With a boisterous laugh, Asshlin ended the situation.

"Easily known you're not a father, James!" he cried. "Why, you'd have given her a kiss and clinched the business fifty seconds ago. But you're starving. Where's that scamp Clo?"

He turned again to the little girl who had drawn nearer to him for protection.

She replied, but in so low a tone that Milbanke heard nothing. A moment later he was enlightened by Asshlin's loud voice.

"Did you ever hear of a thing like that, James?" he exclaimed. "What would you say to a daughter who rides races on the strand in the dark of an October evening, with the mist enough to give your horses their death? 'Pon my word——" His face reddened; then suddenly he paused and laughed. "After all, what's bred in the bone—eh, James?" he said. "I believe I'd have done the same myself at fifteen—maybe worse."

He checked himself, laughed again; then sighed. But catching Milbanke's eye, he threw off the momentary depression, and turned once more to Nance.

"Tell Hannah we won't wait any longer, like a good child!" he said. "There's no counting on that scallywag."

As the child went quickly to the door he motioned Milbanke to the table, and took his own place at its head.

"No ceremony here," he said. "This is Liberty Hall."

Taking up a decanter, he poured some sherry into his friend's glass; then, filling his own, drank the wine with evident satisfaction.

"Gradual decay is what we're suffering from here, James," he went on. "Everything in this country is too damned old. The only things in this house that have stood it are the wine and the silver. The rest—the woodwork, myself, and the linen—are unsound, as you see."

He laughed again with a shade of sarcasm, and pointed to where a large hole in the damask table-cloth was only partially concealed by a splendid salt-cellar of Irish silver.

"Accumulated time is the disease we're suffering from. 'Tisn't the man who uses his time in this country, but the man who kills it who's mastered the art of living. Oh, we're a wonderful people, James!"

He slowly drained and slowly refilled his glass.

As he laid down the decanter, the door opened and Nance appeared and quietly took her place at table. Almost immediately she was followed by Burke in a black coat and wearing a clean collar.

For a second Milbanke marvelled at the domestic arrangements that could compress a valet, a butler, and a coachman into one easy-going personality; the next, his attention was directed to two enormous dishes which were placed respectively before his host and himself.

"Just hermit's fare, James—the product of the land!" Asshlin exclaimed, as Burke uncovered the first dish, revealing a gigantic turkey. "Will you cut yourself a shaving of ham?"

With a passing sense of impotence Milbanke gazed at the great, glistening ham; then the healthy appetite that exposure to the sea air had aroused, lent him courage, and he picked up a carving knife.

But the execution of the ham was destined to postponement. Scarcely had he straightened himself to the task, than a quick bang of the outer door was followed by hasty steps across the hall, and the last member of the household appeared upon the scene.

Almost before he saw her, Milbanke was conscious of her voice—high and clear with youthful vitality, softened and rendered piquant by native intonation.

"Oh, father, such a gallop! Such fun! And I won. The bay cob was nowhere beside Polly. Larry was mad!"

The string of words was poured forth in irresistible excitement before she had reached the door. Once inside, she paused abruptly—her whole animated face flushing.

"Oh, I forgot!" she said in sudden naïve dismay.

She made a quaint picture as she stood there in the light of the candles and the fire—her slight, immature figure arrayed in a worn and old-fashioned riding habit, her hair covered by a boy's cloth cap, her fingers clasping one of her father's heavy hunting crops. But it was neither dress nor attitude that drew Milbanke's eyes from the task before him—that incontinently sent his mind back thirty years to the days when Denis Asshlin had seemed to stand on the threshold of life and look forth, as by Right Divine, upon the pageant of the future. There was little physical likeness between the girl brimming with youth and vitality and the hard, prematurely-aged man sitting at the head of the table; but the blood that glowed in the warm olive skin, the spirit that danced and gleamed in the hazel eyes, was the same blood and the same spirit that had captivated Milbanke more than a quarter of a century before.

The unlooked-for sensation held him spell-bound. But almost rudely the spell was broken. Scarcely had Clodagh's exclamation of dismay escaped her, than Asshlin broke into one of his boisterous laughs.

"Forgot, did you?" he cried. "Well, 'twas like you. Come here!"

He put out his hand, and as he did so, a sudden expression of pride and affection softened his hard face.

"Here's the wildest scapegrace of an Asshlin you've met yet, James," he said.

"Shake hands with him, Clo!" he added in a different voice. "He's a symbol, if you only knew it. He stands for the great glory we must all leave behind us. The glory of youth!" His voice sank suddenly to a lower key, and he raised his glass. "Go on, child!" he added more quickly. "Shake hands with him; tell him he's welcome."

But Clodagh's flow of speech had been silenced. With a suggestion of the shyness that marked her sister, she came round the table as Milbanke rose.

She made no remark as she proffered her hand, and she did not smile as Nance had done. Instead, her bright eyes scanned his face with a quick, questioning interest.

In return, he looked at her clear skin, her level eyebrows and proudly held head; and his awkwardness vanished as he took the slight muscular hand still cold from the night mist.

"How d'you do?" he said. "I've been hearing of you."

Again Clodagh coloured, and glanced at her father.

"What were you telling him, father?" she asked with native curiosity.

Once more Asshlin laughed loudly.

"Listen to her, James," he said banteringly. "Her conscience is troubling her. She knows that it's hard to speak well of her. Isn't that it, scamp? Confess now!"

Clodagh had again passed round the table; and, having thrown her whip and cap into a chair, had seated herself without ceremony in the vacant place that awaited her.

"Indeed it isn't!" she replied with immense unconcern. But an instant later she repeated her question.

"What was it, father? Can't you tell me?"

Asshlin lifted his glass and studied the light through his sherry.

"Ah now, listen to her, James!" he exclaimed again delightedly. "And women will tell you they aren't inquisitive."

Clodagh flushed.

The little sister, seeing the flush, was suddenly moved to assert herself.

"'Twasn't anything, Clo," she said quickly. "He only said you were a scallywag."

Then, as all eyes turned in her direction, she subsided abruptly into confused silence.

"There you are again, James! Look at the way they stick together. A poor man hasn't the ghost of a chance when two of them join forces. One of them ought to have been a boy—if only for the sake of equality."

He shook his head and laughed afresh, while Burke deposited the last plate upon the table, and dinner began in earnest.

That dinner, like his drive from Muskeere, was an experience to Milbanke. More than once his eyes travelled involuntarily from the candle-lit table, with its suggestion of another and an earlier era, to the high walls where the fire cast long shafts of ruddy light and long tongues of shadow upon Asshlin's ancestors, painted in garments of silk and lace that had once found a setting in this same sombre room. There was something strangely analogous in these dead men and women and their living representatives. The thought recurred to him again and again, as he yielded to the pleasant influences of good wine and wholesome food pressed upon him with unceasing hospitality. It was not the first time he had pandered to his taste for past things by comparing a man with his forefathers, but the result had never proved quite so profitable. In their uncommon setting, Asshlin and his children would have appealed to the most unobservant as uncommon types; viewed by the eyes of a student, they became something more; they became types of an uncommon race—of an uncommon class.

With the spur of the old fascination and the goad of the new-born misgiving, he glanced again and yet again from his host's hard, handsome features to the pictures, from the pictures to the warm-coloured faces of the children. The study was absorbing. It supplied him with an agreeable undercurrent of interest while the ham and turkey were removed, and Asshlin, with much dexterity, distributed portions of an immense apple-pie, deluged in cream; it still occupied his mind when—cheese having been placed upon the table and partaken of—Burke proceeded to remove the cloth.

At the moment that the polished surface of the table was laid bare, his glance, temporarily distracted from its study of the nearer pictures, was attracted and arrested by one portrait, that hung in partial shadow above the carved chimneypiece. It was the picture of a tall, slight boy of sixteen or seventeen years, dressed in the black satin knee breeches, the diamond shoe buckles, and powdered queue of a past generation.

Something in the pose of this painted figure, something in the youthful face, caught and held his attention. In unconscious scrutiny, he leant forward to study the shadowed features; then Asshlin, suddenly aware of his interest, leant across the table.

"That was what I meant, James, by saying one of them should have been a boy," he said sharply. "Haven't I justification?"

He nodded half earnestly, half in malicious humour towards the picture above the fire.

For a moment Milbanke was at a loss; then all at once he comprehended his host's meaning. His gaze dropped from the picture to Clodagh, sitting below it. Above the dark riding habit and above the satin coat, it seemed that the same olive skin, the same level eyebrows and clear hazel eyes confronted him.

"I see!" he said quietly. "I see! A very peculiar case of family likeness."

He spoke affably, casually, in all innocence; but scarcely had the words left his lips than he precipitately wished them back. With a loud laugh, Asshlin struck the table with his hand.

"Ah, good!" he exclaimed. "Good! Now, Clo, what have you got to say?"

But with a gesture quite as vehement as his own, the girl raised her head.

"I say that it's not true," she said. "It isn't true. I'm not like him."

She glanced from her father to Milbanke with suddenly kindling eyes.

"I'm not like him!" she repeated. "I won't be like him!"

Asshlin leant back quickly in his chair. He was still laughing, but a shade of temper was audible in the laugh.

"Do you hear that, James?" he said. "We of the present generation are altogether too good for the past. A slip of a girl nowadays thinks herself vastly superior to a great-great-grandfather who was the finest horseman and the most open-handed man in Munster. That's the attitude of to-day."

He moved aside, as Burke re-entered the room and laid a decanter of port and two glasses on the shining mahogany table.

"My great-grandfather, Anthony Asshlin," he went on deliberately, "was as fine a specimen of the Irish gentleman as ever lived—I don't care who denies it. Have a glass of port, James? An appreciation of good wine was the one thing he left his descendants."

There was an awkward silence while he filled the two glasses and pushed one towards his guest.

But Milbanke's ease of mind had already been upset. He held no key to the disconcerting situation; and it puzzled and perplexed him, as his first impression of his old friend had done. Both possessed elements that he vaguely knew to be hidden from his sight—out of focus from his present point of view. For a space he sat warily fingering his glass, but making no attempt to drink. Without openly seeming to observe it, he was conscious of Asshlin's half-humorous, half-aggressive mood; of the nervous attitude of the younger girl, and of Clodagh's flushed face.

To a newly arrived guest, the position was strained. With growing embarrassment he glanced from the rich, dark wine in his glass to its reflection in the polished surface of the table. Finally the awkwardness of the prolonged silence moved him to speech.

"A great-grandfather who was a judge of wine is always worthy of consideration," he murmured amiably, as he lifted the glass to his lips. "I'm afraid mine was a teetotaller."

But his feeble attempt at humour was not destined to be successful. It drew a laugh from his host, but it was a laugh that found no echo.

"You're right, James!" Asshlin cried. "By Jupiter, you're right! Anthony Asshlin was the finest man in the county—and I'm proud of him."

"He was the worst man in the county—and the greatest fool!"

The words, so sudden and unexpected, came from Clodagh. For several seconds she had been sitting absolutely still; but now she lifted her head again, her flushed face glowing, her bright eyes alight with the quick enthusiasm, the hot temper that she had inherited from her race. With a swift movement she turned from her father to Milbanke.

"Do you think it great to be a fool—and a gambler?" she demanded.

Asshlin set down his glass noisily.

"Anthony Asshlin was no gambler," he said. "He was a sportsman."

Clodagh's lip curled.

"A sportsman!" she exclaimed. "Is it sport to keep game-cocks, to play cards, and throw dice? To squander money that belongs to other people? To mortgage your property and to—to—to kill your brother?"

The last words burst from her impetuously, impulsively; then suddenly she paused, shocked by her own daring.

The silence that followed was short. With an equal impetuosity, Asshlin pushed back his chair and rose.

"By Gad, Clo, that's going too far!" he cried. "I'll not hear my great-grandfather called a murderer."

"All the same, he killed his brother."

"In a duel. Gentlemen had to fight in those days."

"Because of cards! Because they quarrelled over cards!"

Then, with a fresh change of expression, she appealed again to Milbanke.

"Do you think that's sport?" she asked. "To get no good out of ordinary things? To get no pleasure out of dogs or horses except the pleasure of making them fight or race so that you can bet on the one you think best?"

She stopped breathlessly; and Milbanke, desperately at a loss, gazed from one angry, excited face to the other. But he was saved the trouble of finding an answer; for immediately Clodagh ceased to speak, Asshlin's loud laugh broke in again.

"Bravo!" he cried boisterously. "All the eloquence and all the lack of logic of your sex! But don't put those propositions to Milbanke; put them to yourself when you've reached his age. If you can't tell at fifty-five why poor human creatures play and kill and make fools of themselves, you'll have been a very lucky woman."

For an instant his voice dropped, the despondency, the restless ennui that Milbanke had previously noticed falling like a brief shadow over his anger. But the lapse was brief. With another laugh and a shrug of the shoulders, he turned suddenly, and, crossing the room, opened the door.

"Burke!" he called loudly across the hall. "Burke, bring more candles and another bottle of port—and the cards!"

At the words Clodagh rose.

"Father!" she exclaimed below her breath. Then her voice faltered. The involuntary note of protest and appeal was checked by some other emotion. With a swift movement she crossed the hearth, picked up her whip and cap, and, without another glance or word, walked out of the room, followed noiselessly by Nance.

Asshlin continued to stand by the door until the figures of his children had disappeared; then he turned back into the room.

"James," he said suddenly, "perhaps you don't think it, but one hair of that child's head is more precious to me than life. She's an Asshlin to the tips of her fingers. She's the whole race of us in one. The very way she repudiates us is proof enough for any man. I tell you the whole lot of us— lock, stock, and barrel—are looking at you out of her eyes."

Again he paused; then again he shook off his passing seriousness with nervous excitability, reseating himself at the table, as Burke entered.

"Ah, here we are!" he cried. "Here we are! Come along, Burke, and show the light of heaven to us. Now, James, for any stakes you like—and at any game! What shall it be? Piquet? Or will we say Euchre, for the sake of the days that are dead and gone? Very well. Euchre let it be—for any stakes you like. It's the land of beggars, but, by Gad, you'll find us game? Pass me your glass for another taste of port."

# CHAPTER IV

The unpleasant sensation of moving in the dark remained with Milbanke while Asshlin, still noisily excited, arranged the stakes, cut for the deal, and, having won the cut, distributed the cards. By nature he was lethargic and placid; by habit he was precise, methodical, and commonplace. The advent into this new atmosphere, with its inexplicable suggestions and volcanic outbursts, left him distressed and ill at ease. He was the type of man who, in every relation of life, likes to know exactly where he stands. Having once satisfied himself upon that point, he was usually content to follow the routine of existence without trouble to those around him; but until it was fully defined, he was a prey to a vague uneasiness.

So absorbed was he by the trend of his own speculations, that for the first five games he gave but small consideration to the play. Then, however, his host jogged his attention with no uncertain hand.

Pausing in the shuffling of the cards, he glanced across the table.

"You're playing like an old woman, James. Are your wits wool-gathering, that you've let me win every blessed game?"

Milbanke looked up. "Forgive me," he said hastily—"forgive me. I was thinking——"

"—Thinking that a broken-down devil of an Irishman isn't high enough game to fly at?" Asshlin laughed. "Well, I'll put some life into you. I'll double the stakes. What do you say to that?"

He leant back in his chair, balancing the pack of cards in his hands.

Milbanke, with suddenly awakened observation, saw that his eyes glittered with excitement and that his lips were set.

"Double the stakes?" he echoed doubtfully. "Oh, certainly if you think it will improve the game. For myself I rarely play for money! I always think that the cards——"

"—Are sufficient in themselves, I suppose?" Asshlin laughed. "Don't you believe it, James? Or if you do, I'll teach you better. Come along! In for a penny, in for a pound! Are you agreeable?"

For a moment Milbanke was thoughtful; then he became conscious of the other's impatient glance.

"Why—why certainly," he said. "Anything you like!"

"Spoken like a man!" Asshlin impulsively threw down the cards, and then gathered them up again. "I see the embalming process isn't completed yet. The antiquarians have left a shred or two of frail humanity in you. Well, we'll have it out. We'll put an edge on it. Come along!" He leant forward, the reckless brightness deepening in his eyes.

But Milbanke hesitated.

"Hadn't we better settle up the first score and start afresh?" he said. "How do we stand?"

He put his hand into his pocket. But the other waived the point.

"Is it paying at this hour of the night?" he cried. "Give me a pencil, and I'll jot down our difference, if you're conscientious. But the balance will be on the other side before the candles are burned out. The devil forgot to bring luck to the Asshlins since poor Anthony went below. But come along, man!—come along! Here's to the youth of us!"

He drained his glass; and turned again to the business of the cards.

During the next half-dozen games neither spoke. With deep absorption, Asshlin followed the run of the cards. Once or twice an exclamation escaped him; once or twice he paused to replenish Milbanke's glass or his own; but in every other respect he had eyes and thoughts for nothing but the business in hand. Milbanke, on the contrary—gambler neither by instinct nor training— was infinitely more interested in his opponent than in the play.

As he watched Asshlin, a score of recollections rose to his mind— recollections that time and advancing age had all but effaced. He recalled the numberless occasions upon which the Irishman, in the exuberance of youth, had sat over a gaming-table until the daylight had streamed in across the scattered cards, the heaped-up cigar-ashes and the emptied glasses; he reviewed the rare occasions on which his cajoleries had drawn him from his own mild pursuits to be a sharer in these prolonged revels; and with the memory came the thought of the headache, the sick sense of weariness that had invariably lain in wait for him the following morning. A wondering admiration for Asshlin had always held a place in these jaded after-sensations—a species of hero-worship for one who could turn into bed at four in the morning and emerge at nine with all the vigour and vitality of the most virtuous sleeper. He had never fully realised that to men of Asshlin's stamp dissipation, excitement, and action are potent stimulants, calling forth all the superfluous nervous energy that by nature they possess. While the tide of life runs high about such men, they are borne forward, buoyed up by their own capacity for living and enjoying. To them, existence at high pressure is a glorious, exalted state, exempt from satiety or fatigue; it is the quieter phases of existence—the phases that to ordinary men mean rest, peace, domestic tranquillity and domestic interests—that these exuberant, ardent human beings have cause to dread.

An hour went by, and still the idea of a past, curiously reflected and curiously contradicted, absorbed Milbanke's perceptions. Then gradually but decisively it was borne in upon his mind that his absorption was blunting his common sense. He was playing execrably.

It has been said that he was no gambler; but neither was he a fool. With something of a shock he realised that he stood a loser to the extent of seven or eight pounds. With the realisation he sat straighter in his chair. It was not that he grudged the money. He was generous—and could afford generosity. It was rather that that admirable quality which urges the Englishman to play a losing game was stirred within him.

"By Jove, Denis!" he said. "I must look to my laurels! I used to play a better game than this."

Asshlin's only answer was a laugh—a laugh from which all the bitterness had dropped away, leaving a buoyant ring of absorption and delight. Under the stimulus of excitement, he had altered. He was exalted, lifted above the petty discontent, the pessimism, the despondency that tainted his empty days.

And so for nearly two hours they played steadily; then Milbanke paused and drew out his watch.

"I don't know what sort of hours you keep in Ireland," he hazarded; "but it's nearly twelve o'clock."

Asshlin had paused to snuff one of the candles that had begun to gutter. At the other's words, he glanced up in undisguised surprise.

"Hours?" he repeated. "Why, any—or none at all. You don't know the glory of having something to sit up for." He paused for a second in a sort of ecstasy. "You don't know it; you can't know it! You have never felt the abomination of desolation."

He laughed feverishly and gathered up the cards afresh.

"Come, James! Your deal!"

And in this manner the night wore on. In the early stages of their play Asshlin's luck stuck to him determinately; but by degrees his opponent's more cautious and level play began to tell, and their positions were gradually reversed. By one o'clock Milbanke had made good his losses and even stood with some trifling amount to his advantage. Here again he had mildly suggested a cessation; but Asshlin, more intoxicated by bad than he had been by good fortune, had demanded his revenge, and called loudly through the quiet house for more candles and more wine.

But with the fresh round of play, the luck remained unaltered. Milbanke continued to win.

With a sleepy face, but no expression of surprise, Burke responded to his master's call, replenishing the light and setting the port upon the table. But the players scarcely noticed his entrance or departure. Asshlin was playing with desperate recklessness; and Milbanke, without intent or consciousness, was slowly falling under the influence of his companion's excitement. As minute succeeded minute and Asshlin sat rigid in his seat— cutting, dealing, marking the result of each game upon a strip of paper— the elder man became more and more the satellite of thirty years ago, less and less the placid archaeologist for whom the follies of the present lie overshadowed by the past.

He forgot the long journey of the afternoon, the peculiar incidents of his arrival. A slight flush rose to his usually bloodless cheeks; he found himself watching the run of the cards with a species of reflected eagerness, roused to an unaccustomed elation when the advantage fell to him.

At three o'clock they played the last round. And it was only then—when the last card had been thrown on the table, and he had risen stiff from long sitting, the winner of something like twenty pounds—that he realised how completely he had been dominated by this resurrected influence; dominated to the exclusion of personal prejudice and even personal comfort. So strong was this impression of past influences that he was roused to no surprise when, glancing at his companion, he saw him temporarily rejuvenated—his expression alert, his whole face vivified by the night's excitement.

Again a touch of the old sympathy arose within him. The reckless, cynical man before him was momentarily effaced; the bright personality of long ago seemed to fill the room.

"Good-night, Denis!" he said gently, holding out his hand.

Asshlin caught it enthusiastically.

"Good-night, James!—good-night! And once more a thousand welcomes and a thousand thanks. You have been a drop of water in the desert to a parching man. Good-night, and pleasant dreams to you! I'll reckon up my losses in the morning and write you a cheque. Good-night!"

Milbanke responded to the pressure of his fingers.

"Don't trouble about the money," he said. "Any time will do—any time. But you're turning in yourself? We'll be upstairs together?"

But Asshlin shook his head.

"Not yet," he said. "Not after this. I'll take a turn across the fields and have a look at the night on the water. I feel too much awake to be smothered by sheets and blankets. It isn't often we feel life here—and the sensation is glorious."

He drew up his tall, powerful figure and stretched out his arms. Then almost at once he let them fall to his sides.

"But what moonshine this is to you, you prosaic Saxon!" he exclaimed. "Let me light you to bed."

He laughed quickly; and, picking up one of the massive candlesticks, moved towards the door.

For an instant Milbanke lingered in the dining-room, grown dimmer with the departing lights; then, hearing his name in his host's voice, he hurried after him into the hall.

Asshlin was standing at the foot of the stairs, the glowing candles held aloft. Above him, the high ceiling loomed shadowy and indistinct; behind him, the dark wainscoted wall threw his figure into bold relief.

It would have demanded but a slight stretch of fancy to picture him as his satin-coated great-grandfather grown to a dissipated maturity, as he stood there, the master spirit in this house of fallen greatness. As Milbanke reached his side, he laughed once more, precisely as Anthony Asshlin might have laughed, standing at the foot of the same staircase nearly a hundred years ago. The taint of heredity seemed to wrap him round—to gleam in his unnaturally bright eyes, to reverberate in his voice.

"Up with you, James!" he cried. "I needn't put your hand on the banister, like I have to do with some of my guests. You never yet drank a swerve into your steps. Well, I don't blame you for it. It's men like you that keep heaven a going concern, while poor devils like me are paving the lower regions. Good-night to you!"

With a fresh laugh he thrust the great candlestick into the other's hand and turned on his heel.

Milbanke remained motionless, while Asshlin passed across the hall and opened the door, letting in a breath of fresh, damp air that set the candle-flames dancing; then, as the door closed again, he turned and put his hand on the banister.

It was with a feeling of unreality, mingled with the borrowed excitement still at work within him, that he began his ascent of the stairs. The natural fatigue consequent on the day's journey had been temporarily dispelled, and sleep seemed something distant and almost unattractive. As he mounted the creaking steps, moving cautiously out of consideration for the sleeping household, he found himself wishing incontinently that he had offered his company to his host in his stroll towards the sea.

As the desire came to him, he paused. He could still overtake Asshlin! He hesitated, glancing from the closed door of his bedroom to the hall lying below him in a well of shadow. Then suddenly he raised his head, attracted by a sound, subdued and yet distinct, that came to him through the silence of the house—the sound of light, hasty steps on an uncarpeted corridor.

In the wave of surprise that swept over him he forgot his recent excitement, his recent wish for action and fresh air. Lifting the candlestick above his head, he peered along the passage that stretched away beyond his own door. But the scrutiny was momentary. Almost at once he lowered the candles and drew back, as he recognised the figure of Clodagh coming towards him out of the gloom. She was wearing a flowing, old-fashioned dressing-gown of some flowered material; one strand of her brown hair had been loosened, and fell across her forehead, shadowing her eyes into something of the beauty they were yet to wear. And as Milbanke looked at her, he realised with a stirring of something like embarrassment, that a touch of promise, very gracious and infinitely feminine, had replaced the first, half-boyish impression that he had received of her.

But if he felt embarrassment, it was evident that she was conscious of none. As she came within a few yards of him she halted for an instant to assure herself of his identity; then, her mind satisfied, she stepped straight onward into the light of the six candles.

"Oh, I'm so glad!" she said quickly. "I was afraid for a minute that it was father. I've been waiting up for you," she added hastily. "I couldn't go to sleep till I'd seen you."

Milbanke was confused. Moved by an undefined impulse, he extinguished three of the six candles.

"Indeed!" he said. "But it's very late. You must—you must be tired."

He glanced uncertainly round the landing, as if seeking a chair to offer her. Then an idea struck him.

"Will you come downstairs?" he suggested. "The fire is still alight in the dining-room. You—you must be cold as well as tired."

He looked hesitatingly at her light gown.

But Clodagh shook her head.

"We mustn't go down," she said. "He might come in and find us—and then we'd have a row. He and I of course, I mean," she added politely.

Then, as if impatient of the preamble, she plunged into the subject she had at heart.

"Mr. Milbanke," she said, "will you promise me not to—not to, after to-night — —?"

Milbanke's face looked blank.

"Not to what?" he asked.

"Oh, not to encourage him—not to play with him. He's ruining himself and ruining us all. Couldn't you guess it from dinner—from the quarrel we had? Oh, he's so terribly foolish!"

Her voice suddenly trembled.

But he was labouring under the shock her revelation had given him.

"Good heavens!" he stammered. "I had no idea—no idea of such a thing."

"No; I know you hadn't—I was sure you hadn't." Her voice thrilled with quick relief.

"No, no. Certainly not. But tell me about it. Dear me!—dear me! I had no idea of such a thing."

"Oh, it began ages ago—before mother died. Burke says 'twas the life— the quiet life after England. He came home, you know, when his father died, and he found the place in a bad way. He has never been rich enough to live out of the country, and he has never stopped fretting for the things that aren't here. But while mother lived he kept pretty good; 'twas after she died that he seemed not to care. First he got gloomy and sad, then he got reckless and terrible. People were frightened of him. His friends began to drop away."

She paused for a moment, glancing down into the hall to assure herself that all was quiet.

"It's been the same ever since. Sometimes he's gloomy and depressed, other times he's wild, like to-night. And when he's wild, he's mad for cards. Oh, you don't know what it's like! It's like being a drunkard—only different— and worse. When he's like that, he'd play with any one—for anything. Last week he had a dreadful man—a horse-dealer from Muskeere—staying here with him for three days. They played cards every night—played till three or four in the morning. Father lost all the ready money in the house, and nearly emptied the stables."

Milbanke stood before her horrified and absorbed. An understanding of many things, before obscure, had come to him while she was speaking; and with the knowledge, a sudden deep pity for this child of his old friend—a sudden sense of guilt at his own blindness, his own weakness.

"Miss Clodagh," he said quickly, in his stiff, formal voice. Then he paused, as she raised her hand with a sharp gesture of attention.

A heavy step sounded on the gravel outside the house. There was an instant's hesitation; then Clodagh leant forward with swift presence of mind and blew out the three remaining candles.

"You understand now?" she whispered.

"Yes," he murmured, below his breath. "Yes; I understand."

A moment later he heard her flit down the corridor, and heard Asshlin open the heavy outer door.

# CHAPTER V

Thus it was that James Milbanke entered on his first night at Orristown. The surprise, the excitement, and the culminating incident of the evening would have been disturbing to a man of even more placid temperament; and rebel as he might against the weakness, he lay awake considerably longer than was his wont in the uncomfortable, canopied bed, listening to the numberless infinitesimal sounds that break the silence of a sleeping house—from the faint, occasional cracking of the furniture to the scurrying of a mouse behind the plaster of the walls. Then gradually, as his ears became accustomed to these minor noises, another sound, unnoticed in the activity of the earlier hours, obtruded itself softly but persistently upon his consciousness—the subdued and regular breaking of the sea on the rocks below the house.

A slight sense of annoyance was his first feeling, for it was many years since he had slept by the sea; then quietly, lingeringly, soothingly the rhythmical persistence of the sound began to tell. Imperceptibly the confusing ideas of the evening became pleasantly indistinct—the numberless contradictory feelings blurred into one delightful sensation of indifference and repose. With the salt, moist air, borne to him through the open window, and the great untiring lullaby of the ocean rising and falling upon his senses, like the purring of a gigantic cat, he fell asleep.

His first sensation upon waking the next morning was one of pleasure— the placid, unquestioning satisfaction that comes to the untroubled mind with the advent of a fine day. To his simple taste, the sights and sounds that met his waking consciousness were possessed of an unaccustomed charm. With daylight, the room that last night had held grim and even ghostly suggestions, took on a more human and more friendly air. The ancient mahogany furniture seemed anxious to reflect the morning sunshine; the massive posts of the bed with their drapery of faded repp no longer glowered upon the intruder. Each object was bathed in, and rejuvenated by, the golden warmth, the incomparable mellow radiance of sea and sky that flowed in at the open window.

For a while he lay in contemplative enjoyment of this early, untainted atmosphere, while the sounds of the awakening day gradually rose above the soft beating of the outgoing tide—falling upon his ears in a pleasant, primitive medley of clacking fowls, joyous, yelping dogs, and stamping horses. For a space he lay still; then the inevitable wish to take active part in this world created from the darkness and the silence of the night aroused him; and, slipping out of bed, he drew on a dressing-gown and walked to the window.

The sight that met his eyes was one of infinite beauty. The delicacy—the poetry—the subtle, unnameable charm that lie in the hollow of Nature's hand were over land and sky and sea; the warmth and wealth of summer stretched before him, but summer mellowed and softened by a golden autumnal haze.

There are more inspiring countries than Ireland—countries more richly dowered in vegetation; countries more radiant in atmosphere and brilliant in colouring: but there is no land where the Hand of the Maker is more poignantly felt; where the mystic spirit of creation—the wonderful, tender, pathetic sense of the Beginning—has been so strangely preserved. As Milbanke stood at the open window, his eyes travelled without interruption over the wide green fields—neither lawn nor meadow—that spread from the house to the shore, owning no boundary wall beyond the low, shelving rocks of red sandstone that rose a natural barrier against the encroachments of the tide. And from the fields his gaze wandered onward, drawn irresistibly and inevitably to the sea itself—the watchful, tyrannical guardian of the silent land.

It lay before him like a tremendous glassy lake, stretching in one untroubled sweep from Orristown to the point, three miles away, where the purple headland of Carrigmore completed the semicircle of the bay. The silence, the majesty of that sweep of water was indescribable. From the rim of yellow sand, which the indolent waves were lapping, to the misted horizon, not one sign of human life marred the smoothness of its surface. Across the bay at Carrigmore a few spirals of smoke rose from the cluster of pink and white cottages lying under the shadow of the Round Tower; on the long, sandy strand a couple of bare-legged boys were leisurely raking up the sea-weed that the waves had left, and slowly piling it on a waiting donkey butt; but the sea itself was undisturbed. It lay as it might have lain on the first day of completed creation—mystical, sublime, untouched.

Milbanke was no poet, yet the scene impressed him. The extraordinary sense of an inimitable and impenetrable peace before which man and man's mere transitory concerns are dwarfed, if not entirely eliminated, touched him vaguely. It was with a tinge of something bordering upon reluctance that he at last drew his eyes from the picture and began to dress.

But once freed from the spell of the ocean, his mind reverted to the other interests that lay closer at hand. He found himself wondering how his entertainers would appear on a second inspection; whether, like his room, they would take on a more commonplace semblance with the advent of daylight. The touch of irrepressible and human curiosity that the speculation aroused gave a spur to the business of dressing; and it was well under the twenty minutes usually devoted to his neat and careful toilet when he found himself crossing the corridor and descending the stairs.

He encountered no one as he passed through the hall; and catching a fresh suggestion of sunshine through the door that stood hospitably open, he paused for an instant to take a cursory glance at the gravelled sweep that terminated the drive, and the grassy slope surmounted by a fringe of beeches that formed the outlook from the front of the house. Then he turned quickly, and, recrossing the hall, passed into the dining-room.

None of the household had yet appeared, but here also the daylight had worked changes.

The curtains were drawn back, permitting the view of fields and sea, that he had already studied from his bedroom, to break uninterruptedly through the three lofty windows. The effect was one of extreme airiness and light; and it was quite a minute before his gaze turned to the darker side of the room, where the portrait of the famous Anthony Asshlin hung above the fire.

Realising that he was alone in the big room, he crossed to the table where breakfast was already laid—the remains of the enormous ham rising from an untidy paper frill to defy the attacks of the largest appetite. In the brilliance of the light, the fineness of the table linen and its state of dilapidation were both accentuated, as was the genuine beauty and intrinsic value of the badly kept silver.

But Milbanke had no time to absorb these details, for instantly he reached the table his eye was caught by a folded slip of paper lying by his place. With a touch of surprise he stooped forward and picked it up; then a wave of annoyance, almost of guilt, succeeded the surprise as he realised that it was a cheque made out in Asshlin's straggling handwriting for his losses of the night before.

As he fingered it uncomfortably a vivid remembrance of his interview with Clodagh rose to his mind. He thought of the poverty, suggested rather than expressed by the girl's words; he thought of the Muskeere horse-dealer who had all but emptied the stables. With a puckered brow he studied his own name scrawled across the cheque; then, with a sense of something like duplicity, he hurriedly pushed it under his plate as he heard the hall door close, and footsteps sound across the hall. A moment later Asshlin, followed by his two daughters, entered the room.

All three greeted him in turn; then Asshlin crossed to the fire and proceeded to stir it to a blaze, while Nance and Clodagh passed to their appointed places.

Both girls looked pleasantly in keeping with the fresh morning—their rich, youthful colouring having nothing to fear from the searching light. Nance was dressed in a very clean blue cotton frock that accentuated the colour of her eyes; but Clodagh was again attired in the old-fashioned riding-habit, though this time the boy's cap was absent, and the sunshine caught reflections in her light brown hair.

"I hope you don't mind my being dressed like this," she said, as she took her seat. "I always have a ride in the mornings, and I generally tidy up for breakfast; but I'm riding a race at ten with Larry—my cousin, you know—so 'twouldn't be worth while to change to-day."

She spoke quite naturally, encountering Milbanke's eyes with no suggestion of embarrassment for last night's adventure.

He met her glance for an instant; then his own wandered guiltily to the corner of the cheque protruding from under his plate.

"Not at all!" he said hurriedly—"not at all! I hope I may be permitted to see the race."

Clodagh smiled.

"Of course—if you like," she said. "But it won't be much to look at." She added this with a quick glance that ineffectually attempted to gauge the guest's tastes and powers of appreciation.

"'Twill be grand!" murmured Nance softly. "And I know who's going to win."

"Nonsense!" said Clodagh. "I won in the practice last night, but the strand was wet, and the cob is only sure on hard ground."

But nevertheless she flushed and threw a quick look of appreciation and affection at her loyal little partisan.

"What are you two chattering about?" said Asshlin, standing up from the fire and straightening his shoulders.

"Is that your notion of hospitality? To keep a stranger waiting for his breakfast? Faith, we knew better in the old days—eh, James?"

He laughed, and passed round the table.

Clodagh presided at the old-fashioned silver urn; and either her confidences of the night before or the prospect of her coming contest affected her, for she forgot the diffidence that had marked her at the dinner of the preceding evening, and talked brightly and with interest on a variety of subjects. Finally, as she handed Milbanke his second cup of tea, she touched upon the object of his visit.

"'Twas to see the ruins at Carrigmore, not us, that you came, wasn't it?" she said with a shade of humour.

He returned her glance seriously.

"Oh no," he said. "At least— —"

"Ah, now you've let it out!" she cried, with a laugh. "I knew it. I said so. Didn't I, Nance? I knew no one would come here just to see us."

Asshlin laughed.

"'Pon my soul!" he cried, "you haven't learned your market value yet, Clo! If I were a girl, I'm hanged if I'd rate myself lower than a fourth-century ruin."

He laughed afresh.

But Clodagh displayed no embarrassment. She was too unversed in the ways of coquetry to see or resent the point of the remark.

"I?" she said naively. "What have I to do with it?"

After this there was a trifling silence, at the end of which, Asshlin looked quickly at his guest.

"By the way, James," he exclaimed, "we were too well amused last night to look ahead. I never thought of asking you about to-day. Have you any pet plans or schemes? Is it to be a pilgrimage to St. Galen? Or what do you say to a day in the saddle? There's a meet not five miles away; and if a good gallop pleases you, I have as neat a little horse for you as ever carried a saddle. What do you say? Of course if you think the Round Tower is likely to collapse or be demolished by a tidal wave, I won't raise a finger; but— —"

Milbanke laughed.

"My dear Denis," he said quickly, "don't you trouble on my account." He glanced deprecatingly over Asshlin's sporting attire. "Don't you trouble about me. I never was a sportsman, as you know. I'll go to my own hunting, and you go to yours. Don't let me interfere with any plans you may have formed. I enjoy a solitary excursion."

But Asshlin's face darkened.

"Oh no," he objected after a short pause—"oh no. If you're not game for it, then the meet is off so far as I'm concerned. I can't have you roaming about the country by yourself. Oh no; I hope I remember my obligations."

Milbanke looked distressed. With a genuine feeling of embarrassment he turned from one face to the other.

"My dear Denis," he objected feebly, "I must really beg of you——"

"Not another word!—not another word!" Asshlin ostentatiously helped himself to some ham, "I hope, James, that whatever our environments, we still understand the traditions of hospitality. If you don't feel on for it, there's no hunting for me to-day."

After this there was another unpleasant pause. Asshlin attempted to hide his chagrin, but his face was unmistakably dark with disappointment.

For a space Milbanke toyed with his breakfast, then he spoke again.

"But, my dear Denis, if you will only allow me——" he ventured.

But before Asshlin could reply, Clodagh's voice broke in.

"Oh! you needn't bother so much, father," she said easily. "You go to the meet, and I'll take Mr. Milbanke to Carrigmore. I'll drive him over in the pony-trap, or we'll walk—whichever he likes best."

She spoke fluently and gaily, and it was difficult for Milbanke to reconcile the high, buoyant tones of her voice with the serious note struck by her the night before. Filled with relief, however, at her timely interruption, he was satisfied to let the discrepancy go unregarded.

"Excellent!" he cried—"an excellent idea, Miss Clodagh! Here's your difficulty solved, Denis. Your Irish sense of chivalry won't allow you to deprive me of so charming a guide."

Clodagh laughed frankly at the stilted compliment, and Asshlin's face brightened perceptibly.

"Oh, well, as you're so amiable," he said magnanimously. "I don't mind admitting that 'twould have been a bit of a sacrifice to give up the hunt. Though if I hadn't been overruled by the majority, I'd have swallowed the ruins without a grimace."

He laughed with restored good-humour, and turned to his daughters.

"When you've done breakfast, Clo," he said, "run round to the stables and tell Burke he need only saddle the bay."

With the decision that he was, after all, to enjoy his day's sport, his spirits had risen; and despite the fact that the daylight revealed many evidences of last night's dissipation that would have been invisible thirty years ago, Milbanke was pleased and reassured by his appearance. His movements were energetic, his expression alert. He suggested one who is interested and attracted by life; and the elder man was too unimaginative—too single of purpose in his own concerns—to suspect that the energy, the suggestion of anticipation were due to his own presence in the house, to the promise of excitement and diversion that that presence offered.

With the definite arrangement of the day's plans, a fresh energy had descended on the party, and but a few minutes passed before Clodagh and Nance rose from table and left the room. Then, as the two men were left alone, Milbanke put into action the resolution that had been gradually maturing in his mind.

Not without a certain trepidation—not without an embarrassed distaste for the task—he bent forward in his precise manner, and drawing the cheque from beneath his plate, began to smooth it out.

"Denis," he said, "I found this on my plate when I came downstairs——"

Asshlin looked up hastily and laughed. He had all the Irishman's distaste to money as a topic of conversation. He was as sensitive in the offering of it to another, as in the accepting of it for himself.

"Oh, that's all right!" he said quickly. "Not another word about that, James—not another syllable."

But Milbanke continued to finger the cheque.

"Denis," he began again, a shade of nervousness audible in his voice, "I am uncertain how to say what I want to say. I am extremely anxious not to offend you, and yet I feel—I fear that you may take offence."

Before replying, Asshlin drained the cup of strong tea that stood beside his plate; then he glanced again at his companion.

"What in thunder are you driving at?" he asked good-humouredly.

Milbanke looked down.

"That's what I want to explain," he answered without raising his head. "And you must not allow it to offend you. I want you, for the sake of old friendship, to let me tear this cheque up. I was excited last night; I infringed on one of my set rules—that of never playing cards for high stakes. It is for my own sake that I ask permission to do this. It—it will put me right with myself."

He laughed deprecatingly.

For a second there was no indication that his laboured explanation had been even heard; then, with alarming suddenness, Asshlin brought his hand down upon the table, ripping out an oath.

"And where the devil do I come in?" he demanded. "Is it because you see the place going to rack and ruin that you think you can insult me in my own house? I'd have you to know that when an Asshlin needs charity, he will ask for it." In the spasm of rage that had attacked him, his eyes blazed and the veins in his forehead swelled. Then, suddenly catching a glimpse of the consternation on his guest's face, he controlled himself by an effort, and with a loud laugh pushed back his chair and rose. "Forgive me, James!" he said roughly. "You don't understand—you never did understand. It's the cursed pride of a cursed country. The less we have to be proud of, the more damned proud we are. We have a sense of humour for everything in creation except ourselves." Again he laughed harshly; then again his mood changed. "James," he said seriously, "put that cheque in your pocket, and if you value my friendship, never mention it again. We may be a bad lot; we may be all Clo says of us—fools, rakes, spendthrifts; but no Asshlin ever shirked his debts of honour." The words were bombastic, the sentiment false, but the natural dignity and distinction of the man—dissipated failure though he might be—were unmistakable, as he stood with high head and erect figure.

By the ironic injustice of such circumstances Milbanke—honest, prosaic, incapable of a dishonourable action—felt suddenly humiliated. With shame-faced haste he muttered an apology, and thrust the cheque into his pocket.

At the moment that he did so, Clodagh re-entered the room.

"It's all right, father!" she exclaimed. "The bay will be round in a second. And Larry has come. Are you ready, Mr. Milbanke?"

He responded with instant alacrity. It was the second time that morning that she had unconsciously come to his relief.

"Oh! quite," he said—"quite ready. Shall we start?"

"This minute, if you like. Good-bye, father! I hope 'twill be a good run." She crossed the room quickly, then paused at the door. "Remember, the race will be nothing at all worth seeing," she added, glancing back over her shoulder at the guest.

# CHAPTER VI

Without ceremony or apology Clodagh led Milbanke to the stables by the shortest route, which entailed the traversing of several long and windy passages and the crossing of the great, draughty kitchen where Hannah, the housekeeper, cook, and general mainstay of the establishment, held undisputed sway.

As they entered her domain, she was standing by an open window engaged in the cleaning of a saucepan—an operation to which she brought an astonishing amount of noisy energy. At sight of the stranger, she dropped the knife she was holding, and made a furtive attempt to straighten her ample and somewhat dirty apron.

"Ah, wisha, Miss Clodagh," she began in a voice that trembled between chagrin and an inherent sense of hospitality, "isn't that a quare thing for you to be doin' now? To be bringin' the gintleman down here—an' me in the middle of me pots? Not but what you're welcome, sir—though 'tis no fit place for you," she added, with a glance that summed the intruder up from head to heel.

Milbanke laughed a little awkwardly.

"So long as you make no objection," he said with amiable haste, "I see nothing to find fault with."

But Hannah gave an incredulous shake of her head.

"Ah! you do be sayin' that," she replied sagely. "But 'tis a quare place you'll be findin' Orristown after England." She added this in a persuasive tone, making a tentative cast for the stranger's sentiments.

But before the fish could rise to her bait, her attention was claimed in another direction. A pellet of mud, aimed with extreme accuracy, came flying through the open window and hit her on the cheek.

Milbanke glanced round quickly; Clodagh laughed; and the victim of the assault gave a gasp, pushed her saucepans aside, and thrust her head through the window.

"Wait till I catch you, Masther Larry!" she cried across the yard. "How can I be doin' the work of six women and three men with the likes of you trapesin' about? 'Pon my word, I'll tell on you—I'll tell your uncle on you. Long threatenin' comes at last!"

But the only response that greeted her was a smothered laugh from the stables opposite—a laugh which Clodagh involuntarily echoed.

Instantly Hannah wheeled round from the window.

"Ah! Miss Clodagh, isn't it a shame for you?" she exclaimed tremulously. "Isn't it a shame for you now to be encouragin' that brat of a boy? Sure, 'tis the third time he thrun his marbles of mud at me this mornin'. So signs, I'll spake to the masther. I will so."

She gave her apron a defiant tug.

Milbanke stood uncertain and embarrassed, nervously curious as to Clodagh's next move. With a certain misgiving he saw her face brim over with delight; then with a sense of complete amazement he saw her step suddenly to the side of the indignant Hannah, throw one arm impulsively round her neck, and give her a hasty kiss.

"Indeed you won't speak to him, Hannah—and you know you won't," she said in her most beguiling tones. "And you'll make a griddle cake for lunch—just to show you aren't angry. Come on, Mr. Milbanke! Larry is waiting."

As they crossed the kitchen, Hannah defiantly passed the corner of her apron across her eyes and ostentatiously resumed her interrupted work.

At the door Clodagh looked back.

"Hannah!" she said persuasively.

Hannah began to scrape her saucepan.

"Go on wid you now, Miss Clodagh!" she cried. "Sure 'tis a pair of ye that's there. I'm out wid ye."

"But the griddle cake, Hannah?"

"Let Betsy over at Mrs. Asshlin's make griddle cake for ye. Maybe she wouldn't put up wid Masther Larry as aisy as me."

"Of course Betsy would make a griddle cake at any time," said Clodagh promptly; "only we couldn't eat it—after yours."

For a moment Hannah made no response; then she gave another disdainful whisk to her apron and attacked the saucepan with renewed force.

Clodagh said nothing, but took a step forward. Her cheeks were bright and her eyes danced with mischief and amusement. As her foot touched the paving stones of the yard, Hannah raised her head.

"I suppose 'twill be at wan ye'll be wantin' the lunch?" she said in a suddenly lowered and mollified voice; and Clodagh responded with a laugh of triumph and delight.

Outside in the sunshine of the yard, she laughed again.

"Hannah is an old duck!" she said. "She is always getting as cross as two sticks, and then forgetting all about it. Nobody could help teasing her. But where's Larry gone to? Larry! Larry!"

There was a pause, a stamping of horse's hoofs, and the sound of a voice whispering affectionate injunctions to an unseen animal; then young Laurence Asshlin emerged from the stables, leading his chestnut cob.

He was a well-made, long-limbed boy of fourteen, with skin as smooth and eyes as clear as Clodagh's own.

"Hullo, Clo!" he exclaimed. "That was a straight shot, wasn't it? Was she mad?"

"Pretty mad," responded Clodagh. "This is Mr. Milbanke. He came last night."

Young Asshlin eyed the stranger frankly and without embarrassment.

"You're not at the meet?" he said with involuntary surprise. "I'd be there, only mother doesn't let me hunt yet. She thinks I'd break my neck or something," he laughed. "But I'll go to every meet within twenty miles when I'm a man," he added. "There's nothing as good as hunting—except sailing. Are you much of a sailor?"

Milbanke looked back into the bright, fearless eyes and healthy, spirited face, and again a touch of aloofness, of age, damped him. There was a buoyancy in this boy and girl, a zest, an enthusiasm outside which he stood the undeniable alien.

"Yes, I am fond of the sea," he responded; "but probably not as you are fond of it."

Try as he might to be natural and pleasant, his speech sounded stilted, his words staid.

The boy looked at him doubtfully.

"Didn't know there were two ways of doing it," he said, rubbing his face against the cob's sleek neck.

But Clodagh came to her guest's rescue.

"Larry doesn't deserve any credit for liking the sea," she said. "His father was a sailor. You go on to the fields, Larry," she added; "you'll find Nance waiting there. I'll saddle Polly in a second, and be after you with Mr. Milbanke. Run now! you're only wasting time."

Larry hesitated for a moment, then he nodded.

"All right!" he acquiesced. "Only don't be long."

Instantly he was gone, Clodagh handed her whip to Milbanke and darted into the coach-house, reappearing with a saddle over her arm and a bridle swinging from her shoulder.

"You are not going to saddle the horse yourself?" he exclaimed in consternation. "Let me call one of the men. Please let me call one of the men."

Clodagh laughed.

"There's no one to call," she said. "Burke is the only proper man-servant we keep, and he drove into Muskeere for provisions as soon as he brought the bay round for father. You don't think I'd let any of the labourers touch the horses!" As she said this she laughed again and, nodding gaily, passed into one of the stalls.

After she had disappeared Milbanke stood silent, listening with an uncomfortable embarrassment to the soft whinnying of the horse, the soft murmuring of Clodagh's voice, the straining and creaking of leather that reached his ears. At last, yielding to his instincts, he stepped forward and spoke again.

"Miss Clodagh, let me help you," he said. "I'm afraid I'm rather useless, but you might let me try."

Again Clodagh's soft, humorous laugh answered him.

"It's done now," she said; "and anyway I've known how to saddle a horse since I was twelve. Stand back a little, please!"

He drew back hastily, and she led out a small grey mare.

"She isn't much to look at," she explained, "but she's grand to go—and I know she's going to win. She must win."

She kissed the animal impulsively on the soft, quivering nostril.

Together they threaded their way between the scurrying fowls and innumerable dogs that filled the yard—Clodagh leading the mare, Milbanke keeping close to her side.

"What is this race for?" he asked, as they passed through the arched gateway. "A mere trial of strength?"

Clodagh's eyes widened.

"Oh no," she said; "that would be silly. There are stakes of course—Larry's telescope against my Irish terrier. The telescope belonged to Uncle Laurence, and is a beauty; but it's nothing at all to Mick—Mick is a pedigree dog, six months old, with the finest coat and the loveliest head you ever saw. If I lost him——" But here she stopped. "It's unlucky to say that, isn't it?" she added quickly. "Of course I'm not going to lose him."

Again she turned and fondled the mare; and a moment later they came into view of the long, level fields that lay between the house and the sea, and saw the erect figure of Larry clearly silhouetted against the sky, as he sat his cob with the ease of the born horseman.

It took Milbanke but a few minutes to place himself in a safe and advantageous position on a ditch that, dividing two of the fields, was to form the last jump of the race. And once ensconced in this pleasant and not uncomfortable seat, he watched the cousins move across the fields to the point where little Nance was waiting to arrange the preliminaries. He saw Clodagh mount the grey mare, observed the one or two inevitable false starts, then became conscious with a quickening of interest that the race had begun.

Had he been possessed of the humorous quality he would undoubtedly have been drawn into a smile at his own position; as it was, he saw nothing ludicrous in the idea of an elderly student seated on an Irish ditch, playing umpire to a couple of children. As the horses started, he merely settled himself more securely in his seat, and drew out his handkerchief in obedience to the instinct that some expression of enthusiasm would be demanded by the winner. He could not picture himself raising a cheer as the conqueror sailed past him; but his dignity affably bent to the idea of a friendly wave of a handkerchief.

A slight breeze was blowing in from the sea, and the intense freshness of the atmosphere again obtruded itself upon him as he watched the horses swing towards him across the fields, the thud of their hoofs upon the grass gaining in volume with every stride.

For a space they galloped neck to neck; then slowly, almost imperceptibly, Clodagh drew away. For a couple of seconds the distance between the animals became noticeable; then young Asshlin, urging the chestnut, regained his lost position, and to Milbanke's eyes the two were again abreast as they crossed the last field.

Once more he settled himself in his place of vantage. Something in the freshness of the morning, something in the youth and vitality of the competitors gave the race an interest and attraction it would otherwise have lacked. With a reluctant sensation—half curiosity, half the alien's unaccountable attraction towards conditions of life other than his own—he found himself straining his eyes towards the two slight figures moving towards him across the short grass. Nearer and nearer they came, maintaining their level positions; then, as the last ditch came clearly into view, the grey mare seemed to gather herself together for the short final gallop and the jump. Leaning forward, he saw Clodagh straighten herself in the saddle as each stride increased the advantage she had gained.

Unconsciously—with the nearer pounding of the hoofs—the excitement of the moment touched him. But it touched him with disastrous results. As the mare neared the ditch, he suddenly leant forward, losing the balance he had so carefully preserved.

The action was instantaneous, and it was but the work of another instant to grasp the sturdy weeds that topped the ditch, and regain his position; but unwittingly the harmless incident had changed the result of the race. As he involuntarily steadied himself, the handkerchief, held in readiness for the victor, slipped from his hand and fluttered down upon the grass.

It fell at the feet of the grey mare. She paused in sudden alarm, then hunched herself together, and shied away from it as from a ghost.

No harm was done. Clodagh kept her seat without a tremor; but in that second of lost time the cob drew level with his rival, then sailed triumphantly over the ditch.

For Milbanke there was a moment of horrible suspense, and a succeeding relief that drove all thought of the race and its result far from his mind. Immediately the field was clear he scrambled from his position and hurried to where Clodagh was soothing the still frightened Polly.

"Miss Clodagh," he began, "I am so sorry. I assure you it—it was not my fault."

Clodagh was bending low over the mare's neck, her flushed face partially hidden. She made no reply to his confused and stammering speech.

"Miss Clodagh," he began afresh, "you are not angry? You don't think it was my fault?"

Clodagh laughed a little tremulously.

"Of course not," she said. "How can you be so silly? I hadn't her properly in hand, that was all."

As she finished young Asshlin cantered back, halting on the further side of the ditch. His face was also flushed and his eyes looked dark.

"Look here," he said, eyeing Milbanke, "what did you mean by balking her like that? What were you doing with your beastly handkerchief? 'Twas no race, Clo!"

But Clodagh looked up.

"Oh yes, it was," she said. "It was all my own fault; I hadn't Polly in hand. I should have pulled her together and sent her over with a touch of the whip. Apologise, Larry! 'Twas a fair race."

But Larry still hesitated, his glance straying doubtfully from one face to the other.

"Honour bright, Clo?" he asked at last.

Clodagh nodded.

"Then I'm sorry, sir," he said frankly, "for saying what I said."

Milbanke made a murmur of forgiveness; and a moment later Nance appeared upon the scene, breathless and full of curiosity. As Larry entered upon a voluble account of the finish in reply to her eager questions, Clodagh wheeled the mare round and trotted quickly across the fields in the direction of the house.

For a moment or two Milbanke stood irresolute; then a sudden impulse to follow the mare and her rider seized him, and ignoring Nance and Larry—still absorbed in heated explanation—he took his way slowly across the green and springy turf.

His crossing of the field was measured and methodical, and he had barely come within sight of the arched gateway of the yard when Clodagh reappeared—this time on foot. The tail of her habit was tucked under one arm, the struggling form of an Irish terrier was held firmly under the other.

She came straight forward in his direction; and, reaching him, would have passed on without speaking. But he halted in front of her.

"Miss Clodagh," he said, "you are hurt and disappointed."

Clodagh averted her eyes.

"I'm not," she said shortly.

"But I see that you are."

"No, I'm not."

"Miss Clodagh, you are. Can't I do something?"

Then at last she looked at him. Her cheeks were burning, and her eyes were brimming with tears that only pride held back.

"It isn't the old race," she said defiantly. "It's—it's Mick."

Two tears suddenly welled over and dropped on the red head of the dog, who responded with an adoring look and a wild attempt to lick her face.

"Oh, I've had him since he was six weeks old!" she cried impulsively. "I reared him and trained him myself! He knows every word I say."

Milbanke suddenly looked relieved.

"Is that all?" he exclaimed cheerfully. "Is that all? We'll soon put that right. Keep your dog. I'll settle matters with your cousin."

He glanced back across the fields to where Larry was walking the cob to and fro.

But Clodagh's face expressed intense surprise.

"But you don't understand," she said. "Mick was the stake. 'Twas a fair race, and Larry won. Mick is—is Larry's now."

He laughed a little.

"Oh, nonsense! You raced for fun."

"Yes, for the best fun we could get," she said seriously. "That's why we staked what we cared most about. Don't you understand?"

For the moment her grief was merged in her unaffected surprise at his lack of comprehension.

But Milbanke was staring at her interestedly. The scene at the breakfast-table, and with it Asshlin's offended pride and ridiculous dignity, had risen before him with her soft, surprised tone, her wide, incredulous gaze. With total unconsciousness she was voicing the sentiments of her race. An Asshlin might neglect everything else in the world, but his debts of honour were sacred things.

He looked more closely at the pretty, distressed face, at the brimming eyes, and the resolutely set lips.

"And simply because you staked him," he said, "you intend to lose the dog?"

Clodagh caught her breath, and a fresh tear fell on Mick's head; then with a defiant lifting of the chin she started forward across the field.

"'Twas a fair race," she said in an unsteady voice.

# CHAPTER VII

Whatever Clodagh may have felt upon the subject, she made no further allusion to the loss of her dog.

An hour after the race, Milbanke, standing at his bedroom window, caught a glimpse of Larry riding slowly across the fields towards the avenue with the evidently unwilling Mick held securely under his arm; and a few minutes afterwards, a noisy bell, clanging through the house, informed him that luncheon had been served.

The two girls were already in the dining-room when he entered. Clodagh had changed her riding habit for a neat holland dress; her hair was smoothly plaited, and only a lingering trace of the morning's excitement burned in her cheeks.

As the guest entered, she came forward at once and pointed to his chair with a pretty touch of gracious hospitality.

"Where is your cousin?" he said, as he responded to her gesture.

She flushed momentarily.

"Gone!" she answered laconically. Then, conscious that the reply was curt, she made haste to amend it. "He's gone home to lunch," she added. "Aunt Fan wanted him back. She's a great invalid and always worrying about him. I suppose invalids are never like other people. Will you please help yourself?"

She smiled and indicated a steaming stew—sufficient to feed ten hungry people—that Hannah, acting in Burke's absence, had planted heavily upon the table.

"We always begin lunch with meat," Clodagh explained; "but we always finish with tea and whatever Hannah will make for us to eat. If you stay long enough you'll be able to tell all Hannah's tempers by what we get at lunch. When she's terribly cross we have bread and jam; when she's middling we get soda bread; but when she's really and truly nice we have currant loaf or griddle cake!"

She glanced round mischievously at the red face of the factotum.

Hannah, who had been wavering between offence and amusement, suddenly succumbed to the look.

"Sure, 'tis a quare notion you'll be givin' him of the place," she said, amicably joining in the conversation without a shade of embarrassment. "If I was you, I wouldn't be tellin' a gintleman that I laves the whole work of the house to wan poor ould woman, an' goes galavantin' over the country mornin', noon, an' night, instead of learnin' meself to be a good housekeeper! So signs, 'tis Miss Nance that'll find the husband first!" With a knowing glance at Milbanke and a shake of the head she left the room, banging the door behind her.

Clodagh laughed. The insinuation in Hannah's words and look passed unnoticed by her. She swept them aside unconcernedly, and proceeded with an inborn tact—an inborn sense of the responsibilities of her position— to fill her *rôle* of hostess and entertain her guest.

So successful was she in this new aspect, that Milbanke found himself thawing—even growing communicative under her influence as the meal progressed. Long before the appetising griddle cake and the heavy silver teapot had been laid upon the table he had begun to feel at home; to meet Nance's shy, friendly smiles without embarrassment; to talk with freedom and naturalness of his small, personal ambitions, his own unimportant, individual researches in his pet study of antiquity.

A reticent man—when once his reticence has been broken down— makes as egotistical a confidant as any other. Before they rose from the table, he had been beguiled into forgetting that the Celtic zeal for the entertainment of a guest may sometimes be mistaken for something more; that Irish children—with their natural kinship to sun and rain, dogs and horses, men and women—may assume, but cannot possibly feel, an interest in monuments of wood or stone, no matter how historic or how unique.

This erroneous impression remained with him until the time arrived for Clodagh to pilot him to Carrigmore; and filled with the knowledge of having a sympathetic listener, he harked back to his earliest experiences while he covered the two miles of firm yellow sand with his young hostess walking sedately beside him and half a dozen dogs—setters, retrievers, and sharp-nosed terriers—careering about him in a joyous band. He entered upon minute and technical details of every archæological discovery of the past decade; he recounted his personal opinion of each; he even unbent to the extent of relating a dry anecdote or two during that delightful walk in the mellow warmth of the afternoon. It was only when the long curve of the strand had at last been traversed and the rocks of Orristown left far behind, that discoveries, opinions, and stories alike faded from his mind in the nearer interest of the Carrigmore ruins.

Even to the pleasure-seeker there is something symbolic and imposing in the tall, grey, symmetrical tower that tops the hill above Carrigmore and faces the great sweep of the Atlantic Ocean; something infinitely ancient and impressive in the crumbling ruins of the church from whose walls the rudely carved figures look down to-day as they looked down in primitive Christian times, when Carrigmore was a centre of learning, and its tower a beacon to the world of Faith. To Milbanke—a student of such things—they were a revelation.

He scarcely spoke as he climbed the steep hill and entered the grass-grown churchyard; and once within the precincts of the ruin all considerations save the consideration of the moment faded from his thoughts. With the mild enthusiasm that his hobby always awoke in him, he set about a minute examination of the place, hurriedly unstrapping the satchel in which he carried his antiquarian's paraphernalia.

During the first half-hour Clodagh sat dutifully on one of the graves, alternately plaiting grasses and admonishing or petting her dogs; then her long-tried patience gave out. With a sudden imperative need of action she rose, shook the grasses from her skirt, and, picking her way between the half-buried headstones, reached Milbanke's side.

"Mr. Milbanke," she said frankly, "would you mind very much if I went away and came back for you in an hour? You see, the ruins aren't quite so new to me as they are to you—people say they've been here since the fourth century."

She laughed, and called to the dogs.

But Milbanke scarcely heard the laugh. There was a flush of delight on his thin cheeks as he peered through his magnifying-glass into one of the carved stones. He waited a moment before replying; then he answered with bent head.

"Certainly, Miss Clodagh," he said abstractedly—"certainly! But make it two hours, I beg of you, instead of one."

And with another amused laugh Clodagh took advantage of her dismissal.

Milbanke's absorption was so unfeigned that when Clodagh came running back nearly three hours later, full of remorse for her long desertion, he greeted her with something amounting to regret.

Twice she had to remind him that the afternoon was all but spent and the long walk to Orristown still to be reckoned with, before he could desist from the fascinating task of completing the notes he had made. At last, with a little sigh of amiable regret, he shut up his book, returned the magnifying-glass to his satchel, and slowly followed her out of the churchyard.

They had covered half a mile of the smooth strand, across which the first long shadows of evening had begun to fall, before the glamour of the past centuries had faded from his consideration, permitting the more material present to obtrude itself.

Then at last, with a little start of compunction, he realised how silent and uninteresting a companion he must seem to the girl walking so staidly beside him; and with something of guilt in the movement, he withdrew his eyes from the long, wet line of sand where the incoming tide was stealthily encroaching.

"Miss Clodagh," he said abruptly, "what are you thinking of?"

With frank spontaneity, she turned and met his gaze.

"I was wondering," she said candidly, "when you'd forget the Round Tower and remember about father."

He started, roused to a fresh sense of guilt.

"You—you mustn't think——" he began stammeringly.

But Clodagh laughed.

"Oh, don't bother about it!" she said easily. "I wasn't really thinking."

For a while he remained silent, watching the noisy dogs as they ineffectually chased the seagulls that wheeled above the unruffled waves; then, at last, urged by his awakened conscience, he half paused and looked again at the girl's bright face.

"Miss Clodagh," he began, "I feel very guilty—I *am* very guilty."

Clodagh glanced back at him.

"How?" she said simply.

"Because last night I unconsciously did what you disapprove of. I played with your father for high stakes, and I am ashamed to say that I won a large sum of money."

For an instant the brightness left her glance; she looked at him with the serious eyes of the night before.

"Much?" she asked impulsively.

"Twenty pounds." Milbanke felt himself colour. Then he rallied his courage. "But that isn't all," he added quickly. "I have something worse to confess. When I came down to breakfast this morning I found a cheque lying on my plate. I felt intensely remorseful, as you can imagine; and determined to make reparation. After breakfast I broached the subject to Denis; I begged him to allow me to cancel our play by tearing up the cheque. He was furiously angry; and I, instead of showing the courage of my opinion, was actually weak enough to succumb. Now, what punishment do you think I deserve?" He paused, looking at her anxiously.

For a while she looked steadily ahead, absorbed in her own thoughts; then slowly she looked back at him with interested, incredulous eyes.

"Don't English people pay when they lose?" she asked after a long pause.

Again he coloured.

"Why, yes," he said hurriedly. "Yes, of course, only——"

"Only what?"

"Nothing—nothing. It was only that I thought you wanted——"

"I wanted you not to encourage him. I never wanted you to think that he isn't a gentleman."

She made the statement with perfect naturalness, as though the subject was one of common, everyday discussion. According to her code of honour, she was justified in putting every possible bar to her father's weakness; but where the bar had proved useless, where the weakness had conquered and the deed she disapproved of had been accomplished, then the matter, to her thinking, had passed out of her hands. Her judgment ceased to be individual and became the judgment of her race.

As she looked at Milbanke's perplexed, concerned face, her expression changed, and she smiled. The smile was gracious and reassuring, but below the graciousness lay a tinge of tolerant indulgence.

"We won't talk about it any more," she said. "I don't suppose you can be expected to understand." And suddenly raising her head, she whistled to the dogs.

During the remainder of the walk Milbanke was very silent. Perplexed and yet fascinated by the problem, his mind dwelt unceasingly upon this strange position into which the chances of a day or two had thrown him. The bonds that drew him to his entertainers, and the gulf that separated him from them, were so tangible and yet so illusive. In every outward respect they were his fellow beings; they spoke the same language, wore the same dress, ate the same food, and yet unquestionably they were creatures of different fibre. He felt curiously daunted and curiously attracted by the peculiar fact.

To appreciate the difference between the Englishman and the Irishman one must see the latter in his native atmosphere. It is there that his faults and his virtues take on their proper values; there that his innate poetry, his reckless generosity, his prodigal hospitality have fullest scope; there that his primitive narrowness of outlook, his antiquated sense of honour and his absurdly sensitive self-esteem are most vividly backgrounded. Outside his own country, he is merely a subject of a great Empire, possessing, perhaps, a sharper wit and a more ingratiating manner than his fellow-subjects of colder temperament; but in his natural environment he stands out pre-eminently as a peculiar development—the product of a warm-blooded, intelligent, imaginative race that by some oversight of Nature has been pushed aside in the march of the nations.

Milbanke made no attempt to formulate this idea or any portion of it, as he paced steadily forward across the darkening sands; but incontinently it did flash across his mind that the girl beside him claimed more attention in this unsophisticated atmosphere than he might have given her in conventional surroundings. She was so much part of the picture—so undeniably a child of the sweeping cliffs, the magnificent sea, and the hundred traditions that encircled the primitive land. In her buoyant, youthful figure he seemed, by a curious retrograde process of the mind, to find the solution to his own early worship of Asshlin. Asshlin had attracted him, ruled him, domineered over him by right of superiority—the hereditary, half-barbaric superiority of the natural aristocrat; the man of ancient lineage in a country where yesterday—and the glories of yesterday—stand for everything, where to-day is unreckoned with, and to-morrow does not exist. Reaching the end of the strand, he turned to her quickly with a strange sensation of sympathy—almost of apprehension.

"Miss Clodagh," he said gently, as she began to ascend the heaped-up boulders that separated the road from the beach, "Miss Clodagh, I grant that I don't quite understand, as you put it; but I knew your father many years before you were born, and I think that gives me some privilege. On one point I have quite made up my mind. I shall not play cards again while I am in your house."

As he spoke, Clodagh paused in her ascent of the boulders and looked at him. In the softly deepening twilight her eyes again held the mysterious promise of great beauty; and in their depths a shade of respect, of surprised admiration had suddenly become visible. As she gazed at him, her lips parted involuntarily.

"I didn't think you were so plucky," she said; then abruptly she stopped, glancing over her shoulder.

From the road behind them came the clicking thud of a horse's hoofs, and a moment later the voice of Asshlin hailed them out of the dusk.

# CHAPTER VIII

It would be futile to deny that the unexpected sound of Asshlin's voice brought a tremor to the mind of his guest. It is disconcerting to the most valiant to be confronted with his antagonist in the very moment that he has laid down his challenge; and at best Milbanke was no hero. Nevertheless he recovered his equanimity with creditable speed, and exchanging a quick glance with Clodagh, scrambled hastily over the remaining stones and reached the road.

As he gained it, Asshlin pulled up sharply and dismounted from his big, bony horse with all the dexterity of a young man. With a loud laugh of greeting, he slipped the bridle over one hand and linked the other in Milbanke's arm.

"Hullo!" he cried. "Now who'd have dreamt that I'd meet you like this? I'm ashamed of you, James. 'Pon my word I am. Philandering across the strand in the fall of the evening as if you were still in the twenties. It's with me you should have been. We had the deuce of a fine run!"

He paused to push his hat from his hot forehead and to rearrange the bridle.

Clodagh, who had followed Milbanke slowly, stepped eagerly forward as she caught the last words.

"Oh, father," she cried, "tell us about it! Who was there? Was the sport good? Did the bay carry you well?"

In her suddenly awakened interest it was clear to Milbanke that the vital question she had been discussing with him—the opinions he had expressed upon it—his very existence even, were obliterated from her mind, her natural, youthful exuberance responding to the idea of any physical action as unfailingly as the needle answers to the magnet. And again the faintly poignant sense of aloofness and age fell upon him as he listened uncomprehendingly to Asshlin's excited flow of words, and watched the bright, ardent face of the girl glowing out of the shadows.

They made a curious trio as they covered the stretch of road that led to Orristown and passed between the heavy moss-grown piers of the big gate, entering the deep shade of the avenue. With an instinctive care for his horse, Asshlin went first, cautiously guiding the animal over the ruts that time and the heavy rains had ploughed in the soft ground. Behind him came Clodagh, Milbanke, and their following of dogs.

Once again the thought of what the evening held came unpleasantly to Milbanke's mind as the shadow of the gaunt beech trees and the outline of the great square house brought the position home to him afresh. Lack imagination as he might, he realised that it was no light task to thwart a man whose faults had been cultivated and whose peculiarities—racial and personal—had been accentuated by a quarter of a century of comparative isolation. But instinctively as the thought came to him, he turned to the girl, whose erect figure had grown indistinct in the gathering gloom.

"Miss Clodagh," he whispered, "though I may not understand, are you satisfied to trust me?"

There was a pause; then, with one of the sudden impulses that formed so large a part of her individuality, Clodagh put out her hand; and for an instant her fingers and Milbanke's touched.

To every one but Asshlin, the dinner that evening was a strain. But the silence or the uneasiness of the others was powerless to damp his enthusiasm. His appetite was tremendous; and as he ate plentifully and swallowed glass after glass of sherry, his excitement and his spirits rose. With the ardour of the born sportsman, he recounted again and again the details of the day's hunt—dwelling lovingly on the behaviour of the dogs and horses, and the prowess of his own mount in particular. Finally, he rose from the table with a flushed face, though a perfectly steady gait, and, crossing the room, pulled the long bell-rope that hung beside the fireplace.

"Now for our night, James!" he cried. "Now for my revenge!

"Clear the table, Burke," he added, as the old man appeared in answer to the summons. "Get out the cards, and bring enough candles to light us all to glory!" He gave a boisterous laugh; and, turning with a touch of bravado, stood facing the picture of his great-grandfather.

Instinctively, as he turned his back upon the party, little Nance drew nearer to her sister, and Clodagh glanced at Milbanke.

As their eyes met, he involuntarily stiffened his small, spare figure, and with a quick, nervous manner nodded towards the door.

For a moment Clodagh hesitated, her fear for her father's self-control dominated by her native interest in an encounter; then Nance decided the matter by plucking hurriedly at her sleeve.

"Don't stop, Clo!" she whispered almost inaudibly, her small, expressive face puckered with anxiety—"don't stop! I'm frightened."

The appeal was instantly effective. Clodagh rose at once, and with one arm passed reassuringly round the child's shoulder, slipped silently from the room.

For some moments after the two had departed, Asshlin retained his position: and Milbanke, intently watchful of his tall figure, held himself nervously in hand for the coming encounter. At last, when the cloth had been removed, the candles renewed, and the cards placed upon the table, Asshlin turned—his face flushed with anticipation.

"That's good!" he exclaimed. "That's good! With a bottle of port and a pack of cards a man could be happy in Hades! Not that I'm forgetting the good comrade that gives a flavour to the combination, James. Not that I'm forgetting that."

His smile had much of the charm, his voice much of the warmth that had marked them long ago, as he drew his chair to the table and picked up the cards.

Milbanke straightened himself in his seat.

"Come along, man! Draw up!—draw up to the table! What shall it be? Euchre again? Are you agreeable to the same stakes?" Asshlin talked on, heedless of the strangely unresponsive demeanour of his guest.

As he ceased to speak, however, Milbanke took the plunge he had been contemplating all day. In the silence of the room, broken only by the faint, comfortable hissing of the peat in the fireplace and the rustling of the cards as Asshlin mechanically shuffled them, he pulled his chair forward and laid his clasped hands on the table.

"Denis," he said in his thin, quiet voice, "I am sorry—very sorry to disappoint you, but I cannot play."

Asshlin paused in the act of shuffling and laid the cards down.

"What in the name of fortune are you talking about?" he asked. His tone was indulgent and amused; it was evident that the meaning in the other's words had not definitely reached him.

"It is not a joke," Milbanke interposed quickly. "I cannot—I do not intend to play."

Then for the first time a shadow of comprehension crossed Asshlin's face—but it was only a shadow. With a boisterous laugh, he leant forward and filled the empty glasses that stood upon the table, pushing one across to Milbanke.

"Have a drop of port, man!" he cried. "Twill give you courage to cut."

He lifted and drained his own glass, and setting it back upon the table, refilled it.

But Milbanke remained immovable. His thin hands were still clasped, his pale face looked anxious.

"Go on, James! You're not afraid of a drop of wine?" Again Asshlin laughed, but this time there was an unpleasant ring audible in his voice.

Mechanically Milbanke lifted his glass to his lips.

"No," he said with embarrassed deprecation, "no, I'm more afraid of your displeasure. I—I'm exceedingly sorry to disappoint you."

But once more his host laughed.

"Nonsense, man! I know your little scruples and your little conscience, and I'm not scared of either. Never meet the devil half way! He covers the ground too quickly as it is." He caught up the cards again, and forming them into a pack, held them out. "Cut!" he said laconically.

Milbanke drew back, and his lips came together, in a thin line.

"Come on! Cut!"

The colour of Asshlin's face became a shade deeper.

Still the other sat rigidly still.

For a moment their eyes held each other; then suddenly the blood surged into Asshlin's neck and face.

"Do you mean to say that you refuse to play?" he asked slowly. "That you refuse to give me my revenge?"

Milbanke met the attack unsteadily.

"My dear Denis——"

But before the words had left his lips, Asshlin flung the cards upon the table with a force that sent a score of them flying across the room.

"And may I ask you for your reasons?" he demanded with alarming calm.

Milbanke fenced.

"I do not wish to play."

"And I don't wish to be treated as a fool."

The other altered his attitude.

"My dear Denis, you surely acknowledge the right of free will? I do not wish to play cards, and therefore beg to be excused. What could be simpler?"

His manner was slightly perturbed, his speech hasty. There was the suggestion of a sleeping volcano in his host's unnatural calm.

In the silence that followed, Asshlin lifted his glass and emptied it slowly.

"I don't know about that," he said as he set it down. "There are unwritten codes that all the free will in the world won't dispose of. One of them is that a gentleman who wins at cards cannot refuse his opponent the satisfaction of his revenge. But perhaps the etiquette has changed since my time."

His manner was still controlled, but his eyes glittered.

Milbanke cleared his throat.

"My dear Asshlin," he said, "we are surely friends of too long standing to split hairs in this fashion. What is this revenge that you talk of? Nothing—a myth—an imaginary justification of honour."

A quick sound of contempt escaped Asshlin.

"And what is every code and every sentiment in the world but an outcome of imagination?" he cried. "What is it but imagination that herds us off from the beasts? I'm satisfied to call it imagination. It tells me that I was worsted last night, and that I'm capable of better things if I try my luck again. I'm satisfied to follow its promptings—and demand my revenge!"

For a while Milbanke sat miserable and undecided; then under the goad of the other's eyes, he did an ill-judged thing. Fumbling nervously for his letter-case, he rose from his seat and walked across to the fireplace.

"There is nothing for you to revenge," he said agitatedly. "There was no play last night. It's cancelled. I cancel it."

With tremulous haste, he pulled out the letter-case, extricated Asshlin's cheque, and dropped it into the fire.

There was a pause—a pause of tremendous moment—in which he stood aghast at his own deed. Then Asshlin turned on him, his face purple and convulsed with rage.

"You dare to insult me? You dare to insult me in my own house? You dare to imply that it was the money—the damned money, that I wanted to win back?"

Milbanke looked up sharply.

"Good God, no!" he exclaimed with unwonted vehemence. "Such a thought never entered my mind."

"Then what's the meaning of all this? What is it all driving at?"

Asshlin's hard, handsome face was contorted by passion and his hands shook.

"Nothing. It's driving at nothing. It is simply that I do not wish to play."

"And why not?" He suddenly rose, his great body towering above the other's. "Why not? By God, I'll have an answer!"

"There is no answer."

"No answer? We'll see about that. Who's been lying to you about me? Who's been carrying scandals about me? Out with it!—out with it!"

Then unexpectedly Milbanke's trepidation forsook him. He suddenly straightened himself.

"No one," he answered.

"No one? Are you quite sure?"

"No-one!"

"Then what do you mean by this? What do you mean by meddling in my affairs?"

He took a menacing step forward.

With a fierce gesture he took another step forward.

Milbanke stood firm.

"I have my reasons," he said quietly.

"Your reasons, have you?" Asshlin laughed harshly. "Then I'll have my answer. What do you mean by it?"

For a second the older man remained silent and unmoved; then a light gleamed in his colourless eyes.

"All right!" he said. "You shall have it. Perhaps it is as well. I came here expecting to see the boy I had known grown into a genial, hospitable, honourable gentleman; instead, I find him an undisciplined, tyrannical egotist."

He said it quickly in a rush of unusual vehemence. All his anticipations, all his suspicions, and their subsequent justification—coupled with the new sense of protection towards the children of his early friend—found voice in these words.

"You are an egotist, Denis," he repeated distinctly. "A weak, worthless egotist—not fit to have children—not fit to have a friend——"

Asshlin stared at him for a moment in speechless surprise; then indignation surmounted every other feeling. With a fierce gesture he took another step forward, his eyes blazing, his hand menacingly clenched.

"How—how dare you?" he stammered. "How dare you? By God, if you were a bigger man I'd—I'd——"

He paused, choked by his fury.

"I know—I know. But I'm not afraid of you. I'm not to be bullied into subjection."

Milbanke's temper, difficult to rouse, was stirred at last. He gave his host glance for glance.

"You realise what you have said?" Asshlin's dark face was distorted, his voice came unsteadily.

"Yes. I regret that I have to say it, but I do not regret saying it. It is wholesome for a man to hear the truth."

"Oh, it's wholesome to hear the truth, is it?"

"Yes; and I won't see you go to pieces for want of a word. You are a man with obligations, and you are neglecting your obligations. There are other things in life besides cards and horses——"

Asshlin suddenly threw back his head.

"By God, you're right!" he cried. "And the other things are a damn sight worse. I'd put a good horse before a self-righteous preacher any day."

Milbanke's usually pallid face flushed.

"You mean that for me?" he asked quietly.

Asshlin shrugged his shoulders.

"If you like," he said. "If the cap fits——" For a moment Milbanke said nothing; then once again he straightened his small, thin figure.

"Very well, Denis," he said, "I quite understand. With your permission I will say good-bye to you now, and to-morrow morning I will catch the earliest train from Muskeere."

He looked at his host steadily. Then, through the temper that still mastered him, a twinge of regret, a sense of parting and loss obtruded themselves. With all his intolerable faults, Asshlin still stood within the halo and glamour of the past.

"Denis!" he exclaimed suddenly.

But the appeal was made too late. Uncontrollable fury—the one power which could efface his sense of hospitality—possessed Asshlin. His pulses pounded; his senses were blurred. With a seething consciousness of insult and injury, he turned again upon his guest.

"You can go to hell for all I care!" he cried savagely.

For a second Milbanke continued to look at him; then without a word he turned, crossed the room, and passed into the hall.

# PART II

# CHAPTER I

It was on a windy March morning three years after his summarily ended visit to Ireland, that James Milbanke stood in the bedroom of his London flat. A perturbed frown puckered his forehead and he held an open letter in his hand.

Outside, the dark sky and cold searching breeze proclaimed the raw English spring; inside, the partly dismantled walls of the room, the emptied drawers and wardrobe, the trunks, bags, and rugs standing ready strapped, all suggested another and more inviting climate. Milbanke was bound for the south.

Three months earlier he had come to the momentous conclusion that a solitary life in London—spent no matter how comfortably—becomes a colourless and somewhat empty thing after a thirty-three years' experience. He had his club and his friends, but he was not a clubman born, and friends must be very intimate to be all-sufficing. The restlessness that sometimes unexpectedly attacks the middle-aged bachelor had fallen upon him. The suggestion that he craved new surroundings and new fields of interest had been slow in coming, and his acceptance of it had been slow. But steadily and inevitably it had grown into his consciousness, maturing almost against his will, until at last the day had dawned on which he had admitted to himself that a change was indispensable. The subsequent events had followed in natural order. His hobby had urged him to leave his own country for one richer in association; the damp cold of the English winter, coupled with the chilled blood of advancing age, had inclined him to the idea of Southern Europe. The result of his triple suggestion was that he stood in his room on that spring morning in the last stages of preparation for a journey to Italy.

He stood there, with the discomfort of packing pleasantly accomplished, and his belongings neatly surrounding him; yet his attitude and expression were those of a man who is faced by an unlooked-for difficulty. With a nervous gesture, he shook out the letter that he held, and began to read it hastily for the fourth time. It was a long letter, written in a careless, almost boyish hand on thin paper, and bore the address of "Orristown, Ireland." It was dated two days earlier, and began:

"Dear Mr. Milbanke,—

"You will be very much surprised to get this, but I write for father, not for myself. He had a bad accident yesterday while out riding, and is terribly hurt and ill. The doctor from Carrigmore is with him all the time, and my aunt—as well as Nance and I; so he is well cared for. But he seems to get worse instead of better, and we are dreadfully frightened about him.

"There is one thing he constantly craves for—and that is to see you. Ever since that night, three years ago, when you and he quarrelled and you went away, I think he has been fretting about you. Of course, he has never spoken of it, but I don't think he has ever forgotten that he treated you badly.

"This morning he talked a great deal about the time when you and he were young together; so much so, that I asked him if he would like to see you. The moment I spoke his face lighted up, but then at once it clouded over again, and he muttered something about never giving any man the chance of refusing him a favour.

"Dear Mr. Milbanke asking you to come here, but I feel differently. I would risk anything a hundred times over on the chance of bringing you to him. And if you are in London, please do come, if only for one night. Don't refuse, for he is very, very bad. Any time you send me a telegram, the trap can meet you either at Muskeere or Dunhaven.

"This is a dreadful letter, but I have been up all night, and scarcely know what I am writing.

"Answer as soon as possible,

"Yours,

"Clodagh Asshlin."

Milbanke scanned the letter to the last line; then, as he reached the signature, the inertia that had pervaded his mind was suddenly dispersed. His own shock of sorrow and dismay, his own interrupted plans faded from his consideration; and in their place rose the picture of a great white house on the lonely Irish coast; of a sick—perhaps a dying—man; of two frightened children and a couple of faithful, inefficient servants. With an energy he had not evinced for years he crossed the room, stumbling over straps and parcels, and rang the bell with imperative haste.

When a surprised maid appeared at the door he turned to her with unwonted excitement.

"I have a telegram to send," he said; "one that must go at once."

The rest of that day, with its suddenly altered plans, its long railway journey from Paddington to New Milford, and its stormy night crossing from the latter point to the town of Waterford, was too beset with haste and confusion to contain any definite recollections for Milbanke. It was not until he had taken his seat at eight o'clock next morning in the small and leisurely train that transports passengers from Waterford to the seaport of Dunhaven that he found time to realise the significance of his journey; and not until he descended from his carriage at this latter station and was greeted by old Burke, the Orristown retainer, that he fully appreciated the gravity of the incident that had occasioned it.

There was no change apparent in Burke's familiar face save the gloom that overhung his expression. But this was obvious to Milbanke at a first glance.

"You're welcome, sir!" were his opening words; then the underlying bent of his thoughts found vent. "'Tis a sorrowful house you'll be findin'," he added in a subdued voice.

Milbanke glanced up sharply from the rug he was unstrapping.

"How is he?" he asked. "Not worse?"

Burke shook his head.

"'Twouldn't be wishin' for me to give you the bad word——" he began deprecatingly.

"Then he is bad?"

The old man pursed up his lips.

"Ah, I'm in dread 'tis for his long home he's bound," he said reluctantly. "Glory be to God an' His Holy Ways! But 'tis of thim two poor children that I do be thinkin'."

But Milbanke's mind was occupied with his first words.

"But how is he?" he demanded. "What is the injury? Has he an efficient doctor?"

Again Burke shook his head.

"Docthors?" he said dubiously. "Wisha, I don't put much pass on docthors! not but what they say Docthor Gallagher from Carrigmore is a fine hand wid the knife. But, sure, when the Almighty takes the notion to break every bone in a man's body, 'tisn't for the like of docthors to be settin' up to mend them."

With this piece of pessimistic philosophy, he picked up Milbanke's bags and rug, and guided him through the small station into the open, where the Orristown trap stood waiting in a downpour of rain.

He imparted little more information during the long drive, and Milbanke had to sit under his dripping umbrella with as much patience as he could muster while they ploughed forward over an execrable road.

The gateway of Orristown, when at last it was reached, looked mouldy and forlorn in the chilly damp of the atmosphere; and as they plunged up the avenue at the usual reckless pace, a perfect torrent of rain-drops deluged them from the intersecting branches of the trees. Yet despite the gloom and the discomfort, a thrill of something like pleasure filled Milbanke as a whiff of pure, cold air brought the scent of the sea to his nostrils, and the turn of the avenue showed the square house, white and massive against the grey sky.

But he was given little time to indulge in the pleasure of reminiscence, for instantly the trap drew up, the hall door was thrown open, showing a face and figure that sent everything but the moment and the business in hand far from his mind.

It was Clodagh who stood there waiting to greet him—Clodagh, curiously changed and grown in the three years that had passed since their last meeting. In place of the spirited, unformed child that he remembered, Milbanke saw a very young girl, whose boyishness of figure had disappeared in slight feminine curves, whose bright, fearless eyes had softened into uncommon beauty.

With a glow of relief lighting up her face, she stepped forward as the horse halted, and, heedless of the rain that fell on her uncovered head, laid one hand on the shaft of the trap.

"Oh, it's good of you!—it's good of you!" she exclaimed. "We can never forget it."

Then the colour flooded her cheeks, and her eyes filled.

"Oh, he's so bad!" she added. "It's so terrible to see him—so terrible."

She looked up with alarm and impotence into Milbanke's face.

But it was not the guest, but old Burke who found words to calm her fear and grief. Leaning down from his seat, he laid a rough hand on her shoulder.

"Whist now, Miss Clodagh!" he said softly—"whist now! Sure God is good. While there's life there's hope. Don't be believin' anythin' else. Sure, what is he but a young man yet?"

"That's true, Burke—that's true!" Clodagh exclaimed quickly. "Won't you come in, Mr. Milbanke?" she added. "You know how welcome you are."

Once inside the hall, she turned to him quickly and confidingly.

"I can never forget that you've done this," she said. "It's a really, really generous thing. But all my mind is full of father. You can understand, can't you?"

Her agitation, her alarm, her evident helplessness in presence of a contingency never previously faced, all touched him deeply. His tone was low and gentle as he responded.

"I understand perfectly—perfectly," he said. "Poor Denis! Poor Denis! How did the thing occur?"

"Oh, just an accident—just an accident. About six months ago he took a fancy for riding late at night. He used to ride for miles along the most dangerous paths of the cliff. I knew it wasn't safe; I said so over and over again. But you know father!" She gave a little hopeless shake of her head. "On Monday night he saddled one of the young horses at about ten o'clock, and went out by himself. It came to twelve and he hadn't returned. Then we began to get uneasy, and at one o'clock we started to look for him. After a search all along the cliff, we found him wedged between two of the upper ledges of the rocks, terribly—terribly hurt." She shuddered palpably at the recollection. "We didn't know—we don't know even now—quite how it happened. But we think the horse must have lost his footing and fallen over the cliff, throwing father; for the poor thing was found dead on the shingle next morning. 'Twas a miracle that father escaped with his life, but he's terribly injured."

She paused again, as though the subject was too painful to be pursued.

Milbanke looked at her compassionately.

"Has he had proper medical advice?" he asked.

"Oh yes! Doctor Gallagher from Carrigmore has done everything, and we have a trained nurse from Waterford."

"That's right. I must have a talk with the doctor. But how is Denis now? Will he know me, do you think?"

"Oh yes! Ever since the first night he has been quite conscious. He expects you. He's longing to see you."

"Then may I go to him?"

Clodagh nodded; and, turning, led the way silently up the remembered staircase. On the landing, the recollection of their curious interview on his first night at Orristown recurred forcibly to Milbanke. He glanced at his guide to see if it had any place in her mind; but her thoughts were evidently full of other things. With a quick gesture that enjoined silence, she led him down the corridor, upon which rough fibre mats had been strewn to deaden sound.

With that peculiar sensation of awe that serious illness always engenders, he tip-toed after her, a sense of apprehensive depression growing upon him with every step. As they neared the end of the passage, a door opened noiselessly, and two figures emerged from a darkened room. The taller of the two—a pale, emaciated woman, dressed in mourning—was unknown to him; but a glance told him that the latter was little Nance, grown to pretty, immature girlhood.

On catching sight of him, she drew back with a passing touch of the old shyness; but, conquering it almost directly, she came forward and shook hands in silence. In the momentary greeting, he saw that her vivacious little face was red and marred by tears; but before he had time for further observation Clodagh touched his arm.

"My aunt, Mrs. Asshlin!" she whispered.

Milbanke bowed, and Mrs. Asshlin extended her hand.

"We meet on a sad occasion, Mr. Milbanke," she murmured in a low, querulous voice. "My poor brother-in-law was always such a rash man. But with some people, you know, there is no such thing as remonstrating. Even this morning when Mr. Curry, our rector from Carrigmore, came to have a little talk with him, he was barely polite; and it was only yesterday that we dared to tell him that Doctor Gallagher insisted on having a nurse. Now, what can you do with a patient like that?"

Milbanke murmured something vaguely unintelligible; and Clodagh stirred impatiently.

"Did you give him the medicine, Aunt Fan?" she asked.

"I did; but with great difficulty. My brother-in-law has always been averse to medical aid," she explained to Milbanke.

"He's never had any need of it," Clodagh whispered sharply. "Will you come, Mr. Milbanke? He's quite alone. The nurse is resting."

With great dignity Mrs. Asshlin moved away.

"I shall ask Hannah to get me a cup of tea, Clodagh," she murmured. "I get such a headache from a sick-room."

Without replying, Clodagh turned again to Milbanke.

"He's not to get excited," she whispered. "And mind—mind—don't say that you think him looking badly."

She paused and laid her fingers lightly on his arm; then with a swift movement, she stepped forward, drawing him with her into the big, darkened room with its sense of preternatural quiet, and its pungent, suggestive smell of drugs and antiseptic dressings.

# CHAPTER II

With a strange blending of curiosity and shrinking, Milbanke obeyed the pressure of Clodagh's hand, and moved forward into the room. The cold March daylight was partly excluded by drawn blinds, but a glow from the fire played upon the walls and the high four-post bedstead.

With the same mingling of curiosity and dread, his eyes fell at once upon this prominent article of furniture and remained fixed there in doubt and incredulity. For the moment his senses refused to acknowledge that the feverish, haggard face that stared at him from the pillows was the face of Asshlin—Asshlin, tyrannical, passionate, greedy of life.

In the hours of agony that he had passed through, the sick man's features had become shrunken, causing his eyes to stare forth preternaturally large and restless; his hair had been cropped close, to allow of the dressing of a wound over the temple, and the tight white bandages lent a strange and unfamiliar appearance to his finely shaped head. With a sick sensation, Milbanke went slowly forward.

The patient made no attempt to move as he drew near the bed, but his feverishly bright glance seemed to devour his face.

"Here he is, father!" Clodagh exclaimed softly and eagerly. "Here's Mr. Milbanke! Now, aren't you happy? He's not able to move," she explained, turning to the guest. "It gives him terrible agony to stir."

Milbanke had reached the bed; and with a sensation of awkwardness and impotence impossible to describe, he stood looking down upon Asshlin.

"My poor Denis!" he said. "My poor, poor friend! This is a bad business; I had no idea——"

Then he paused confusedly, remembering Clodagh's warning.

"But we'll see you laughing at it all before we're much older," he added, in awkward haste to make amends.

A gleam of something like irony crossed Asshlin's watchful eyes.

"I'm done for this time, James!" he said feebly. "I suppose I've had my day, and, like every other dog, must answer to the whistle. I don't complain! I'm getting more than my deserts in seeing you again. You're as welcome as the flowers in——"

His voice failed.

"I know—I know! Don't trouble! Don't try to speak!" Milbanke bent over him anxiously.

But Asshlin glanced back.

"Ah, but that's what I must do, James!" he said sharply. "That's what I want you for. I have something that must be said."

Milbanke turned to Clodagh.

"Is it right of him to excite himself?" he asked in distress. "If it's anything that you reproach yourself with, Denis——"

But Asshlin interrupted with a weak echo of his old intolerance.

"Send Clo away!" he said. "There's something I want to say."

Again Milbanke looked helplessly at Clodagh, but her eyes were fixed passionately on her father's face.

"He'll excite himself more if we cross him," she said hesitatingly. "I think I'd better go."

Still Milbanke hesitated.

"But the doctor?" he hazarded. "If the doctor insists on quiet——"

She glanced at him quickly, her clear eyes brimming.

"Oh, I don't know!" she exclaimed; "I can't cross him—I can't cross him! He's wanted you so badly."

She turned quickly towards the bed.

"Father," she said tenderly, "won't you promise not to talk much? Won't you promise to take care?"

For answer, Asshlin looked up, meeting her glance.

"I'll promise, child—I'll promise. Run away now—and God bless you!" He added the expressive native phrase in a suddenly lowered voice.

Clodagh bent quickly and kissed his hot, drawn face with passionate affection; then, as if fearing to trust herself, she turned hastily and passed out of the room.

Instantly the two men were alone, Asshlin turned to his guest.

"James," he said agitatedly, "I haven't thought much about the Almighty in these last years; but I give you my word, I have prayed that I might see you before I die."

"My dear Denis, don't! I beg you not to excite yourself. I implore you——"

Asshlin made a harsh sound of impatience.

"Don't waste breath over a dying man," he said roughly. Then, seeing the distress in the other's face, he altered his tone. "Don't take it to heart, James! It's the road we must all travel. They think there's life in me yet, but I know better. You may blindfold a sheep as much as you like, but 'twill know that you're dragging it to the slaughter. I tell you I'm done for—as done for as if the undertaker had measured me for the coffin."

He moved his head slightly and painfully, his feverish glance brightening.

"James," he exclaimed suddenly, "I'm in a terrible position! But 'tisn't death that's troubling me."

"Denis!"

"'Tis true! I'm not frightened of death—I hope I'm man enough to face a natural law. 'Twould have been better if I'd had to face it thirty years ago."

"Denis, don't! I beg you to keep quiet——"

"Quiet? I tell you there's not much quiet for a man like me. 'Tisn't what I'm going to that's troubling me, but what I'm leaving behind. I'll be paying me own score on the other side; but here 'tis others will be paying it for me."

His burning eyes fixed themselves on Milbanke's.

"But, my dear old friend——"

"Don't talk to me, James! Don't waste words on me. I'm broke inside and out. I'm smashed. I'm done for." A spasm of pain, mental and physical, twisted his features. "The weak, worthless egotist has come to the end of his rope!" He tried to laugh.

Milbanke, in deep apprehension, laid his hand lightly on his shoulder.

"Denis," he pleaded, "don't talk like this! Don't torture yourself like this!"

Asshlin groaned.

"'Tis involuntary!" he cried. "'Tis wrung from me. Every time they come into the room—every time I see the tears in their eyes—every time they kiss me, I tell you I taste hell."

"Who?"

"The children. My children." Another spasm crossed his face. "You once told me I was not fit to have children, James—and you were right. By God, you were right!"

"Denis, I refuse to listen. I insist—I——"

"Don't bother yourself! 'Tisn't of my damned health I'm thinking."

"Then what is it? What is troubling you?"

"The children—the children. I've been a blackguard, James—a blackguard." He moved his head sharply, regardless of the agony the movement caused. "I tell you I don't care what's before myself. I've always been a reckless fool. But 'tis the children—the children."

"What of the children?"

A sound of mockery and despair escaped Asshlin.

"Ah, you may well ask!" he said—"you may well ask! 'Tis the question I've been putting to myself every hour since they laid me here. You know the world, James. You know what the world will be to two pretty, penniless girls. And they're so unconscious of it all! That's the sting of it. They're so unconscious of it all! They care for me; they cling to me as if I were a good man, and in five years' time they may be cursing the hour they were born." A fresh groan was wrung from him.

A look of apprehension crossed Milbanke's face.

"Oh no, Denis!" he exclaimed quickly. "No. Things can't be as bad as that. Your suffering has told upon your nerves. Things can't be as bad as that."

"They are worse. I tell you these two children will face life without a penny."

"No, no! You exaggerate. Why, even if you were to die they would still have the place. The place must be worth something."

"Ah, if I could only drug my conscience with that thought! But I can't—I can't! Before I'm cold in my grave my creditors will be down on the property like a swarm of rats."

"No, no!"

"Yes! I tell you yes! The children will be homeless as well as penniless."

Milbanke glanced about him in deep perplexity.

"There's your sister-in-law," he hazarded at length.

"Fan?" Asshlin made a contemptuous grimace. "Fan is as poor as a church mouse already. Laurence had nothing to leave her: the Navy beggared him. No, Fan could do nothing for them. And, anyway, she and Clodagh couldn't stand each other for a twelvemonth. You might as well try to blend fire and water. No, there's no way out of it. I'm reaping the whirlwind, James. I'm reaping it with a vengeance."

The fever of his suffering and the excitement of his remorse were burning in his eyes. In the three days of his illness his natural exuberance of mind had been directed towards one point—the tardily aroused knowledge of the future that awaited his children. And the consequence had been a piteous intermingling of realisation and partial delirium. His agony and helplessness were pitiable as he turned to his friend.

"What am I to do, James?" he asked—"what am I to do?"

Milbanke bent over him.

"Denis! Denis!" he pleaded.

"But what am I to do? Advise me while there's time. 'Tis for that I've wanted you. You've always been a good man. What must I do?"

Milbanke tightened his lips.

"You have friends," he said.

"Ah! but how many? And where?"

There was no response for a moment, as Milbanke slowly straightened himself and glanced across the room towards the fire. Then very quietly he turned towards the bed.

"You have one—here," he said in a low voice.

For an instant Asshlin answered nothing; then an odd sound—something between a laugh and a sob—shook him.

"James!" he cried. "James!"

But Milbanke leant forward hastily.

"Not a word!" he said. "Not one word! If thanks are due, it is from me to you. It is not every day that human responsibilities fall to an old bachelor of my age."

Asshlin remained silent. Dissipated, blunted, degenerate though he might be, his native intuition was unimpaired; and in a flash of illumination he saw the grade of nobility, the high point of honour to which this prosaic, unimaginative man had attained in that moment of need. With a pang of acute pain, he freed his uninjured arm and shakingly held out his hand.

"There are no friends like the old friends, James!" he said in a broken voice.

# CHAPTER III

Asshlin scarcely spoke again during the early portion of that day. The immense effort of his explanation to Milbanke left him correspondingly weak; though through all his exhaustion, a look of peace and satisfaction was visible in his eyes.

During the whole morning Milbanke remained at his bedside, only leaving the room to partake—at Clodagh's urgent request—of a hurried meal in the deserted dining-room. At twelve o'clock the nurse resumed her duties, and soon afterwards the dispensary doctor from Carrigmore drove over to see his patient. Before he came into the sick-room Milbanke left it; but when—his examination over—he departed with a whispered injunction to the nurse, he found the stranger waiting for him in the corridor.

Milbanke stepped forward as he appeared, and silently motioned him down the passage to his own room, inviting him to enter with a punctilious gesture.

"Doctor Gallagher, I believe?" he said. "Allow me to introduce myself. My name is Milbanke. I am a very old friend of your patient."

With a slow but friendly gesture, the young man held out his hand.

"Oh, I know all about you!" he said. "I'm glad to make your acquaintance."

His voice, with its marked Irish accent, was soft and pleasant, and his glance was good-natured; but his tanned skin and rough shooting-suit suggested the sportsman rather than the medical practitioner.

Milbanke eyed him quickly.

"Then you won't misunderstand anything I may say?"

Gallagher smiled.

"Not a bit of it!" he answered nonchalantly. "And what's more, I think I know what it's going to be."

A shade of confusion passed over the Englishman's face. His understanding was still unattuned to the half-shrewd, half-inquisitive tendencies of the Irish mind. With a shadowy suspicion that he was being unobtrusively ridiculed, he became a degree colder.

"I am grieved beyond measure at Mr. Asshlin's condition, Doctor Gallagher," he said, "and it has struck me—it has been suggested to my mind that possibly——" He stopped uncertainly. "That possibly——"

"That perhaps there ought to be another opinion?" Gallagher looked at him complacently. "Well, maybe you're right. 'Tisn't because *I* condemn him that he shouldn't appeal to a higher court."

Milbanke started.

"Then you think poorly of his chances?"

Gallagher shook his head expressively.

"You despair of him?"

A pang of unexpected grief touched Milbanke. He realised suddenly how distant, vague, and yet how real a part the ideal of his youth had played in his life and thoughts; how deep a niche, unknown to them both, Asshlin had carved for himself. With a sense of loss altogether disproportionate to circumstances, he turned again to the doctor.

"Yes, I should like another opinion," he said quickly. "The best we can get—the best in Ireland. We can't get a man from town sooner than to-morrow, and time is everything. I suppose Dublin is the place to wire to? Not that I am disparaging you," he added. "I feel confident you have done everything."

Gallagher smiled.

"Oh, I'm not taking offence. It's only human nature to think what you do. I'll meet any one you like to name. But he'll say the same as me."

"And that is?"

"That he's done for." Gallagher lowered his voice. "He hasn't the stamina to pull through, even if we could patch him up. He's been undermining that big frame of his for the last ten years. No man nowadays can sit up half the night drinking port without paying heavily for it. Many a time, driving home from a late call, I've seen the light in these windows at three in the morning."

Milbanke pulled out his watch.

"But these Dublin doctors," he said. "Tell me their names."

Gallagher pondered a moment.

"Well, there's Dowden-Gregg and Merrick," he said. "And of course there's Molyneaux. Molyneaux is a magnificent surgeon. If any man in Ireland can make a suggestion, he will. But of course his fee——"

Milbanke interrupted sharply.

"Molyneaux let it be," he said decisively. "Wire for him when you get back to Carrigmore. Wire urgently. The expenses will be my affair. What they may amount to is of no consideration."

A look of involuntary respect crossed Gallagher's face.

"I understand," he said. "I'll wire at once. And you can comfort yourself that you'll have the best opinion in the country."

He nodded genially, the new considerations for Milbanke tinging his usually careless manner; and with an inaudible word of farewell, turned on his heel.

Once alone, Milbanke went in search of Clodagh. He suffered no small trepidation at the thought of communicating his action to her, and he bestowed much silent consideration upon the manner in which he should couch his information. Failing to find her in the house, he wandered out into the grounds. The rain had ceased, and a watery gleam of sunshine was falling on the wet gravel of the drive. Picking his way carefully, he turned in the direction of the yard; but he had scarcely reached it, when Clodagh's clear voice reached him, directing Burke as to some provisions required from Muskeere.

On seeing her guest, she came forward at once. Her face looked brighter and happier than he had seen it since his arrival. Her mercurial nature had responded instantly to the apparent change in Asshlin.

"Oh, isn't it lovely that he's so much better?" she cried. "You must have the gift of healing; it's like as if you had set a charm."

Milbanke made no response.

"Why don't you say something?" she asked quickly. "Don't you think he's better? Doesn't the doctor think he's better?"

Her quick mind sprang like lightning from one conclusion to another.

"Mr. Milbanke," she added, "you're keeping something back! There's something you don't like to say!"

Then at last Milbanke found voice.

"Indeed no, Miss Clodagh. You are wrong—quite wrong, believe me. There is nothing to be alarmed at—nothing. It is only— —"

"Only what?"

"Now don't be alarmed! I beg you not to be alarmed!" The sudden whiteness that had overspread her face unnerved him. "It is only that I, as a Londoner, am a little doubtful of your village doctor. A mere prejudice, I know. But Gallagher is broadminded and willing to humour me. And he—I—that is, we both think that another opinion will do no harm. It's nothing to be alarmed at. Nothing, believe me! A mere formality."

But Clodagh's lips had paled. She stood looking at him silently, her large, questioning eyes reminding him disconcertingly of Asshlin's.

"Miss Clodagh," he said again, "don't be alarmed!—don't be alarmed! It's only to satisfy an old sceptic——"

"Oh no, it isn't!" she said suddenly. "Oh no, it isn't! I know—I know quite well. It means that he's going to die."

Her voice caught; and, with a swift movement, she turned and fled out of the yard, leaving Milbanke pained, bewildered, and alarmed.

The afternoon passed in weary, monotonous waiting. Half an hour after the conversation in the yard, Clodagh appeared in her father's room. She was pale and subdued, and her eyelids looked suspiciously red, but she took her place quietly at the foot of the bed. She sat very still, her eyes fixed on Asshlin's face, apparently heedless of both the nurse's deft movements and Milbanke's silent, unobtrusive presence. At three o'clock the acute pains that had tormented the patient at intervals ever since the accident had occurred, returned with a violence that seemed accentuated by the respite he had obtained during the morning. For an hour or more he writhed and groaned in unspeakable agony, while those about him suffered a reflected torment, and chafed impotently at the distance that cut off Carrigmore and the possibility of any fresh medical relief. The nurse was unceasingly vigilant; but the mild and cautious remedies ordered by Gallagher were powerless to soothe the violent pain. At last Nature mercifully intervened, and the exhausted sufferer fell into a sleep that lasted for several hours.

At seven o'clock there was a stir of excitement through the house, as the whisper passed from one to another that the Dublin surgeon had arrived. When the news reached the sick-room, Milbanke drew a breath of intense relief; but Clodagh's pale face went a shade whiter.

The great man arrived attended by Gallagher, and was shown directly to the patient's room. There was a confused moment of introduction; then Milbanke and Clodagh slipped quietly into the passage, leaving the doctors and nurse to their work.

During a long interval of indescribable suspense Molyneaux made his examination. Then, without a word, he and Gallagher emerged from the room and descended solemnly into the dining-room.

While this final conference lasted Clodagh—who had returned to her vigil immediately the doctors had left the sick-room—sat silent and motionless beside the bed; outside in the corridor, Mrs. Asshlin wandered to and fro, weakly tearful and agitated, while Nance stood beside her father's door, afraid to enter and yet reluctant to remain outside. Downstairs in the hall, Milbanke paced up and down in nervous perturbation, awaiting his summons to the conclave.

At last the door opened, and Gallagher looked out.

"Mr. Milbanke," he said, "Doctor Molyneaux would like to see you."

With a little start of agitation Milbanke went forward.

In the dining-room a great peat fire was burning as usual, lighting up the faces of Asshlin's ancestors; but the candles in the silver sconces were unlighted and the window curtains had not been drawn. In the dull light from the three long windows the large, placid face of Molyneaux looked preternaturally long and solemn. Milbanke felt his heart sink.

In formal silence the great man rose and motioned him forward, and the three sat down at the centre table.

"Mr. Milbanke," he began in slow and unctuous tones, "I suppose you would like me to come to the point with as little delay as possible? Professional details will not interest you."

Milbanke nodded mechanically.

Molyneaux hesitated, studying his well-kept hands; then he looked up with the decorous reserve proper to the occasion.

"I regret to inform you, Mr. Milbanke," he said softly, "that my visit is of little—I might say of no—avail. Doctor—er—Gallagher's diagnosis of the case is satisfactory—perfectly satisfactory. Beyond mitigating his sufferings, I fear we can do nothing for our poor friend."

"Nothing!" Milbanke felt a sudden dryness in his throat.

Molyneaux shook his head with becoming gravity.

"Nothing, Mr. Milbanke. The injuries to the ribs and hip we might have coped with, but the seat of the trouble lies deeper. The internal——"

But Milbanke held up his hand.

"I beg you to give me no details," he said weakly. "This—this is a great shock to me."

He covered his face with his hands and sat silent for a few seconds.

Molyneaux tapped lightly upon the table with his finger-tips.

"It was merely that your mind might be fully satisfied, Mr. Milbanke — —" he said a trifle pompously.

Milbanke started.

"Forgive me! I understand — I fully understand. It is only the thought of what lies before us — the thought of his children's grief — —"

Molyneaux made a gracious gesture of comprehension.

"Ah, yes," he murmured. "Very distressing! Most distressing!"

He looked vaguely round the room; and Gallagher, as if anticipating his thought, pulled out his watch.

Milbanke rose quickly.

"I thank you very much, Doctor Molyneaux," he said, "for your — your valuable opinion. I think Miss Asshlin wishes to know if your train will permit you to partake of some dinner before you leave us?"

Molyneaux smiled with the air of a man who has put an unpleasant duty aside.

"Ah, thank you!" he said suavely. "Thank you! If Doctor — Gallagher gives me permission I shall be charmed. He understands your local time-tables, and has promised that I shall catch the night mail to Dublin."

He smiled again and glanced genially round the firelit room.

"What interesting family portraits our poor friend possesses!" he added with pleasant affability.

But Milbanke did not seem to hear.

"If you will excuse me for a moment," he said hastily, "I will see that you are caused no unnecessary delay. You can understand that we — that we are a somewhat demoralised household."

His voice was agitated, his step uneven as he crossed the room and passed into the hall.

Molyneaux followed him with a conventional glance of sympathy; then his eyes turned again to the pictures with the gratified glance of a dilettante.

"Do you happen to know if this is a Reynolds?" he said to Gallagher, rising and crossing the room.

# CHAPTER IV

To the last day of his life, that evening, with its horde of harassing and unfamiliar sensations, remained stamped upon Milbanke's mind; and not least among the unpleasant recollections was the visit of Molyneaux, and the dinner at which he himself unwillingly played host.

It may have been that his usually placid susceptibilities had undergone a strain that rendered him over sensitive; but whatever the cause, the atmosphere diffused by the great man jarred upon him. In his eyes, it seemed little short of callous that one who had just passed sentence of death upon his patient could so far remain unmoved as to partake with relish of the dinner set before him, and comment with affable appreciation upon the quality of the patient's wines.

Milbanke spoke little during the course of that meal. Try as he might to enact the part entrusted to him, his thoughts persistently wandered to the room upstairs, with its doomed sufferer and its anxious watchers, as yet mercifully ignorant of the verdict that had been pronounced. But if the host was silent, the guests made conversation. Gallagher was assiduous in his attentions to the man who, in his eyes, stood for the attainment of all ambition; and Molyneaux—under the unlooked-for stimulus of good, if homely food and wines that even as an epicure he admitted to be remarkable—was graciously pleased to accept the homage of his humble colleague, and to display a suave glimpse of the polished wit for which he was noted in society.

His expressions of regret were perfectly genuine when at last the sound of wheels on the gravel of the drive broke in upon his discourse, and Gallagher deprecatingly drew out his watch.

"The way of the world, Mr. Milbanke!" he murmured as he rose. "Our pleasantest acquaintances end the soonest. I must wish you good-bye—with many thanks for your delightful hospitality. So far as our poor friend is concerned," he added, in a correctly altered tone, "Doctor Gallagher may be relied upon to do everything. In a case like this, where physical pain is recurrent and violent, we can only have recourse to narcotics. We have already allayed the suffering consequent on my examination and you may rely upon some hours of calm; for any subsequent contingency Doctor Gallagher has my instructions. Of course, if you wish me to have one more glimpse at him before I go— —"

But Milbanke, who had also risen, held out his hand mechanically.

"Oh no," he said quietly. "No, thank you! I don't think we will trouble you any further. It has been a great satisfaction to have obtained your—your opinion."

Molyneaux waved his hand magnanimously.

"Do not mention it!" he murmured. "My regret is deep that I have been of so little avail. Good-bye again, Mr. Milbanke! It has been an honour as well as a pleasure to meet you."

He smiled blandly, and added the last remark as Gallagher solicitously helped him into his furlined travelling coat. Then, still suavely genial, he passed out of the dining-room towards the hall door.

Gallagher hurried after him, but, in passing Milbanke, he paused.

"I'll be back in an hour, Mr. Milbanke," he said. "I'm just going as far as Carrigmore with Doctor Molyneaux to get an additional supply of morphia."

Milbanke nodded silently, and in his turn stepped into the hall.

When the two men had entered the waiting vehicle, when Molyneaux had waved a courtly farewell and the coachman had gathered up the reins, he turned and slowly began to mount the stairs.

Instantly his foot touched the landing, Mrs. Asshlin darted from the shadowy corridor.

"What news?" she asked agitatedly. "Oh, Mr. Milbanke, what news? The suspense has been dreadful."

Her voice trembled. Tears came very easily to Mrs. Asshlin, and her habitual attitude of mourning had heretofore irritated Milbanke. But now her thin face and faded black garments came as a curiously welcome contrast to the bland affluence, the genial, complacent superiority of Molyneaux. He turned to her with a feeling of warmth.

"Forgive my delay, Mrs. Asshlin!" he said gently. "One is never in a hurry to impart bad news. Doctor Molyneaux holds out no hope—not a shadow of hope."

There was a pause; then Mrs. Asshlin made a tragic gesture.

"Oh, the children!" she murmured. "The poor, poor children! What will become of them?"

"The children will be provided for," Milbanke said hastily. Then, without giving her time for question or astonishment, he went on again:

"Don't say anything of this to Clodagh," he enjoined. "She must have these last hours in peace."

"Certainly—certainly! Poor Denis! Poor Denis! I always said he would have an unfortunate end. But go in and see him, Mr. Milbanke. Clodagh is in the room."

Milbanke silently acquiesced, and moved slowly down the corridor.

At the door of her father's room, he found Nance still patiently watchful. He paused, arrested by his new sense of obligation, and looked down into the upturned, wistful little face.

"What are you doing here, Nance?" he asked kindly.

She made a valiant attempt to conjure up her pretty, winning smile, but her lips began to tremble.

"I don't know!" she said shyly and softly; then in a sudden burst of confidence she stepped close to him. "Clo doesn't like me to go in," she murmured. "She thinks it makes me sad to see father; and I don't know where to go. I'd be in Hannah's way in the kitchen, and I don't like being with Aunt Fan, and—and I'm frightened to be by myself. There's a horrid sort of feel in the house."

Her dark blue eyes searched Milbanke's face appealingly; and with a sensation of pity and protection, he stooped and took one of her cold, limp hands.

"You may come in," he said gently. "It is very lonely out here. I think we can make Clodagh understand."

Without hesitation her fingers closed round his in a movement of confidence and gratitude, and together they passed into the room where Asshlin lay peacefully under the influence of the narcotic administered by Molyneaux. By Gallagher's orders the nurse—who had been deprived of her necessary rest in the morning—had retired to her room again in preparation for the night, and only Clodagh was in attendance. Having quietly closed the door, Milbanke halted hesitatingly, expecting a flood of questions. But to his intense surprise she did not even glance in his direction. She sat motionless and pale, her eyes on her father's face, her attitude stiff and almost defiant. He wondered for a moment whether, by the power of instinct, she had divined Molyneaux's verdict, or whether, through some source unknown to him, the news of it had already reached her. With a sense of trepidation, he tightened his fingers round Nance's small hand, and drew her silently into a corner of the room.

For more than an hour the three watchers sat regarding their patient. No one attempted to speak—no one appeared to have anything to say. Once or twice Mrs. Asshlin flitted agitatedly in and out of the room, but none of them took heed of her presence. Occasionally a clock struck in the silent house or a cinder fell from the fire, causing them all to start nervously. But, except for these interruptions, the quiet was preternatural.

It was with a throb of relief at his heart that Milbanke at last caught the sound of Gallagher's horse trotting up the avenue, and knew by the shutting of the hall door that the doctor had entered the house.

He walked into the sick-room a few minutes later, and with a casual nod to all present, moved at once to the bed.

Bending over Asshlin, he felt his pulse, then glanced significantly at Milbanke, who had risen on his entrance.

"I think we must inject a stimulant," he said. "The pulse is a little weak."

With a faint sound of consternation Clodagh stood up.

"Oh, he's not worse?" she said. "Doctor Gallagher, he's not worse?"

Gallagher looked at her, and his expression changed. The distress of a pretty girl is always difficult to resist.

"No, Miss Asshlin," he said kindly. "No. You see, he has gone through a lot. We must expect him to be weak."

Clodagh looked relieved, though the alarm still lingered in her eyes.

"Of course," she said. "Yes, of course. Is there anything I can do?"

Gallagher glanced at her again.

"Well," he said quietly, "perhaps you will call the nurse for me? There's no real need for her, but it is just as well we should have her on the spot."

Again Clodagh's eyes darkened with apprehension, but she made no remark. Signalling to Nance to follow her, she left the room.

As the two girls disappeared, Gallagher bent again over Asshlin, making another rapid examination; then once more he glanced up at Milbanke.

"He may not last the night," he said below his breath. "Molyneaux expected that it wouldn't be a long business, but we didn't look for the change so soon as this."

Milbanke did not alter his position.

"You'll stay on, of course?" he said mechanically.

"Yes. Oh yes, I'll stay on!"

As he said the last word Clodagh reappeared.

"The nurse will be here in a minute," she said in a steady voice.

The unrelaxed, monotonous vigil lasted until two o'clock; then, as Asshlin showed a disposition to rally, the doctor asserted his authority, and dismissed Mrs. Asshlin, Nance, and Milbanke for a much-needed rest—Clodagh alone refusing to leave the room.

Though he would not have admitted it, the command came as a boon to Milbanke. His long and arduous journey, coupled with the strain and excitement of the day and evening, had culminated in intense weariness; and when Gallagher's order came, it would have been a superhuman effort to offer any protest.

Reaching his room, he took off his boots, and, partially undressing, threw himself upon his bed.

How many hours he slept the deep sleep of utter exhaustion he did not know. His first effort at awaking consciousness was a thrill of nervous fright that made him sit up in bed, aware with a sudden shock that some one was knocking imperatively on his door and calling him by name in low, agitated tones.

"Mr. Milbanke! Mr. Milbanke! Wake, please! Quick! Mr. Milbanke!"

He stared into the darkness for an instant in dazed apprehension; then he slid out of bed, fumbling blindly for his dressing-gown.

"Coming!" he called. "Coming!"

Having found the garment, he crossed the room stumblingly, thrusting his arms into the sleeves as he went.

Opening the door, he realised the situation with a sick sinking of the heart. Clodagh stood in the corridor with a blanched face, holding a candle in her shaking hand.

"Oh, come, please!" she exclaimed. "Come quick!"

Without a word he stepped forward, and the two hurried down the passage.

In the sick-room the fire was glowing and additional candles had been lighted. For a second Milbanke paused at the door; then, as his eyes grew accustomed to the access of light, the scene became clear to him. On the bed lay Asshlin, his head partly propped up by pillows, his eyes wide, his breath coming in slow, difficult gasps; Gallagher was moving about the room with more quickness and deftness than the Englishman could have believed possible; Mrs. Asshlin, unnerved, and yet fascinated, leaned upon the end of the bed; while Nance—crying silently—followed the nurse to and fro in dazed, half-comprehending fear; and Hannah, the household factotum, crouched behind the door, weeping and murmuring inarticulate prayers.

The picture turned Milbanke cold. With an instinctive gesture he paused, with the intention of shielding it from Clodagh's sight. But at the very moment that he turned towards her, a convulsion shook the dying man. He half-lifted himself in bed, his eyes staring wildly; as Gallagher rushed forward, a faint sound escaped him, his head fell forward, and his body collapsed in the doctor's arms.

There was a breathless, appalled silence—a silence that seemed to extend over years. At last Gallagher looked up.

"It's all over," he said in a hushed voice.

For a minute no one spoke, no one moved. It seemed as if the whole room was petrified. Then Gallagher quietly laid the body back upon the pillows, and as though the action broke the spell, Clodagh gave a sudden sharp cry and ran forward to the bed.

# CHAPTER V

The three days that followed Asshlin's death resolved themselves into so many hours of gloom and confusion, that found their culmination in the funeral ceremony.

To Irishmen of every class, a funeral is invested with an almost symbolic importance, and a solemn consideration is bestowed upon its most minute details. And Milbanke, deeply imbued with the horror and suddenness of the whole disaster, was filled with a growing astonishment at the numberless preliminaries—the amount of precedence and prestige requiring consideration—before one poor human body could be hidden away. But he rose dutifully to the occasion and proved himself unfailingly patient and conscientious in every emergency, from the first repugnant interview with the undertaker to the woeful breakfast, partaken of in the early hours of the funeral morning, with the curtains drawn across the dining-room windows and the candles in the massive silver sconces shedding an unnatural light upon the table laden with eatables.

The guests who partook of this meal were men of varied and interesting types; but whatever their characteristic differences, it was remarkable that the same air of responsibility and solemnity inspired them all. It did not matter that many of them had been personal enemies of the dead man; that many, with that jealous distrust of unconventionality that reigns in Ireland, had markedly drawn away from him in the last ten years of his life; death had obliterated everything. Asshlin's eccentricities, his lawlessness, his contempt for the little world in which he lived were all forgotten. He was one of themselves—deserving, in death at least, the same consideration that the county had bestowed upon his father, his grandfather, and those who had gone before them.

The faces of these men were unfamiliar to Milbanke, though each on entering the dining-room shook him cordially and sympathetically by the hand. The meal was partaken of almost in silence; and it was with obvious relief that, one after another, the members of the party rose from table and passed into the darkened hall, and from thence to the sweep of gravelled drive that fronted the house, where the less privileged of those who had come to do Asshlin honour lounged singly or in groups.

The funeral was timed to start at nine; but the concourse of mourners—well accustomed to the delays inevitable on such an occasion—evinced no sigh of impatience when half-past nine, and then ten arrived, and no move had yet been made.

But all things come to those who understand the art of patience. At a quarter past ten a thrill galvanised the lethargic crowd; and with the recognition of the great moment for which they waited, the men began to jostle each other and push forward towards the house, while all hats were respectively removed.

A faint murmur of admiration and awe went up from the gathering as the great brass-bound coffin was borne solemnly through the door and laid upon the open bier. In silence Milbanke and young Laurence Asshlin took their places as chief mourners, and with the inevitable confusion and uncertainty of such a moment, the crowd of men and vehicles formed up behind them, the horses under the bier moved slowly forward, and the body of Denis Asshlin passed for the last time down the avenue and through the gates of Orristown.

The funeral over, Milbanke walked back from Carrigmore alone. The servants, who had followed their master to his resting-place in the old graveyard, had remained in the village to enjoy the importance that the occasion lent them; young Asshlin had disappeared at the conclusion of the burial service; while the daughters and sister-in-law of the dead man—in accordance with the custom of the country—had remained secluded in their own rooms at Orristown, appearing neither at the breakfast nor the funeral.

In a house of death, the hours that succeed the burial are, if possible, even more melancholy than those that precede it. The sensations of awe and responsibility have been dispersed, but as yet it is impossible to resume the commonplace routine of life. As Milbanke passed through the gateway and walked up the drive, ploughed into new furrows by the long procession of cars that had followed the coffin, he was deeply sensitive to this impression; and it fell upon him afresh with a chill of desolation as he entered the door, still standing open, and moved slowly across the deserted hall.

In the dining-room the curtains had been drawn back and the candles extinguished; but the daylight seemed to fall tardily and unnaturally upon the room after its three days' exclusion. He stood for a moment looking at the débris of the breakfast that had not yet been removed, at the disarray of the chairs that had been hurriedly vacated; then, with a fresh and poignant sense of loss and loneliness, he turned hastily and walked out of the room.

In the hall he attempted to pause afresh; but the sound of muffled sobbing from the upper portion of the house sent him incontinently forth into the open. With an overwhelming desire for human fellowship — for any companionship in this abode of desolation, he passed without consideration of his dignity round the corner of the house in the direction of the stable-yard.

He walked calmly, but there was a pucker of anxiety on his usually placid brow — an expression of concern, apart from actual sorrow, in his tightly set lips. To the most casual observer it would have been obvious that something weighed upon his mind.

Still moving with his habitual precision, he entered the yard by the arched gateway, picking his way between the scattered array of rubbish, food, and implements that encumbered the ground.

When he appeared, a dozen rough or glossy heads were thrust out of kennels or outhouses, as the dogs accorded him a noisy welcome; but paying only partial heed to their demonstrations, he passed on to the vast coach-house, with the vague hope that some labourer connected with the farm or stables might possibly have been left behind in the general exodus. But here again he was doomed to disappointment. The coach-house, with its walls festooned with rotting harness, its ghostly row of cumbersome antiquated vehicles, was as empty of human presence as the yard itself.

Conscious of the isolation that hung over the place — disproportionately aware of his own aimlessness, he stood uncertain in what direction to turn. For the moment, the household had no need of him; there were no legal formalities to succeed the funeral, Asshlin having left no will; and of personal duties he had none to claim his attention.

He stood by the coach-house door woefully undecided as to his next move, when all at once relief came to him from the most unexpected quarter of the outbuildings. One of the dairy windows was opened sharply, and a head was thrust through the aperture.

"Wisha, what is it you're doin' there, sir?" a voice demanded kindly. "Sure that ould yard is no fit place for you!"

Turning hastily, Milbanke saw the broad, plain face of Hannah; her small eyes red, her rough cheeks stained with weeping.

"Why, Hannah!" he exclaimed, "what are you doing here? I thought you were at the funeral."

Hannah passed the back of her hand across her eyes.

"Wisha, what would I be doin' at it?" she demanded huskily. "Sure I don't know what they do be seein' in funerals at all."

Milbanke glanced up with interest, recognising the originality of the remark.

"Why, you and I are of the same opinion," he said. "The Celtic delight in the obsequies of a friend has been puzzling me for the last three days——" Then he paused suddenly, conscious of Hannah's fixed regard. "That is," he substituted quickly—"that is, I have been wondering, like you, what they see in it."

Hannah's small, observant eyes did not waver in their scrutiny.

"You've been wonderin' about somethin', sure enough!" she said. "I seen it meself every time I'd be carryin' in the dinner or doin' a turn for the poor corpse. God be good to him this holy and blessed day!" Again she wiped her eyes. "But 'tisn't wonderin' alone that's at you," she added more briskly. "'Tis some other thing that's lyin' heavy on your mind. I seen it meself at every hand's turn."

Milbanke started. This sympathetic onslaught was as disconcerting as it was unexpected.

"I—I won't contradict you, Hannah," he said waveringly. "No doubt you are right."

For the space of a minute Hannah was profoundly silent; then she broached the subject that had been filling her mind for a day and a half.

"Wisha, now, is it thrue what they do be tellin' me?" she asked softly and warily—"that you're goin' to be father and mother an' all to thim two poor children?"

Again Milbanke started almost guiltily; then the personal anxiety that mingled with and almost dominated his grief for Asshlin rose irrepressibly in response to the persuasive tones, the kindly human interest and curiosity.

"Yes, Hannah," he said quickly. "Yes, it is my intention to try and fill my poor friend's place."

The tears welled suddenly into Hannah's eyes, and with an awkward movement she wiped her rough hand in her apron and held it out.

"God Almighty will give it back to you, sir!" she exclaimed, with impulsive fervour.

Strangely touched by the expression of understanding and appreciation, he responded to the gesture and took her hand.

But instantly she withdrew it.

"Don't be mindin' an ould woman like me, sir," she said deprecatingly. "'Twas the thought of the children that come over me. I couldn't help it. I had the both of thim in me arms before they could cry. Small wonder me heart would be in thim! Many's the sad day I put over me, thinkin' what would become of them, wid the poor masther goin' to the bad. God forgive me for sayin' it! And sure now 'tis all settled and done for—and the heavth of it off of our minds. Praise be to God!"

She paused to dry her tears.

"And what would you be thinkin' to do wid thim?" she asked presently in a new and more personal tone.

Milbanke did not answer at once. His eyes strayed uneasily from one object in the yard to another, while the frown of perplexity that had puckered his brow since Asshlin's death reappeared more prominently than before. At last, with a certain expression of puzzled resolution, he looked up and met Hannah's attentive gaze.

"To tell you the truth, Hannah," he said, "that is the precise question I have been asking myself ever since your poor master died."

There was a wait of some seconds while his listener digested the information; then she nodded her head with slow impressiveness.

"I seen it meself," she said again. "Sure, I seen it as plain as daylight. 'There's somethin' on his mind,' I says to meself. An' if it isn't the poor masther's death,' I says, 'thin it's nothin' more nor less than the natural feelin's of a single gentleman that finds himself wid two grown daughters.'"

It was characteristic of Milbanke that he did not smile. He recognised only one fact in the old servant's words—the fact that the state of affairs over which he had been worrying in lonely perplexity had suddenly been accurately, if roughly, voiced by some one else. He glanced up with quick relief into the round, red face framed in the dairy window.

"Hannah," he said honestly, "your surmise was perfectly correct."

For the first time a smile broke over her tear-stained face.

"I was right thin? 'Tis the children was troublin' you?"

A sharp gleam of inquiry shot from her eyes.

"Yes," he answered simply.

"An' why, now?" Again her tone changed, the irrepressible undercurrent of native humour, native inquisitiveness and familiarity welling out unconsciously. "Sure, they're good children."

"I do not doubt it. I do not doubt it for one moment."

The Gambler | 91

"But they're troublin' you all the same?"

"Well, yes. Yes, I confess they are troubling me."

"Both of thim?" she asked innocently.

He hesitated.

"Well, no," he replied artlessly. "No, not both of them."

"Ah, I thought that same!" Hannah gave a nod of understanding. "Sure, 'twas to be tormentin' men she was brought into the world for. I said so meself the first day I took her into me arms."

"But—but I haven't said anything. How do you know that it is——?"

"How do I know that it's Miss Clodagh that's botherin' you? Sure, how do I know that you're standin' before me? Faith, by the use of me eyesight! Haven't I seen you lookin' at her and ponderin'—and lookin' at her agin?"

Milbanke's lips tightened, and he drew himself up.

"I should be sorry if any thought I have bestowed on your young mistress——" he began coldly; then suddenly the intense need of help and sympathetic counsel over-balanced dignity. "Hannah," he said abruptly, "I'm in a terribly awkward position, and that is the simple truth. My mind is quite at rest about the younger girl. She is a child—and will be a child for years. A good school is all she needs. But with the other it's different—with Clodagh it's different. Clodagh is no longer a child."

Hannah remained discreetly silent.

"If I had a sister," he went on, "or any friend to whom I could entrust her. But I have none."

Again Hannah shook her head.

"Why, thin, that's a pity!" she murmured. "Sure, 'tis lonesome for a gintleman to be by himself."

"It is a pity—a great pity. You do not know how it is weighing upon me. Of course, there is her aunt——"

Hannah made an exclamation of horror.

"Is it Mrs. Laurence?" she cried. "Is it tie her to Mrs. Laurence you would? Sure, you may as well put her in the grave and be done wid it."

Milbanke's harassed face grew more perplexed.

"No," he said hurriedly—"no; I understand that that arrangement is impossible. I was merely wondering whether there is any other—any more distant relative with whom she might be happy——"

He looked anxiously into her broad, shrewd face.

For a moment the small eyes met his seriously, then involuntarily they twinkled.

"Faith, when I was a young woman, sir," she said slowly, "men wasn't so sat on findin' relations for a girl like Miss Clodagh—unless maybe 'twas a relation of their own makin'!"

Milbanke suddenly looked away.

"What—what do you mean?" he asked confusedly.

"Why, that 'tisn't aunts and cousins that a girl like Miss Clodagh wants, but a good husband."

"A—a husband?"

"Why, thin, what else? Instid of throublin' yourself and frettin' yourself till your heart is scalded out of you, why don't you marry her? That's what I've been askin' meself ever since the poor masther died. It's out now, if I'm to be killed for it!"

She eyed him almost defiantly.

But Milbanke stood stammering and confused, his gaze fixed nervously on the ground, an unaccustomed flush on his worn cheeks.

"But—but, Hannah, I—I am an old man!"

His tone was deprecating and meant to be ironic; but unconsciously it had an undernote of question; unconsciously, as he raised his eyes to his mentor's face, he straightened the shoulders that age and study had combined to bend.

"I am an old man!" he said again. "Why—why, I am five years older than her father——"

Hannah continued to search his face.

"An' sure what harm is that?" she said. "Wasn't me own poor man as ould as me grandfather?—an' no woman ever buried a finer husband—God rest him!"

Milbanke's lack of humorous imagination stood him in good stead.

"But she's a child," he stammered—"a child——"

For answer, Hannah leant out of the window until her face was close to his.

"Listen here to me!" she said softly. "Child or no child, you thought about marryin' her before ever I said it. But you'd never riz the courage to do it. You're not like the Asshlins, that would tear down the walls of hell if they wanted to be gettin' at the divil; you'd like somebody to take him be the hand and draw him out nice and aisy for you— —

"There she is up in that lonesome house, frettin' her heart an' cryin' her eyes out. Why can't you go up an' take her, before somebody else does?"

As she came to the last words her rough voice dropped. Her loyalty to her dead master, her anxiety to see his child in a place of safety poured from her in crude eloquence. To her primitive mind Milbanke appeared as the ideal husband—a man of dependable years, of wealth, of good social position; and all her affections, all her energies yearned to make the marriage. She could not have framed the fear that possessed her; but her instinct, her acute native intuition warned her unanswerably that the daughter of Denis Asshlin would need protection, and would need it before long. With an impulsive gesture she stretched out her hand, and, touching Milbanke's shoulder, pushed him gently forward into the yard.

"Go on, sir!" she urged softly. "Go on up an' take her, before somebody else does!"

# CHAPTER VI

It may be surmised without fear of misconception that never during the smooth course of his uneventful existence had Milbanke been so rudely shaken into self-comprehension as by Hannah's unlooked-for onslaught. Left to the placid guidance of unaided instinct, it is almost certain that he would have left Orristown whenever the hour of departure arrived, innocently unconscious that any parting pangs could be attributed to a personal cause. It is possible that, with the passage of time, he might have acknowledged that somewhere in the inner recesses of his mind there was a shrine where one face, more changeful and alluring than any other he had known, reigned in solitary state; but beyond that tardy acknowledgment he would not have dared to venture. Later still, perhaps, if circumstances had compelled him to resign his guardianship over Clodagh in favour of some possible husband, it is within the bounds of reason to conjecture that understanding of his feelings might have come to him when, having said good-bye to the young girl just crossing the threshold of life, he returned to his home, newly and bitterly alive to his age and loneliness. But now, in the light of present events, all such suppositions had become valueless. As if by some powerful outside pressure, his eyes had been opened, and he stood dazed and elated before the new road that opened upon his vision.

His brain felt light and unsteady, his limbs were imbued with a sensation of unaccustomed buoyancy as he turned, impelled by Hannah's words, and moved across the yard towards the arched gateway. A half-admitted, intoxicating sense of imminent action possessed him; and as he walked forward it seemed that he scarcely felt the ground beneath his feet.

Almost without volition, he passed from the stone-paved courtyard into the sweep of gravelled pathway that fronted the house. For the first time in his existence he was conscious of being borne forward on the tide of his emotions; and the knowledge had an exhilarating, unbalanced daring that suggested youth.

As though he feared the evaporation of his mood, he made no pause on gaining the pathway, but went straight forward towards the house with a haste and impetuosity very foreign to his formal nature. On his second entry into the hall, he paid no heed to the chill desolation of the place, but crossing the intervening space, began immediately to mount the stairs.

Scarcely had he reached the highest step, however, than he halted incontinently. For, as though in direct response to the thoughts that were filling his mind, a door on the corridor opened, and Clodagh appeared.

Seeing him, she too paused; and in the moment of mutual hesitation he had opportunity to study her.

In her new black dress, she looked slighter and more immature than he had expected; and the pathetic effect of her appearance was enhanced by the paleness of her face and the heavy, purple shadows that sleeplessness and tears had traced below her eyes. As the impression obtruded itself upon him, his own nervous excitement dropped from him suddenly.

"My poor child!" he said involuntarily.

At the words and the tone, she turned to him impulsively.

"Oh! Mr. Milbanke——" she began.

Then her loneliness, her sense of bereavement and desolation, inundated her mind. With a short sob, she moved abruptly away, and turning her face to the wall, broke into a passion of tears.

The action was the action of a child; and without hesitation Milbanke responded to it. Stepping across the corridor, he put his arm about her shoulder and drew her gently towards the stairs.

"Come!" he said soothingly—"come! The house is quite quiet, and you are badly in want of a little daylight and fresh air. Come! Let me take you out."

Clodagh sobbed on; but she suffered herself to be led down the stairs and across the hall towards the open door. There, however, she paused, newly arrested by her grief.

"Oh, Mr. Milbanke," she cried, "I can't believe it! I can't believe that we'll never see him again. Poor father! Oh, poor father!"

But Milbanke was equal to the situation.

"You must be brave," he said kindly. "You must remember that he would like you to be brave."

The words were an inspiration; with marvellous efficacy they checked the torrent of Clodagh's tears. For a moment she stood looking at him in a dazed, uncertain way; then she lifted her head in a pathetic attempt at decisive action.

"You are right," she said unevenly. "He *would* like to know that I was brave."

The declaration seemed to cost her an immense effort; for instantly it was made, she turned away from Milbanke, freeing herself from his detaining arm. And as though fearing to trust herself to any further onrush of emotion, she stepped through the open door and walked quickly forward to where the gravelled drive merged into the long and narrow glen in which the Orristown woods met the sea.

Down the wide track leading to this glen she walked, with head rigidly erect and with resolutely set lips, while Milbanke followed. Now that the immediate need for his protection had been removed, his mind involuntarily reverted to his earlier and more tumultuous thoughts. With a strange, half-timid excitement, he acknowledged the personal element in his surroundings, and exulted with a certain tremulous joy in the keen air that blew inland from the sea; in the pleasant earthy smell of the moss that clothed the rough stones of the boundary wall skirting the path; in the promise of spring, suggested by the hardy green of the wild violet plants clustering at the roots of the beech trees. And with his eyes fixed upon Clodagh's slim black figure, he walked forward in a vaguely intoxicating dream.

For the full course of the path she went on steadily; but reaching the glen, she paused; and there, as if by a pre-arrangement of destiny, Milbanke overtook her.

With a quiet, unostentatious movement he stepped to her side, and stood looking upon the scene that spread before them.

The view was not imposing, but it was beautiful with the brooding, solemn beauty that emanates from Ireland. Upon one hand, the sea stretched away green, invincible, and cold as it so often looks in early spring; upon the other, the woods lay a mass of leafless, interlacing boughs that formed a clean, brown silhouette against the grey sky; while directly in front, the first undulation of the rugged Orristown cliffs stood up, an impregnable rampart against the outer world.

For a long silent moment Clodagh surveyed the picture; then with one of the impulsive, unstudied gestures that were so characteristic of her, she looked round; and for the first time since they had left the house, her eyes rested on Milbanke's face.

"You are very kind to me," she said suddenly. "Why are you so kind?"

The words, spoken with complete ingenuousness, came at a singularly appropriate moment. To Milbanke, nervously conscious of his own emotions, they seemed inspired. With a quick, unsteady gesture he wheeled round, and putting out his hand, caught hers.

"It—it is easy to be kind to some people," he said, almost inarticulately.

Clodagh looked at him in some surprise; but it did not occur to her to withdraw her hand. She stood perfectly calm and unembarrassed; and presently, as he made no attempt at further speech, her glance wandered back to the cool stretch of green water.

"Yes," she said slowly, "I suppose it is easy to be nice to some people; but not to selfish people like me."

At her words, Milbanke's hand tightened abruptly.

"You must not say that," he murmured. "I have never seen any faults in your character. And even—even if I had"—his voice quickened confusedly—"even if I had seen them, you would still be the—the child of my oldest friend."

He spoke disjointedly and agitatedly; but at his words, Clodagh turned to him afresh with a grateful, impulsive movement.

"Ah, then I understand!" she said warmly. "You are very kind—you are very good——"

At her movement and her tone, a mental giddiness seized upon Milbanke. A flush rose to his temples.

"Clodagh," he said suddenly, "let me be kind to you always! Let—let me marry you—and be kind to you always!"

The appeal came forth with volcanic suddenness. He had not meant to be precipitate; it was entirely alien to his slow, methodical nature to plunge headlong into any situation. But the occasion was unprecedented; circumstances overwhelmed him. For a long space he stood as if transfixed, his eyes straining to catch the expression on Clodagh's face, his pale, ascetic features puckered with anxiety.

The pause was long—preternaturally long. Clodagh stood as motionless as he, her hand still resting passive in his clasp, her clear eyes staring into his in stupefied amazement. It was plainly evident that no realisation of the declaration just made had penetrated her understanding. To her mind—unattuned, even vaguely, to the idea of love, and temporarily numbed by her grief—the thought that her father's friend could consider her in any light but that of a child was too preposterous, too unreal to come spontaneously. The belief that Milbanke's extraordinary words but needed some explanatory addition held her attentive and expectant. And under this conviction, she stood unconscious of his close regard and unembarrassed by the pressure of his hand.

At last, as some shadowy perception of her thoughts obtruded itself upon him, he stirred nervously, and the flush upon his face deepened.

"Clodagh," he said, "have I made myself plain? Do you understand that I—that I wish to marry you? That I want you for my—my wife?"

The final word with its intense incongruity cut suddenly through the mist of her bewilderment. In a flash of comprehension the meaning of his declaration sprang to her mind. Her face turned red, then pale; with a sharp movement she drew away her hand.

"You want to marry me?" she said in a slow, amazed voice.

Before the note of blank, undisguised incredulity, Milbanke shrank into himself.

"Yes," he said hurriedly—"yes; that is my desire. I know that perhaps it may—may seem incongruous. You are very young; and I——"

He hesitated with a painful touch of embarrassment. At the hesitation, Clodagh's voice broke forth.

"But I don't want to marry," she cried; "I don't want to marry—any one."

There was a sharp, half-frightened note audible in her voice. For the moment, her whole attitude was that of the inexperienced being who clings instinctively to the rock of present things, and obstinately refuses to be cast into the sea of future possibilities. For the moment, she was blind to the instrument that was forcing her towards those possibilities. To her immature mind it was the choice between the known and the unknown. Then suddenly and accidentally her eyes came back to Milbanke's face, and the personal element in the choice assailed her abruptly.

"Oh, I couldn't!" she cried involuntarily—"I couldn't!—I couldn't!"

She did not intend to hurt him; but cruelty is the prerogative of the young, and she failed to see that he winced before the decisive honesty of her words.

"Am I so—so very distasteful?" he asked in a low, unsteady voice.

She looked at him in silence. It was the inevitable clash of youth and age. She was warm-hearted, she was capable of generous action; but before all else, she was young—the triumphant inheritor of the ages. Life stretched before her, while it lay behind him. She looked at him; and as she looked a wave of revolt—a strong, sudden sense of her individual right to happiness—surged through her.

"Oh, I couldn't!" she cried again—"I couldn't!"

And before Milbanke could reply—before he had time to comprehend the purport of her words—she had turned and fled in the direction of the house, leaving him standing as he was, dazed and petrified.

Upward along the path, Clodagh ran. Her impulse towards flight had been childish, and her thoughts as she sped forward were as unreasonable and confused as a child's. She was vaguely, blindly filled with a desire to escape—from she knew not what; to evade—she knew not what. Her one clear thought was that the prop upon which she had leaned in these days of sorrow and despair had unaccountably and suddenly been withdrawn; and that she stood woefully alone and unprotected.

On she ran, until the archway of the courtyard broke into view; then, without a moment's hesitation, she swerved to the left, sped across the yard, and burst unceremoniously into the kitchen.

In the kitchen Hannah was busying herself over the fire that, in the confusion of the morning's event, had been suffered to die down. At the tempestuous opening of the door she turned sharply round, and for a second stood staring at the disturbed face of her young mistress; then, with the intuitive tact of her race, she suddenly opened her ample arms, and with a sob Clodagh rushed towards her.

For a long moment Hannah held her as if she had been a baby, patting her shoulder and smoothing her ruffled hair, while she cried out her grief and bewilderment. At last, with a slow sobbing breath, she raised her head.

"Oh, Hannah, I want father!" she said—"I want father!"

Hannah drew her closer to her broad shoulder.

"Whisht, now!" she murmured tenderly—"whisht, now! Sure, he's betther off—sure, he's betther off."

But Clodagh's mind was too agitated to take comfort. With a change of mental attitude, she altered her physical position—freeing herself abruptly from Hannah's embrace.

"Hannah," she cried suddenly, "Mr. Milbanke wants me to marry him. And I won't! I can't! I won't!"

Hannah's eyes narrowed sharply. But whatever her emotion, she checked it, and bent over her charge with another caress.

"Sure you won't, of course, my lamb. Who'd be askin' you?"

"No one."

"Thin why would you be frettin' yourself?"

"I'm not fretting myself. Only——"

"Only what?"

"Only — — Oh! nothing, nothing." With a distressed movement Clodagh pushed back her hair from her forehead. Then she turned to the old servant afresh. "Hannah," she demanded, "why does he want to marry me? Why does he want to?"

Hannah was silent for a space; then her shrewd, ugly face puckered into an expression of profound wisdom.

"Men are quare," she said oracularly. "The oulder, the quarer. Maybe he's thinkin' of himself in the matther; but maybe" — her voice dropped impressively — "maybe, Miss Clodagh, 'tis the way he's thinkin' of you — —"

She paused with deep significance.

The effort after effect was not wasted. Clodagh looked up sharply.

"What do you mean?" she asked.

"Mane?" Hannah turned away, and, picking up a poker, began softly to rake the ashes from the fire. "Sure, what would I be manin'?"

"But you do mean something. What is it?"

Hannah went on with her task.

Clodagh stamped her foot.

"Hannah, what is it?"

"Nothin'. Sure, nothin' at all. I'm only sayin' what quare notions men takes."

"But you mean something else. What is it?"

Hannah stolidly continued to rake out the remnants of the fire.

"I know nothin'," she said obstinately. "Ask Mrs. Laurence."

"But you do. I know by your voice. What is it?"

An alert, unconscious note of apprehension had crept into Clodagh's tone. Her lips suddenly tightened, her eyes became wide.

"What is it, Hannah?" she exclaimed. "What's the reason he wants to marry me?"

"Sure no rason at all."

"Oh!"

Clodagh made a gesture of anger and disgust. Then she made a fresh appeal.

"Hannah, please — —"

But Hannah went on with her work. Years of shrewd observation had taught her the power of silence.

"Then you won't tell me?"

There was no response.

"Hannah!"

At last the old servant turned, as though pressed beyond endurance.

"Well," she said, with seeming reluctance, "maybe he'd be thinkin' 'twould be aisier for wan of the Asshlins to be drawin' out of her husband's pocket than to be——"

But Clodagh interrupted. She turned suddenly, her cheeks burning, her eyes ablaze.

"Hannah!" she cried in sharp, pained alarm.

But Hannah had said her say. With her old, imperturbable gesture she turned once more to her task.

"I know nothin'," she murmured obstinately. "If you're wantin' more, ask Mrs. Laurence."

For a while Clodagh stood, transfixed by the idea presented to her mind. Then, action and certainty becoming suddenly indispensable, she turned on her heel. "Very well!" she said tersely—"very well! I will ask Aunt Fan."

And with as scant ceremony as she had entered it, she swept out of the kitchen.

As the door banged, Hannah glanced over her shoulder, her red face brimming with tenderness.

"Wisha, 'tis all for the best!" she murmured aloud—"'tis all for the best. But God forgive me for hurtin' a hair of her head!"

With feet that scarcely felt the ground beneath them, Clodagh sped along the stone passages that led to the hall, and from thence ascended to the bedrooms. Her senses were acutely alive, her mind alert with an unbearable apprehension. A new dread that, by the power of intuition, had almost become a certainty impelled her forward without the conscious action of her will. Without any hesitancy or indecision, she traversed the long corridor, and, pausing before the room occupied by her aunt, knocked peremptorily upon the door.

After a moment's wait Mrs. Asshlin's querulous voice was raised in response.

"Well?" she asked. "What is it? Who's there?"

"Clodagh."

There was an audible sigh. And the usual "Come in!" followed somewhat tardily.

Clodagh instantly turned the handle and opened the door.

In this room the blinds had not yet been drawn up, and only a yellowish light filtered in from outside; in the grate a fire burned unevenly; and close beside sat Mrs. Asshlin, a cup of tea in her hand, a black woollen shawl wrapped about her shoulders. As her niece entered, she glanced round irritably, drawing the wrap more closely round her.

"Shut the door, Clodagh!" she said. "I hate these big, draughty houses."

Clodagh obeyed in silence; then walking deliberately across the room, paused by her aunt's chair. Her face was still burning, her heart was beating unpleasantly fast.

"Aunt Fan," she said, "I want to ask you something. Why should Mr. Milbanke bother about me—about us?"

Mrs. Asshlin, startled by the suddenness of the unlooked-for attack, turned in her seat and peered through the yellow twilight into her niece's excited face.

"What on earth is the matter with you, child?" she demanded.

"Nothing. But I want to know."

Mrs. Asshlin made a gesture tantamount to shrugging her shoulders.

"It is quite natural that Mr. Milbanke should be interested in you. He was your father's oldest friend."

"Yes, yes." Clodagh bent forward uncontrollably. "And, Aunt Fan, has father died poor? Has—has he left debts? That's what I want to know."

Mrs. Asshlin moved nervously in her chair.

"My dear child——" she began weakly.

"Has he? Oh! Aunt Fan, has he left debts?"

Mrs. Asshlin was taken at a disadvantage.

"Well," she stammered—"well——"

"He has left debts?"

"Well, yes. If you must know—he has."

Clodagh caught her breath.

"Of course, as I often said," Mrs. Asshlin continued, "poor Denis was a terribly improvident man——"

But Clodagh checked her.

"Don't!" she said faintly. "I couldn't bear it—just to-day. Are the debts big?"

"Immense."

Mrs. Asshlin made the reply sharply. She was not an ill-natured woman, but her sense of dignity had been hurt.

As the word was spoken, Clodagh swayed a little. The black cloud of vague liabilities that hangs over so many Irish houses had suddenly descended upon her. And in the consequent shock, it seemed that the ground rocked under her feet. After a moment she steadied herself.

"Must the place go?" she asked in an intensely quiet voice.

"Yes. At least——"

"What?"

"It would have had to go, only——"

"Only for what?" In her keen anxiety Clodagh stooped forward and laid her hand on her aunt's shoulder. "Only for what, Aunt Fan?"

Shaken and unnerved at the interrogation, Mrs. Asshlin sat up with a start.

"Why do you do that, Clodagh?" she cried—"why do you do that? You gave me a palpitation of the heart."

But Clodagh's eyes still burned with inquiry.

"Why won't the place have to go?" she demanded. "How will the debts be paid?"

Mrs. Asshlin freed herself nervously from her niece's hand.

"Mr. Milbanke will pay them," she said impulsively; then instantly she checked herself. "Oh! what have I said?" she exclaimed. "Don't pretend that I told you, Clodagh. He is so particular that you shouldn't know."

But Clodagh scarcely heard. Her hand had dropped to her side, and she stood staring blankly at her aunt.

"You mean to say that he's going to pay father's debts—our debts?"

"Yes. He even wants to put the place into good repair. Poor Denis seems to have cast a perfect spell over him."

"Then we'll owe him something we can never possibly repay!"

Mrs. Asshlin drew herself up.

"Not exactly owe," she corrected. "It is an—an act of friendship. The Asshlins have never been indebted to any one for a favour. Of course Mr.

Milbanke is a wealthy man; and it's easy to be generous when you have money——"

She heaved a sigh.

But Clodagh stood staring vacantly at the opposite wall.

"It's a debt all the same," she said, after a long pause. "I suppose it is what father used to call a debt of honour."

She spoke in a slow, mechanical voice; then, as if moved to action by her train of thought, she turned without waiting for her aunt's comment, and walked out of the room.

Traversing the corridor, she descended the stairs and passed straight to the hall door. Once in the open, she wheeled to the right with a steady deliberate movement and began slowly to retrace the steps she had taken nearly half an hour earlier.

Steadily and unemotionally she went forward, skirting the courtyard, until, at the dip of the path, the glen came into view, and with it Milbanke's precise, black figure, standing exactly as she had seen it last.

The fact caused her no surprise. That he should still be there seemed the natural—the anticipated thing; and without any pause—any moment of hesitation or delay—she moved directly towards him.

As she reached his side, her cheeks were hot, her heart was still beating unevenly; and, absorbed by her own emotion, she failed to see the dejected droop of his shoulders, the slight, pathetic suggestion of age in his bent back.

Her footsteps were scarcely audible on the damp earth, and she was close beside him before he became conscious of her presence; as he did so, however, he started violently, and the blood rushed incontinently over his forehead and cheeks.

"Clodagh!" he stammered.

But Clodagh checked him, laying her hand quickly on his arm.

"Mr. Milbanke," she said hurriedly, "will you forgive me for what I said? I want to take it back. I want to say that, if you still like, I—I will marry you."

# CHAPTER VII

And thus it came about that Clodagh Asshlin entered upon a new phase of that precarious condition that we call life. The impulse that had induced her to accept Milbanke's proposal was in no way complex. The knowledge had suddenly been conveyed to her that, through no act of her own, she had been placed under a deep obligation; and her primary—her inherited—instinct had been to pay her debt as speedily and as fully as lay within her power, ignoring, in her lack of worldly wisdom, the fact that such a bargain must of necessity possess obligations other than personal, which would demand subsequent settlement.

However unversed she may be in the world's ways, it is scarcely to be supposed that any young girl, under normal conditions, can look upon her own marriage as an abstract thing. But the circumstances of Clodagh's case were essentially abnormal. Milbanke's proposal—and the facts that brought her to accept it—came at a time when her mind and her emotions were numbed by her first poignant encounter with death and grief; and for the time being her outlook upon existence was clouded. The present seemed something sombre, desolate, and impalpable; the future something absolutely void.

For two days after the scene in the glen, she and Milbanke avoided all allusion to what had taken place between them. He appeared possessed by an insurmountable nervous reticence; while she, immersed in her trouble, seemed almost to have forgotten what had occurred.

On the evening of the third day, however, the subject was again broached.

Milbanke was sitting by one of the long, dining-room windows, reading by the faint twilight that filtered in from the fast-darkening sky. The light in the room was fitful; for though the table was already laid for dinner, the candles had not yet been lighted.

With his book held close to his eyes, he had been reading studiously for close upon an hour, when the quick opening of the door behind him caused him to look round. As he did so, he closed his book somewhat hastily and rose with a slight gesture of embarrassment, for the disturber of his peace was Clodagh. But it was not so much the fact of her entry that had startled him, as the fact that, for the first time since her father's death, she was arrayed in her riding-habit.

Shaken out of his calm, he turned to her at once.

"Are you—are you going for a ride?" he asked in unconcealed surprise.

Clodagh nodded. She was drawing on her thick chamois gloves, and her riding-crop was held under her arm. Had the light in the room been stronger, he would have seen that her lips were firmly set and her eyes bright with resolution. But his mind was absorbed by his surprise.

"But is it not rather—late?" he hazarded anxiously, with a glance towards the window.

She looked up astonished.

"Late?" she repeated incredulously.

Then the look of faintly contemptuous tolerance that sometimes touched her with regard to him passed over her face.

"Oh no; not at all!" she explained. "I'm used to riding in the evening. You see, Polly must be exercised; and I'd rather it was dark, the first time I rode after——"

Her voice faltered.

Milbanke heard the tremor, and, as once before, his sense of personal timidity fled before his spontaneous pity.

"Clodagh," he said suddenly, "allow me to ride with you. I was a fairly good horseman in—in my day."

There was pathos in the deprecating justification; but Clodagh's attention was caught by the words alone.

"You!" she said in blank amazement.

Then something in the crudeness of her tone struck upon her, and she made haste to amend her exclamation.

"Of course it's very, very kind of you," she added awkwardly.

At her lowered tone, Milbanke coloured, and took a step forward.

"Clodagh," he began, with a flash of courage, "I think you might allow me to be more kind to you than you do. I think I might give you more protection. And it has occurred to me that perhaps we ought to announce our—our engagement——"

He halted nervously.

As soon as he had begun to speak, Clodagh had walked away from him across the room; and now she stood by the mantelpiece looking down steadily into the fire.

"Do you agree with me?" he asked, moving nervously towards her.

There was an embarrassed silence. And in his perturbation he glanced from her bent head to the picture above the chimneypiece from which Anthony Asshlin's ardent face showed out a vague patch of colour against its black background.

"Clodagh," he said suddenly, "allow me to tell Mrs. Asshlin that you have promised to marry me."

But still Clodagh did not answer; still she stood gazing enigmatically into the burning logs, her slight figure and warm youthful face fitfully lighted by the capricious, spurting flames.

"Clodagh!" he exclaimed. And there was a note of uneasiness in his low, deprecating voice.

Then at last she turned, and their eyes met.

"Very well!" she said quietly. "You may tell Aunt Fan. But, if you don't mind, I'll ride by myself."

That night, at the conclusion of dinner, the engagement was announced. All the members of the Asshlin family were seated round the table when Milbanke, who had practically eaten nothing during the meal, summoned his wavering courage and leaned across the table towards Mrs. Asshlin, who was sitting at his right hand.

"Mrs. Asshlin," he began almost inaudibly, "I—that is, Clodagh and I"—he glanced timidly to where Clodagh sat erect and immovable, at the head of the table—"Clodagh and I have—have an announcement to make. We, that is I——" He stammered hopelessly. "Mrs. Asshlin, Clodagh has made me very—very proud and very happy. She has consented to—to be my wife."

He took a deep, agitated breath of wordless relief that the confession was made.

There was a long pause. Then suddenly Mrs. Asshlin extended both hands towards him in an hysterical outburst of feeling.

"My dear—dear Mr. Milbanke," she said. "What a shock! What a surprise, I should say! What would my poor brother-in-law have thought! But Providence ordains everything. I'm sure I congratulate you—congratulate you both." She turned to Clodagh. "Though of course it is not the time for congratulations——" She hastily drew out her handkerchief.

As she did so, little Nance rose softly from table and slipped unobserved from the room. At Milbanke's words, the child's face had turned terribly white, and she had cast an appealing, incredulous look at Clodagh. But Clodagh, in her self-imposed stolidity, had seen nothing of the expressions round her; and now, as her sister left her place and crossed the room, the significance of the action went unnoticed.

For a moment the only sound audible in the room was the cracking of the fire and Mrs. Asshlin's muffled weeping; but at last, Milbanke, agonised into action, put out his hand and touched her arm.

"Please do not give way to your feelings, Mrs. Asshlin!" he urged. "Think—think of Clodagh!"

Thus appealed to, Mrs. Asshlin wiped away the half-dozen tears that had trickled down her cheek.

"You must forgive me," she murmured. "We Irish take things too much to heart. It—it brought my own engagement back to me—and of course my poor Laurence's death. I hope indeed that it will be a very long time before Clodagh——"

But the words were broken by a clatter from the other side of the table, as young Laurence Asshlin opportunely knocked one wine-glass against another. And in the moment of interruption, Clodagh pushed back her chair and stood up.

"If you don't mind, Aunt Fan," she said, "I think I'll go to bed. The— the ride has tired me. Good-night!" And without a glance at any one, she walked out of the room.

But she had scarcely crossed the hall, when a step behind her caused her to pause; and, looking back, she saw the figure of her cousin, a pace or two in the rear.

In the half light of the place, the two confronted each other; and Clodagh lifted her head in a movement that was common to them both.

"What do you want?" she asked.

Asshlin stepped forward.

"'Tisn't true, Clo?" he asked breathlessly.

Clodagh looked at him defiantly and nodded.

"Yes," she said. "'Tis true."

For a moment he stared at her incredulously, then his incredulity drove him to speech.

"But, Clo," he cried, "he's sixty, if he's a day! And you——"

Clodagh flushed.

"Stop, Larry!" she said unevenly. "Father was nearly sixty."

But Asshlin's sense of the fitness of things had been aroused.

"That's all very well!" he cried. "Uncle Denis was all right for a father or an uncle. But to marry! Clo, you're mad!"

Clodagh turned upon him.

"How dare you, Larry?" she cried. "You are horrible! I hate you!"

Her voice caught, and with a sudden passionate gesture she wheeled away from him and began to mount the stairs.

The action sobered him. With impetuous remorse, he thrust out his hand to detain her.

"Clo!" he said. "I say, Clo!"

But she swept his hand aside.

"No!—no!" she exclaimed. "I don't want you!—I don't want you! I never want to speak to you again. You are hateful—detestable——"

With a swift movement, she pushed past his outstretched arm and flew up the stairs.

In her bedroom Hannah was hovering about between the washstand and dressing-table, a lighted candle in one hand, a carafe of water in the other. At the sight of her mistress she laid both her burdens down with a cry of delight.

"My darlin'!" she exclaimed. "An' is it thrue? Tim heard the word of it an' he carryin' the cheese out of the dinin'-room; but sure I wouldn't belave him——"

But Clodagh checked her.

"Don't be a fool, Hannah!" she cried, almost fiercely; and turning her face from the old servant's scrutinising eyes, she walked across the room towards the bed.

For a moment Hannah stood like an ungainly statue; then she nodded to herself—a nod of profound and silent wisdom—and tip-toeing out of the room, closed the door behind her.

Instantly she was alone, Clodagh began to undress. With hysterical impetuosity she tore off each garment and threw it untidily upon the floor; then slipping into bed, she buried her hot face in the pillows and burst into a violent, unreasoning torrent of tears.

For ten minutes she cried unceasingly; then the storm of her misery was checked. The door handle was very softly turned, and little Nance stole into the room.

She entered eagerly, then paused, frightened by the scene before her; but her hesitation was very brief. With a sudden movement of resolution she sped across the space that divided her from the bed, and laid a cold, tremulous hand on Clodagh's shoulder.

"Clo," she said, "is it true? Are you going to marry him? Are you going away from here?" Her voice sounded thin and far away.

Clodagh raised herself on one elbow, and looked at her sister. Her face was flushed, her eyes were preternaturally bright.

"Why do you want to know?" she demanded angrily. "Why is everybody bothering me like this? Can't I do what I like? Can't I marry if I like?"

Her voice rose excitedly. Then suddenly she caught sight of Nance's quivering, wistful little face; and her anger melted. With a warm, quick movement, she held out her arms.

"Nance!" she cried wildly — "little Nance! — the only person in the world that I really love!"

# CHAPTER VIII

That night Clodagh fell asleep with her wet cheek pressed against her sister's, and her arms clasped closely round her.

Next morning she woke calmed and soothed by her outburst of the night before; and after breakfast she was able to enter into the primary discussion concerning her marriage without any show of emotion. The conclave, at which she, her aunt, and Milbanke alone were present, took place in the drawing-room and was of a weighty and solemn character. The first suggestion was put forward by Mrs. Asshlin, who, with the native distaste for all hurried and definite action, pleaded that an engagement of six months at least would be demanded by the conventionalities before a marriage could take place; but here, to the surprise of his listeners, Milbanke displayed a fresh gleam of the determination and firmness that had inspired him during the days of sickness and death. With a reasonableness that could not be gainsaid, he refuted and disposed of Mrs. Asshlin's arguments; and, with a daring born of his new position, made the startling proposal that the wedding ceremony should be performed within the shortest possible time; and that, to obviate all difficulties, Clodagh and he should leave Ireland immediately, journeying to Italy to take up their residence in the villa that he had already rented at Florence for his own use.

Immediately the suggestion was made, Mrs. Asshlin broke forth in irresistible objection.

"Oh, but what would people say?" she cried. "Think of what people would say, with the funeral scarcely over."

Milbanke looked at her gravely. His matter-of-fact mind was as far as ever from comprehending the ramifications of the Irish character.

"But, my dear Mrs. Asshlin," he urged, "do you think we need really consider whether people talk or not? Surely we who knew and loved poor Denis——"

"Oh, it isn't that! No one knows better than I do what a friend you have been——"

Milbanke stirred uncomfortably.

"Please do not speak of it. I—I did no more than any Christian would have done. What I mean to suggest— —"

But again she interrupted.

"Yes, yes; I know. But we must consider the county—we must consider the county."

But here Clodagh, who was standing by the window, turned swiftly round.

"Why must we?" she asked. "The county never remembered father till he was dead. If I'm going to be married, it's all the same to me whether it's in three weeks or three months or three years."

Milbanke coloured—not quite sure whether the declaration was propitious or the reverse.

"Certainly!—certainly!" he broke in nervously. "I think your view is a—a very sensible one."

Mrs. Asshlin shook her head in speechless disapproval.

"And what is to become of Nance?" she asked, after a moment's pause.

Again Milbanke glanced uncertainly at Clodagh.

"My idea," he began deprecatingly, "was to place the child at a good English school. But for the first year or two I think that perhaps Clodagh might be allowed to veto any arrangement I may make."

Clodagh stepped forward suddenly and impulsively.

"Do you mean that?" she asked.

He bent his head gravely.

"Then—then let us take her with us to Florence. 'Twould make me happier than anything under the sun."

The words were followed by a slightly dismayed pause. Although he strove bravely to conceal the fact, Milbanke's face fell. And Mrs. Asshlin became newly and markedly shocked.

"My dear Clodagh— —" she began sternly.

But Milbanke put up his hand.

"Pray say nothing, Mrs. Asshlin!" he broke in gently. "Clodagh's wishes are mine."

The blood surged into Clodagh's face in a wake of spontaneous relief.

"You mean that?" she said again.

Once more he bent his head.

"Then I'll marry you any time you like," she said with a sudden, impulsive warmth.

And in due time the day of the marriage dawned. After careful consideration, every detail had been arranged and all difficulties smoothed away. The ceremony was to take place in the small, unpretentious Protestant church at Carrigmore, where, Sunday after Sunday, since the days of her early childhood, Clodagh had listened to the Word of God, and had sent up her own immature supplications to heaven. The marriage—which of necessity was to be of the most private nature—was fixed for the forenoon; and it had been arranged that immediately upon its conclusion, Clodagh, Nance, and Milbanke should repair to Mrs. Asshlin's cottage, from which—having partaken of lunch—they were to start upon their journey without returning to Orristown.

The wedding morning broke grey and mild, presaging a typical Irish day. After a night of broken and restless sleep, Clodagh woke at six; and slipped out of bed without disturbing Nance.

For the first moment or two she sat on the side of her bed, her hands locked behind her head, her bare feet resting upon the uncarpeted floor. Then suddenly the sight of the long cardboard box that had arrived from Dublin the day before, containing the new grey dress in which she was to be married, roused her to the significance of the hour. With a swift movement she rose, and crossed the room to the window.

The view across the bay was neutral and calm. Over the sea to the east a pale and silvery sun was emerging from a film of mist; while on the water itself a white, almost spiritual radiance lay like a mystic veil. Clodagh took one long, comprehensive glance at the familiar scene; then, as if afraid to trust herself too far, she turned away quickly and began to dress with noiseless haste.

Twenty minutes later, she crept downstairs arrayed in her old black riding-habit.

Where she rode on that morning of her marriage; what strange and speculative thoughts burned in her brain; and what secrets—regretful or anticipatory—she whispered into Polly's sensitive ears, no one ever knew!

At half-past eight she re-entered the stable-yard, slipped from the saddle unaided, and threw the mare's bridle to Burke.

For a full minute she stood with her gloved hand upon the neck of the animal that had carried her so often and so well; then, with a sudden, almost furtive movement, she bent forward and pressed her face against the cropped mane.

"Take care of her, Tim!" she said unsteadily—"take care of her! I'll come back some day, you know."

And without looking at the old man, she turned and walked out of the yard.

She met no one on her way to the house; but as she passed across the hall, she was suddenly arrested by the sight of Milbanke descending the stairs, already arrayed in a conventional frock-coat.

Unconsciously she paused. From the first she had vaguely understood that he would discard his usual serge suit on the day of the wedding; but the actual sight of these unfamiliar clothes came as a shock, bringing home to her the imminence of the great event as nothing else could possibly have done. He looked unusually old, thin, and precise in the stiff, well-cut garments—a circumstance that was unkindly enhanced by the fact that he was palpably and uncontrollably nervous.

There was a moment of embarrassed silence. Then, mastering her emotions, Clodagh advanced to the foot of the stairs, holding out her hand.

He responded to the gesture with something like gratitude.

"You have been out early," he said hurriedly. "Have you been taking a last look round?"

Clodagh nodded and turned aside. The pain of her recent farewell still burned in her eyes and throat.

He saw and interpreted the action.

"Don't take it to heart, my dear!" he said quickly. "You shall return whenever you like. And—and it will be my proud privilege to know that you will always find everything in readiness for you."

Clodagh's head drooped.

"You are very good," she said in a low, mechanical voice.

For a space Milbanke made no response; then suddenly his fingers tightened nervously over the hand he was still holding.

"Clodagh," he said anxiously, "you do not regret anything? You know it is not too late—even now."

Clodagh glanced up, and for one instant a sudden light leapt into her eyes; the next, her lashes had drooped again.

"No," she said, "I regret nothing."

Milbanke's fingers tightened spasmodically.

"God bless you!" he said tremulously. And leaning forward suddenly, he pressed his thin lips to her forehead.

The hours that followed breakfast and saw the departure from Orristown were too filled with haste and confusion to make any deep impression upon Clodagh's mind. The last frenzied packing of things that had been overlooked, the innumerable farewells, all more or less harassing, the scramble to be dressed, and the entering of the musty old barouche, that had done duty upon great occasions in the Asshlin family for close upon half a century, were all hopelessly—and mercifully—confused. Even the drive to Carrigmore with her aunt and sister filled her with a sense of dazed unreality. She sat very straight and stiff in the new grey dress, one hand clasped tenaciously round Nance's warm fingers, the other holding the cold and unfamiliar ivory prayer-book that had been one of Milbanke's gifts. It was only when at last the carriage drew up before the little church, and she passed to the open gateway between two knots of gaping and whispering villagers, that she realised with any vividness the inevitable nature of the moment. As she walked up the narrow path to the church door, she turned suddenly to her little sister.

"Nance——" she said breathlessly.

But the time for speech was passed. As Nance raised a questioning, excited face to hers, Mrs. Asshlin hurried after them across the grass; and together the three entered the church. A moment later Clodagh saw with a faint sense of perturbation that the building was not empty. In a shadowy corner close to the altar rails Milbanke was talking in nervous whispers to the rector, who was to perform the ceremony.

A few minutes later, the little party was conducted up the aisle with the usual murmur of voices and rustle of garments; and, in what seemed an incredibly—a preposterously—short space of time, the service had begun.

During the first portion of it Clodagh's eyes never left the brown, clean-shaven, benevolent face of the rector. Try as she might, she could not realise that the serious words, pouring forth in the voice that a lifetime had rendered familiar, could be meant for her who, until the day of her father's accident, had never personally understood that life held any serious responsibilities. It was only when the first solemn question was put to her; and, startled out of her dream, she responded almost inaudibly, that her eyes turned upon Milbanke standing opposite to her—earnest, agitated, precise. For one second a sense of panic seized her; the next, she had blindly extended her left hand in obedience to the rector's injunction, and felt the chill of the new gold ring as it was slipped over her third finger.

After that all-important incident, it seemed but a moment before the ceremony was over, and the whole party gathered together in the vestry. With a steady hand she signed her name in the register; then, instantly the act was accomplished, she turned instinctively towards the spot where Nance was standing.

But before she could reach her sister's side, she was intercepted by Mrs. Asshlin, who stepped forward, half tearful, half exultant, and embraced her effusively.

"My dear child!—my dear, dear child!" she murmured disjointedly. "May your future be very happy!"

Clodagh submitted silently to the embrace; then, as her aunt reluctantly withdrew into the background, she became conscious of the old rector's kindly presence. Looking closely into her face, he took her hand in both his own.

"God bless you, my child!" he said simply. "I did not preach you a sermon just now, because I do not think you require one. You are a dutiful child; and I believe that you have found a very worthy husband."

At the word husband, Clodagh looked up quickly; then her eyes dropped to her wedding ring.

"Thank you!" she said almost inaudibly. And an instant later Milbanke stepped forward deferentially and offered her his arm.

In silence they passed down the aisle of the church, in the centre of which stood the old stone font at which Clodagh had been christened, and on which she had been wont to fix her eyes during the Sunday service while the rector preached. All at once this inanimate friendly object seemed to take a new and unfamiliar air—seemed to whisper that Clodagh Asshlin existed no more, and that the stranger who filled her place was an alien. Her fingers tightened nervously on her husband's arm and her steps involuntarily quickened.

Outside, in the calm, grey, misty atmosphere, they lingered for a moment by the church door, in order to give Nance and Mrs. Asshlin the opportunity of gaining the cottage before them; but both were ill at ease, self-conscious, and acutely anxious to curtail the enforced solitude. And it was with a sigh of relief, that Clodagh saw Milbanke draw out his watch as an indication that they might start.

About the gate, the little group of curious idlers had been augmented. And as Clodagh stepped to the carriage an irrepressible murmur of admiration passed from lip to lip, succeeded by a cold and critical silence as the bridegroom—well bred, well dressed, but obviously and incongruously old—followed in her wake.

Clodagh comprehended and construed this chilling silence by the light of her own warm appreciation of things young, strong, and beautiful. And as she stepped hastily into the waiting carriage a flush of something like shame rose hotly to her face.

The drive to the cottage scarcely occupied five minutes; and even had they desired it, there was no time for conversation. Milbanke sat upright and embarrassed; Clodagh lay back in her corner of the roomy barouche, her eyes fixed resolutely upon the window, her fingers tightly clasping the ivory prayer-book. One fact was occupying her mind with a sense of anger and loneliness—the fact that her cousin Larry had not been present in the church. Since the night on which her engagement had been announced, the feud between the cousins had continued. During the weeks of preparation for the wedding Larry had avoided Orristown; but though no overtures had been made, Clodagh had never doubted that he would be present at the ceremony itself. And now that the excitement was passed, she realised with a shock of surprise that she had been openly and unmistakably deserted.

The thought was uppermost in her mind as the carriage stopped; and when her aunt came forward to greet them, her first question concerned the absent member of the family.

"Where's Larry, Aunt Fan?" she asked.

"My dear child, that's just what I have been asking myself. But come in!—come into the house!"

Mrs. Asshlin was fluttered by the responsibilities of the moment.

"Why wasn't he in church?" Clodagh asked, as she followed her into the narrow hall.

Mrs. Asshlin threw out her hands in a gesture of perplexity.

"How can I tell?" she said. "Boys are incomprehensible things. I'm sure—er—James is not old enough to have forgotten that?"

She glanced archly over her shoulder.

Milbanke looked intensely embarrassed, and Clodagh coloured.

"Well, we'd better not wait for Larry," she interposed hastily. "You know what a time it takes to get round to Muskeere with that big barouche."

Mrs. Asshlin became all assiduity.

"Certainly!—certainly, my dear child! Mr. Curry and his brother are already waiting. Won't you come in?"

With hospitable excitement she marshalled them into the dining-room.

The room into which they were ushered, though small, was bright and cheerful; and, notwithstanding the season, there were flowers upon the table and mantelpiece. But even under these favourable conditions, the lunch was scarcely a success. Mrs. Asshlin was genuine enough in her efforts at entertainment; but the guests were not in a condition to be entertained. Milbanke was intensely nervous; Clodagh sat straight and rigid in her chair, uncomfortably conscious of insubordinate emotions that crowded up at every added suggestion of departure. Even the rector's brother—a bluff and hearty personage, who, out of old friendship for the Asshlin family, had consented to act as best man at the hurriedly arranged wedding—felt his spirits damped; while little Nance, who sat close to her sister, made no pretence whatever at hiding the tears that kept welling into her eyes.

It was with universal relief that at length they rose from the table and filed out into the hall. There, however, a new interruption awaited them. In the shadow of a doorway they caught sight of Hannah, arrayed in her Sunday bonnet and shawl, and still breathless from the walk from Orristown.

At sight of the little party she came forward with a certain ungainly shyness; but catching a glimpse of Clodagh, love conquered every lesser feeling.

"Let me have wan last look at her!" she exclaimed softly. "That's all I'm wantin'."

And as Clodagh turned impulsively towards her, she held out her arms.

"Sure, I knew her before any wan of ye ever sat eyes on her!" she explained, the tears running down her cheeks. "Go on now, miss—ma'am," she added brokenly, pushing Clodagh forward towards the door, and turning to Milbanke with an outstretched hand. "Good-bye, sir! And God bless you!" Her sing-song voice fell, and her hard hand tightened over his. "Take care of her!" she added. "An' don't be forgettin' that she's nothin' but a child still, for all her fine height and her good looks."

She spoke with crude, rough earnestness; but at the last words her feelings overcame her. With another spasmodic pressure, she released his fingers and, turning incontinently, disappeared into the back regions of the cottage.

For a moment Milbanke remained where she had left him, moved and perplexed by her hurried words; then, suddenly remembering his duties, he crossed the hall and punctiliously offered his arm to Clodagh. "The carriage is waiting," he said gently. But Clodagh shook her head.

"Please take Nance first," she murmured in a low, constrained voice.

He acquiesced silently, and as he moved away from her, she turned to Mrs. Asshlin.

"Good-bye, Aunt Fan!" she said. "And tell Larry that I'm—that I'm sorry. He'll know what it means."

Her carefully controlled voice shook suddenly, as pride struggled with affection and association. Suddenly putting her arms round Mrs. Asshlin's neck she kissed her thin cheek; and, turning quickly, walked forward to the waiting carriage.

There was a moment of excitement; a spasmodic waving of handkerchiefs, the sound of a stifled sob and the tardy throwing of a slipper; then, with a swish of the long driving whip, the horses bounded forward, and the great lumbering carriage swung down the hill that led to the Muskeere road.

As they bowled through the village street, Clodagh shrank back into her corner, refusing to look her last on the scene that for nearly eighteen years had formed a portion of her life's horizon. The instinctive clinging to familiar things that forms so integral a part of the Celtic nature, was swelling in her throat and tightening about her heart. She resolutely refused to be conquered by her emotion; but the emotion—stronger for her obstinate suppression of it—threatened to dominate her. For the moment she was unconscious of Milbanke, sitting opposite to her, anxious and deprecating; and she dared not permit herself to press the small, warm fingers that Nance had insinuated into her own.

With a lurch, the carriage swept round the curve of the street, and emerged upon the Muskeere road. But scarcely had Burke gathered the reins securely into his hands, scarcely had the horses settled into a swinging trot, than the little party became suddenly aware that a check had been placed upon their progress. There was an exclamation—from Burke; a clatter of hoofs, as the horses were hastily pulled up; and the barouche came to a halt.

With a movement of surprise, Clodagh turned to the open window. But on the instant there was a scuffle of paws, the sharp, eager yap of a dog, and something rough and warm thrust itself against her face.

"Mick!" she cried in breathless, incredulous rapture. Then she glanced quickly over the dog's red head to the hands that had lifted him to the carriage window.

"Larry!" she said below her breath.

Young Asshlin was standing in the middle of the road—red, shy, and excited.

"I want you to take him, Clo," he said awkwardly, "for a—for a wedding present."

For one instant Clodagh sat overwhelmed by the suggestion; and next her eyes unconsciously sought Milbanke's.

"May I?" she said hesitatingly. It was her first faltering acknowledgment that her actions were no longer quite her own.

Milbanke started.

"Oh, assuredly!" he said—"assuredly!"

And Clodagh opened the carriage door, and took Mick into her arms.

For one moment the joy of reunion submerged every other feeling; then she raised a glowing, grateful face to her cousin.

"Larry——" she began softly.

But old Burke leant down from his seat.

"We'll be late for the thrain," he announced imperturbably.

Again Milbanke started nervously.

"Perhaps, Clodagh——" he began.

Clodagh bent her head.

"Shut the door, Larry," she said. "And—and you were a darling to think of it."

Asshlin closed the door.

"Good-bye, Nance! Good-bye, sir! Good-bye, Clo!"

He looked bravely into the carriage; but his face was still preternaturally red.

Clodagh turned to him impulsively.

"Larry——" she began again.

But the horses started forward; and the boy, lifting his cap, stepped back into the roadway.

Clodagh stooped forward, waved her hand unevenly, then dropped back into her seat.

While the horses covered a quarter of a mile, she sat without movement or speech. But at last, lifting his adoring eyes to her face, Mick ventured to touch her hand with a warm, reminding tongue.

The gentle appeal of the action—the hundred memories it evoked—was instantaneous and supreme. In a sudden irrepressible tide, her grief, her uncertainty of the future, her home-sickness inundated her soul. With a quick gesture she flung away both pride and restraint; and, hiding her face against the dog's rough coat, cried as if she had been a child.

# PART III

## CHAPTER I

It was nine o'clock on a morning four years after the wedding at Carrigmore; the season was late spring; the scene was Italy; and Florence— the city of tranquillity made manifest—lay at rest under its coverlet of sun and roses. In the soft, early light, the massed buildings of the town seemed to blend together until, to the dazzled eyes, the Arno looked a mere ribbon of silver as it wound under its bridges; and the splendid proportions of the Duomo became lost in the blue haze that presaged the hot day to come.

The scene was vaguely beautiful, viewed from any of the hills that guard the city; but from no point was its soft picturesqueness more remarkable than from the terraces and windows of a villa that nestled in a curve of the narrow, winding road between San Domenico and Fiesole. This villa, unlike its neighbours, was long and low in structure; and in addition to the stone urns, luxurious flowering plants, and wide, painted jalousies common to Italian houses, it boasted other and more individual attractions—to be found in a flight of singularly old marble steps that led from one level of its garden to another; and in the unusual magnificence of the cypresses that grew in an imposing semi-circle upon the upper terrace.

It was under the shade of these sombre trees that a breakfast table stood, awaiting occupation, on this particular morning at the hour of nine. The table in itself formed a picture, for in the warm shafts of sun that slipped between the cypress trees, silver and glass gleamed invitingly, while in their midst an immense Venetian bowl filled with roses made a patch of burning colour. Everything was attractive, refined, appetising; and yet, for some undiscernible reason, the inmates of the villa appeared in no haste to enjoy the meal that awaited them.

For fully ten minutes after the coffee had been laid upon the table, the Italian man-servant stood immovably attentive, his back stiff, his glance resting expectantly upon the verandah; then his natural interest in the meal caused him to alter his position and cast a sympathetic eye upon the coffee in imminent danger of growing cold.

Five more minutes passed. He looked again at the villa; sighed, and gracefully flicked a fly from the basket of crisp rolls. Then suddenly he stood newly erect and attentive, as his quick ear caught the swish of a skirt and the sound of a light step. A moment later Clodagh emerged upon the sunny terrace, followed by her dog Mick.

At any period of existence, four years is a span of time to be reckoned with. But when four years serves to bridge the gulf between childhood and womanhood, its power is well-nigh limitless. As Clodagh stepped through the long window of her room and came slowly out into the morning light, it would have been a close observer who would, at a first glance, have recognised the unformed girl of four years ago in the graceful, well-dressed woman moving forward through the Italian sunshine. On a second glance, or a third, one would undoubtedly have seen traces of the long, undeveloped limbs in the tall, supple figure; caught a suggestion of the rough luxurious plait in the golden-brown hair coiled about the well-shaped head; and have been fascinated by numerous undeniable and haunting suggestions in contour and colouring. But there memory would have hesitated. The Clodagh who had scoured the woods, scrambled over the rocks, and galloped across the lands of Orristown was no longer visible. Another being, infinitely more distinguished, infinitely more attractive— and yet vaguely deprived of some essential quality—had taken her place. In the four years that had passed since she left Ireland she had, from being a child, become a woman; and below the new beauty that nature had painted upon her face lay an intangible, a poignantly suggested regret for the girlhood that had been denied her.

As she stepped out upon the terrace, she paused for a moment and her eyes travelled mechanically over Florence—warm, beautiful, inert. Then, with the same uninterested calm, she turned slowly towards the breakfast table; but there her glance brightened.

"Oh, letters!" she said aloud; and with an impulsive movement, she hurried forward, letting her elaborate muslin dress trail unheeded behind her.

Scarcely seeing the profound bow with which the man-servant greeted her, she picked up the letters, and scanned them one by one. Then as she disappointedly threw the last back upon the table, she half turned, in acknowledgment of a measured step that came across the terrace from the direction of the house. At the same moment Mick pricked up his ears and slowly wagged his tail, while the Italian servant bent his body in a fresh salutation.

Milbanke—for his was the second step that had disturbed the silence—came forward without haste. Reaching the table, he took Clodagh's left hand and pressed it; then he stooped methodically and patted the dog's head.

"Good-morning!" he said gravely. "Are there any letters?"

"Yes, four; and all for you—as usual."

He smiled, unobservant of the slightly tired irritability of Clodagh's tone.

"Ah, indeed!" he said. "That is pleasant. Is there one from Sicily? Scarpio promised to let me have the latest details of the great work."

He took up the four letters and carefully studied the envelopes. As he came to the last, his thin face became animated.

"Ah, this is satisfactory!" he exclaimed. "I knew he would not fail me. What wonderful—what fascinating work it must be!"

He tore the envelope open and began to peruse the letter.

While he scanned the opening lines, Clodagh watched him absently; but as the first page fluttered between his fingers, she gave a slight, involuntary shrug of the shoulders and, moving round the table, sank into the seat that the servant drew forward for her. Then, with an uninterested gesture, she poured out two cups of coffee.

For a while there was silence save for the turning of the letter in its recipient's hand; the occasional snap of Mick's teeth as he attempted to catch a fly; and the thousand, impersonal sounds of lazy, outdoor life that rose about them. At last Milbanke looked up, his face tinged with mild excitement.

"This discovery is very remarkable," he said. "Sicily will obtain a new importance."

Clodagh smiled faintly.

"In the antiquarian's eyes," she said with unconscious irony. There was no bitterness and no impatience in her voice. She spoke as if stating a fact that long familiarity had rendered absolutely barren.

Looking back over the four years of her marriage, it seemed to her that her life had been one round of archaeological discoveries—all timed to take place at the wrong season. She vividly remembered the first of these events; the discovery of some subterranean passages in the neighbourhood of Carrara, which had taken place two months after her arrival in Italy, while life yet retained something of the dark, vague semblance usually associated with a nightmare. Still desperately home-sick and unreasonably miserable in her new position, she had eagerly grasped at Milbanke's suggestion that they should visit the scene of these excavations. But with this first essay, her interest in discoveries had taken permanent flight.

The heat had been tremendous; the country parched and unsympathetic; the associations terribly uncongenial. She remembered the first morning, when she and Nance, stifling in their black dresses, had by tacit consent stolen away from the party of fellow enthusiasts to which Milbanke had attached himself; and climbing to the summit of a low, olive-crowned hill, had sat tired, silent, and unutterably wretched, looking out upon the arid land.

But that excursion had been the prelude to a new era. Visits to various antiquities had succeeded each other with dull regularity, broken by long, uneventful sojourns in the green seclusion of the villa at Florence. Then the first break had occurred in the companionship of the trio. Nance had been sent home to an English school.

Clodagh's acceptance of this fiat had been curiously interesting—as had been her whole attitude towards Milbanke and his wishes. From the day on which she recognised that the state of matrimony was something irrevocably serious, she had taken upon herself an attitude of reserved surrender that was difficult to analyse—difficult even to superficially understand. By a strangely immature process of deduction, she had satisfied herself that marriage was a state of bondage, more or less distasteful as chance decreed—a state in which, by a fundamental law of nature, submission and self-repression were the chief factors necessary upon the woman's side.

As sometimes happens when there is a great disparity in years, the wedded state had widened instead of lessening the gulf between Milbanke and herself. It had cast a sudden, awkward restraint upon the affection and respect that his actions had kindled in her mind, while inspiring no new or ardent feelings to take its place. Ridiculously—and yet naturally—her husband had become an infinitely more distant and unapproachable being than her father's friend had been. And to this new key she had, perforce, attuned her existence.

With a greater number of years—even with a little more worldly experience—she might have made a vastly different business of her life; for, at the time of his marriage, Milbanke had been hovering upon the borderland of that fatuous love in which an old man can lose himself so completely. If, in those first months, she had permitted any of the ardour, any of the fascination of her nature to shine upon him, she might have led him by a silken thread in whatever direction she pleased. But three factors had precluded this—her youth, her inexperience, her entire ignorance of artifice. In her primary encounter with the realities of life, she had lost her strongest weapon—her frank, unswerving fearlessness; and in lieu of this she had, in the moment of first panic, seized upon the nearest substitute, and had wrapped herself in an armour of reserve.

And on this armour, the weapons of Milbanke's love had been turned aside. There had been no scenes, no harassing disillusionment; but gradually, inevitably his original attitude with regard to her—his shy reticence, his uncertainty, as in the presence of some incomprehensible quality—had returned. He had slowly but surely withdrawn into himself, turning with a pathetic eagerness to the interests that had previously usurped his thoughts. With the nervous sensitiveness that warred continuously with his matter-of-fact precision, he became uncomfortably conscious of occupying a false position, of having made an indisputable—almost a ridiculous—mistake; and he had taken a blind leap towards the quarter in which he believed compensation to lie. While Clodagh, vaguely divining this—vaguely remorseful, of what she scarcely knew—had held her own enthusiasms more rigidly in check, schooling herself into acquiescence with every impersonal suggestion that he chose to make.

From this had arisen the pursuit of the antique in whatever corner of Europe—and at whatever season of the year—circumstances might decree. To Clodagh, the pilgrimages had seemed unutterably wearisome and unutterably foolish; but there is a great capacity for silent endurance in the Irish nature. Quick-blooded though it may be, it possesses that strong fatalistic instinct that accepts without question the decree of the gods. The spirit of revolt is not lacking in it; but it requires a given atmosphere—a given sequence of events—to bring it into activity. At two-and-twenty Clodagh was weary of her husband, of herself, of her life. But precisely as her father had fretted out his existence in the quiet monotony of Orristown, she had accepted her fate without thought of question.

In the second year, when they had travelled to England with Nance, Milbanke had suggested a visit to Ireland, but this proposal she had declined. The days when every fibre of her being had yearned for her own country were passed; and the idea of return had lost its savour.

As she sat now, sipping her coffee and gazing abstractedly down to where the hot sun glinted on the Arno, it seemed to her that her life—the glorious, exuberant state that she had been accustomed to call her life—had drifted incredibly far away; that it lay asleep, if not already dead, in some intangible realm widely beyond her reach. She thought of Nance away at her English school, and unconsciously she envied her. To be fifteen, and to be surrounded by young people! Involuntarily she sighed; and Mick, ever acutely sensitive to her change of mood, turned and pressed his cold nose against her knee.

Mechanically she put down her hand and pulled one of his soft ears; then suddenly she raised her head, attracted by an exclamation of impatience in Milbanke's usually placid voice. Looking up, she saw that he had opened a second letter.

"What is it?" she asked, her momentary curiosity dropping back to indifference. "Was that last intaglio unauthentic after all?"

Milbanke glanced up with an annoyed expression. "This does not concern the intaglio," he said. "This is from Barnard—David Barnard, who acts as my broker, and looks after my business affairs. You have heard me speak of him."

"Of course. Often." An expression of interest awakened in Clodagh's face.

"Well, this letter is from him—written from Milan. Most tiresome and annoying its coming at this juncture!" He scanned the letter for the second time. "I particularly want to run down into Sicily before Scarpio leaves."

"And does the letter prevent you?" There was interest and a slight hopefulness in the tone of Clodagh's voice.

"I am very much afraid that it does."

"But why?"

He folded the letter carefully and returned it to its envelope.

"Because Barnard is coming to Venice in two days, and suggests that I should meet him there."

"Venice!" Clodagh said the word softly.

"Yes. Most tiresome!—most annoying! But he thinks it an opportunity that should not be lost. I have not had an interview with him since we left Nance at school. He came then to our hotel in London; I do not think you met him."

"No. But I remember his coming to see you. I remember Nance and I thought he had such a jolly laugh; we heard it from her bedroom—the one that opened off our sitting-room."

With the mention of this new subject, trivial though it was, Clodagh's manner had changed.

"But what about Venice?" she asked, after a moment's pause. "Will you go?"

Milbanke looked thoughtful.

"Well, I—I scarcely know what to say. Of course I could refuse on the ground of this business in Sicily. But it is a question of expediency. A few days with Barnard now may save me a journey to London next year. Still it is very provoking!"

"But Venice!" Clodagh suggested, and again her tone was soft. More than any other in Italy, the beautiful city of the Adriatic had appealed to her curiosity and her imagination. With a quick glance her eyes travelled over the sheltered, drowsy garden, sloping downward, terrace below terrace.

"I should love to see Venice," she said suddenly. "I always picture it so wide and silent and mysterious."

Milbanke looked up from the opening of his third letter.

"Venice is unhealthy," he said prosaically.

For one moment her lip curled.

"Perhaps that is why it appeals to me," she said with a flash of the old, insubordinate spirit. Then suddenly her eyes met her husband's quiet, puzzled gaze and the passing light died out of her face. With a hasty gesture she lifted her coffee cup to her lips and set it down empty.

"Come along, Mick!" she said, pushing back her chair and speaking with unconscious sarcasm. "Come and let us see whether we can find any roses in the garden!"

# CHAPTER II

Clodagh's manner was careless and her gait nonchalant as she rose from table and crossed the terrace followed by her dog; but inwardly she burned with a newly kindled sense of anticipation. There was no particular reason why the idea of a journey to Venice, for the purpose of seeing a stock-broker—even though that stock-broker was a personal friend of Milbanke's—should be instinct with any promise; yet the idea excited her. With the exception of the journey to England with Nance, it was the first time in four years that her husband had seriously contemplated any move not ostensibly connected with his hobby. And the thought of Venice; the suggestion of encountering any one whose interests lay outside antiquities, had power to elate her. As she left the breakfast table, her steps unconsciously quickened; and Mick, attentively sensitive to her altered gait, wagged his short tail, gave one sharp, incisive bark of question, and looked up at her with ears inquisitively pricked.

She paused and looked down at him.

"Mick, darling," she whispered, "imagine Venice at night—the music and the water and the romance! And just think—" her voice dropped still lower—"just think what it would be to meet some one—any one at all—who might happen to notice that one's clothes were new, and that one's hair was properly done up!"

She bent down in a sudden impulse of excitement and kissed his upraised head; then with a quick laugh at her own impetuosity, she turned and ran down the first flight of time-worn marble steps.

That was her private and personal reception of the news. Later, returning with her arms full of the roses that ran riot in the garden, she was able to meet Milbanke with a demeanour of dignified calm; and to answer his questions as to whether her boxes could be packed in two days, in a voice that was dutifully submissive and unmoved.

But the two days of preparation were imbued with a secret joy. There was a new and unending delight in selecting the most beautiful of the dresses in her elaborate wardrobe, and in feeling that at last they were to be seen by eyes that would understand their value. For Milbanke, while never restraining her craving for costly clothes, had, since the day of their marriage, been totally unobservant and indifferent as to whether she wore silk or home-spun; and on the occasions when outside opinions might have been brought to bear upon the matter—namely, the moments when the archaeological excursions were undertaken—necessities of season or expediency had invariably limited her supply of garments to the clothes that would not show the dust or the clothes that would keep out the rain. But now the prospect was different. It was still the season in Venice; she would be justified in bringing the best and most attractive clothes she possessed. The thought was exhilarating; life became a thing of bustle and interest. Two and three times a day she drove into Florence to make totally unnecessary purchases; she wrote more than one long letter to Nance; and indulged in many a protracted and confidential talk with Mick as they sat together on the edge of the old marble fountain that dripped and dozed in the sun.

By a hundred actions, obvious or obscure, she made it plain in those days of preparation that, despite the fact that her childhood lay behind her, and that she had known none of the intermediate pleasures of ordinary girlhood, she was a being whose heart, whose capacity for enjoyment, whose comprehension of life was extraordinarily—even dangerously—young.

At last the day dawned upon which they left the villa on the sunny hill—said good-bye to the wide, slow river, the riotous roses and the slow-tolling bells of Florence—and took train for the north.

Through the hours of that railway journey Clodagh sat almost silent. To her eager mind, already springing forward towards the enchanted city, there was no need for speech; and the quiet, prim husband seated opposite to her, made no call upon her imagination. He was essential to the journey—as the padded cushion behind her head, or the English books and magazines by her side were essential to it—and for this reason he occupied that most fatal of all positions, the position of an accepted, familiar accessory. The early days of their marriage, when in her eyes, he had taken in a new and dreaded aspect, were entirely past. With his super-sensitiveness and constitutional self-distrust, he had withdrawn somewhat hastily from the position of lover, to shelter behind the cloak of his former guardianship. And Clodagh had hailed the change of attitude with obvious relief.

Now, as she sat eagerly alert to gain her first glimpse of Venice, she had almost forgotten that those early days had ever existed. For the moment Milbanke was a cipher; and she an ardent appreciative individual undergoing a new sensation.

Such was her precise mental position when at last the scene for which she waited broke upon her view. Rising straight out of the water, Venice seemed to her ardent eyes even more the product of a visionary world than her dreams had made it. The hour was seven; and from the many spires and domes of the city warm gleams of bronze or gold shot forth at the touch of the setting sun. But the prevailing note of colour that gleamed through the mauve twilight was white—the wonderful, semi-transparent white of ancient marble back-grounded by sea and sky.

The effect made upon Clodagh's mind by this white city wrapped in its evening veil was instantaneous and deep. With the exception of Florence, her knowledge of the beauties of Italy was very limited; and her first glimpse of Florence had been gained under such unpropitious circumstances that its sheltered loveliness had never appealed to her as it might otherwise have done. Now, however, her condition of mind was tranquil, if not happy; and as the train sped forward, she gazed spell-bound at this beauty at once so tangible and so unreal.

To every traveller it must come with the sense of desecration, that this most magical of cities is approached by nothing less prosaic than an ordinary railway terminus. And Clodagh gave a little involuntary gasp of disappointment as the train swerved suddenly, exchanging the glamour of the outer world for a noisy station that might have belonged to any town; and as she rose from her seat, arranged her hat, and collected her books, she wondered for one moment whether the vision just hidden from her view was in reality the handiwork of man and not some mirage conjured up by her own imagination. So strong was the feeling, that she remained silent as she descended from the train, and waited while Milbanke saw to the collecting of the luggage; then, still without speaking, she followed him down the flight of steps that lead to the water. But there, as the station vanished from consideration, and the picturesque crowd of waiting gondolas met her gaze, her pleasure and excitement woke again; and with a quick gesture, she laid her hand on her husband's arm.

"Oh, isn't it wonderful?" she said in a hushed voice.

Milbanke turned to her uncertainly.

"Yes, my dear," he said absently—"yes. But——" He sniffed critically—"but do you not detect a distinctly unhealthy odour?"

Clodagh's hand dropped suddenly and expressively to her side, and she wheeled round with unnecessary haste towards the gondola into which the luggage was being piled.

But even this jarring incident could not mar the first journey in the stately black boat. Every portion of the way was instinct with its own especial charm. From the wide dignity of the Grand Canal with its ancient palaces, its mysterious stream of silent traffic, its occasional note of modern life, to the fascinating glimpses of narrower waterways where the women of the people, with uncovered heads, leaned out of their windows to exchange the day's gossip with a neighbour across the water—all was a delight, something engrossing and unique. Clodagh had no desire to speak as they glided forward; and when the hotel steps were reached, she suffered herself to be assisted from the gondola scarcely certain whether she was dreaming or awake.

Outside the hotel, half a dozen visitors were seated upon the small stone terrace, indolently watching the arrival of new guests; but so absorbed was Clodagh in the scene before her, that she scarcely observed their presence. And when Milbanke, murmuring an excuse, departed to see after their rooms, she turned again towards the canal that she had just left; and, leaning over the balustrade of the terrace, paused for a moment to study the picture afresh.

But as she stood there, unconscious of everything but the wonderful, noiseless pageant passing ceaselessly through the purple twilight, more than one glance strayed in her own direction. And two at least among the hotel visitors changed their lounging attitudes for the purpose of observing her more closely.

The two—both men—were simultaneously and noticeably attracted. The elder, who, by his extremely fastidious and studied appearance, might almost have belonged to another and earlier era than our own, was a man of nearly seventy; the younger was his junior by forty-five years. But—so levelling a thing is spontaneous admiration—the expression upon the two faces, as they leant suddenly forward, was strikingly similar.

The old man held a gold-rimmed eyeglass close to his eye; the younger meditatively removed his cigarette from his mouth. But at this critical moment of their close observation, Milbanke reappeared, and, moving stiffly across the terrace, touched Clodagh's arm.

"My dear," he said, "our rooms are ready. If you will go upstairs, I will find Barnard. I will not dress for dinner to-night. It is after seven o'clock."

Clodagh turned, her face glowing with the enthusiasm that filled her mind.

"All right!" she said. "But I think I'll just change into something cool. It won't take ten minutes."

Without waiting for his assent, she turned quickly and Walked across the terrace to the vestibule of the hotel.

As she passed the two men in the lounge chairs, the elder again lifted his eyeglass; while the younger, leaning forward, stared at her with that superb lack of embarrassment or reserve that the young Englishman can at times assume.

"By Jove!" he said very softly, as the two new arrivals disappeared into the hotel.

His companion turned to him with a thin laugh that belied his carefully preserved appearance.

"Attractive—eh?" he said.

The other replaced his cigarette in his mouth.

"What nationality is she?" he asked after a moment's pause. "I'd feel inclined to say Italian myself, but the old father's so uncompromisingly Saxon."

Again the older man laughed—a laugh that expressed unfathomable worldly wisdom.

"Father!" he said satirically. "Fathers don't shuffle round their womenfolk like that. They are husband and wife."

"Husband and wife!" The other smiled. But the older man pursed up his lips.

"You'll find I'm right," he said. "She walked three steps ahead of him, to avoid seeing him—and she did it unconsciously. Proof conclusive!"

The young man laughed.

"Doesn't carry conviction, uncle!" he said. "I'll bet you a fiver you're wrong. Will you take me on?"

His companion smiled languidly.

"As you like," he responded.

The young man nodded; then he looked down lazily at his flannel suit.

"I suppose it's time to change," he said reluctantly. "Awful bore being conventional abroad."

With another careless nod, he lounged off in the direction of the hall.

Exactly a quarter of an hour later, Clodagh emerged from her bedroom, looking fresh and cool in a dress of rose-coloured gauze that, cut high in the neck and possessing sleeves that reached the wrist, was yet light and diaphanous in effect. She opened her door and, mindful of the lateness of the hour, moved quickly out into the corridor. But scarcely had she taken a step in the direction of the stairs, than a door exactly opposite to her own was opened with equal haste; and the young Englishman of the terrace appeared before her. Seeing her, he halted involuntarily, and for a second their eyes met.

The glance was momentary; there was not a word spoken; but irresistibly the colour rushed into Clodagh's face. It took her but an instant to regain her composure, and to pass down the empty corridor with a touch of hauteur; but long after she had gained the stairs, her heart was beating with a new excitement. The glance that the stranger had given her had been almost ill-bred in its absolute directness; but ill or well bred, there had been no mistaking the unqualified admiration it conveyed. The personality of the man had escaped her attention; the fact that his hair was dark, his face attractive, and his figure tall, slight, and graceful had made no impression upon her. All she was conscious of—all that set her pulses throbbing, was the suddenly awakened knowledge that, within herself, she possessed some subtle, and previously unrealised power that could compel a man's regard.

She descended the stairs with a new sensation of elasticity and elation; and at its foot found Milbanke awaiting her in conversation with a suave, elderly man.

As she came within speaking distance, the two turned towards her.

"My dear!" Milbanke said quickly, "allow me to introduce Mr. David Barnard! David, this is my—my wife!"

Clodagh looked up curiously, and met the florid face, bland smile, and observant eyes of Barnard—a man who for nearly a quarter of a century had managed to prosper in his profession, and at the same time to retain a prominent place in fashionable society. As their glances met, she held out her hand.

"How d'you do!" she said. "I believe I've been wanting to know you ever since I heard you laugh one day two years ago."

She spoke warmly—impulsively—almost as Denis Asshlin might have spoken. Involuntarily Milbanke glanced at her with a species of surprise. In that moment she was neither the frank, fearless child he had first known, nor the self-contained, unfathomable girl who had since become his daily companion. In the crowded, cosmopolitan atmosphere of the hotel, she seemed suddenly to display a new individuality.

Barnard took her outstretched hand, and bowed over it impressively.

"It is very charming of you to say that, Mrs. Milbanke," he murmured. "But I'm afraid James has told me that you come from Ireland!"

Clodagh laughed.

"He'll also tell you that I lived quite forty miles from the Blarney stone!"

She looked up, her face brimming with animation. Then suddenly and involuntarily she coloured. The young Englishman of the terrace was coming slowly down the stairs.

He descended nonchalantly, and as he reached the hall, he deliberately paused in front of the little group.

"Hallo, Barney!" he said easily. "Been playing much bridge this afternoon?"

Barnard looked round with his tactfully affable smile.

"Haven't had one rubber," he said.

"No?"

"No."

There was a pause—a seemingly unnecessary and pointless pause—in which Barnard looked suavely at the newcomer; the newcomer looked at Clodagh; and Clodagh looked fixedly out across the hall. Then at last the older man seemed to realise that something was expected of him. With a gay gesture, he metaphorically swept the silence aside.

"Mrs. Milbanke," he said affably, "will you permit me to present my friend Mr. Valentine Serracauld?"

# CHAPTER III

Clodagh looked up, colouring afresh; and the young man bowed quickly and eagerly. He belonged to a type new to her, but familiar to every social Londoner: the type of young Englishman who, gifted with unusual height and fine possibilities of muscular development, saunters through life—physically and morally—exerting his energy and his strength in one direction only—the eternal, aimless, enervating search after personal pleasure.

To be explicit, the Honourable Valentine Serracauld was suffering from that most modern of complaints—the lack of surmountable obstacles. The nephew of one of the richest peers in England, he had started life heavily handicapped. A sufficiency of money had rendered work unnecessary; good looks and a naturally ingratiating manner had precluded the need for mental equipment; while his social position had unfairly protected him from any share in the rough and tumble existence that moulds and hardens a man's character. At fifteen, he had been an average healthy public schoolboy; at five-and-twenty, he was a fashionable young aristocrat, whose only business in life was the aiding and abetting of his uncle in the absorbing pursuit of killing time.

He bowed now to Clodagh with the extreme impressiveness that men of his type bestow upon a new and promising introduction.

"Charmed to meet you, Mrs. Milbanke!" he said. "Are you a resident here—or a bird of passage like ourselves?" He indicated Barnard.

Clodagh met his intent gaze with a renewed thrill of speculative pleasure.

"My husband and I live at Florence," she explained. "We are only here on business—which sounds a desecration."

Serracauld continued to watch her.

"Not if you have any share in it," he said in a low voice.

She laughed and blushed.

"I'm afraid you speak from inexperience," she said. "To the people who know me, I am a very prosaic person."

She looked involuntarily at Milbanke.

But Milbanke's eyes were on the groups of hotel guests, already moving towards the dining-room.

"Don't you think we might—might make a move— —?" he hazarded vaguely.

There was a very slight pause; then Serracauld responded to the suggestion.

"You are quite right!" he said easily. "I expect my uncle is looking for me; he usually gets fidgety about feeding time. Will you excuse me, Mrs. Milbanke? Perhaps later on I shall have the chance of correcting that inexperience you accuse me of."

He laughed pleasantly; and with a courteous gesture, disappeared into the crowd that was fast filing out of the hall.

As he disappeared, Clodagh turned towards the dining-room, leaving Milbanke and Barnard to follow; but she had scarcely crossed the hall, when the latter overtook her.

"Well, Mrs. Milbanke," he said genially, "what do you think of our young friend? I believe he usually finds favour in ladies' eyes."

She glanced up.

"I think him very charming," she said candidly. "Who is he? Do you know him well?"

Barnard smiled.

"I have known him since he was a boy at Eton. He is nephew of the famous Earl of Deerehurst who, according to rumour, spends three hundred a year on silk socks, and bathes every morning in scented milk."

Clodagh made an exclamation of disgust.

"What an abominable person!"

Again Barnard smiled.

"Well, I don't quite know," he said tolerantly. "Rumour is generally a yard or two in front of reality. Perhaps Deerehurst is rather a mummified old *roué*; but then, you know, embalming is a clean process, Mrs. Milbanke, before, as well as after, death. I sometimes wonder whether Valentine won't put the family money to even less harmless use if he ever succeeds to the title. He is next in the succession, but for one feeble life."

Clodagh's eyes opened.

"Really!" she said. "I should never have connected him with so much responsibility."

Barnard looked down at her.

"Responsibility!" he said. "I don't think I should call it responsibility! But what has become of James?"

He paused, and glanced round the fast emptying hall.

As he did so, Milbanke hurried up, his manner newly interested, his thin face flushed.

"Who do you think I have just seen, Clodagh?" he asked excitedly. "Mr. Angelo Tombs—that interesting scientist who joined our party at Pisa last year!"

Clodagh looked round.

"What?" she said in surprise. "The big, untidy-looking man, who had written a book on something terribly unpronounceable?"

Milbanke nodded gravely.

"Yes," he said. "A most interesting and exhaustive work. I shall make a point of congratulating him upon it directly we have finished dinner."

"And what about me?" Barnard eyed him quizzically.

"You! Oh, you must wait, David! You will understand that a man like Mr. Tombs is not to be met with every day."

They were entering the dining-room as Milbanke spoke; and involuntarily Barnard glanced from the precise, formal figure of his friend, to the youthful, attractive form of his friend's wife.

"And you, Mrs. Milbanke?" he asked in a undertone. "Are you an equally great enthusiast? Does the antique appeal very forcibly to you?"

As he put the question, he was conscious of its irony; but an irrepressible curiosity forced him to utter it. He was still labouring under an intense surprise at Milbanke's choice of a wife; and the desire to probe the nature of the relationship was strong within him.

"Are you like the man in the Eastern story?" he added. "Would you barter new lamps for old?"

Clodagh was walking in front of him as he put the question, and Milbanke was left momentarily behind. For a second she made no reply; then suddenly she turned and cast a bright glance over her shoulder.

"If you had asked me that question this morning, Mr. Barnard," she said, "I don't believe I could have answered it. But now I can. I would not part with one new, bright lamp for a hundred old ones—no matter how rare. Am I a great vandal?"

Her eyes were shining with the excitement of the moment, and her face looked beautifully and eagerly alive.

"Am I a great vandal?" she repeated softly.

There was an instant's pause; then Barnard stepped closer to her side.

"No, Mrs. Milbanke," he said. "But you are a very unmistakable child of Eve."

The dinner that night was a feast to Clodagh. She sat between Milbanke and Barnard; and though the former was silently engrossed in the thought of his coming interview; and, for the time being, the latter confined his talk to impersonal subjects, she felt as she had never felt before in the span of her twenty-two years. For the first time she was conscious of being a woman — privileged to receive the homage and the consideration of men. It was a wonderful, a thrilling discovery; all the more thrilling and all the more wonderful because shrouded as yet in a veil of mystery.

Dinner was half way through before Barnard returned to his task of studying her individually; then he turned to her with his most suavely confidential manner.

"Have you been very gay in Florence this season?" he asked.

She looked up quickly.

"Gay?" she repeated. "Oh no! I don't think we are ever exactly gay."

He raised his eyebrows.

"Indeed!" he said. "You surprise me. There used to be quite an amusing English crowd at Florence."

Clodagh coloured, feeling vaguely conscious of some want in her social equipment.

"Oh, I didn't mean the other English residents," she corrected hastily. "I meant ourselves — James and I."

Barnard's face became profoundly interested.

"But don't you care for society?" he said, his eyes travelling expressively over her pretty dress.

Again she coloured.

"It isn't that," she said in a low, quick voice. "James doesn't care about parties — or people — —"

Barnard's lips parted to express surprise or sympathy; but she finished her sentence hastily.

" —And of course I like what he likes."

Barnard bent his head.

"Of course," he said enigmatically, and dropped back into silence.

For a time he remained apparently absorbed in his dinner. Then, as Clodagh began to wonder uncomfortably whether she had unwittingly offended him, he turned to her again.

"Mrs. Milbanke," he said softly, "would you think me very presumptuous if I were to make a little proposal?"

Clodagh brightened.

"Of course not! Say anything you like."

"You will be here for a week?"

"I—I hope so." She glanced covertly at Milbanke.

"Oh yes, you will! I shall arrange it."

She looked at him quickly.

"You?" she said. "How?"

"Never mind how!" He smiled reassuringly. "You will be here for a week; and my proposal is that, while Milbanke is settling his business, I should be allowed to introduce you to some English friends of mine who are in Venice just now. It may be presumptuous, but I seem to feel" —he hesitated for a moment—"I seem to feel that you want to make some new friends—that you want to have a good time. Forgive my being so very blunt!"

Clodagh sat silent. She felt no resentment at his words, but they vaguely embarrassed her. The new possibility thrilled her; yet insensibly she hesitated before it.

"But ought I to want new friends?" she asked at last in a very low and undecided voice.

Barnard laid down the glass that he was lifting to his lips, and looked at her quickly. Her freshness charmed, while her *naïveté* puzzled him.

"Well, Mrs. Milbanke," he said suddenly, "suppose we find that out?"

And, leaning forward, he addressed Milbanke.

"James," he said, "I have just been making a little suggestion. While you and I are putting our ancient heads together, don't you think Mrs. Milbanke ought to study her Venice—local colour—atmosphere—all that sort of thing?"

Milbanke turned in his seat.

"Eh, David?" he exclaimed. "What's that you say?"

"I was suggesting that Mrs. Milbanke should see a little of Venice now that she is here."

He indicated the long windows of the dining-room through which the sound of voices and music was already being borne on the purple twilight.

Milbanke's face became slightly disturbed.

"Of course!—of course!" he said vaguely. "But—but neither of us care much for conventional sight-seeing; and then, you know, my time here is limited."

"Exactly!—exactly what I was saying. Your time is valuable. All the more danger of Mrs. Milbanke's hanging heavy on her hands. Now, there are some charming people staying here at present, who would only be too delighted to make her visit pleasant."

Milbanke's expression cleared.

"Oh, well——" he began in a relieved voice.

"Exactly! Lady Frances Hope is here. You remember Lady Frances who married my cousin Sammy Hope—the red-headed little beggar who went into the Navy? She would be intensely interested in Mrs. Milbanke. I wish you would let me make them known to each other."

He smiled suavely, thoroughly in his element at the prospect of working a little social scheme.

Milbanke looked at Clodagh.

"What do you think, my dear?" he asked vaguely.

Clodagh looked down at her plate.

"I don't quite know," she murmured.

Barnard leant close to her in a confiding manner.

"Quite right, Mrs. Milbanke!" he said. "Never trouble to analyse your feelings. Just give them a free rein. Lady Frances Hope is a most charming woman. Always bright, always good-natured, always in the swim—if you understand that very expressive phrase."

Clodagh smiled as she helped herself to an ice. During their conversation, the dinner had drawn to its close; and here and there people were already rising from table and moving towards the hall or the long windows that opened on to the canal. Unconsciously her eyes turned in the direction of these open windows, through which a flood of light streamed out upon the water, bringing into prominence the dark gondolas that flitted perpetually to and fro like great black bats.

Seeing her glance, Barnard turned to her again.

"Shall we charter a gondola?" he asked. "It's the thing to do here?"

Her eyes sparkled.

"Oh, how lovely!" she said; then involuntarily her face fell and she looked at her husband.

"But perhaps——" she began deprecatingly.

As the word escaped her, Milbanke—who had been oblivious of the conversation—pushed back his chair and rose from table with a faint exclamation of excitement.

"Ah, there he is!" he said, his eyes fixed upon a distant corner of the room. "There he is! I must not run the risk of missing him!"

Clodagh turned to him eagerly.

"James," she began, "Mr. Barnard says——"

But Milbanke's mind was elsewhere.

"My dear," he said hurriedly, "you must really excuse me. A man like Mr. Angelo Tombs is a personage of importance."

"Yes; but, James——"

She paused, disconcerted. Milbanke had left the table.

For quite a minute she sat silent, her cheeks burning with a sudden sense of mortification and neglect. To a reasoning and experienced mind, the incident would have carried no weight; at most it would have offered grounds for a passing amusement. But with Clodagh the case was different. Circumstances had never demanded the cultivation of her reason, and experience was an asset she was not possessed of. To her sensitive, youthful susceptibilities, the incident could only wear one complexion. Her husband had obviously and wittingly humiliated her in presence of his friend.

She sat with tightened lips, staring unseeingly at the table.

Then suddenly and softly some one crossed the room behind her, and paused beside her chair. Turning with a little start, she saw the pale, clean-cut features and searching dark eyes of Valentine Serracauld.

"Mrs. Milbanke," he said at once in his easy, ingratiating voice. "If you are not doing anything else this evening, may I place my uncle's gondola at your disposal? Both he and I would be considerably honoured if you and your husband——"

Clodagh looked up into his face with a quick glance of pleasure and relief.

"Oh, thank you!" she said. "Thank you so very much! I should love to come, only my husband is—is busy to-night."

She paused; and in the pause Barnard leaned close to her again, with his most friendly and reassuring manner.

"After all, Mrs. Milbanke," he said, "do you think that need preclude you from the enjoyment? James is perfectly happy; Lord Deerehurst's gondola is quite the most comfortable in Venice; and I'm sure *I'm* staid enough to play propriety! Suppose we make a party of four?"

Serracauld laughed delightedly.

"How splendid!" he said. "Mrs. Milbanke, may I find my uncle and bring him to be introduced?"

He bent forward quickly, leaning across Milbanke's empty chair.

For one second Clodagh sat irresolute; then she glanced swiftly from one interested, admiring face to the other, and again the blood rushed into her face in a wave of self-conscious pleasure.

"Yes," she said softly—"yes. Bring your uncle to be introduced."

# CHAPTER IV

Serracauld smiled his acknowledgment of the granted permission, and departed in search of his uncle; while Barnard looked at Clodagh with amused interest.

"If you can waive your prejudices against the milk baths, Mrs. Milbanke," he said, "you'll find old Deerehurst quite a delightful person. But, of course, when one is very young, prejudices are adhesive things."

He finished his coffee meditatively, stealing a glance at her from the corner of his eye.

She remained silent for a moment, tentatively fingering her cup.

"Do I seem so very young?" she asked at last, without raising her eyes.

At the words, he turned and looked at her fully.

"Do you know, Mrs. Milbanke," he said seriously, "I am literally devoured by a desire to ask you your age? When I saw you come downstairs to-night, I felt—pardon the rudeness!—like laughing in James's face when he introduced you as his wife. You scarcely looked eighteen. But a little while ago, when you spoke of your life at Florence, I suddenly felt out in my calculations. Your face, of course, seemed just as fascinatingly young; but from your expression I could have believed you to be twenty-four. And now again—Please *do* be lenient to my impertinence!—now again, as you spoke to Serracauld, you looked like a child turning the first page in the book of life. Are you an enigma?"

During the first portion of his speech, Clodagh had looked grave; but at his last words she laughed with a touch of constraint.

"No," she answered. "I am nothing half so interesting—and it's four years since I was eighteen. But hadn't I better get my cloak before Mr. Serracauld comes back?"

With another slightly embarrassed laugh, she rose; and without waiting for Barnard's escort, walked out of the room.

Ten minutes later, she descended the stairs, wrapped in a light evening cloak. Her cheeks were still flushed with excitement, and her hazel eyes were dark with anticipation. Yesterday—only yesterday—she had been a mere item in the secluded, unimportant life of the villa at Florence; now, to-night, three men—each one of whom must, in his time, have known superlatively interesting and beautiful women—awaited her pleasure!

As she stepped across the hall, Serracauld darted forward to meet her.

"This is very gracious of you!" he murmured. "I hear it is your first evening in Venice."

She glanced up at him, as they moved slowly forward across the hall.

"My very first evening," she said softly. "And I so want to enjoy it."

He paused deliberately, and looked at her.

"May I take that as permission to make it enjoyable—if I can?"

Her lashes drooped in instinctive, native coquetry.

"Aren't you going to introduce your uncle to me?" she said in a lowered voice.

He looked at her, mystified and attracted.

"If I knew you better, Mrs. Milbanke——" he began.

But without replying, Clodagh moved away from him across the hall and out on to the terrace. There, transfixed by a new impression, she paused involuntarily.

Venice is beautiful in the morning and exquisite in the twilight, but it is at night that the mystery of Venice—that most subtle of its many charms— enwraps and envelops it like a magic web. There is nothing in Europe to rival the literal, tangible romance of Venice at night: the faint, idle, infinitely suggestive lap of water against a thousand unseen steps; the secret darkness, revealed rather than dispersed by the furtive, uneven lights shed forth from windows or open doors; the throb of music that seems woven into the picture—an inseparable, integral part of the enchanted life. All is a wonder and a joy.

To Clodagh, with her inherent love of things mystic and beautiful, the scene was curiously impressive. In an ecstasy of appreciation, she stood drinking it in; then, suddenly touched with the warm desire of sharing her sensations, she turned to her companion.

"Isn't it—wonderful?" she said below her breath.

Serracauld looked at her for a moment in puzzled doubt; then he smiled indulgently.

"Yes!" he said vaguely. "Yes! It is rather great—the water and the gondolas and—and all that sort of thing——"

146 | The Gambler

Her large, clear eyes rested on his face, then slowly returned to their scrutiny of the canal. A momentary sense of disappointment had assailed her—she was conscious of a momentary jar. But as she stood, silent and uncertain, a burst of low, throbbing music broke across the darkness, and at the same moment she became conscious of a large gondola gliding up to the hotel steps.

With the excitement of anticipation, the cloud passed from her face.

"Come!" she cried—"come! I see Mr. Barnard."

It was at the head of the flight of stone steps leading to the water, that Lord Deerehurst was introduced to her; and in the semi-darkness, it struck her that he made a distinctly interesting figure, with his black hair worn a shade lower on the forehead than modern fashion permits; his pale, aristocratic, unemotional face; his cold, penetrating eyes; and the somewhat unusual evening clothes that fitted his tall figure closely and, by a clever touch of the tailor's art, conveyed the suggestion of a period more picturesque than our own. She studied him with deep attention; and bent her head in gratified acknowledgment of the profound bow with which he marked the introduction. A moment later, he offered her his hand, and himself assisted her to the waiting gondola.

With a pleasant, excited sense of dignity and importance, she passed down the steps and entered the boat, noting, as she took her seat, its costly and elaborate fittings and the sombre livery of the two gondoliers; then, as she leant back against the cushions, her eyes passed back interestedly to the three men to whom she owed the night's adventure.

Lord Deerehurst came first, moving with a certain stiff dignity, and appropriated the seat by her side; Barnard and Serracauld followed, placing themselves on the two smaller seats that flank the stern; and a moment later, she saw the gondoliers swing lithely round into their allotted positions, and felt the gondola shoot out swiftly and silently into the dark waters.

Following the custom of the place, they headed for the point where the idle and the pleasure-seeking of Venice gather nightly to listen to the music, and lazily watch the swaying paper lanterns of the musician's gondolas.

Clodagh sat silent as they skimmed onward. She was bending slightly forward, her whole attitude an unconscious typifying of expectancy; her hands were lightly clasped in her lap, and again the hazel of her eyes was darkened by their dilated pupils.

As the gondola slackened speed and the music became nearer, more distinct, Lord Deerehurst, who had been covertly studying her, leant suddenly close to her.

"You are a great appreciator of the beautiful, Mrs. Milbanke!" he said in his thin, high-bred voice.

Clodagh started; and, glancing from one to the other of the three men, laughed shyly.

"Why do you say that?" she asked.

"Because I have presumed to watch your face."

She blushed; and Barnard, feeling rather than seeing her embarrassment, made haste to reassure her.

"Mrs. Milbanke is an adept in the appreciation of beauty," he said with a laugh. "She was brought up on the study of it."

Again Clodagh coloured, and again she gave a shy laugh.

"If you say that, Mr. Barnard," she said, "I shall accuse you of being a fellow-countryman. I am Irish, you know." She turned and looked up at Deerehurst.

The old peer again bent forward interestedly.

"Indeed!" he exclaimed. "Then we have a bond of sympathy. Some of my best friends come from Ireland."

His voice was high and possessed no fulness, but he had the same courteously ingratiating manner that belonged to his nephew; while a larger acquaintance with the world had taught him an adaptability to circumstances—and persons—that Serracauld had not troubled to acquire. As he spoke now, he brought a tone of deference and friendliness into his words that touched Clodagh to a feeling of companionship.

"Then you know Ireland?" she said quickly.

"Very well indeed."

Her expression softened.

"When were you there last?" she asked in a low voice.

"Last autumn. I was staying at Arranmore with——"

"—With Lord Muskeere. I know—I know. Why, you were in our county. My father often and often stayed at Arranmore before——" She checked herself hastily. "Oh, long ago, before—before I was born," she added a little awkwardly. "It was from a stream that runs near there that he took my name—Clodagh."

"Indeed! What a charming idea!"

Deerehurst raised his gold-rimmed eyeglass, and peered at her through the dusk.

At the same moment, Serracauld leaned forward in his seat.

"Clodagh!" he repeated — "Clodagh! What a pretty name!"

Once more, and without apparent reason, Clodagh felt her heart beat unevenly. With a short laugh, she turned to Barnard.

"And you, Mr. Barnard," she said hastily, "do you like the name?"

Barnard made a suave gesture.

"I say that it fits its owner."

Once more she laughed with a tinge of nervous excitement.

"A very guarded statement!" she said brightly. "I think we had better talk about something else. Who are the people I am to meet here? Mr. Barnard kindly wants to provide me with new friends."

She turned again to Deerehurst.

"Indeed!" Once more he lifted the gold-rimmed glass, this time to study Barnard.

"Yes," broke in Barnard genially. "Mrs. Milbanke's husband and I have met here to talk shop; and I have a shrewd presentiment that, unless we provide her with a diverting channel or two, Mrs. Milbanke may find Venice a bore."

"I could never do that."

Clodagh turned an animated face towards the dark flotilla, on the outskirts of which their own gondola was hovering.

"But, my dear lady, even Venice can become uninteresting and dry — paradoxical as it may sound," Barnard returned airily. "My proposal," he explained, "is that I should make Frances Hope and Mrs. Milbanke known to each other. Don't you think the idea brilliant?"

"Quite! — quite!" Serracauld looked up interestedly. "You are a man of ideas, Barny!"

Lord Deerehurst said nothing, but again his eyeglass gleamed in the uncertain light.

"What is Lady Frances Hope like?" Clodagh asked, suddenly withdrawing her gaze from the massed gondolas that swayed in the musicians' lantern light.

"Like?" Serracauld repeated vaguely. "How would you describe her, uncle? The sort of woman who does everything twice as well as anybody else — and at half the cost — eh?"

Lord Deerehurst gave one of his thin, metallic laughs.

"I always think," he said slowly, "that if Frances Hope had been the child of a milkman instead of a marquis, she would have made a singularly successful adventuress. No reflections cast upon the late Sammy, my dear Barnard!"

He waved his white hand, and the dim, uncertain light gleamed on a magnificent diamond ring.

Barnard laughed with a tolerant air.

"Rather an apt deduction!" he admitted. "I am inclined to agree with you. Frances is just one of those shrewd, plain-looking, attractive women who enjoy climbing steep ladders. It is rather a pity she was born on the top rung. But I believe we have frightened Mrs. Milbanke!"

He turned suddenly and caught Clodagh's expression, as she sat forward, listening intently.

At the mention of her name, she laughed quickly, and leant back against the cushions of her seat.

"What do you mean?" she asked with a touch of constraint. "Am I as childish as all that?"

They all looked at her; and Barnard gave an amused laugh.

"Come!" he cried banteringly. "There's no use telling me you weren't just a little shocked."

"Shocked?"

"Yes, shocked." He nodded his head once or twice in genial gaiety. "There's no denying that the word 'adventuress' has a daunting sound. There was a danger signal in the very thought of a lady who might—under any conditions—have been notorious. Come now, confess!"

Clodagh looked from his amused, quizzical eyes to Serracauld's satirical, laughing ones, and a shadow of uncertainty—of doubt—crossed her own bright face. There was an element in this social atmosphere that she did not quite understand.

"Indeed— —" she began hotly.

But Serracauld, whose glance had never left her own, bent forward quickly, looking up into her face.

"I say, Mrs. Milbanke," he cried, "let's refute the insinuation of this old inquisitor! Let's waive ceremony, and storm Lady Frances Hope in her citadel! She is always at home at this hour of night."

Clodagh looked up.

"To-night?" she said. "Oh, but how could I? I don't know her!"

Serracauld laughed.

"Oh, as for that, we're abroad, not in England! The greatest stickler for etiquette allows that there's a difference in the two conditions."

"But I couldn't. How could I?" Her eyes sought Barnard's.

"Oh yes!" he cried. "I knew it!—I knew it! We have frightened you off!"

She flushed uncomfortably.

"It isn't that!" she cried in distress. "You know it isn't that!" Involuntarily she turned to Lord Deerehurst; but in the dim light she detected a smile on his pale, cold face.

With a sudden change of emotion, self-reliance came to her.

"Where does Lady Frances Hope live?" she asked in a careless voice.

Barnard was studying her intently.

"She has apartments in the Palazzo Ugochini," he said. "Quite close at hand."

For a moment Clodagh looked fixedly in front of her; then her lips closed suddenly, and she raised her head.

"Very well!" she said shortly. "Take me to the Palazzo Ugochini—just to prove that you were wrong."

# CHAPTER V

The decision was no sooner made, than it was carried into execution. The order was given to the gondoliers, and instantly the long dark gondola swung round, disengaging itself from the tangle of surrounding craft, and headed for the quieter spaces of the middle stream.

The Palazzo Ugochini was on the Grand Canal; and as they glided westward, past the beautiful church of Santa Maria della Salute, Barnard leant forward and directed her attention to their destination.

"There is the Palace of the Ugochini," he said. "It contains some of the finest frescoes in Italy. It was bought up some years ago by an enterprising Frenchman who lets it out in sections. Just now Lady Frances Hope is the proud occupier of the first floor."

With a movement of interest, she followed his glance looking silently at the long line of irregular, imposing buildings that stretched away before her.

"What a beautiful old place!" she said. "Are those your friend's windows?"

She indicated the first floor of the palace, from the open windows of which a warm stream of light poured downwards upon the water.

"Yes. I expect they're playing bridge up there. Frances is an enthusiast. By the way, do you gamble, Mrs. Milbanke?"

Involuntarily Clodagh started and looked round; then, as she met Barnard's bland, amiable face, she blushed at her own emotions.

"Oh no!" she said in a low voice. "I—I never play cards."

Serracauld looked up quickly.

"What!" he exclaimed. "You don't play bridge?"

"I have never played any game of cards since I was a child."

The three men looked at her in unfeigned surprise.

"Not really, Mrs. Milbanke?"

Serracauld's eyes were wide with astonishment.

"Really !—quite really!"

"Why you are ethereal, Mrs. Milbanke," Barnard said laughingly, as the gondola glided up to the palace steps. "The passport to humanity nowadays is an inordinate love of risk."

Clodagh laughed nervously.

"Then I must be inhuman," she said.

The gondola stopped, and Lord Deerehurst rose. As he offered her his hand, he looked searchingly into her face.

"Only time can prove the truth of that statement, Mrs. Milbanke!" he said in his thin voice.

In the mystery of her surroundings, the words seemed to Clodagh to possess a curious, almost a prophetic ring; and their echo lingered in her ears as she stepped from the gondola and entered the palace. But she was young; and to the young, action must ever outweigh suggestion. She had scarcely mounted the old marble staircase before the excitement of her impending ordeal sent all other ideas spinning into oblivion. There was adventure and experience in every succeeding moment.

At the head of the stairs they were met by an English man-servant. He stepped forward gravely, as if accustomed to the arrival of late callers; and, relieving Clodagh of her cloak, ushered her down a long corridor and through an arched doorway hidden by a velvet curtain.

The salon into which they were shown was large and high ceiled. The walls displayed some allegorical studies in the fresco work of which Barnard had spoken; the floor was bare of carpet and highly polished, reflecting the elaborately designed but scanty furniture and the wonderful glass chandeliers that hung from the ceiling; and in the three long windows that opened on the canal, stood groups of statuary.

During the moment that followed their entrance, Clodagh almost believed that the room was unoccupied, so wide and formal did it look; but a second glance convinced her of her mistake. At its further end four persons were playing cards at a small table, partly sheltered from the rest of the room by a massive leather screen.

When their names were announced, no one at the table moved or even looked round; but immediately afterwards there was a stir amongst the players, and the light sound of cards thrown hastily down, followed by a quick laugh in a woman's voice.

"Game—and rubber! Well done, partner! How does the score stand, Tory?"

The owner of the laugh rose from her seat, and almost instantly turned to the door, revealing to Clodagh's curious eyes a strong, energetic face, redeemed from ugliness by a pair of intensely intelligent eyes and a mouth that displayed strong white teeth. It was the somewhat disconcerting face of a clever woman to whom life represents an undeniable—if an invigorating—struggle. Seeing the little group by the doorway, she hurried forward with an almost masculine assurance.

"You poor, dear people!" she exclaimed in her strong voice. "A thousand apologies! We were on the point of finishing a most exciting rubber——" Her voice broke off short, as her eyes rested on Clodagh.

"Who is this, Barny?" she asked interestedly.

Barnard stepped forward, laying his hand smilingly on Clodagh's arm.

"This, my dear Frances," he said, "is a new friend that I want you to make! The wife of an old friend of mine. You may have met her husband—Mr. Milbanke—one of the Somerset Milbankes. Poor Sammy knew him well."

Lady Frances Hope puckered her strong, assertive eyebrows.

"I believe I do remember meeting a Mr. Milbanke, but I scarcely think——" She looked scrutinisingly at Clodagh.

"Oh yes, it's the same!—it's the same!" Barnard's interruption was somewhat hasty. "Mr. Milbanke is a great archaeologist. He and Mrs. Milbanke are only in Venice for a week. I had intended bringing you to call formally at their hotel; but circumstances——"

Here Clodagh broke in.

"You must please, please forgive my doing such a very extraordinary thing as this," she said. "It was all Mr. Barnard's fault——"

But Lady Frances Hope cut the explanation short by holding out her hand.

"You are extremely welcome!" she said cordially. "And if the truth must be told, I owe you a debt of gratitude for saving me an afternoon call. It's a hundred times pleasanter to meet like this. Now, let me see! You play bridge, of course. We can make up another four."

She glanced over her guests with an organising eye.

Clodagh stepped forward deprecatingly and cast a beseeching look at Barnard. But in the slight pause that followed, it was Lord Deerehurst who came to her rescue.

"Mrs. Milbanke has just been confessing to us that she never plays cards," he said smoothly. "If you will go on with your game, Lady Frances, I shall do my best to amuse her."

He turned his unemotional glance from one to the other.

The surprise that his announcement had brought to their hostess's face, changed instantly to an expression of hospitality.

"No!—no, indeed!" she cried. "I would infinitely prefer to talk to Mrs. Milbanke. Come!" she added, smiling at Clodagh. "Come and let me introduce you to these bridge-playing people. Perhaps they will convert you."

She laughed, and followed by the four, moved across the salon.

At their approach, the three at the card-table—two women and a man—turned to look at them, and the latter, a square-built, thick-set youth, wearing a pince-nez and possessing a quick, inquisitive manner, rose to his feet.

"Mrs. Milbanke!" said Lady Frances, "this is Mr. Victor Luard! Miss Luard! Mrs. Bathurst!"

Luard bowed; and the two women looked at Clodagh, each acknowledging the introduction after her own fashion. Miss Luard gave a quick, friendly nod, Mrs. Bathurst a slow and graceful inclination of the head, accompanied by a faint, insincere smile.

"Are you a bridge player?" she asked, raising a pair of pretty, languid brown eyes to Clodagh's. "I wish so much you would take my place. I've been having the most appalling luck."

Her glance wandered on to Serracauld, Barnard, and Deerehurst.

"Ah, here is Lord Deerehurst!" she cried in a suddenly animated voice. "Lord Deerehurst, do come and tell me what you would have done with a hand like this!"

She picked up her scattered cards, and began to sort them; then, with a graceful movement, she drew her skirts aside, and indicated a vacant chair that stood beside her own.

Lord Deerehurst hesitated, lifted his eyeglass, and scrutinised her pretty pink and white face, then languidly dropped into the empty chair. At the same moment Clodagh, Serracauld, Luard, and his sister fell into conversation; and Lady Frances and Barnard moved away together towards one of the open windows.

For a quarter of an hour the formation of the party remained unchanged; then a slight incident caused a distraction in the assembly. Clodagh—who had shaken off her first shyness, and was beginning to enjoy the conversation of her new acquaintance—heard the curtain at the arched entrance drawn back; and, looking round, was surprised to see two servants enter, solemnly carrying a table and a painted board, which they proceeded to set up in the middle of the room.

Her wonder and curiosity were depicted on her face, for Luard looked at her quickly and interestedly.

"Don't you know what that is, Mrs. Milbanke?" he asked. "Hasn't Barny told you of Lady Frances' famous roulette? Lady Frances!" he called, "come and initiate Mrs. Milbanke!"

At the words, every one turned and looked at Clodagh. And Lord Deerehurst, with a murmured word to Mrs. Bathurst, rose and came round the card-table.

"Are you going to tempt the gods?" he asked in his peculiar voice.

Clodagh looked round, a little embarrassed by the general interest.

"Well, I—I suppose I should like to see roulette played," she admitted guardedly.

He bent his head, and looked at her with his cold, penetrating smile.

"Ah, I see!" he said softly. "Judicious reservations!"

But at that moment Lady Frances crossed the room, and pausing by the roulette-table, set the ball spinning.

"Come along, people!" she cried gaily. "Fortune smiles!"

They all laughed and strolled across the room.

"Come along!" Lady Frances urged again—"come, Rose!" She smiled at Mrs. Bathurst. "Unlucky at bridge, lucky at roulette! Come, Tory!—come, Val!"

She glanced from Luard to Serracauld.

There was another amused laugh, and all the party with the exception of Clodagh stepped forward and placed one or many coins upon the table.

Lady Frances' eyes were quick to detect the exception. With her fingers poised above the board, she waited smilingly.

"Won't you stake, Mrs. Milbanke?" she asked.

Clodagh blushed, and stepped back shyly. At the same instant, Serracauld moved forward to her side.

"Oh, Mrs. Milbanke, but you must!" he cried.

Again confusion covered Clodagh, as all eyes were turned upon her.

"No, please!" she said. "I—I think I'd rather not."

Barnard laughed suavely.

"Mrs. Milbanke is wise!" he said. "She wants to see which way the gods are pointing."

"Then Mrs. Milbanke is unwise! The gods are jealous beings; we must not treat them with suspicion. I'll stake for her!"

It was Lord Deerehurst who spoke. And regardless of Clodagh's quick, half-frightened expostulation, he stepped forward out of the little circle, and placed a gold coin on the number thirteen. A moment later Lady Frances gave a short amused laugh, and with a dexterous movement of the fingers set the ball whizzing.

To Clodagh it was a supreme—an extraordinary—moment. Until Lord Deerehurst had made the stake—until the first click of the spinning ball had struck upon her ear—she had been conscious of only one feeling: a prejudiced, innate dread of every game—whether of chance or skill—upon which money could be staked; but the simple placing of the coin, the simple turning of the pivot had marked for her a psychological moment. With a quick catching of the breath, she stepped involuntarily forward, aware of but one fact—the keen, exhilarating knowledge that the stopping of the ball must mean loss or gain—individual loss or gain.

During the dozen seconds that it spun round the circle, she stood silent; then a faint sound of uncontrollable excitement slipped from between her lips. Hers was the winning number!

As in a dream, she extended her hand, and took the little heap of money from the fingers of Luard, who had come to Lady Frances' assistance; then, on the instant that the coins touched her palm, her excitement evaporated; her sense of elation fell away, to be succeeded by the first instinctive shrinking that had swayed her imagination.

Acting purely upon impulse, she turned to Lord Deerehurst; and before he could remonstrate, pressed the money into his hand.

"Please take it!" she said urgently—"please take it! It isn't mine. It oughtn't to be mine. I—I don't wish to play."

# CHAPTER VI

The little incident, trivial in itself, damped the general ardour for roulette. After a dozen turns of the wheel, Lady Frances declared herself satisfied.

"Mrs. Milbanke has regenerated us—for the moment!" she cried. "I can't play roulette to-night. But our turn will come; Mrs. Milbanke. We will be revenged on you!"

Her shrewd, smiling glance passed rapidly over Clodagh's face.

Again the whole company laughed.

"Mrs. Milbanke is a feminine Sir Galahad!" said Luard. "By the way, Lady Frances, when is our irreproachable knight to honour Venice with his presence?"

He turned and looked banteringly at his hostess.

Lady Frances smiled.

"Oh, any day now," she returned. "But aren't you rather incorrigible?"

"So Sir Galahad thinks!" he retorted, unabashed. "Is he an acquaintance of yours, Mrs. Milbanke?"

Clodagh smiled uncertainly; and Lady Frances laughed.

"How ridiculous of you to expect Mrs. Milbanke to read your riddles!" she said sharply. "The person this very disrespectful young man is speaking of, Mrs. Milbanke, is Sir Walter Gore——"

"The most admirable Sir Walter Gore!" interjected Luard.

Lady Frances' sallow face flushed very slightly.

"—Sir Walter Gore," she went on, ignoring the interruption, "who is only twenty-nine—has been ten times round the world—and is imbued with the deepest contempt for all modern social things."

She laughed again, as she finished; but a fleeting change of expression had passed over her face.

Clodagh looked up smilingly.

"And where is the likeness to me?" she asked.

"Oh, you are both above mere human temptations, Mrs. Milbanke!" Luard broke in irrepressibly.

Lord Deerehurst, who had been listening to the conversation, lifted his eyeglass.

"But then Sir Walter Gore has been ten times round the world," he remarked in his thin, dry voice. "And this is Mrs. Milbanke's first visit to Venice."

Again they all laughed, and Clodagh coloured.

"You think my stoicism would not wear well?" she asked.

Deerehurst looked at her searchingly.

"Stoicism may be born of many characteristics," he said. "I am not in a position to say from what yours springs. But"—he lowered his voice.—"I do not think you are a natural stoic."

She laughed and glanced uneasily round the little company, already beginning to break up into groups of two and three.

Observing the look, Lady Frances turned to her tactfully. "Come, Lord Deerehurst!" she cried. "We are getting too serious. If you *must* philosophise, take Mrs. Milbanke on to the balcony, where she will have something to distract her thoughts. For myself, I want to hear Valentine sing. Val!" she called. "Come to the piano and make some music! I'm surfeited with stringed instruments and Italian voices."

She moved across the salon; and Lord Deerehurst turned to Clodagh.

"May I follow our hostess's suggestion? May I talk philosophy on the balcony?"

She smiled. The slight strain, of which she had been conscious ever since the incident of the roulette, lifted suddenly, and her earlier sensation of elated excitement returned.

"Yes, if you like," she responded brightly. "The balcony sounds very tempting. And as for the philosophy, I can promise to listen—if I can't promise to understand."

She smiled afresh, and crossed the wide room, Deerehurst following closely.

As she passed the group of statuary and stepped through the open window, Serracauld struck a chord or two on the piano, and an instant later, his voice—a full strong voice, intensely passionate and youthful—drifted across the salon and out into the night.

At the first note Clodagh halted, surprised and enchanted by the sound; and sinking silently into one of the balcony chairs, rested one arm on the iron railing.

The music Serracauld sang was French, and possessed much of the distinction that marks that nation's art. The song was a hymn to life—and its indispensable coadjutors, youth and love; and it went with a peculiar lilt that stirred the blood and stimulated the fancy. He sang it as it should be sung—easily and arrogantly; for, as frequently happens with those who possess voices, he could express in music thoughts, ideas, and emotions that never crossed his own selfish, somewhat narrow soul.

Clodagh, staring down into the dark waters in an attitude of wrapt attention, drank in the song to its last note; and as the final vibration died away, she looked round at Deerehurst with an expression infinitely softened and enhanced.

"How beautiful!" she said. "Oh, how beautiful!"

Deerehurst, who had seated himself beside her, leant forward and rested his own arm upon the balcony railing.

"It is not the song that is beautiful, Mrs. Milbanke," he said, "but the thoughts it has wakened in you."

Clodagh looked at him in silent question. She was still under the spell of the music, and saw nothing to resent in his cold gaze.

"You were the instrument," he went on in the same lowered voice. "The notes were not played upon the piano, but upon your brain. Your brain is a network of sensitive strings, waiting to be played on by every factor in life—music, colour, sunshine, emotion— —" His tone sank.

Clodagh glanced quickly at his tall, thin figure, seated so close to her own, and at the wax-like, inscrutable face showing through the dusk.

"You seem to know me better than I know myself," she said uncertainly.

He watched her intently for a moment; then he leant forward, his long, pale fingers toying with the ribbon of his eyeglass.

"I do know you better than you know yourself."

She gave a little embarrassed laugh.

"Then explain me to myself!"

Again he seemed to study her; then he leant back in his chair with a decisive movement.

"No!" he said—"no! Not now! In a year—or two—or even three, perhaps. But not now."

She laughed again; and unconsciously a note of relief underran her laugh—a relief that, by a natural sequence of emotion, brought a fresh reaction to the coquetry of an hour ago.

With a quick turn of the head, she looked up at him. "But how shall I find you in a year—or two—or three?"

She was distinctly conscious that the words held a challenge; but the thought was fraught with the new intoxication that the evening had created.

With a swift movement, he bent closer to her.

"The world is very small, Mrs. Milbanke—when one desires to make it so."

In the half light of the balcony, his pale eyes seemed to search hers.

Involuntarily she blushed, but her glance met his steadily enough.

"Not until one has been ten times round it!" she reminded him.

He laughed his thin, amused laugh; then suddenly he became grave again.

"Don't you feel," he said, "that when we desire a thing very greatly, our own will power may bend circumstances?"

Her eyes faltered, and her gaze moved to the gondolas flitting silently below them.

"I think I have given up desiring things greatly," she said in a low, uneven voice.

Deerehurst's eyelids narrowed.

"Would it be presumptuous to ask why?"

"No. Oh no!"

"But you will not throw light upon my darkness?"

She turned her head, and once more her gaze rested on his face.

"No," she said softly, "it isn't that. It is that I don't believe I could enlighten you—even if I would. I am a puzzle to myself."

"The deeper a riddle, the more tempting its solution."

Very quietly he drew still nearer, until his foot touched the hem of her skirt.

The action, more than the words, startled her. With a little laugh, she drew back into her seat.

"Perhaps it is no riddle after all!" she said quickly. "Perhaps it is the lack of human nature—the likeness to Mr. Luard's 'Sir Galahad.'"

She laughed again nervously. Then suddenly her own words suggested to her a new and less dangerous channel of talk.

"When is this wonderful person to be in Venice?" she asked. "I should like to see him."

But Lord Deerehurst had no intention of allowing another man's name to interfere with his pleasure.

"Mrs. Milbanke," he said earnestly, "may I ask you another question—-a serious one?"

"Not till you've answered mine."

"But this is personal—personal to you and me. The other is not."

He bent over her chair; and, seemingly by accident, his hand brushed her sleeve.

"Mrs. Milbanke——"

But even as his thin voice articulated her name, a shadow fell across the lighted window behind them; and Serracauld, characteristically easy and nonchalant in his movements, stepped on to the balcony.

Clodagh turned with a short, faint laugh. The beating of her heart was uneven, and her face felt hot.

"Mr. Serracauld," she said impulsively, "when is Sir Walter Gore coming to Venice? I have been asking Lord Deerehurst, but he cannot—or will not tell me."

Deerehurst, who at his nephew's approach had drawn quietly back into his seat, looked up with perfect composure.

"Yes, Valentine," he said smoothly, "I believe Gore has been making an impression by proxy."

Serracauld laughed.

"Really!" he said. "How interesting! I shall look forward to the meeting in the flesh."

Again he laughed, as at something intensely amusing. And as Clodagh turned towards him doubtfully, she saw him shoot a swift, satirical glance at his uncle.

"Why?" she asked quickly—"why should our meeting be interesting?"

Once more a vague sense of antagonism assailed her—a vague distrust of this new atmosphere.

Serracauld answered at once in his light, ingratiating tone.

"For no reason, Mrs. Milbanke, that you can possibly cavil at!"

"But for what reason?" Her glance rested inquiringly on his face. "Do tell me. I hate things that I cannot understand."

Deerehurst smiled a little cynically.

"A very youthful sentiment!" he murmured. "The older one grows, the more one seeks the incomprehensible."

His eyes rested upon her with a fixed regard.

For a space she sat very still, attempting no rejoinder. Then, as if suddenly moved to decisive action, she rose and turned towards the lighted salon.

"It's very late," she said quickly. "I must think about getting home."

Serracauld stepped aside, and Deerehurst, who had risen with her, moved forward.

But with a swift gesture that ignored them both, she crossed the balcony and stepped through the open window.

After she had left them, the two men stood for a moment looking at each other; then, with an elaborately careless gesture, Lord Deerehurst raised his eyeglass and peered out across the dark canal.

"Rather a pleasant little gathering to-night!" he said casually. "Rose Bathurst looks particularly well."

Serracauld's lips parted; then pursed themselves together, while he cast one comprehensive glance at his uncle's stiff back.

"Oh yes!—yes! Quite!" he rejoined vaguely; then, very swiftly, he turned and hurried across the salon after Clodagh.

She was bidding her hostess good-night as he reached her side; and his attentive glance noted her heightened colour and her nervously alert manner.

"To-morrow night, then!" Lady Frances was saying; and he saw Clodagh nod and smile.

"To-morrow night!" she repeated. "Mr. Barnard, are you ready?"

As she looked round for her cavalier, Serracauld stepped softly to her side.

"Mrs. Milbanke," he said, "you will not discard my uncle's gondola? He is waiting to know if we may convey you home."

She looked up at him with a faint suggestion of coldness and distrust. Then, across the silence of her indecision, the low notes of the Venetian night music broke forth again, as the musicians' gondola passed the Palazzo Ugochini on its way homeward. For one moment it seemed to sweep across the salon through the open windows; then it faded into the distance, as the boat passed on up the canal. At the sound, Clodagh's face involuntarily softened, her lips parted, and she smiled.

"Very well!" she acquiesced below her breath. "Tell Lord Deerehurst that he may take me home."

# CHAPTER VII

During the night that followed, Clodagh's excited thoughts scarcely permitted her to sleep; but with that extraordinary reserve of strength that springs from the combination of youth and health, she rose next morning as fresh and untired as though she had enjoyed unbroken rest.

Coming downstairs at half-past eight, the first person she encountered was Milbanke, entering the hotel from the terrace. And spurred by her own exuberant spirits, roused to a sense of general good-will by her own rosy outlook upon life, she went quickly forward to greet him.

"Good-morning, James!" she said. "I hope you haven't been tiring yourself."

It struck her as an after impression that he looked slightly worn and fatigued.

As he took her hand, he smiled, gratified by her concern.

"Not at all, my dear!" he responded—"not at all! I have had an hour's excursion with Mr. Tomes. I assure you I had no idea that the bye-ways of Venice were so interesting."

"All Venice is heavenly."

Clodagh's glance wandered across the terrace to the canal, radiant in the early light.

Milbanke raised his head, arrested by the fervour of her tone.

"Then you—you enjoyed yourself last night?" he ventured with unusual penetration.

"Oh, so much!" She turned to him with a glowing smile that betrayed a warm desire for universal confidence and sympathy. "So much! Mr. Barnard and the tall, dark-haired boy that you met last evening took me round the canals in the most beautiful gondola belonging to Lord Deerehurst. We saw all the interesting people from the hotels, and heard the music; and afterwards Mr. Barnard brought me to the Palazzo Ugochini and introduced me to Lady Frances Hope. She was charmingly kind and hospitable; and made me promise to go again to-night—and to bring you."

Milbanke's face fell.

"But, my dear——" he began deprecatingly.

"Oh, you must come!—you must! Lady Frances Hope feels sure she has met you before. You must come!"

Milbanke looked distressed.

"But, my dear——"

"Yes, I know you hate society. But just this once—I—I *wish* you to come——"

She made the appeal with a sudden anxious gesture, born of a very subtle, a very instinctive motive—a motive that had for its basis an obscure and quite unacknowledged sense of self-protection.

Milbanke—materialist born—heard only the words, noting nothing of the undermeaning.

"But, my dear," he expostulated, "the thing is—is impossible. Mr. Angelo Tomes has promised to expound his theories to me after dinner to-night——"

He looked at her nervously.

She was silent for a minute or two—suddenly and profoundly conscious that, in all the radiant glory of her surroundings, she stood alone. At the painful consciousness, she felt her throat swell, but with a defiant refusal to be conquered by her feelings, she gave a quick, high laugh.

"Oh, very well!" she cried—"very well! As you like!"

And without looking at him again, she turned and entered the coffee-room of the hotel.

Having partaken very hastily of her morning meal, she returned to the terrace, where—among the other early loungers—she found Barnard, reading his English newspapers. Seeing her, he threw the papers down, jumped to his feet, and came forward with evident pleasure.

"Good-morning!" he said cordially—"good-morning. You look as fresh as a flower, after last night's dissipation."

She took his hand and met his suave smile with a sense of relief.

"Good-morning!" she returned softly. "Have you seen James? He breakfasted hours ago."

"Yes," he said—"oh yes! I was talking to him just now. He has gone to write letters."

"To write letters!"

There was no curiosity and very little interest audible in Clodagh's tone.

"So he said. And you? What are you going to do?"

She looked up and smiled again.

"To idle," she said. "I have an inherited gift for idling."

Barnard smiled, then glanced along the terrace with an air of pretended secrecy.

"Take me into partnership!" he said in a whisper. "My clients don't know it, but I'm constitutionally the laziest beggar alive. Do let me idle in your company for half an hour? The canals are delightful in the early morning— —"

He indicated the flight of stone steps, round which one or two gondolas were hovering in expectation of a fare.

Clodagh's glance followed his; and her face insensibly brightened.

"I should love it," she said.

"Truly?"

She nodded.

"Right! Then the thing is done."

He hurried forward. And with a little thrill of pleasureable anticipation, she saw one of the loitering gondolas glide up to the steps.

For the first few moments after they had entered the boat, she was silent; for in the iridescent morning light, Venice made a new appeal; then gradually—insidiously—as the charm of her surroundings began to soothe her senses, the encounter with Milbanke melted from her mind; and the subtle environment bred of last night's adulation rose again, turning the world golden.

As they passed the Palazzo Ugochini, she looked up at the closed windows of the first floor; then almost immediately she turned to her companion.

"Mr. Barnard," she said suddenly, "I want to ask you a question. I want you to explain something."

And Barnard, closely studious of her demeanour, felt insensibly that her mood had changed—that, by a fine connection of suggestions, she was not the same being who had stepped into the gondola from the hotel steps. With a genial movement, he bent his head.

"Command me!" he said.

Before replying, she took another swift glance at the closed windows; then she turned again and met his eyes.

"Tell me why this friend of Lady Frances Hope's is called 'Sir Galahad'?"

He smiled.

"Gore?" he said with slightly amused surprise. "I didn't know you were interested in Gore."

"I am not. But please tell me. I want to know!"

His smile broadened.

"The nick-name surely explains itself."

"Somebody with an ideal? Somebody above temptation?"

"Precisely."

She pondered over this reply for a moment; then she opened a fresh attack.

"Then why should Lord Deerehurst and Mr. Serracauld have smiled when they spoke of his meeting me?"

Barnard looked up in unfeigned astonishment; then he laughed.

"Upon my word, Mrs. Milbanke," he cried, "you are absolutely unique!"

Clodagh flushed. For one second she wavered on the borderland of offence; then her mood—her sense of the ridiculous and the sunny atmosphere of the morning—conquered. She responded with a laugh.

"I suppose I'm not like other people," she said.

"—For which you should say grace every hour of your life!" Barnard turned and looked into her glowing face. "But I'll satisfy your curiosity. Gore is known in his own set as a man who obstinately—and against all reason—refuses to believe in—well, for instance, in the interesting young married woman."

Clodagh's lips parted.

"But what——" she began impetuously; then she stopped.

Barnard continued to look at her.

"Isn't the inference of the smile somewhat obvious?"

Her glance fell.

"Oh!" she said—"oh! I suppose—I suppose I see."

"Precisely."

"But surely——" she began afresh; then again intuition interfered, though this time to a different end. It was not the moment—it was not the atmosphere—in which to parade one's sentiments! With the too ready facility of her nation for adapting itself to environment, she laughed suddenly and gaily at her own passing prudery, and raised a bright face to Barnard's.

"And when he meets these interesting young married women?" she asked amusedly.

"Ah, there he dubs himself 'Sir Galahad'! Some people call him a saint, for keeping his eyes on the ground; others call him a sinner, for not picking up what he sees there. In reality, he is neither sinner nor saint; but just that enviable creation—a man who is self-sufficing."

While he spoke, and for some time after he had ceased to speak, Clodagh sat silent. She was leaning over the side of the gondola and looking down into the calm water, her warm face touched by a mischievous expression, her hazel eyes half closed. At last she spoke, but without raising her head.

"And you are all waiting for the person who will make him see the need for some one else?"

She waited for Barnard's answer, but it did not come. Sensitive to the silence, she raised her head. Then her self-consciousness left her, superseded by curiosity. As she looked up, she saw her companion lean forward and wave a cheerful greeting to the occupant of a gondola approaching them from the direction of the railway station. Involuntarily she changed her position and her glance followed his.

The passing of the two gondolas occupied no more than a minute. But the incidents comprised in some minutes remain with us all our lives. The approaching boat was a large one, rowed by two gondoliers; for, though it had only one passenger, it carried a pile of luggage, much travel-worn. Clodagh's eyes noted this, but they did so very briefly; for instantly the gondola drew level with her own, her glance lifted itself to the owner of the luggage—the man to whom Barnard had waved his greeting.

She saw him with great distinctness, for the early light in Italy is peculiarly penetrating; and her first thought—a purely instinctive one—was that he possessed a sailor's face. His strong, clean-cut features suggested a keen and intimate relationship with natural elements; his healthily clear skin was tanned by sun and wind; and his eyes looked out upon the world with the quiet reliance that seems a reflexion of the steadfast ocean. The first impression of the man was vaguely daunting. There was something self-contained, even cold, in the erect pose of his tall, muscular figure, in the manner in which he held his head. Then, quite unexpectedly, his critic gained a new impression of him. As the gondolas passed each other, he leant forward in his seat and his lips parted in a very pleasant smile.

"Ubiquitous as usual, Barnard!" he called in a strong, fresh voice. "I might have known you would be the first man I should run across!"

He raised his cap, and Clodagh saw that his hair was crisp, close-cut, and very fair, giving an agreeable touch of youthfulness to his sunburnt face.

Barnard laughed, and responded with some words of welcome.

The stranger smiled and nodded.

"Come round and see me this afternoon!" he cried, as the gondolas drew apart. "I'm staying at the Danieli!"

"Who was that?" Clodagh asked involuntarily, as the stranger's boat glided out of sight. Then she blushed suddenly. "Why are you laughing?" she demanded.

Barnard smiled.

"I am not laughing, Mrs. Milbanke," he murmured. "I assure you I am not laughing. It is the merest smile at nature's little bit of stage management. That interestingly bronzed young Englishman is Sir Walter Gore!"

# CHAPTER VIII

This little incident—this small and yet significant interlude—in Clodagh's day of new-born freedom, possessed a weight and an importance all its own. It is quite possible that, taken as a mere note in the tuneful, inconsequent symphony of her social life in Venice, Barnard's expression of his sentiments might have glanced across her mind, leaving no definite impression. But the web of fate is wonderfully woven. Barnard had propounded those sentiments through the medium of a name—a name which was to be indelibly printed upon Clodagh's memory by the strangely opportune appearance of its owner.

At the moment when the gondolas passed, at the moment when Barnard laughingly explained the stranger's identity, the name of Walter Gore took on a new significance, became a personal element in touch with her own existence.

In studying the effect of this incident upon her actions, it must be borne in mind that Clodagh's moral position was strangely incongruous—a position to which not one amongst her new acquaintances possessed a key. She was a married woman with the vitality, the curiosity, the sense of adventure of a girl in her first season. She was like a plant that, having been shut for long in dark places, is suddenly exposed to the influences of warmth and light. She glowed, she blossomed, she expanded under every passing touch.

As she leant back against the cushions of the gondola and met the amused and quizzical glance that accompanied Barnard's explanation, her thoughts sprang forward under a certain stimulus of excitement; her blood—the blood of a reckless, adventurous race—leaped suddenly in response to a new idea. She looked up at her companion, her face glowing, her hands clasped lightly in her lap.

"Mr. Barnard," she said, "will Sir Walter Gore be at the Palazzo Ugochini to-night?"

Barnard met her glance. For a moment he studied her whimsically, then he responded by putting a question of his own.

"Mrs. Milbanke," he asked, "is it true that when you dare an Irishwoman to do a certain thing, that thing is as good as done?"

Clodagh's lashes fluttered, and she coloured hotly; then with the naïve defiance, the intoxication of youthful assurance, she lifted her eyes again and gave another bright, clear laugh.

"Two unanswered questions should be as good as one reply!" she said, looking straight into his face.

All that day Clodagh went about her concerns with a delightful, furtive sense of things to come. In the evening she came down to dinner arrayed in a dress of lace and embroidery that had come from Vienna only three weeks before. The dress possessed sweeping lines that defined her slight figure; and above the jewelled lace of the bodice her graceful shoulders, smooth as ivory, and as warm in tone, showed bare of any ornament. The faint olive of her skin was enriched by the neutral colour of her dress, and in the bright light of the hotel rooms, the underlying gleam of gold was distinctly visible in her brown hair. Her whole appearance as she entered the dining-room was subtly attractive; and in every detail of her expression pleasure and anticipation gleamed like tangible things. From the colour that wavered in her cheeks to the dilated pupils that turned her eyes from hazel to black, she was the embodiment of eager expectation.

Neither Deerehurst, Serracauld, nor Barnard dined at the hotel that night, but from the eyes of more than one stranger she read the assurance that she had not arrayed herself in vain; and youthfully conscious of a subtle, impersonal success, her eager spirits rose high.

Regardless of Milbanke's monosyllabic answers, she kept up a stream of conversation; and at last, when she rose with the general company, she did not leave the room, but paused with her hand on the back of his chair.

"I am going for my cloak, James," she said. "Mr. Barnard is to call for me. Shall we say good-night now?" Her face, as she bent forward, leaning over his shoulder, was filled with a bright preoccupation.

The scene was no new one—nor was its lesson new. It merely expounded the eternal disparity between the present generation and the past. On the one hand, was the patient surrender of the being who has known life with its poor compensations and its tardy requitals; on the other, the impatience, the ardour, the egotism of the being who longs to understand, to tear the bandage from his blind, curious eyes, to shake the fetters from his eager, groping hands. It was a scene that is enacted every day of every year by fathers and daughters, mothers and sons. A scene in which, daily and yearly, a merciful nature mitigates the tragic truth by means of a blessed sanity—an instinctive renunciation. But this was no case for natural healing balm; this was no case of father and daughter, but of husband and wife.

"Shall we say good-night?" Clodagh asked again.

Milbanke started and looked up; and something in her warm beauty—something in her gracious youth affected him.

"Clodagh," he said timidly. "Clodagh, are you—are you very anxious? Will you enjoy this party very much?"

Clodagh looked down on him in frank surprise.

"Why, of course!" she said. "Why do you ask?"

His gaze wavered before her level glance. He looked round at the fast emptying room.

"No reason, my dear!" he murmured—"no reason, I assure you! Go to your party. Enjoy yourself!"

At his words she bent quickly and brushed his forehead with her lips, but so lightly, so unthinkingly that the act was valueless.

"Good-night!" she said—"good-night, James! And thank you!"

She straightened herself quickly; and with a mind already speeding feverishly forward towards the night's amusement, she turned and walked out of the room.

It was nine o'clock when she and Barnard arrived at the Palazzo Ugochini, and already the deep purple of the Venetian night was wrapping the waterways in mysterious shade. But to-night she was less absorbed in outward things. An engrossing idea occupied her mind. She felt at once surer—and less sure—of herself than she had felt the night before.

The time occupied in reaching the palace and mounting the marble steps seemed to her very brief; and almost before she realised that the moment had come, she heard her own and Barnard's names announced by Lady Frances Hope's English servant.

Her first sensation upon entering the salon, was an almost childish satisfaction in the thought that she had dressed so carefully; for it needed but a glance to show her that the evening's gathering was of a very much more important nature than that of the previous night. Quite fifty people were grouped about the lofty room, whose centre and pivot was again the gaudy, modern roulette-table; and towards this table, with its surrounding group of gay and noisy votaries, she and Barnard turned as if by instinct.

Nearing the circle of players, she saw that Luard—her acquaintance of last evening—was officiating at the game to the delight and amusement of his clients; while at a little distance from the table, she caught sight of her hostess in conversation with a tall man whose remarkably fair and close-cropped hair gave her a sudden thrill of recognition.

As in duty bound, she walked straight forward to where Lady Frances was standing. And as she murmured her greeting, her hostess turned quickly, appraising in a single rapid glance her dress, her hair, her complexion, while she extended her hand with a cordial gesture. It may be possible that the cordiality cost Lady Frances an effort—that the smile with which she greeted her radiant guest covered a suggestion of feminine chagrin; but if so, no one detected it. Her welcome sounded genuine and even warm.

"My dear Mrs. Milbanke!" she exclaimed. "How charming of you to remember! And how charming you look!" she added in a whisper meant for Clodagh's ear alone.

Then with a movement of seemingly spontaneous hospitality, she turned to the fair-haired stranger, who had fallen into conversation with Barnard.

"Walter!" she said, "I should like you to know Mrs. Milbanke! Mrs. Milbanke, allow me to introduce Sir Walter Gore!"

It was the affair of a moment. The stranger made a gesture of excuse to Barnard; turned quickly, and bowed with well-bred deference. Then he raised his head, and for the first time Clodagh met his glance—the clear, fearless glance, slightly reserved, slightly aloof, that carried with it the suggestion of the sea. His look was quiet, steady, and absolutely impersonal.

And Clodagh, instantly conscious of this polite reserve, felt her face redden. She was aware of a distinct sensation of being smaller—less important to the scheme of things—than she had been five minutes earlier. Her vanity was inexplicably—yet palpably—hurt. Her first feeling was a distressed humility, her second an angry pride. Then a new expression leaped into her eyes. Smartingly conscious of Barnard's interested, quizzical glance fixed expectantly upon her, she challenged the stranger's regard.

"How d'you do?" she said. "I think I have seen you before."

He smiled politely.

"Indeed!" he said. "In England?" His tone was courteous and attentive, but neither curious nor interested.

Her colour deepened.

"No. Here in Venice—this morning. I was in Mr. Barnard's gondola when you were coming from the station to your hotel."

He looked at her, then at Barnard—a perfectly honest, unaffected glance.

"Indeed!" he said again. "I certainly remember seeing that Barnard was not alone, but I was remiss enough not to notice who the lady was."

For one second a feeling of resentment—almost of dislike—stung Clodagh. The next, her old daring mood of years ago sprang up within her.

"Where I come from," she said, "no man would have the courage to say that."

Barnard laughed.

"Assume a virtue, if you have it not! Is that the Irish code?"

Gore smiled.

"If that *is* the Irish code," he said gravely. "I'm afraid Ireland only echoes the rest of Europe. Assumption is the art of the twentieth century. The man who can assume most, climbs highest! Isn't that so, Lady Frances?"

He turned to their hostess.

Clodagh stood silent. She was filled with a humiliating, childish sensation of having been rebuked—rebuked by some one whose natural superiority placed him beyond reach of childish temper or childish violence. The sensation that many a time in old and distant days had sent her flying to the shelter of Hannah's arms, rose intolerably keen. With a defiant sense of futility and loneliness, she turned away from the little group—only to encounter the pallid face and stiff, distinguished figure of Lord Deerehurst, as he came slowly towards her across the room.

Extending his hand, he took her fingers and bowed over them.

"Mrs. Milbanke," he said, "I have just been mentally accusing Lady Frances of surrounding me by so many acquaintances that I could not find one friend. Now I desire to retract!"

In the sudden relief—the sudden touch of unexpected flattery—Clodagh's mobile face underwent a change.

"Then you have found a friend?" she said.

At sound of the words, Sir Walter Gore involuntarily turned; and, seeing the old peer, made a slight movement of surprise and extended his hand.

"Lord Deerehurst!" he said. "I did not know you were in Venice!"

They shook hands without cordiality; and having murmured some conventional remark, the older man turned again to Clodagh.

"Yes," he said, "I have found a friend!"

His cold eyes gave point to the words.

She laughed and coloured. Again she was conscious of Barnard's amused, speculative gaze; but also she was conscious of the quiet, slightly critical eyes of her new acquaintance. Goaded by the double spur, she glanced up into Deerehurst's face.

"Well?" she said. "And now?"

"Now I am in my friend's hands."

He made a profound and eloquent bow.

Again she coloured, but again vanity and mortification stirred her blood. With a winning movement, she took a step forward.

"Your friend would like to listen to philosophy on the balcony," she said in a recklessly low voice.

# CHAPTER IX

To the superficial student of Clodagh's character, this development of a phase in her mental growth may present itself as something distasteful—even unworthy; but to the serious student of human nature, with its manifold and wonderful complexities, it must perforce come clothed in a different guise.

Placed by circumstances in a singularly isolated position—springing from a race in whom love of power, love of admiration, love of love itself are inherent qualities—it is not to be wondered at that, in the first flush of her realised sovereignty over men, she should view the world from a slightly giddy altitude.

No one grudges her triumphs and her innocent intrigues to the girl in her first season. Humanity looks on indulgently while she breaks her first lance with the candid joy, the pardonable egotism that is bred of youth. And, incongruous as it may sound, Clodagh's was the position of the debutante. She was comprehending for the first time—and comprehending with accumulated emotion—the fact that she possessed an individual path in life. And with the arrogance of inexperience, she sprang to the conclusion that every foot crossing that path, should yield her a toll of homage.

And now one foot had crossed it without pause, without even a desire to linger! Her cheeks burned under the smart of her hurt vanity, as she turned from the little group that surrounded Lady Frances Hope, and allowed Deerehurst to lead her across the salon. Her emotions were many and confused, but one personality occupied her thoughts against the angry expostulations of her reason. By an illogical, but very human sequence of impressions, Sir Walter Gore had, in one moment, become the most objectionable—and the most interesting—person of her acquaintance.

As she stepped out upon the balcony, Deerehurst drew forward the low chair that she had occupied the night before; and she sank into it with a little sigh. For the first time in the glamour of her new-found excitement, she felt glad to escape from the crowd and the lights of the salon.

For a while her companion made no effort to break the silence that she seemed anxious to preserve, then at last he changed his position, stepped softly forward, and laid his hand on the back of her chair.

"Is what Barnard tells me true?" he asked. "Are you really leaving Venice in a week?"

She bent her head without looking up.

"But surely we can persuade you— —"

His voice quickened, then broke off, as Clodagh turned to him.

"Does it matter to any one whether I go or stay?" she asked in a slightly tremulous voice.

The only surprise that Deerehurst betrayed, was shown in the narrowing of his cold eyes. He studied her penetratingly for a moment; then he spoke again very quietly.

"Mrs. Milbanke," he said, "can you ask that question in good faith?"

A faint touch of last night's embarrassment wavered across her mind, but this time she swept it defiantly aside.

"Yes; I mean it."

She turned, and again looked up into his face.

"And am I to answer in good faith?"

She bent her head, still looking at him.

"Then judging by the one case of which I can confidently speak, yes!— distinctly yes!"

There was a pause; and Clodagh gave a faint laugh.

"And whose is the one case?"

Her voice sounded cool, high, even slightly indifferent. It piqued Deerehurst to a further step. He answered her question with another.

"Mrs. Milbanke," he said, "have you ever heard of Circe?"

Again she laughed.

"My education was extensive, if very intermittent," she said. "Yes, I have heard of Circe—and her wild beasts."

He echoed the laugh in his thin, expressive voice.

"I see the implication! But I would willingly play even wild beast—to your Circe!"

He bent over her chair.

She drew away with a slight, sharp movement; but he did not alter his position.

"Do you know that a man would follow you—anywhere?"

"Anywhere?"

"Anywhere."

He let his hand glide softly from the back of the chair to her shoulder.

At the touch of his fingers, she slipped away from him with a noiseless movement, and rose to her feet.

"Then follow me back to the salon!" she said in a voice that still sounded high and light.

There was a constrained pause, but it was one of short duration. Deerehurst was not the man to be easily taken at a disadvantage. For one instant a glimmering of chagrin showed on his composed face; the next it was gone. He straightened his dignified figure, and felt mechanically for his eyeglass.

"'Pon my word!" he said. "I believe you *are* Circe. Use your prerogative!"

He turned, laughed a little, and indicated the salon with a courtly gesture.

Clodagh looked at him. He puzzled and disconcerted her. To one whose innate instinct was a yielding to impulse, his absolute impassivity in face of disconcerting situations was something incomprehensible. And now, as he stepped aside to give her passage, she gave a quick laugh, expressive of both embarrassment and relief; and crossed the balcony with a certain instinctive haste.

During their absence, the crowd in the salon had increased; the press about the roulette-table had become denser; while at half a dozen card-tables, sheltered from the general gathering by large screens of old Italian leather-work, parties of four were playing bridge.

Ignoring these latter groups, Clodagh crossed the room towards the roulette-table, and paused upon the outskirts of the crowd that surrounded it.

Deerehurst, following her closely, narrowed his eyes with a touch of interest as he saw that, either by intention or accident, she had halted beside Sir Walter Gore.

"Well," he said in his thin, satirical voice, as he gained her side—"well, shall we combine forces as we did last night? I brought you luck, remember!"

She turned upon him almost sharply.

"No!" she said—"no! I don't play roulette."

At the vehemence of her denial, he raised his eyebrows; and Sir Walter Gore looked round. Seeing the speaker, an involuntary gleam of surprise crossed his face.

"Surely you are not so unfashionable as to disapprove of gambling, Mrs. Milbanke?" he asked.

Clodagh raised her eyes; and this time her glance was free from coquetry.

"I have not been fashionably brought up," she said.

"Indeed!"

The surprise—and, with it, a reluctant interest—deepened in Gore's glance. But his eyes wandered doubtfully over her dress.

Invariably quick to follow a train of thought, she gave a short, comprehending laugh.

"Oh, I know what you are thinking of!" she cried. "I don't look as if I belong to the wilds. People never understand that dressing is a knack that comes to women, and does not really mean anything."

He smiled, amused against his will.

Again she laughed, like a child who has been praised.

"Oh, it's quite true!" she added. "I could tell you of dozens of cases——"

But her flow of confidence was suddenly terminated. Valentine Serracauld, catching sight of her through the throng of people, had made a hasty way towards her. His finely cut colourless face was animated and his dark grey eyes looked excited.

"How d'you do?—how d'you do, Mrs. Milbanke?" he exclaimed. "Please congratulate me! I've had a run of luck! Netted seventy pounds!"

Clodagh's lips parted.

"Seventy pounds!" she said breathlessly, and instinctively she turned to Gore. But Gore's place was empty. At Serracauld's approach, he had moved unostentatiously away.

At the knowledge that he was gone, a sense of disappointment fell upon her. She glanced uncertainly at Deerehurst.

The old peer, who had been a cynical observer of the little scene, gave a thin laugh.

"Our friend Gore is fearful of contamination," he said, glancing at his nephew.

Serracauld laughed.

"Gore!" he said contemptuously. "Oh, Gore and I never did chum up! But where have you been hiding yourself all day?" He turned again to Clodagh. "We have had dark suspicions that old Barny has been buying up your society with Stock Exchange tips. Come, now, confess!" He paused and laughed, looking with intent admiration into her expressive face.

And Clodagh—sailing upon the tide of present things, elated by the eager interest of two men, and excited by the grudging interest of a third— forgot that, for every frail craft such as hers, there is an ultimate harbour to be gained, a future to be reckoned with. She lifted her head, met Serracauld's searching glance, and echoed his inconsequent laugh.

# CHAPTER X

The next day Clodagh made one of a party to the Lido, and the same night accompanied Lady Frances Hope, Deerehurst, and Serracauld to a theatre; but on neither occasion did she meet, or even see, Sir Walter Gore.

On the afternoon of the second day, however, he again appeared upon the scene of her interests, and in an unexpected manner.

The hour was six; and she, with Barnard and Milbanke, was seated on the hotel terrace, chatting desultorily in the warmth of the early evening.

While they talked, a gondola glided up to the hotel steps; and in the glow of the waning sun, they saw Gore step from the boat, pause to give some order to the gondolier, and then mount the stone steps.

They all three saw him simultaneously. Clodagh, to her own annoyance, coloured; and Barnard smiled in his observant, quizzical fashion.

"I didn't tell you that Gore was coming to see me this afternoon, Mrs. Milbanke," he said in an undertone. "I had a fancy that you might run away."

The flush on Clodagh's face deepened.

"Run away?" she exclaimed in angry haste.

But Barnard rose without replying, and went forward to meet his visitor.

Having greeted his host, Gore turned to Clodagh.

"How d'you do, Mrs. Milbanke?" he said, raising his hat. Then he looked interrogatively at Milbanke.

Barnard made a sweeping gesture.

"My old friend Mr. James Milbanke!" he said. "James, Sir Walter Gore!"

Milbanke looked up quickly; and the younger man held out his hand with a pleasant touch of cordiality.

"How d'you do, sir?" he said. "Are you making a long stay in Venice?"

With a friendly movement, he pulled forward one of the wicker chairs and seated himself beside Milbanke.

Clodagh, leaning far back in her own long, low seat, looked at him curiously. Unconsciously the remembrance of Serracauld's careless manner upon a similar occasion of first introduction recurred to her mind, coupled with the knowledge of Barnard's contemptuous idea of her husband—his fads and his peculiarities. What could this man see to attract him in a dry archæologist of twice his age? She found herself waiting intently for his next remark—his next action.

"Are you making a long stay?" he repeated, settling himself in his chair.

Milbanke, surprised and pleased at the unexpected attention, sat up stiffly in his seat.

"Oh no!" he said—"no! We are leaving in three or four days. I—I am interested in antiquity, and should, properly speaking, be in Sicily at the present moment. Perhaps you have heard of the very remarkable researches that are being carried on there?"

Gore smiled.

"No, I'm afraid I must confess ignorance. I know disgracefully little about the past."

Barnard, fearing a dissertation from Milbanke, interrupted with a laugh.

"I'm afraid most of us find the present more alluring!"

He cast a swift glance at Clodagh.

But Clodagh, still annoyed with him, and with herself—still puzzled by Gore's attitude—lifted her head sharply.

"At least," she said, "we can be sure that the present is genuine."

Gore turned and looked at her.

"Are you quite sure of that, Mrs. Milbanke?" he asked quietly. "Don't you think there is trickery and deception in the manufacture of many things besides the antique?"

Her glance faltered.

"I have seen a lot of unauthentic relics," she said with a touch of obstinacy.

"And I, a lot of unauthentic life."

He looked at her with a slight smile. The smile stung her unreasonably.

"Some people can never become connoisseurs," she retorted quickly.

Gore laughed, but without offence.

"Not of treasures, perhaps, but with experience and observation, surely any one can become a judge of men—and women."

Clodagh forced herself to smile.

"You disapprove of women?"

"Disapprove! Indeed, no!"

But here Barnard interposed with one of his suave gestures.

"He only disapproves of the modern woman, Mrs. Milbanke!"

Gore turned to him good-humouredly.

"Wrong, Barnard!" he said. "I admire the modern woman—the truly modern woman. It is the society woman—of any period—that I lose patience with."

Barnard smiled.

"The present-day woman is very proud of her complex life," he said smoothly, "her big card debts and her little intrigues."

Gore's healthy face turned a shade redder.

"I know!" he said tersely. "But to me, a woman with no higher ambition than the playing of cards winter and summer, afternoon after afternoon, is—is pitiable."

Clodagh leant forward.

"Perhaps they play cards because they have no real interests."

He looked at her quickly.

"And why have they no real interests, Mrs. Milbanke? Isn't it because they reject all simple, natural, wholesome things? Such women do not know the meaning of the word home. They do not want a home—or home life, as the women of the last generation understood it."

"Ah, there you touch bottom, my dear Gore! There you are in your depth!" Again Barnard gave one of his smooth, tactful laughs. "This young man has a great pull over us, Mrs. Milbanke, when he compares the present generation with the past."

At the suave words, Gore made a slightly embarrassed gesture, and looked instinctively towards Milbanke.

"Forgive my tirade, sir!" he said a little confusedly. "Mr. Barnard is right. I have rather a high ideal of womanhood. I am possessed of a—a very remarkable mother."

"A mother!" Clodagh looked round impulsively. "Oh, tell me what she is like!"

With a certain spontaneity, Gore turned to respond to her question; but before his eyes met hers, their glance was intercepted by a shrewd, amused, inquiring look from Barnard. The effect of the look was strange. His emotion so suddenly aroused, died suddenly. His face became passive, even a little cold. He straightened his shoulders, and gave the restrained, self-conscious laugh that the Englishman resorts to when he feels that his sentiments have entrapped him.

"Oh, you must not ask me what my mother is like, Mrs. Milbanke," he said. "I could not give you an unbiassed opinion. As it is, I have been wasting your time unpardonably. Barnard, do you think Mrs. Milbanke will excuse you for ten minutes?"

Barnard rose slowly.

"Do not put me to the pain of saying 'yes,'" he exclaimed. "Let me imagine that I am tearing myself away against Mrs. Milbanke's express desire. Au revoir, Mrs. Milbanke! Au revoir, James!"

He nodded, and sauntered off in the direction of the hotel door.

A moment later Gore shook hands silently with Clodagh and her husband, and moved away in the same direction.

As he disappeared into the hotel, Milbanke folded his newspaper with interested haste.

"What a well-mannered young man!" he said. "Who is he? What is his name?"

Clodagh was sitting very still, her hands clasped in her lap, her eyes fixed upon some distant object.

"Gore," she said shortly—"Gore. Sir Walter Gore."

"Gore!" Milbanke repeated the name as though it pleased him. "A fine young fellow! Very unlike the majority of young men of the present day."

Clodagh said nothing.

"Don't you agree with me, my dear?"

As if by an effort, she recalled her wandering gaze, turned her head slowly, and looked at her husband.

"He—he certainly seems unlike other people," she admitted in a low voice.

After this rejoinder there was silence. Clodagh, her brows drawn together in a perplexed frown, relapsed into her former absorbed contemplation; while Milbanke, having changed his position once or twice, shook out the sheets of his newspaper and buried himself in the lengthy report of a scientific meeting.

But scarcely had he reached the end of his first paragraph, than a large shadow fell across the page, and, looking up quickly, he saw the ponderous figure of Mr. Angelo Tomes.

At the sight of his hero he started, coloured with pleasure, and rose hastily.

"Mr. Tomes!" he exclaimed. "Clodagh, my dear, here is Mr. Tomes!"

Clodagh turned without enthusiasm, and looked at the loose figure and unkempt hair of the scientist.

"I do not think you and my—my wife have met, Mr. Tomes!" Milbanke broke in with a nervous attempt at geniality.

Mr. Tomes bowed.

"No; but I have many times seen Mrs. Milbanke," he said ponderously.

Clodagh bent her head, noting with the fastidious intolerance of youth that his clothes were baggy and his hands unclean.

Milbanke gave a nervous, conciliatory laugh.

"I—I have noticed that great men are always observant," he said jocularly.

Mr. Tomes smiled.

"That is scarcely a compliment to Mrs. Milbanke," he interposed consciously.

Clodagh looked up and met his eyes.

"I don't wish to be paid compliments, Mr. Tomes," she said. "Please don't try to think of any. Did you come to take my husband out?"

Mr. Tomes stammered, visibly crestfallen.

"Well," he began, "there is a certain archway in one of the smaller churches, which I think Mr. Milbanke ought to see. But as an archway is not too weighty for a lady's consideration, it struck me—it occurred to me——"

But Clodagh cut him short.

"Oh, Mr. Tomes, I'm much too frivolous even for archways. Don't take me into your calculations; I should only spoil them. Of course it's very kind of you," she added with tardy remorse, "but the experiment would be a failure. Ask my husband——"

Milbanke looked distressed.

"Oh, my dear——" he began.

But Clodagh's nerves were jarred.

"I know!" she broke in—"I know it's awfully kind of Mr. Tomes! But I couldn't go to see an archway to-day. I couldn't. I really—really couldn't."

Mr. Tomes relapsed into a state of pompous offence.

Milbanke looked from one to the other in nervous misery.

"Certainly not—certainly not, my dear!" he agreed. "You are tired; you have been doing too much." He peered at her through the softly falling twilight with a look of helpless concern.

She felt, rather than saw the look; and that sensitive dread of being rendered conspicuous that attacks us all in early life, caused her to shrink into herself.

"Nonsense!" she said a little coldly. "I am perfectly well. Please go and see Mr. Tomes's archway. I don't mind being left alone. I would like to be left alone."

Milbanke stirred uneasily.

"Of course, my dear, if you wish it!" he murmured. "Mr. Tomes, shall we—— Are you ready——"

He waved his hand towards the canal.

Mr. Tomes drew his loose limbs together, and bowed formally to Clodagh.

"Certainly, if you wish it, Mr. Milbanke!" he said stiffly; and walked off along the terrace.

Milbanke did not follow him at once. He stood looking at his wife in pained uncertainty.

"Clodagh, my dear," he began at last, "if there is anything I can do——"

But Clodagh turned away.

"No," she said almost inaudibly; "no, there is nothing. I'd like to be alone. I want to be alone."

And Milbanke—perplexed, embarrassed, vaguely unhappy—turned slowly, and walked across the terrace after his scientific friend.

Clodagh waited until the last sound of Mr. Tomes's loud, rolling voice had melted into the distance with the departure of his gondola; then with a stiff, tired movement she rose, walked in her own turn across the terrace, and, leaning upon the stone parapet, gazed out into the purple twilight, as she had gazed on the evening of her first arrival.

How long ago—how infinitely far away—that first arrival seemed to her! With the capacity for the assimilation of new emotions that belongs to all her race, she had lived more keenly during the last three days, than during the preceding four years. To one of her temperament, life is not a matter of time, but of experience. At eighteen she had been a child; on her twenty-second birthday she had been a girl; and now, when that birthday was past by but a few months, she was conscious of the stirring of her womanhood—roused into swift activity by the first approach of the world with its men and women, its laxities and prejudices, its infinite potentialities for good or evil.

Some vague foreshadowing of this idea was casting itself across her mind, when the thread of her musings was suddenly broken by a quick step sounding across the deserted terrace, and with a slight, involuntary movement, she straightened herself, and brought her hands together upon the cold surface of the parapet.

Sir Walter Gore had parted with Barnard in the hall of the hotel; and now he crossed the terrace quickly, conscious of the fast falling twilight. He was close to the flight of stone steps that led to the water, before the flutter of Clodagh's light dress caught his preoccupied attention.

Seeing her, he paused and raised his hat.

"You look very mysterious, Mrs. Milbanke," he said. "Has your husband gone indoors?"

Clodagh felt herself colour. Unreasonably, and seemingly inexplicably, the mention of Milbanke's name jarred upon her.

"My husband has gone to see an archway in one of the churches," she said with a tinge of sharpness.

Caught by the inflexion of her voice, Gore looked at her more closely through the gathering dusk.

"And you do not share his taste for the antique?"

She turned towards him, her eyes alight with a sharp, cold brightness.

"I hate the antique!" she said with sudden vehemence.

Almost against his will, Gore looked at her again.

"And yet you come from Ireland? Isn't everything there very old?"

For an instant she looked away across the darkening waters; then her glance flashed back to his.

"Yes, old," she said passionately; "but so naturally old, that its age is not thrust upon you. Where I come from, there is a ruined chapel on the edge of a cliff that dates from the fourth century. And at the present day the peasants pray there, just as their ancestors prayed centuries and centuries ago. They don't stare at it, and read about it, and write about it, like the antiquarians do. They pray there. The chapel isn't a curiosity to them; it's a part of their lives."

Gore was silent. An unconquerable surprise—a reluctant fascination—held him chained, forgetful of the gathering darkness and of the gondola that awaited him at the foot of the steps.

As he stood hesitating, Clodagh spoke again.

"Don't you believe that things should be lived—not merely looked at?" she asked, her voice low and tense. Almost unconsciously the desire to interest this man, to win his attention, to compel him to share her opinions, had sprung into her mind.

Gore answered her with directness. "No," he said. "All things cannot be lived."

His voice was quiet and controlled; the pose of his body, the look in his eyes, all suggested a tempered strength—a curbed vitality. The desire to dominate him rose higher, overshadowing every other sensation in Clodagh's brain.

She stepped nearer to him, her hand resting on the stone balustrade, her body bending forward.

"Don't you think that when life is so very short, we are justified in taking all we can—when we can?"

Her warm lips were parted, her eyes shone with an added light. She was walking on the edge of an abyss with the ardour of one whose gaze is fixed upon the sun. But Gore—seeing only the abyss—girded on his armour.

"No," he said slowly and deliberately. "No; that has never been my standpoint."

"Then you refuse the good things of life when they come your way?"

"Good is a very elastic word."

He was fencing, and she realised it. With a subtle change of tone, she made a fresh essay.

"Isn't the meaning of every word merely a matter of inflexion?"

He hesitated.

"I—I suppose so," he admitted guardedly.

She smiled suddenly, looking up into his face.

"Then to me, the word 'good' means all that is warm and light and happy. And to you, it means something cold—or unattainable?"

"Indeed no! You have made a wrong deduction."

"Well, what does it mean to you?"

"Mean? I—I am not sure that I can tell you."

"Perhaps you have not found the meaning?"

"Perhaps not."

"But you are seeking for it?"

He laughed a little constrainedly.

"I may be—unconsciously."

Again she averted her eyes, and turned towards the mysterious canal.

"Now I understand one thing!" she said in a soft, slow voice.

"What is that?" Gore was curious, despite himself.

"Why they call you 'Sir Galahad'?"

There was a moment of silence. His face flushed, then turned cold.

"Indeed!" he said stiffly. "And, if it is not indiscreet, may I ask who calls me 'Sir Galahad'?"

At the tone of his voice, Clodagh wheeled round.

"Didn't you know?" she asked. "I thought—oh, I was sure you knew——"

He laughed.

"No!" he said with elaborate indifference—"no! To whom am I indebted for the name?"

But his companion was silent. Acutely conscious of having struck a wrong note, she felt angry with herself—angry with him.

"Who gave me the name?" he asked again.

"I had better not say. I thought you knew of it."

"Then I am at liberty to guess. It was Lord Deerehurst?"

His tone was curt—even contemptuous.

Clodagh flushed. It seemed as if, by a subtle insinuation, he had scorned her.

"And if it was Lord Deerehurst?" she asked sharply.

Gore made an exclamation of contempt.

"You dislike Lord Deerehurst?"

He shrugged his shoulders.

"You dislike Lord Deerehurst?" She was persistent, remembering keenly and uncomfortably the favour she had shown the old peer in his presence the night before.

Gore gave a short, indifferent laugh, and the sound galled her.

"Lord Deerehurst is a friend of mine," she said unwisely.

He bent his head with a stiff movement.

"If I have transgressed," he said, "please forgive me! I have already trespassed on your time. Good-bye! Perhaps we shall meet later at the Palazzo Ugochini."

His voice was cold and very reserved.

The blood beat hotly and uncomfortably in Clodagh's veins, but she raised her head and answered in a voice as indifferent as his own.

"Good-bye! It's quite possible that you may *see* me at the Palazzo Ugochini; but I can't promise more."

Gathering up her light skirt, she turned and walked across the terrace to the door of the hotel.

Gore stood and watched her until the last gleam of her dress was lost in the lighted hall; then slowly—thoughtfully, almost reluctantly—he began his descent of the steps.

# CHAPTER XI

Clodagh's mood was inexplicable even to herself as she entered the hotel, ran upstairs to her own room, and began to dress for dinner.

She changed her dress with an almost feverish haste, giving herself no time for thought; and then, scarcely waiting to take a final look into the mirror, left the room and hurried down into the hall. There she encountered Barnard.

"I have just been speaking to your husband," he said, greeting her with a smile. "He has been lured into attending some secret conclave of Italian scientists. He asked me to make his excuses to you."

Clodagh's glance fell.

"Oh!" she said with a curious little inflection of the voice.

"Of course he knew that you were going out to-night?"

"Oh yes! Of course!" She still kept her lashes lowered.

Barnard smiled.

"Mrs. Milbanke," he exclaimed in a cheerful voice, "suppose we have a gay evening! Lord Deerehurst has asked me to dine with him and Serracauld at the 'Abbati.' Let's form an even party! The old man will be absolutely charmed; and you have never dined at a restaurant. Say I may arrange it!"

For a moment longer Clodagh studied the ground; then very quickly she raised her eyes, and in their depths Barnard read a new expression.

"After all," she said tentatively, "why shouldn't we take what comes our way?"

He extended his hands.

"Why, indeed? Let me spread the good news?"

Again she let her lashes droop.

"Very well!" she said—"very well! Say that I want to enjoy myself."

The dignified and placid serenity of Venice had been intruded upon that season by the establishment of a fashionable dining-place, which, under the name of the Abbati Restaurant, had taken up its position in a beautiful old house on one of the narrower waterways.

Its distance from Clodagh's hotel was short; and the journey thither—taken in Lord Deerehurst's gondola, in company with the old peer, Serracauld, and Barnard—occupied but a few minutes. Clodagh's first impression, on gliding up the still, dark waterway and stepping out upon the time-worn garden steps, was one of delight. And as she stood for a moment in the shadow of the ancient wall, above which the tree-tops rose, casting black reflections into the water that ran beneath them, she was conscious of the subtle touch of the warm night wind upon her face; of the subtle poetry in the scent of unseen flowers; of the subtle invitation conveyed by the long row of lighted windows, seen through a screen of magnolias.

She had momentarily forgotten her companions, when Deerehurst—the last to leave the gondola—stepped softly to her side.

"This appeals to you?" he said.

She started slightly at his unexpected nearness; then, with a quick impetuosity, she responded to his question.

"I think it is exquisite," she said. "The light through the trees suggests such wonderful, mysterious things."

He smiled under cover of the darkness.

"It suggests an enchanted banquet. Let us find the presiding genius!"

He laid his fingers lightly on her arm and guided her up the long, dim garden.

Followed by Serracauld and Barnard, they traversed the shadowy pathways and emerged upon an open space of lawn that fronted the house.

Three or four of the private rooms were already occupied; and with the faint streams of light that poured from their open windows, came the pleasant murmuring of talk and laughter.

As the little party stepped into the radius of this light, a stately personage came forward deferentially; and, recognising Deerehurst, made a profound bow.

The old nobleman nodded amiably, as to an acquaintance of long standing, and, drawing the man aside, addressed him in French.

The explanation was brief, and almost at once Deerehurst turned back to his companions.

"Come, Mrs. Milbanke!" he said. "Our friend Abbati proves amenable to persuasion. He will give us his prettiest room—though we are unexpected guests."

Clodagh stepped forward with eager curiosity.

"I never thought a restaurant could be like this," she said.

"Very few of them are, Mrs. Milbanke," murmured Barnard, close behind her. "The usual restaurant is an ostentatious place of white enamel, palms, and lights, where a hundred tongues are vainly endeavouring to drown a band. This little corner will scarcely outlive another season. It's too perfect—too quiet to find favour with the crowd. It was opened under the patronage—rather, at the suggestion—of Prince Menòf, a sybarite millionaire temporarily out of sorts with Paris. But now Paris smiles once more; Menòf has wearied of Venice; and poor Abbati begins to tremble."

Clodagh looked round.

"But could anything so exquisite be a failure?"

"Easily, my dear lady! People like to eat their expensive dinners where others can comment on their extravagance! It's a very vulgar world!"

The three men laughed; and Clodagh, slightly distressed, slightly puzzled, stepped through the wide hall to the room that Deerehurst indicated.

It was a small chamber, long and narrow in shape. The walls were panelled in faded brocade, and the lights were shrouded in silk of some soft hue; the floor was covered with a carpet in which wreathed roses formed the chief design; and the furniture consisted of one oval table, four beautiful old chairs, and a couple of ancient French mirrors. As Deerehurst stepped forward to relieve Clodagh of her cloak, four waiters entered noiselessly; and almost immediately dinner was served.

It was a dinner such as Prince Menòf would have delighted in. There was nothing tedious, nothing monotonous in the six or seven courses that comprised its menu; each stimulated and gratified the appetite, without a hint of satiety. It was an Epicurean feast. And it was interesting to study the varying ways in which the guests responded to its appeal.

Barnard—placid man-of-the-world, indulgent connoisseur of all the luxuries—openly lingered over the delights of the meal; Serracauld ate quickly and almost greedily, as many men of slight build, and thin, sensual faces do eat; Deerehurst alone toyed with his food, giving serious attention to nothing beyond the dry toast with which he was kept supplied; while Clodagh—young enough and healthy enough to have an appetite that needed no tempting—frankly enjoyed her dinner, without at all comprehending its excellence.

During the first portion of the meal, conversation was fitful and impersonal; but as the waiters left the table to carry in one of the last dishes, the tone of the intercourse underwent a change. Deerehurst turned to Clodagh with a sudden gesture of concern and intimacy.

"I see you do not endorse my choice of wine!" he said in a gently solicitous voice.

She looked up with slight confusion; then looked down at her untouched glass, in which the champagne bubbles were rapidly subsiding.

"I—I never drink champagne," she said a little diffidently.

"Oh, Mrs. Milbanke! And my poor uncle has been sacking the Abbati cellars for this particular vintage!" Serracauld glanced up quickly and almost reproachfully.

Barnard laughed, as he blissfully drained his own glass.

"You are really very unkind, Mrs. Milbanke," he murmured. "You make one feel such a deplorable worldling."

But Deerehurst looked round towards a waiter who was re-entering the room.

"Bring this lady another glass and some more champagne!" he said.

Clodagh turned to him sharply and apprehensively. But he touched her wrist with his finger-tips.

"Please!" he said in his thin, high-bred voice—"please! I want you to taste this wine. I generally have some difficulty in getting it outside my own house."

His pale, far-seeing eyes rested on her face; and it seemed to her excited fancy that their glance supplemented his words. That, as plainly as eyes could speak, they added the suggestion that some day she might honour that house with her presence. The idea confused her. She turned away from him in slight uneasiness; and at the same moment one of the waiters filled her long Venetian glass with the light golden wine.

"To please me!" Deerehurst murmured again—"to please me!"

She looked round, confused and still embarrassed; gave one unsteady, yielding laugh; then lifted the glass.

"If—if I must——" she said deprecatingly.

Barnard and Serracauld smiled, and Deerehurst raised his own glass.

"To the next occasion upon which you consent to be my guest!" he said with a profound and impressive bow.

On the surface, this incident seems scarcely worth recording; yet for Clodagh it marked an epoch—an epoch not evolved through yielding to her host's persuasions, not evolved through drinking a single glass of unfamiliar wine; but evolved through the fact that one item in the sum of her prejudices had gone down before that potent fetish, the dread of appearing conspicuous.

With her action, a fleeting shadow of self-distrust fell across her mind; but she swept it aside, as she had previously swept the memory of her interview with Gore. Deep within her lay the specious knowledge that, for her, this bright existence was only transitory—that somewhere behind the lights and music and laughter lay her own individual groove, to which she must return like a modern Cinderella, when the enchanted interlude of brilliant days was ended. And in this knowledge lay the secret of her greed for joy. Certain of the monotony to come, she caught passionately at every proffered pleasure.

Ten o'clock had struck before the little party left the restaurant; and although she had drunk no more champagne, and had refused the liqueurs that had been served with coffee, her eyes were excitedly bright, as she stepped from the gondola at the steps of the Palazzo Ugochini.

Mounting the marble stairs with Deerehurst close behind her, she was filled with an exhilarating sense of confidence in herself—of defiance towards the world at large. The memory of the afternoon, when she had stood on the dark terrace and listened to Gore's contemptuous voice, had left her—or remained only as a spur to her enthusiasm.

The animation—the zest for pleasure—was plainly visible in her eyes, as she entered the salon, and went forward towards her hostess. And Lady Frances Hope, looking round at sound of her guest's names, saw this peculiar expression with a stirring of curiosity.

"Where have you all been?" she asked, as she took Clodagh's hand.

Barnard laughed.

"We are shocking truants!" he said gaily. "We have been dining at the 'Abbati.'"

She looked at him quickly.

"All four of you?" she asked shrewdly.

He smiled.

"You have a suspicious mind, Frances! Yes; all four of us."

Lady Frances laughed.

"No," she said. "I never harbour suspicions. It is Mrs. Milbanke's air of having just discovered some delicious secret that is always prompting me to curiosity."

"How do you manage to look so triumphant?" She turned again to Clodagh with a long, puzzled glance. "I wish you would impart the secret."

Clodagh's bright eyes met hers.

"My father used to say that the secret of happiness is never to look beyond the present hour."

"A philosopher!" murmured Deerehurst.

"I should say a bold man." Barnard looked from the old nobleman to his hostess.

But almost as he spoke, the name of Sir Walter Gore was announced, and Lady Frances looked sharply towards the door.

With a quiet, unembarrassed bearing, Gore crossed the salon.

As he approached the little group, Lady Frances stepped towards him with outstretched hands.

"How nice of you!" she said softly. "I began to fear you had forgotten about to-night."

He took her hand calmly.

"But I had promised to come," he said simply.

And at the words, his eyes turned involuntarily towards Clodagh.

"Good evening, Mrs. Milbanke!" he added in the same level voice.

At his glance and his words, Clodagh's expression changed. The vague excitement of the past hours seemed suddenly to focus itself. She realised abruptly that she had not yet vindicated her right to the joy of life. With exaggerated difference she bent her head in acknowledgment of his greeting; and almost immediately turned to Deerehurst.

"Lord Deerehurst!" she said, very softly and distinctly, "I want you to do me a favour to-night! I want you to teach me to play roulette!"

It was her declaration of war—the moment towards which she had unconsciously been tending ever since the interview of the afternoon. She knew it instantly the words had left her lips—knew it by the quick surprise in Barnard's eyes, the sharp curiosity in Lady Frances Hope's, the veiled triumph in Deerehurst's, and the cold disapprobation in Sir Walter Gore's. Without another glance she turned away and walked slowly forward across the salon, to where a couple of dozen people were grouped about the roulette-table.

As she moved deliberately forward, many heads were turned in her direction, but she was heedless and almost unobservant of the interest she evoked. Her heart was beating fast, she was rejoicing recklessly in her vindicated independence.

Deerehurst overtook her, as she halted by the roulette-table. And she was conscious of his presence without looking round.

"Will you stake for me?" she said in a quick undertone. "You were lucky the other night."

He stepped forward, smiling with a cold touch of wisdom, and took the coin she handed to him.

"What! A convert!" cried Luard, who was again officiating at the game. "Luck to you, Mrs. Milbanke!"

He gave a pleasant laugh, as her coin touched the table, and a moment later set the ball spinning.

Clodagh waited, holding her breath. The ball slackened speed—hesitated over the gaily painted board—and finally dropped into its place. There was a general laugh of excitement; the little crowd pressed closer to the table, and she saw her coin swept into Luard's hands.

The incident was eventful. Quite suddenly the colour leaped into her face and her eyes blazed. In total unconsciousness of self, she stepped forward to the table.

Deerehurst, closely watchful of her, moved to her side.

"Shall I stake again?" he asked in a whisper.

But she did not turn her head.

"No!—no!" she cried. "I'll stake for myself."

Her voice sounded distant and absorbed. It seemed in that brief moment that she had forgotten her companion and herself.

Thrice she staked, and thrice lost; but the losses whetted her desires. She played boldly, with a certain reckless grace born of complete unconsciousness. At last fortune favoured her, and she won. Deerehurst, still standing close beside her, saw the expression of her face, saw the careless—the almost inconsequent—air with which she accepted her spoils; and, noting both, he touched her arm.

"You are a true gambler!" he said very softly. "You care nothing for gain or loss. You play for the play's sake!"

And Clodagh, with her mind absorbed and her eyes on the roulette-board, gave a quick, high-pitched, unthinking laugh.

# CHAPTER XII

At nine o'clock on the night following her first venture in the world of gambling, Clodagh was again standing by the roulette-table in Lady Frances Hope's salon. She had been playing for two hours, with luck persistently against her; but no one who had chanced to glance at her eager, excited face would have imagined even for a moment that the collection of coins in her gold purse was dwindling and not increasing.

Deerehurst had been correct in his deductions. She played for the play's sake. The losing game—the hazardous game was the one which appealed to, and absorbed, her; the savour of risk stimulated her; the faint sense of danger lifted her to an enchanted realm. And on this night she made an unconsciously picturesque figure as she stood fascinated by the chances of the play—her face flushed, her eyes intensely bright, her fingers restlessly eager to make their stakes. Round about her was gathered a little group of interested and admiring men—Deerehurst, Luard, Serracauld, and a couple of young Americans who had come to Venice with introductions to Lady Frances Hope; but on none of them did she bestow more than a pre-occupied attention. She permitted them to stand beside her; she laughed softly at their compliments and their jests; but her eyes and her thoughts were unmistakably for the painted board over which Barnard was presiding. Another half-dozen rounds of the game were played; then suddenly she turned away from the table with a quick laugh.

"The end!" she said to Serracauld, who was standing nearest to her; and with a quick gesture, she held up the gold netted purse, now limp and empty.

With an eager movement, he stepped forward.

"Let me be useful!" he whispered quickly.

"Or me! I represent your husband, you know!" Barnard leant across the roulette-table.

"Oh, come, Barny! I spoke first——"

But Clodagh looked smilingly from one to the other, and shook her head.

"No!—no!" she said hastily. "I—I never borrow money."

Serracauld looked obviously disappointed.

"Nonsense, Mrs. Milbanke——" he began.

But Deerehurst intervened.

"If Mrs. Milbanke does not wish it, Valentine——" he murmured soothingly. "Mrs. Milbanke, let me take you out of temptation!"

He bowed to Clodagh, and courteously made a passage for her through the crowd that surrounded them. If any cynical remembrance of her first vehement repudiation of the suggestion that she should gamble, rose now to confute her newer denial, no shadow of it was visible in his face.

As they freed themselves from the group of players, they paused simultaneously, and looked for a moment round the large, cool salon, about which the elder or more serious of the assembly were scattered for conversation or cards. Neither spoke; but after a moment's wait, Deerehurst turned his pale eyes in the direction of the open windows, and by the faintest lifting of his eyebrows conveyed a question.

Clodagh laughed; then silently bent her head, and a moment later they moved forward together across the polished floor.

As they passed one of the many groups of statuary that brightened the more shadowed portion of the room, she caught a glimpse of her hostess, once again in conversation with Sir Walter Gore, and she was conscious in that fleeting moment of Gore's clear, reflective eyes resting on her in a quick regard.

With a swift, almost defiant movement she lifted her head, and turned ostentatiously to Deerehurst.

"Is it to be philosophy to-night?" she asked in a low, soft voice.

He paused and looked at her, his cold, pale eyes slow and searching in their regard.

"Not to-night—Circe," he said almost below his breath.

Clodagh coloured, gave another quick, excited laugh, and, moving past him, stepped through one of the open windows.

Gaining the balcony, she did not, as usual, drop into one of the deep lounge chairs; but, moving forward, stood by the iron railing and looked down upon the quiet canal.

The night was exceptionally clear, even for Italy. Every star was reflected in the smooth dark waters; while over the opposite palaces a crescent moon hung like a slender reaping-hook, extended from heaven to garner some mystic harvest.

For a moment Deerehurst hesitated to disturb her; but at last, waiving his scruples, he went softly forward, and stood beside her.

"Are you offended?" he asked in a very low voice.

"No!"

Her answer came almost absently; her eyes were fixed upon the moon.

"Then sad?"

"I don't know! Perhaps!"

He drew a little nearer.

"And why sad?"

She gave a quick sigh, and turned from the glories of the night.

"I have only two days more in Venice. Isn't that reason for being sad?"

"But why leave Venice?"

"My husband is leaving."

He smiled faintly.

"And is he such a tyrant that you must go where he goes?"

She laughed involuntarily.

"A tyrant!" she said. "Oh no! I can scarcely say he is a tyrant."

"Then why do you go with him?"

She looked round for a moment, then her eyes returned to the pageant of the sky.

"Why does one do anything?" she said suddenly in a changed voice.

With a quiet movement Deerehurst leant forward over the railing, and looked into her face.

"Usually we do things because we must," he said softly. "But compulsion is not always disagreeable. Sometimes we are compelled to action by our own desires— —"

Clodagh, conscious of his close regard, felt her breath come a little quicker. But she did not change her position; she did not cease to study the sky. She knew that his arm was all but touching hers; she was sensitive to the faint and costly perfume that emanated from his clothes. But she felt these things vaguely, impersonally, as items in a drama unconnected with herself. When his next words came, it was curiosity rather than dread that stirred in her mind.

"It is my desires that are forcing me to speak now. The desire to see you again after you leave Venice—the desire to see more of you than a mere acquaintance sees—to be something more than a mere friend——"

Clodagh still looked intently at the stars, but unconsciously her lips parted.

"Why?" she asked below her breath. And it seemed to her that the word was not spoken by her, but by some one else.

With an eager gesture, Deerehurst extended his hand, and his long, pale fingers closed over her own.

Then out across the darkness and the silence of the balcony floated the strong, decisive voice of Lady Frances Hope.

"Lord Deerehurst!" it called. "Lord Deerehurst! So sorry, but Rose wants you to give an expert opinion upon one point in a game of bridge. It won't take two minutes."

The voice faded away again as its owner moved back into the room.

At the sound of his name, Deerehurst had drawn himself erect. Now, bending forward silently and swiftly, he lifted the hand he was still holding and kissed it vehemently. The next moment he had crossed the balcony and entered the salon.

Left alone, Clodagh stood motionless. With a vivid physical consciousness, she could still feel the pressure of his cold lips upon her hand; but her mental sensations were benumbed. That something had occurred she dimly realised; that some point—some climax—had been reached she was vaguely aware. But what its personal bearing upon her own life might be, she made no attempt to guess. With a dazed mind she gazed out across the quiet canal, striving to marshal her ideas.

For several seconds she stood in this state of mental confusion; then, with disconcerting suddenness, a new incident obtruded itself upon her mind. With a violent start, she became conscious that some one had passed through the open window, and was coming towards her, across the balcony.

She turned sharply. But as she did so, her fingers slipped from the railing, and all thought of Deerehurst's kiss was banished from her mind. With a sense of acute surprise, she recognised the figure of Sir Walter Gore.

Taking no notice of her dismayed silence, he came quietly forward.

"Good-evening, Mrs. Milbanke," he said. "Have you been enjoying yourself?"

With a certain vague confusion, she met his gaze.

"Yes," she answered. "I—I suppose so."

There was a short silence; and Gore, moving to the balcony railing, rested his arm upon it.

"It is getting late," he said. "Time for us all to be thinking of our hotels."

Again she looked at him in faint bewilderment.

"Yes. I—I suppose so," she said once more.

Another pause succeeded her halting words; then, with a gesture of decision, Gore stood upright, bringing his glance back to her face.

"Mrs. Milbanke," he said suddenly, "let me take you home! I have a gondola waiting at the steps."

The words were so totally unexpected that Clodagh remained mute, and, leaning forward, looked down into the heavy shadows cast by the ancient palace. There was a strange sensation of triumph in this unlooked-for moment—in this sudden capitulation of a man who had previously ignored her: a sensation before which all lesser things—Deerehurst's passion, Serracauld's ardour, Barnard's friendship—became meaningless and vague.

But Gore, guessing nothing from her bent head, glanced behind him towards the salon.

"Well?" he said. "May I be your escort?"

Under cover of the dusk, Clodagh smiled.

"Mr. Barnard generally takes me home——"

Involuntarily Gore's figure stiffened.

"—But," she added in a low, quick whisper, "I—I would very much rather go back with you!"

Under many conditions, the words would have seemed bold. But the manner in which she uttered them disarmed criticism. Gore's face relaxed.

"Then let us make our escape!" he said. "Lady Frances is settling a bridge dispute; and quite a dozen people have slipped away in the last ten minutes. No one will question which of them has taken you home."

And Clodagh gave a short, light laugh of sudden pleasure. The small conspiracy made Gore so much more human—drew them so much closer together than they had been before.

"Yes!—yes!" she said eagerly. "And I am lunching with Lady Frances to-morrow. I can explain then."

"Yes! Quite so! Now, if you are ready!"

He moved to the window.

Very quietly they re-entered the salon; and a flush crossed Clodagh's face as she saw Deerehurst bending over a card-table with the nearest approach to boredom and impatience she had ever known him to evince. Her heart, already beating to the thought of her new conquest, gave an added leap at this silent evidence of her power.

In the corridor outside the salon Gore took her cloak from the servant, and himself wrapped it about her as they descended the stairs; then, passing to the flight of worn steps that led to the water, he signalled to a waiting gondolier.

"Mrs. Milbanke," he said, as he offered her his hand, "I am going to make a strange request. I want to talk to you for half an hour before taking you home. Will you give me leave to make a tour of the canals?" He spoke very quietly and in a tone difficult to construe.

At his curious appeal, her heart gave another quick, excited throb, though instinctively she realised that neither Deerehurst, Serracauld, nor Barnard would have proposed a midnight excursion in quite his voice or manner. But the very mode of the request enhanced its charm. She looked up into his face as she laid her hand in his.

"I give you leave!" she said gently.

He met her glance, but almost immediately averted his eyes. And as he handed her to the seat, he turned swiftly to the gondolier, addressing him in Italian.

The colloquy lasted but a few seconds, and at its conclusion the boat shot silently out into the canal.

"This man does not understand a word of English," he said, as he dropped into his place by Clodagh's side.

Again his words were peculiarly suggestive, and again his tone was curiously frank. Why should he suggest that their conversation was unintelligible? And suggest it in so impersonal a tone? She leant back in her cushioned seat and let her eyelids droop. Her mind was full of puzzling and delightful thoughts. Never had she tasted the mystery of Venice as she tasted it to-night. Every passing breath of wind, every scent blown from the dark and silent gardens, every distant laugh or broken word, was alive with unguessed meanings. The feverish excitement of the past week seemed to fall away. This was romance! This drifting with an inscrutable companion through an unfathomable night!

Her eyes closed; she lay almost motionless, filled with an aimless, vague delight. All creation—with all creation's limitless possibilities—lay in the warm darkness that enveloped her. Then, with the instinct of senses newly and sharply astir, she became conscious that Gore was watching her. With a thrill of expectancy and anticipation, she opened her eyes.

There is something very curious—something subtle and almost intimate—in the opening of one's eyes upon the steady scrutiny of another. As Clodagh raised her lids, her glance encountered Gore's; but on the instant that their eyes met, her joy in the moment—her exultant triumph— was suddenly killed. For the look that she surprised was not the look she had anticipated. It was interested, it was attentive, it was grave, but it held neither subjugation nor passion. As her brain woke to this realisation, she involuntarily raised herself in the cushioned seat.

At the same moment, her companion leant slightly forward.

"Mrs. Milbanke," he said quickly, "I have been watching you and thinking about you ever since I came to Venice. And at last I have decided, that I must tell you what my thoughts have been.

"I am not very old—perhaps I have no right to speak. But a man sees a good deal of life, even if he wants to keep his eyes shut; and I have seen a great many people throw away their chances—take the false and refuse the true. I have seen some men do it, and I have seen many women—many, many women." He paused, but did not look at her. "It is a common, everyday occurrence; so common that one generally looks on at it with indifference. But sometimes—just sometimes—one stops to think. One feels the great, great pity of it!"

He paused again, looking fixedly down at the strip of carpet beneath their feet.

Clodagh glanced at him—a swift, searching, almost surreptitious look.

"There are times when one stops to think." He raised his head and looked at Clodagh, sitting erect and pale, her large eyes wide open, her hands clasped in her lap. "There are times when it seems cruel—when it seems a sacrilege to see a girl going down the easy road of lost illusions and callous sentiments. I know this sounds incomprehensible—sounds impertinent. But I cannot help myself. I must tell you what no one else will tell you. I must put out my hand."

He paused, but Clodagh did not speak.

"You are very young, you are very high-spirited, you—you are very attractive. And the world is full of people ready—waiting—to take advantage of your youth, your high spirits, your attractiveness. You are not fit for this society—for this set that you have drifted into— —"

"This set? Isn't it your own set?" At last Clodagh's lips parted.

He made an impatient gesture.

"A man has many sets."

Her pale face flushed suddenly.

"I don't think I understand," she said.

"No. But I am trying to make you understand. I am not disparaging Lady Frances Hope—or her social standing. She is a charming woman—a clever woman, but she is a woman of to-day. Her pleasures, her ambitions, her friends— —"

Clodagh lifted her head.

"—Her friends?" she said faintly.

"—Are not the friends for you—for any inexperienced girl. Take them one by one. There is Serracauld—indolent, worthless, vicious; Barnard—decent enough as a man's friend, and as honest as his clients permit him to be, but no proper guide for a girl like you; Deerehurst— —"

But Clodagh checked him.

"Lord Deerehurst? What about Lord Deerehurst?" Her voice was high and strained.

Gore made a gesture of contempt.

"Deerehurst— —" he began hotly; then suddenly his tone changed.

"Mrs. Milbanke," he said earnestly, "whatever you may say, whatever you may do, I cannot believe that in your heart you are in sympathy with these people, whose one object in life is to gamble—to gamble with honour, money, emotion—anything, everything that has the savour of risk and the possibility of gain.

"You have no justification for belonging to these people. You have the good things of life, the things many women are forced to steal—position, a home, a good husband— —"

At the last word Clodagh started violently. And with a quick impulsive movement, Gore turned to her afresh.

"You are intoxicated with life—or what seems to you to be life! You are forgetting realities. I have seen your husband. He is an honest, simple, trustworthy man—who loves you."

The tone of his voice came to Clodagh with great distinctness. It seemed the only living thing in a world that had suddenly become dead. While she had been sitting rigid and erect in the stern of the gondola, everything had altered to her mental vision—everything had undergone a fundamental change. The purple twilight; the mysterious night scents; the breezes blown in from the lagoon had become intangible, meaningless things. She was conscious of nothing but Gore's clear words, of her own soul, stripped of its self-deception. At last, with a faint movement, she turned towards him.

"Take me home," she said in a numbed voice. "I wish to go home."

At the words, he wheeled round in sudden protest. But as his eyes rested on her cold face, a tinge of self-consciousness chilled his zeal—self-consciousness, and the suddenly remembered fact that his own action was, after all, unjustifiable. His own figure suddenly stiffened.

"As you wish, of course!" he said quietly. "I suppose my conduct seems quite unpardonable."

For one fleeting second an impulse—a desire—crossed Clodagh's face; but as it trembled on the brink of utterance, Gore leant forward in his seat and gave a quick, imperative order to the gondolier. A moment later they had glided up a narrow waterway and emerged again upon the Grand Canal.

From the door and windows of Clodagh's hotel, a stream of light was still pouring out upon the water. As they drew level with the terrace, she turned her face away from this searching radiance, and rose quickly to her feet.

"Good-night," she said in an almost inarticulate voice—"good-night! Don't stir! Don't help me!"

But Gore had risen also. And in a sudden return of his earlier, more impulsive manner, he forgot the self-consciousness that had chilled him.

"Mrs. Milbanke——" he said quickly.

But Clodagh evaded his eyes; and with a sharp nervous movement, shook her head.

"No!" she said—"no! Don't help me! I don't want help!"

Stepping past him with an agile movement, she ran up the steps, and across the terrace to the door of the hotel.

Obeying a dominant impulse, Gore turned to follow her. But as his foot touched the side of the boat, he paused, drew slowly back, and dropped into his former seat.

With almost breathless haste, Clodagh ran up the silent staircase of the hotel, and entering her own room, turned on the light; then, walking straight to the dressing-table, she paused and stared into the mirror at her own reflection.

The sight of that reflection was not reassuring. Her face looked colourless, as only olive-tinted skin can look; her wide eyes with their narrowed pupils seemed almost yellow in their intense clearness; while her whole air, her whole appearance, was frightened, tired, pained. As she looked, a nervous panic seized her, and she turned her gaze away.

With freedom to look elsewhere, her eyes roved over the dressing-table, and suddenly fixed themselves upon a large, square envelope bearing her name, which stood propped against a scent bottle.

In nervous haste she picked it up, and looked at it uncomprehendingly. It was unusually large and thick and addressed in an unfamiliar hand. With the same unstrung haste she turned it about between her fingers, halting with new apprehension, as she saw that its flap bore an elaborate black coronet and monogram.

At last, with a strange sense of apprehension, she tore the envelope open.

"Circe," the letter began.

"I will not reproach you for deserting me. Life is too brief for reproaches—when one longs to fill it with pleasanter things. But be kind to me! Give me the opportunity of finishing that broken sentence. I shall smoke a cigar on the terrace at eleven to-night. If you are generous, wrap yourself up, and keep me company for ten minutes. I shall wait—and hope.

"Deerehurst."

She read to the end, and stood for a space staring at the large, straggling writing; at last, as if suddenly imbued with the power of action, she tore the letter across—tearing and retearing it into little strips; then, throwing the fragments on the ground, she turned and fled out of the room.

Milbanke's bedroom was on the same floor as her own, though separated from it by half the length of the corridor. Leaving her own apartment, she hurried towards it; and pausing outside the door, knocked softly and insistently. A delay followed her imperative summons; then Milbanke's voice came faint and nervous, demanding the intruder's name.

She answered; and a moment later the door was opened with a confused sound of shooting bolts.

Milbanke's appearance was slightly grotesque, as the opened door disclosed him, silhouetted against the lighted room. He was garbed in a loose dressing-gown; his scanty hair was disarranged; and there was an expression of alarm on his puckered face. But for once Clodagh was blind to these things. With a swift movement she entered the room, and closing the door, stood leaning against it.

"James," she said breathlessly, "you finished your business with Mr. Barnard to-day, didn't you?"

Milbanke, suddenly conscious of her white face, began to stammer.

"Clodagh! my dear—my dear——"

But Clodagh waved his anxiety aside.

"Tell me!" she said. "It's finished, isn't it?"

"Yes!—yes! But, my dear——"

She threw out her hands in a sudden, vehement gesture.

"Then take me away!" she cried—"take me away! Let us go in the morning, by the very first train—before any one is up."

Milbanke paled.

"But, my dear," he said helplessly, "I thought—I believed——"

Clodagh turned to him again.

"So did I!" she cried—"so did I! I thought I loved it. I thought I loved it all—the music and the gaiety and—and the people. But I don't. I hate it!—I hate it!—I hate it!"

In a strangled sob, her voice gave way; and, with it, her strength and her self-control. She took a few steps forward; then, like a mechanical figure in which the mechanism has suddenly been suspended, she stopped, swayed a little and, dropping into the nearest chair, broke into a flood of tears—such tears as had shaken her four years ago, when she drove out of Carrigmore on the day of her wedding.

# PART IV

## CHAPTER I

The penetrating Florentine sunshine was enveloping the villa that stood upon the hill above San Domenico; but it was not the full, warm sunshine of late April that had opened the roses in the garden and deepened the shadows of the cypress trees nearly two years earlier, when Clodagh had dreamed of her visit to Venice. It was the cool sunlight of February, and it fell across the polished floors, and threw into prominence the many antique and curious objects that filled the rooms, with a searching clearness that almost seemed like a human scrutiny.

In a small salon that opened upon the terrace Clodagh sat at a bureau. In front of her was a formidable array of letters and business papers, neatly bound into packets by elastic bands, and under her hand was spread a sheaf of unused, black-bordered note-paper.

Whether it was the multitude of her own thoughts that retarded the task she had in hand, or a certain air of absolute stillness that seemed to brood over the villa, one could not say; but certain it is that for nearly half an hour she sat in an attitude of abstraction, her fingers poised above the note-paper, the tip of her pen held against her lips.

At last, however, a new idea seemed born in her mind, for she laid down her pen, rose suddenly to her feet, and moving across the room, paused beside the window.

For a long, silent space she stood at this closed window, her gaze wandering over the scene that custom had rendered so familiar, — the hillside, cut into characteristic tiers of earth, until it sloped downwards almost like a flight of steps, from which the grey olive trees and the black cypresses rose sharply defined in the brilliant atmosphere; at its foot, Florence, with its suggestion of dark-roofed houses and clustering spires; and beyond all, encircling all, the low chain of mountains, blue and purple in the sun. Quite suddenly, with a swift, impulsive movement, she unfastened the latch and threw the window open.

In the added radiance that poured into the room, she stood more distinctly revealed, and the slight changes that even two years can make became visible in her face and figure. The pose of her body and the carriage of her head were precisely as they had been, but her cheeks were a little thinner, and some of her brilliant colouring was gone; but the fact that would most speedily have appealed to one who had not seen her for the two years was the circumstance that she wore deep mourning—a mourning that lent an unfamiliar, almost a fragile air to her whole appearance.

That would have been the first impression; and then, as one studied her more closely, it would have been borne in upon one that these were mere outward signs—that the true, the real alteration lay not in dress, not in the thinness of her face nor in the unwonted pallor of her skin, but in the very curious expression with which she gazed out over the distant hills; the look of kinship—of comprehension—of that illusive, subtle sentiment that we call anticipation, with which her eyes met the far-off sky line.

For many moments she stood as if fascinated by the sense of promise that breathed and vibrated in the spring air; then, at last, with a quickly taken breath, she turned away from the open window, and, recrossing the room, seated herself again at the bureau, picked up her pen, and with new inspiration began to write.

"Larry—dear cousin,—

"I, the worst correspondent in all the world, am going to write you a long letter—because my heart is so full of thoughts that I must unburden it to some one who will listen. Who better than my friend—my brother—of the old dear, dear days?

"It was good of you and Aunt Fan to write me those two long affectionate letters; and I needed them. For though there was no horror in James's death, death itself is—and always must be—terrible to me. Terrible—but also very, very wonderful! Wonderful beyond words, when one realises that somebody one has known as good and kind and unselfish—but ordinary, Larry, ordinary as oneself—is suddenly transformed into something infinitely wise and mysterious, with a mystery one can only think about and fear.

"One month ago, James was in his usual health, going about his little daily tasks, losing himself in his little daily interests. And now he understands the million things that puzzle you and me and the rest of the world of living people!

"His death—as I told you in my first short note—was painless and quiet, and unselfish like his life. He held my hand and knew me to the very end, and spoke to me quite lucidly of his affairs half an hour before he died. And, Larry—I think he was happy! You cannot imagine what it is to be able to say that! Death brings so many regrets. It frightens me when I look back now over the years, and think of our marriage. It was so terribly, cruelly unwise. A man of his age, a girl of mine! And, knowing what I know now, the first years must have been very bitter for him. Since then, things have been better—and worse. Two years ago we were perilously near disaster—he and I—when something—it does not matter what—saved us both.

"How sincerely I thank God, now, that it was so. At the time I suffered horribly; but it was good for me. It made me see that duty is not merely a negative thing. And now it is all over—all over, like a dream that is past. I am as I was. I am free!

"I seem heartless to say that. I could not say it to any one except you—or Nance. And I even wonder if Nance could quite understand. I feel that she must be so very much younger than myself. But you will not misunderstand, Larry, will you? You will see that it isn't want of heart, but just the knowledge that there is a future—a future for me, who had ceased to believe in one!

"Just before I began this letter I stood for a long time at an open window, looking out over Florence, lying below me in the wonderful sunshine that comes to Italy in the spring; and quite suddenly, Larry, I thought of England in May. England in May! It seems to suggest a hundred, thousand things. Don't say I am disloyal! For, of course, I want to go home to Orristown; but not just yet—not just yet. I feel—I cannot quite explain it to you—just a little afraid of going back to Ireland. Just at the moment it is too full of memories. But I want to see England. I want to live in England.

"Yes; I *shall* live in England—for the present at least. And you and Aunt Fan must come and stay with me; and then you will report on your stewardship! For, of course, you are still to manage Orristown—as well and capably as you have managed it during the last three years. I always think it was one of James's kindest actions to me to give that management to you, though I shall always regret that you and Aunt Fan will not make use of that big empty house. But what is the good of talking! The Asshlins are all disgustingly proud.

"I can see you smile as you read this, and perhaps I can hear you say: 'How like Clo!' I hope—oh, Larry, I hope I can!

"Give them all my love—Hannah, Burke, the dogs, and Polly. Dear, pretty Polly! How I crave sometimes for just one long, wild gallop. She must be eight years old by now; and yet she looks as fit as ever—you said so in your letter of a month ago. Dear, pretty Polly!

"I can do very much as I like now, Larry, in every way. James has been more than generous. I am to have the interest on sixty thousand pounds, although I may not touch the capital. A wise precaution. Was there ever an Asshlin who could keep money? But, as it is, I shall be rich. Two thousand pounds a year! Why, it is wealth. And then again there is another thing in which James has been good to us. He has placed a thousand pounds to my credit, apart from my own money, which I am to give to Nance on her twenty-first birthday, or on her engagement, should she marry with my consent before she comes of age. Was it not a kindly, thoughtful act? But does it not seem incredible to talk about Nance—little Nance—being of an age when she might think of marrying? I often long to see her—and sometimes I feel ridiculously shy and a little bit afraid; it is so strange that we have never in all these years visited England, and that some plan of poor James's should always have prevented her spending her holidays with us—though, so far as that goes, Carrigmore was a more homelike place than Italy to spend them in.

"What is she really like? You say she has grown very pretty, but you never say more than that. Men don't realise how women crave for details. But I shall see her for myself in a few weeks. She leaves school next month, you know, and will join me at once. Before James's death she had been asked on a visit to America by the mother of a school friend of hers—a girl named Estcoit, who is leaving school on the same day as Nance. But now that is all changed. She writes begging me to let her come to me directly; and her letter has made me know that, beneath all the silly feelings of shyness and uncertainty, I too want her.

"So now I have said all. Now you see me as I am, Larry—more the old Clodagh than I have been for years. The Clodagh who remembers and loves you always, as her dear cousin—her dear, dear brother."

The letter ended unconventionally, without a signature; but the writing of the last lines was strong and bold, with a vigorous upward curve.

With a touch of impetuosity, Clodagh picked up an envelope and addressed it to Laurence Asshlin at Orristown; then, rising from the bureau, she rang a bell.

An Italian man-servant responded to the summons—the same man-servant who had waited at breakfast on the morning that Milbanke had received Barnard's summons to Venice. Entering the room with sympathetic deference, he paused just inside the door.

"Signora!" he murmured.

Clodagh turned to him, the black-edged envelope in her hand.

"Tell Simonetta to bring me my hat and cloak," she said. "I'm going down into Florence—to post a letter." And without waiting to see what expression her declaration brought to the man's face, she crossed the room and stood once more in the flood of clear, cool sunlight that poured through the open window.

# CHAPTER II

Exactly one week later Clodagh arrived in Paris on her way to England. Simonetta Ottolenghi—an Italian woman, who had been in her service as maid for nearly four years—was her only companion; there was no friend to meet or welcome her in the unfamiliar city, and even the dog Mick— the companion of so many solitary hours—had been left behind in Florence until she could conveniently send for him; yet, incongruous as it may sound, her feelings were happy—her mind was free from loneliness as her train steamed into the crowded railway station and she found herself free to drive to her hotel. After all, life undeniably stretched before her, and there was no prohibition against letting her eyes dwell upon the vistas it opened up!

Knowledge of duty done—be the doing ever so tardy—is the best stimulus for the wayfarer in the world's by-ways; and Clodagh, as she stepped from her train on that February afternoon, was conscious of some such reassuring certainty.

In the last two years, life for her had been a thing of physical inaction, accompanied by a subtle process of mental development. The night of tempestuous excitement—when, in a whirl of pain, chagrin, and passionate self-contempt, she had repudiated Venice and her newly made friends—had been the birth of a fresh phase in her existence. With all the ardour, all the enthusiasm, whereof her vivid nature was capable, she had veered from her former point of view to another almost as extreme. The return to Florence, the taking up of existence in the secluded villa, had been like the incidents of a dream; then, in the days that had succeeded—in the early mornings, or the late evenings—as she sat upon the marble rim of the drowsy fountain in the garden, gazed down from Fiesole upon the sleeping Roman amphitheatre, or knelt in a dim recess of the old church of San Dominico, rendered mystical by the smell of incense and the flicker of wax tapers, the dream had shaped itself. It had become a tapestry, into the pictures of which many figures were woven, but where only two took place and prominence—her own and one other.

For in those silent hours the thought of Gore—the remembrance of Gore—had come back to her as tangible things. In that solitude peopled by imagination, she had forgotten the hurt vanity, the bitter disappointment, that had clothed her last interview with him; and remembered only that, seeing fit to reprove her, he had dared to do so—that, seeing the brink upon which she had stood, he had put out his hand to draw her back.

And, standing in this new light, Gore became an ideal, a being apart, endowed with endless power to inspire high deeds. An idealist born, Clodagh was created to make-believe. The make-believes were probably the swaying of an impulsive mind from one emotional pole to the other; but in this case, at least, benefit accrued. She developed a sudden gentle tolerance of Milbanke—an altogether unprecedented care for his comfort and well-being.

The working of this profoundly subtle emotion was far too deep to be even guessed at by herself. And had any student of human nature told her that the new tenderness for the timid, unassuming husband, who made so few demands upon her consideration, arose from the fact that another man had crossed her life—rousing at once her imagination, her antagonism, and her admiration, showing her new depths in the world around her, new possibilities within herself—she would have been both incredulous and indignant.

But no student of human nature visited the villa. And she lived undisturbed in her atmosphere of dreams. Whether the vague, subconscious thought that Gore, away in his own world, might hear of her graver attitude towards life and might secretly approve, ever lent zest to her self-imposed duties, it would have been impossible to say; but certain it is that if the thought came, it came unbidden and stayed unrecognised.

And now Milbanke was dead. And life—not the mythical life of memories, of dreams, even of ideals, but the life of hope and warm human possibilities—was hers, as it had been long ago, before her husband's name had ever been spoken in her presence.

Her mind was at peace, as she drove through the narrow streets of Paris, with their cheerful characteristic chorus of shouting newsvendors, and cracking whips.

The hotel she had chosen was a small one, close to the Place Vendome; and when her fiacre stopped and she entered the vestibule, her sense of pleasure and contentment increased. The quiet air of the place contrasted agreeably with her previous experience of hotel life.

Still conscious of this impression of security, she turned away from the bureau where she had registered her name, and crossed the vestibule to the lift. Taking her place on the velvet-covered seat, she watched the attendant close the iron doors and turn to set the lift in motion. But at the moment that he laid his hand upon the button, she saw the swinging doors of the hotel open, to admit a lady.

The new-comer, seeing that the lift was about to ascend, hurried towards it; and Clodagh, idly interested by the sound of rustling silk, leaned forward in her seat. But the light in the vestibule was dim, and she caught nothing beyond the outline of a large hat and the suggestion of a pale green dress. Then, suddenly, the stranger spoke, and her heart gave a tremendous leap.

"Wait!" she called in French—"wait! I am coming!"

It needed but the five words, spoken in a clear, dictatorial voice, to assure Clodagh that the speaker was known to her; and as the attendant paused in his task, and, turning promptly, opened the grilled door, her mind was prepared for the vision of Lady Frances Hope.

But if she was prepared for the encounter, the new-comer was taken completely by surprise. Entering the lift, she glanced casually at its other occupant; then her whole face changed.

"It is—— It can't be! It *is* Mrs. Milbanke!" Her glance passed rapidly over Clodagh's deep mourning and her expression altered in accordance. "My dear Mrs. Milbanke," she said softly, "how thoughtless of me not to realise at once! I heard through Mr. Barnard. How are you?—how are you?"

She pressed the hand Clodagh had offered her, and looked sympathetically into her face. Then, as the lift, gliding upwards, stopped at the first floor and Clodagh rose, her expression changed again.

"Are you located on this floor? How delightful! We are neighbours. I am number five. What are you?"

"Seven," Clodagh said gently, speaking for the first time. There was something very strange to her in this meeting—something not altogether unpleasant. In the two years since they had met—and in the light of her last evening in Venice—the image of Lady Frances Hope had become slightly distorted. And there was a sense of surprise, of reassurance in finding her so kindly, so gracious, so unalarming.

"Seven!" Lady Frances repeated. "Delightful! You must dine with me to-night. I have a private room, and am quite alone. It will be an act of charity. I am on my way south. By the way, where are you bound for?"

Clodagh smiled.

"I am going home."

"Home?"

"To England."

"England! My dear child, not England in February? Why, the atmosphere is a combination of fog and sleet; and the people— —" She made a gesture of horror. "Everybody who hasn't influenza is either expecting it or shaking it off."

Clodagh laughed a little.

"I have never had influenza. It will be an experience. But I must look after my maid. Travelling is new to her."

She glanced down the corridor to where Simonetta was awaiting her beside a mountain of luggage.

Lady Frances made haste to echo her laugh.

"Well, well!" she said. "It's good to have the enthusiasm of youth. But you will dine with me? Dinner in an hour."

Clodagh hesitated. Yesterday she would have ardently avoided a meeting with Lady Frances Hope. Now that it had been thrust upon her, it seemed to possess no danger. What was it Gore had said on that memorable night? "I am not depreciating Lady Frances Hope or her social standing— —" Very swiftly she recalled the words and construed them in the light of her present feelings. After all, she was not the child she had been two years ago. And it was not Lady Frances, but the set that surrounded her, to which Gore took exception.

Her companion, seeing the hesitation in her eyes, gave a quick, bright smile.

"Do come! I will give you news of—every one."

Clodagh coloured slightly.

"Very well!" she said. "In an hour. Thank you very much!"

And with an agreeable, unfamiliar sense of interest and excitement, she turned and passed down the corridor to where Simonetta stood.

Before opening her own door, Lady Frances Hope stood for a few seconds watching the retreating figure; then, apparently without reason, she frowned, drew her lips together, and pushing her door hastily open, passed out of sight.

Still imbued with the sense of contentment, Clodagh changed her heavy black travelling dress for one of lighter texture, allowed Simonetta to rearrange her hair, and, at the appointed hour, presented herself at Lady Frances Hope's door.

Lady Frances had also discarded her elaborate costume for something lighter and more comfortable, and was ensconced on a low divan, reading a French novel, when her guest was announced. Immediately Clodagh's name reached her, she threw the book aside, and rose with great cordiality.

"How sweet you look!" she exclaimed. "You are the first dark woman I've ever liked in black. But then, of course, you are not exactly dark. Sit down! Dinner will be served in a moment. How did you know of this place? Have you stayed here before?"

Clodagh had come forward and seated herself beside her hostess. Now, as she looked about her, she noticed with a feeling of restfulness that the room was pretty and homelike, and that there were flowers on the tables and soft yellow shades on the electric lamps.

"No; I have never been here before. Mr. Barnard gave the address to my—my husband, when we were in Venice; and I came across it among his papers after—after——" She hesitated.

Lady Frances leaned forward sympathetically.

"Poor child!" she murmured. "Don't talk of it! You have had a most trying time. Barny told me all about it only a week ago. But this place is really quite good," she added, in a cheerful voice; "better now than ever. They have just secured the chef from the 'Abbati' Restaurant in Venice. But, of course, you knew 'Abbati's.'"

Her quick glance passed over Clodagh's face. Then she rose and moved to the table, as two waiters entered, and dinner was announced.

Clodagh coloured, and crossed the room in her hostess's wake.

"Yes," she said, taking her seat at the table—"yes; I once dined there. It was a wonderfully fascinating place. Has it been a failure?"

Lady Frances shrugged her shoulders.

"Vanished! But tell me about yourself!" She turned to her guest with a change of manner. "You are not seriously contemplating England at this time of year?"

Clodagh smiled calmly.

"Quite seriously."

"But, my dear child, why, if one may be inquisitive?"

"Because I want to know England—to know the English."

Lady Frances's eyes narrowed very slightly; then she gave one of her bright laughs.

"Then come back with me to the Riviera! Any English people worth studying will be found there. Change your plans! Come back with me!"

Clodagh looked up. She was uncertain whether the suggestion had been made in jest or earnest, and the smiling, searching glance of her hostess did not enlighten her. With a slight feeling of embarrassment, she broke off abruptly into another channel of talk.

"And how is Mr. Barnard?" she asked.

"Barny! Oh, optimistic as ever!"

"Then there is one amusing person left in England!"

Lady Frances laughed.

"Only temporarily. He takes his holiday next month. Last March he joined the Luards and me in Naples, and we all went on to Sicily. It was tremendous fun."

She laughed again over some recollection; and entered upon a history of her Sicilian adventures that occupied the rest of dinner.

At the termination of the meal, however, when the waiters had brought in coffee and silently retired, she dropped her reminiscent tone, and, rising from table, moved back to the divan, which was drawn pleasantly near to a bright wood fire.

"Come here, and let's be comfortable!" she said. "I always have a cigarette after dinner. I forget whether you smoke."

Clodagh smiled, as she came slowly forward.

"Not since my cousin and I used to smoke in the top branches of an apple tree in Ireland. I should be afraid to try the experiment again; I might lose an illusion. No other cigarettes could taste like those stolen ones!"

She gave a little sigh, then a little laugh, and seated herself.

Lady Frances looked up from the cigarette she was drawing from her case.

"Illusions!" she said. "Why, life is all illusions at your age!" She paused; then, after a moment's silence, went on again, but in a slower, more considered voice: "You thought I was jesting at dinner, when I asked you to come south with me. But I wasn't. I meant it." She struck a match and lighted her cigarette. "You don't know how you would enjoy Nice. You lost yourself in the delights of roulette at Venice. Think what Monte Carlo would be!"

With a sudden tumultuous confusion, Clodagh flushed.

"I—I have ceased to care about things like that," she said in a hurried voice.

Lady Frances's expression changed to one of deep interest, sharpened by surprise.

"Ceased to care?" she repeated softly. "Since when? And why?"

"Since"—Clodagh hesitated—"oh, since that time in Venice."

Her hostess flicked the ash from her cigarette.

"Some new influence?"

Clodagh was taken unawares.

"I—I have got to know myself better since that time in Venice," she said below her breath. "Some one—something—has made me see that it was not my true self that showed then. I was foolish in those days. I was carried away——"

A very faint smile flitted across Lady Frances's lips.

"That idea belongs to the some one else?" she said in a quiet, cordial tone that invited confidence.

Moved by a sudden impulse, Clodagh leant forward in her seat and clasped her hands. As on the day in Florence—the day when she had written her letter to Laurence Asshlin—her soul thirsted for confession. After two long years of silent thought, the temptation to open her heart in speech was overmastering. The room was comfortable, dimly lighted, almost homelike; the hour was propitious; her hostess's voice was extraordinarily kind. She stole one half-shy, half-eager glance at the averted face.

"Lady Frances," she said suddenly, "I was very childish, very foolish, that time in Venice. I knew it even before I—before I left."

With extreme tact, Lady Frances refrained from looking at her. Smoking quietly, she made her next remark in a low, reassuring voice.

"Then that was why you left so suddenly?"

"That was why."

"Walter Gore must have been very eloquent!"

Lady Frances spoke in the same even tone; but, as she felt the thrill of surprise with which Clodagh received her words, she turned quickly and decisively, and met her startled eyes.

"I always knew that Walter Gore went back with you to your hotel on that last night," she said. "I always knew that he read you a very moral lecture."

Clodagh drew a quick breath.

"But how did you know?"

Lady Frances studied her face for a moment; then she gave a direct answer to the question put to her.

"Walter himself told me," she said.

After she had spoken there was silence in the room. On her part it was the silence of the experimenter, who has taken a step in a new direction and is waiting for results; on Clodagh's, it was the silence of incredulity, of doubt, of dread. That Gore should have spoken of that last night in Venice to any third person was a circumstance that, at very least, needed explanation. She sat breathlessly waiting that explanation.

During the moment of fruitful silence Lady Frances Hope remained very still, fingering her cigarette, drawing in fitful puffs of smoke, avoiding with elaborate carelessness any observation of her companion's manner.

Then, as if some psychological crisis for which she was waiting had been achieved, she altered her position and her expression; and, turning, laid her hand upon Clodagh's.

"Dear Mrs. Milbanke," she said, "I am glad all this has happened; I am glad we have met. You are at a moment in your life when you need a friend—a friend who understands——"

Her fingers tightened upon Clodagh's in a warm, sympathetic pressure.

"You are young; you are free; you have the whole world at your feet. Don't spoil your life by taking it too seriously!

"When I was your age, or only a little older than you, I was left a widow—as you have been left; but I was unlike you in one particular: I had a very wise and far-seeing mother to help me with her advice. Do you know what her advice was?"

Clodagh sat silent.

"It was comprised in one sentence. 'Avoid scandal, but fly from sentiment!' Do you see all the wisdom in that advice to a woman who has just become her own mistress?"

Still Clodagh was silent, filled by a sense of uncertainty, of loneliness, of fear. She waited for Lady Frances's explanation with the numb sense of helplessness that is born of ignorance.

"Of course, I may be wrong," the strong, reliant voice went on; "but I feel you are in need of just such counsel. You are emotional; you are an idealist; you are coming out into life expecting it to be a fairy tale—and it is not a fairy tale. It is a realistic story—sometimes a long one, sometimes a short one, but always realistic. Take my advice! Make the best of it as it is! Don't break your heart because there are no dragons, or castles, or princes."

She paused at last; and at last Clodagh spoke.

"You are very kind—very good. But I don't see what it all has to do with me."

With a frank, almost an affectionate gesture, Lady Frances took both her hands, and, looking into her face, spoke the words for which she had so carefully prepared the way.

"If what I am going to say hurts you, you must forgive me. I feel such centuries older than you, that I can risk a great deal. Don't spoil your life, don't throw away your pleasure, because of one moral lecture! It isn't worth while. I know what I am saying. People like Walter Gore are reprehensible. They take themselves so seriously, that sometimes other people make the mistake of taking them seriously too; and then things go wrong."

Clodagh's face became a shade paler.

"I—I am stupid," she said. "I don't seem to understand."

"My dear! It is so hard to say it bluntly."

"Please say it bluntly."

For an instant the older woman hesitated before the coldness of Clodagh's tone; but the next, she took the opening offered her.

"You are deliberately turning away from the best in life because some one, in a moment of enthusiasm, preached you a sermon. You make the mistake of thinking that Walter Gore did something unusual when he warned you against cards and roulette—against Lord Deerehurst and Val Serracauld and me—whereas, Walter was born to preach!"

Clodagh's lips parted. Lady Frances had justified herself. Gore *had* spoken of that last interview. But why? And how?

"Lady Frances," she said very quietly, "why did Sir Walter Gore tell you all these things?"

Lady Frances freed the hands she had continued to hold.

"Oh, we are old friends. He tells me many things. I fought more than one battle for you, while you were in Venice—and afterwards."

"For me? After I left Venice?"

"Oh, many battles. Walter is so extreme in his judgments of men and things. I lose patience with him sometimes."

"And what was Sir Walter Gore's judgment of me—after I left Venice?"

Lady Frances gave a little deprecating laugh.

"Would that be quite fair?"

"Yes, I think so, if I wish to know."

The older woman took a fresh cigarette from the case beside her.

"And you won't be offended?"

"I won't be offended." Clodagh's voice sounded a little dry.

"Well, then—oh, really, it's very stupid! Perhaps I'd better not."

Clodagh rose quietly from the divan and walked to the mantelpiece.

"Please tell me," she said.

At her tone, her hostess ceased to dally. She struck a match and raised the cigarette to her lips.

"Well," she said, with another little apologetic laugh, "I think Walter has always imagined you a very pretty, very fascinating—little fool!"

There was another silence—very short but very tense. Lady Frances laid down her cigarette unlighted, and blew out the match.

"Mrs. Milbanke, you don't mind?"

Clodagh laughed—suddenly and almost loudly.

"Mind? Mind? Why *should* I mind?"

Had her denial been a shade less intense, its steadiness might have deceived her companion; as it was, the faintest flickering smile touched her lips, as she also rose and came slowly forward.

"My dear child!" she murmured reproachfully—"my dear child, you have misunderstood. I never implied that Walter interested you personally; I merely used him as an illustration—as a means of conveying the folly of taking serious people seriously. But you are tired. I have been cruelly unreasonable. I shall send you straight to bed. You are fagged after that long journey."

She put out her hand and laid it on Clodagh's arm; but Clodagh was not in a mood to be caressed.

"It's all right!" she said abruptly. "I suppose we both misunderstood. I *am* a little tired. I think I *will* say good-night!"

"Good-night, dear child!" Lady Frances pressed her hand, and walked with her slowly across the room. As she passed out into the corridor, she waved a gay farewell. "Sleep well!" she called. "But dream of an English February—and wake with a changed mind!"

As she said the last words, Clodagh paused for a moment; then went on again without speaking, and entered her own room.

Tired though she was, she scarcely slept that night; and in the early hours of the morning she saw the bright dawn break over Paris. At eight o'clock she rang for Simonetta, and asked for ink, pen, and note-paper.

Sitting up in bed, she wrote the following note.

> "Dear Lady Frances,
>
> "As we are both women, I can hope that you won't call me variable. If you still want me as a companion, I think I will, after all, go with you to Nice. Looking into the matter more closely, I find I really have no affinity for sleet or influenza!
>
> "Yours,
>
> "Clodagh Milbanke."

Having despatched the note to Lady Frances Hope, she wrote two long, feverishly hasty letters—one to Laurence Asshlin at Orristown, the other to Nance at her school near London.

# CHAPTER III

It was in the middle of February that Clodagh arrived in Paris on her journey home; and it was the end of April before that ardently planned return to England at last took place.

On a fresh, showery April afternoon when all London looked renewed and beautified by soft air and fitful brilliant sunshine, she alighted from the train at Charing Cross.

Her arrival in the lofty, unfamiliar station was very different from her arrival at the bustling, exciting Parisian terminus two months earlier. Then, she had descended from her train with the rapidity of one who sees in the least promising object the hope—if not the certainty—of interest; now, she left her carriage with the quiet indifference to outward circumstance that acquaintance with society teaches. Unconsciously she had learned to move as the women of the world move—the women who know themselves possessed of a certain value, and are faintly flattered, faintly amused, perhaps faintly wearied by the knowledge.

As she walked down the platform a momentary glimmering of disappointment crossed her face; and she turned to Simonetta who had come hurrying towards her.

"I thought Lady Frances would have met us," she said. "But I suppose she is waiting at the flat."

Simonetta looked up solicitously at her mistress. "And the signora?" she hazarded. "She is not tired?"

Clodagh smiled a little absently.

"Oh no, Simonetta! You must not trouble about me. I have come home, you know!" She gave a little laugh. "But we must not delay," she added. "Have you the keys of all the boxes?"

"Yes, signora."

"Then you can see to the examining of the luggage. When it is done, this porter will put you into a cab. I have given him the address."

"Yes, signora."

"Then I shall see you at the flat?"

"Yes, signora."

Clodagh smiled again; and, turning away, wended her way through the crowd of passengers surrounded by eager relatives and friends.

Reaching the courtyard of the station, she unostentatiously hailed a hansom, and, having given her new address to the cabman, took her seat. A moment later, the cab swung out into London—became one with the concourse of traffic that, in the season, seems to overflow the streets. For the instant Clodagh felt herself merged in the teeming life, which the open doors of the vehicle permitted to approach so nearly; for the instant she stifled the sense of isolation that had been slowly gathering force. And, leaning forward in her seat, fixed her attention upon the passing scene.

Across Trafalgar Square, up Waterloo Place, and into the traffic of Piccadilly she was borne with exhilarating speed—the cabman avoiding with extreme dexterity the throng of carriages, motor cars, and omnibuses that seemed momentarily to increase. To Clodagh, sitting rigidly attentive, the scene appeared like an impressive pageant—a pageant of magnificent wealth and abundant prosperity, a splendid, characteristic picture, in which the budding English trees, the imposing English clubs, the gorgeous English equipages, and the beautiful English women made up the background and the central figures. It was the great procession of a life she had seen only in imagination; and as her curious eyes drank in its details, she found herself almost mechanically repeating in her mind the formula to which for the past two months she had clung with passionate persistence.

"I *will* live! I *will* enjoy!"

For the two months this had been her philosophy. Unconsciously, it had been her philosophy since the night in Paris, when, in one hour, her castle of imagination had fallen about her feet, and she had stood, as it were, houseless. In that brief space of time she had realised that she had been inhabiting a fool's paradise. A fool's paradise! The name had seemed curiously apt; and through the long, dark hours of that hateful night her cheeks had burned as she recalled how she had peopled her enchanted realm, while all the time its unconscious creator had forgotten its creation— or remembered it only as one self-righteous act among many. Lady Frances Hope was right! Deerehurst had been right! Barnard had been right! Ideals were a mistake—things made to be shattered, as hopes were made to be broken! To live—to live fully, heedlessly, extravagantly—was the only wisdom. Gore had spoken truly! She had been a fool. She had been wrong in supposing that she had a debt to work off; on the contrary, life was her debtor. It was she who had a score against life!

In this fever of mind, she had written the letters that sent Nance on her interrupted journey to America; cancelled her invitation to her aunt and cousin to stay with her in England; and set her own feet on the road to the south. And in the weeks that followed, the same fever had burned in her blood. During the preparations for the Riviera and during the journey to Nice, she had been possessed by a frenzy of energy. She had craved for incessant action and excitement with a pertinacity that had seemed insatiable.

And in the crowded Casino at Monte Carlo she had at last attained her object—she had at last succeeded in losing herself; there, day after day, night after night, she had sat in the stifling, scented atmosphere, listening to the incessant, significant click of gold and silver, watching the artificial light glare down upon the hideously artificial faces pressed in densely packed circles round the long green tables. The place had fascinated her with its outward immobility, its hidden sea of greedy passion. It was, she had fiercely told herself, life!

After six weeks, Lady Frances Hope had announced her intention of returning to London. But Clodagh had implored her to postpone her departure for another week; and when she had laughingly declared the delay impossible, had announced her own determination to remain on alone—a determination which no argument of her companion's had been powerful enough to alter.

And now, after nearly eight weeks spent between Monte Carlo and Nice, she was returning to take up her residence in a London flat, chosen for her by Lady Frances.

Her brain felt feverishly active as the cab, having skirted the park railings from Hyde Park Corner to Knightsbridge, turned into the square courtyard belonging to the large, quiet building where she was to find her home.

Descending quickly, she entered the big doorway and glanced curiously at her new surroundings. The vestibule was imposing, but a little lonely. And although the hall porter came almost immediately to her assistance, and listened attentively to the information that she was the new tenant of the second floor flat, and that her maid and her luggage were following in another cab, his impersonal air daunted her. She was annoyed—and almost frightened—by the sudden, poignant desire that assailed her to see even one familiar face.

However, she listened in her own turn to the polite assurance that all was in readiness for her arrival; and in due course she passed sedately to the lift, and was borne upwards.

As she stepped out upon the richly carpeted passage that led to her own door, she looked round in the half-formed expectation that Lady Frances Hope might be waiting for her outside her rooms; but almost at once she dismissed the idea. English people were not demonstrative! She would find Lady Frances awaiting her beside a cosy tea-table—or a bright fire! With the haste of anticipation, she crossed the corridor, and pressed the electric bell.

There was a slight delay before the summons was answered; then the door was opened by a well-dressed, unemotional-looking maid.

Clodagh stepped forward.

"I am Mrs. Milbanke—your mistress," she said quickly.

The woman looked at her without curiosity.

"Will you kindly walk in, madam?" she said. "I hope you will find everything in order."

A chill—a chill that painfully suggested home-sickness—fell upon Clodagh; but she thrust it resentfully aside and entered the pretty panelled hall of the flat.

"Where is Lady Frances Hope?" she asked, pausing just inside the threshold.

The maid came forward respectfully, but without enthusiasm.

"Her ladyship has not been here to-day, madam. Can I attend to you, madam, until your maid arrives?"

Clodagh stood very still. She was conscious of a horrible, inordinate disappointment; but aware that the servant's eyes were still upon her, she rallied her self-control.

"Thanks!" she said. "I shan't want anything but a cup of tea. Bring me some tea to my own room. Did Lady Frances Hope leave no message?"

"No message, madam."

The maid hesitated for an instant longer; then, feeling herself dismissed, moved noiselessly away to the servant's quarters.

Left alone, Clodagh stood irresolute. This was her home! Her eyes wandered round the hall, from the walls of which the pictures of the former tenant looked down as though they criticised the intruder. This was her home coming! A home coming devoid of one friendly hand, one welcoming word! Unable to quell the passion of loneliness that swelled within her, she turned blindly and opened the door that stood nearest to her.

It was the dining-room that she had chanced upon—a charming white-panelled room, furnished with Sheraton furniture. But in her present mood, its graceful severity failed to please her; to her lonely gaze it had an uninhabited look—it seemed almost to resemble a very perfect room upon the stage. Drawing back hastily, she closed the door; and, moving down the hall, entered another room.

This proved to be her own bedroom—a bright, high-ceiled apartment decorated and furnished in old French fashion and possessing two large windows, looking upon Hyde Park. But here again she was confronted by the sensation of unfamiliarity. And as she paused just inside the door, looking from the long windows to the stately bed, she was suddenly and completely dominated by her feelings. In a tempestuous wave of emotion, her hunger for happiness rose menacingly, while the tide of her philosophy suddenly ebbed. In that moment, as she stood alone in the wide room, she swayed between trust in her own heart and faith in the world's healing power. Then, as so frequently happens, the world snatched the laurels before they had been held out.

With the same unmoved demeanour, the maid who had admitted her, appeared at the door.

"If you please, madam, the housemaid tells me that her ladyship *did* send a note for you this morning. You'll find it on the dressing-table."

At the woman's words, Clodagh started, and her whole face coloured and changed. Hurrying across the room, she saw the letter, picked it up, and tore it open.

"Dearest Clodagh," she read.

"I must seem a perfect beast. But my old Aunt Deborah—with whom I can't afford to quarrel!—has announced her stupid intention of spending a day in town. And of course it must be this day of all days! *Do* be a darling and show you forgive me by coming round to dine at eight-thirty. Lord Deerehurst returned yesterday from the famous two months' rest-cure, looking younger than ever. He and Val will be here to-night. Bridge after dinner. Don't fail to come.

"Yours,

"F. H."

As Clodagh read the last line of the letter, she lifted her head, and turned with a quick gesture to the maid who was waiting by the door.

"I want a fire lighted here and my tea brought to me immediately it is ready," she cried in a changed voice. "And send my maid in directly she arrives. I'm dining out!"

Without waiting for a reply, she crossed the room and paused beside one of the windows, looking down upon the park. Her spirits had risen; her excitement had been rekindled; she had been saved from the companionship she had learned to dread—companionship with herself.

# CHAPTER IV

Lady Frances Hope's house was situated in Curzon Street; and thither Clodagh departed shortly after eight o'clock.

Again she chose a hansom as a means of conveyance, for as yet there had been no question of her procuring a carriage of her own; and again she became conscious of the peculiar stimulus, the peculiar power that the great tide of London life exercises upon its observers. The last glimmering of daylight was lingering in the sky as the cab passed up Knightsbridge, but already the houses and hotels were brilliantly lighted, and the stream of diners and theatre-goers was forming into its nightly procession.

During that short drive, she encountered many glances—glances of interest, criticism or curiosity from women well-dressed as herself and bound upon some such mission as her own—glances of sharp speculation or sudden admiration from men driving, west or southward. And something of London's immensity, something of London's secrecy, came to her in those brief moments; she was stirred by the fact that has moved many another dweller in the vast city—the fact that every day, every night, some thousands of lives brush our own in a passing glance, in a stray word, in a chance touch, and then drift on into mystery, never to reappear.

Her thoughts were confused and excited as she descended from the cab and entered the Curzon Street house; but on the moment that she stepped into the hall, her dreams were banished. A door on her right opened, and her hostess hurried forward and kissed her effusively.

"You dear thing!" she cried. "Wasn't it abominable of me? Was the arrival desperately weary? Come up to my bedroom. The men haven't come yet. What ages it seems since we said good-bye at Nice! How are you?" She talked in her masterful voice, without waiting for a reply, until they entered the bedroom. There her maid, who was busying herself at the dressing-table, came forward to assist Clodagh; but Lady Frances checked her at once.

"Mrs. Milbanke won't need you, Rees. I'll take off her cloak."

Rees moved obediently towards the door; but there she ventured to pause for a moment.

"I hope you had a comfortable journey, madam," she said.

Clodagh, invariably gracious to her inferiors, turned to her warmly.

"Thank you, Rees! An excellent journey! But I'm glad to see everybody look so well." She added the last with a little smile, to which the maid responded as she closed the door.

Lady Frances laughed.

"You have bewitched Rees!" she said. "But you do that as you eat or sleep—by instinct. Let me look at you!" She laid her hands on Clodagh's shoulders and turned her towards the light.

"You've been playing every night since I left you," she said with decision.

Clodagh laughed with some constraint.

"And losing?"

Clodagh flushed.

"I have no luck," she said shortly. Then, almost at once, she turned away, freeing herself from her companion's detaining hands.

"Lady Frances," she said in a different tone, "please don't think I forget about—about——" she hesitated. "I get my first allowance at the beginning of July, you know——"

She paused; and Lady Frances gave a seemingly careless laugh. "My good child, don't speak of it! Any time!—any time!"

"You are very kind. I had hoped to settle up on my return, but the last week was shocking. But everything will be right at the beginning of July. She walked over to the dressing-table and looked at herself in the long glass.

"What a sweet house you have!" she said suddenly in an entirely different voice.

Lady Frances had been watching her with a close scrutiny; but now, with a good deal of ready dissimulation, she threw off her attentive manner and answered in Clodagh's own light tone.

"Yes; it is a nice little place. But what about the flat? Isn't that perfect?"

"Yes."

"You are not enthusiastic? Oh, I *am* disappointed!"

Clodagh turned from the mirror.

"Forgive me!" she said impulsively. "Of course the flat is perfectly sweet—and exactly what I want. It was just the arriving alone that made it seem a little—a little——"

"Of course!—of course! Poor dear child! But wait!—wait till you begin to know people!"

Clodagh's expressive face brightened.

"Yes. And when Nance—when my sister comes back! Oh! I *must* enjoy myself! I *must* be happy!"

"Why should you be anything else? When have you heard from your sister?"

"The day I left Nice—a most dear letter. She is having a heavenly time in America. The Estcoits are such delightful companions; the girl is seven months younger than she is—and the boy is seven years older. Curious difference, isn't it?"

"Very. But I didn't know there was a boy. I thought it was only the school friend and the mother."

"Oh no! There's the brother—Pierce. Nance's letters are full of him."

Lady Frances gave a little half-sarcastic laugh.

"Then Nance is presumably still learning—though she has left school?"

Something in the utterance of the words made Clodagh flush.

"Don't!" she said involuntarily—"don't! Nance is—is different from me."

Then, as her hostess remained silent, she turned and looked at her.

"Don't be offended!" she added. "It is only that I can't have anything cynical said of Nance. I know you don't understand. It seems that because I sent her to America, I don't really care— —" She halted again.

"But I don't make you understand!—I don't seem to make any one understand." Her voice dropped slightly; and Lady Frances, as though fearing some emotional outburst, broke in hastily.

"My dear child!—my dear Clodagh!" Then she paused, for the door opened and her maid Rees reappeared.

"Excuse me, my lady! But Lord Deerehurst and Mr. Serracauld are in the drawing-room. Franks thought your ladyship would wish to know."

"Quite right. Thank you, Rees! Clodagh, are you ready?"

Clodagh's face was slightly flushed from her momentary outbreak, as she left the bedroom. Descending the stairs, Lady Frances moved to her side and passed her hand through her arm: and at the touch, a sharp repulsion to this friendship—this fair weather, effusive, superficial friendship—surged through her. And yet where was she to find a firmer sentiment? Where, in all the world, was there a being who had any real need of her? Her aunt? Her cousin? She knew instinctively that their world and her own were inevitably sundered. Nance? Had not even Nance—the little Nance of childish days—

already begun to gather interests of her own—to form her own friendships? No; there was no niche that especially claimed, that especially needed her!

At this point in her hasty and confused speculations, the door of the drawing-room was thrown open: and, after an interval of two years, she saw Lord Deerehurst and Serracauld.

More than once she had pictured the meeting with the old peer; but, as is invariably the case, the reality was much more vivid than the imagination had been. Deerehurst came forward with the stiff, courtly manner that brought back with almost painful clearness the balcony of the Venetian palace—the Venetian salon with its polished floor and glittering chandeliers—the Venetian night-music borne across the waters. It all surged back in a wave of memory—first a pang of pain, then a pang of reckless self-contempt. After all, who cared? What did her action—her manner of living—even her existence—matter to any living soul? She held out her hand and allowed him to bow over it.

He bowed over it for a long time; then he raised his head and looked at her. His pale, inscrutable face was as waxlike as ever; his eyes were as cold, as penetrating, as old in their look of supreme wisdom.

"So we meet again," he said. "My hope has been fulfilled!"

For a moment Clodagh stood, permitting him to clasp her fingers and look into her face, while she herself made no effort to speak; then, as if suddenly conscious of something strange in the position, she freed her hand with a little, nervous laugh, and turned to where Serracauld was waiting to greet her.

With a smile and a gesture of easy familiarity the younger man came forward.

"Welcome to England!" he said. "Only yesterday a man at my club was telling me of the prettiest woman on the Riviera this year. I won't be personal, but the lady was at Monte Carlo only a week ago—turning other people's heads and emptying her own pockets with the most delightful impartiality."

Clodagh laughed, but this time without embarrassment.

"Be as personal as you like!" she said carelessly. "It wasn't my fault if luck was dead against me."

Deerehurst came forward slowly.

"But the turned heads?" he asked.

She smiled.

"Was it my business to put them straight again? I'm not a surgeon."

They all laughed; and at that moment dinner was announced.

Lady Frances Hope touched Clodagh's arm.

"Lord Deerehurst will play host, Clodagh! Val, I consign myself to you!"

Serracauld moved to her side with his usual indolent ease; and Deerehurst offered Clodagh his arm.

They had to traverse the length of a large double drawing-room before the dining-room was reached. And during that passage he found opportunity for a whispered word or two. As they moved forward he avoided looking at Clodagh; but his arm slightly and unmistakably pressed hers.

"Am I not forgiving—to be so glad to see you?" he murmured in his thin, cold voice. "I waited on the terrace until twelve o'clock, that night in Venice."

Involuntarily her face flushed. His voice was as potent as ever to express infinitely more than the words it uttered.

"I—I wish to forget Venice," she said.

He stole a swift glance at her.

"Then shall we make a compact? Shall we forget it jointly?"

She said nothing.

Again, almost imperceptibly, his arm pressed hers.

"Why try to ignore me? I am in your life."

The words were few and very simple: so simple and so few that they conveyed a peculiar impression of power—of weight.

A faint, half-comprehended chill fell upon Clodagh; such a chill as had fallen upon her once before in the "Abbati" Restaurant, when Deerehurst had drunk to their next meeting as host and guest.

She laughed suddenly, with a quick, nervous lifting of the head.

"But it is life itself that I wish to ignore."

Again he glanced at her—very swiftly, very searchingly.

"So be it!" he said. "I take that as a challenge—to life and to me."

At the conclusion of dinner that night, the little party of four sat down to bridge. And an hour after midnight Clodagh rose from the card-table, a loser to the extent of over forty pounds.

# CHAPTER V

On a certain morning in the last week in June, Lady Frances Hope rode into the courtyard of the Knightsbridge flats. Throwing her bridle to the man-servant who was attending her, she dismounted from her horse, gathered up her habit, and entered the doorway of the building.

Seating herself in the lift, she was borne upwards, and a few seconds later stepped out upon the second floor, and, going briskly forward, pressed the bell of Clodagh's hall door.

The summons was answered by the same maid who had admitted Clodagh on the day of her arrival; and seeing the visitor, she drew back instantly, throwing the door wide.

"Is Mrs. Milbanke up, Barkes?" Lady Frances asked. "I did not see her in the park this morning."

"Mrs. Milbanke didn't ride this morning, my lady. She is having breakfast in her own room. Shall I say your ladyship is here?"

Lady Frances replied by walking into the hall.

"No, thanks! I'll announce myself."

Stepping forward without ceremony she passed down the hall and opened the door of Clodagh's bedroom. But on the threshold she paused, interested by what she saw.

The two windows that looked upon the park were wide open, and through them the beautiful warm sunshine was pouring across the room, touching the old French furniture into a renewal of its glories. Drawn into the full radiance of this light, stood a small round table set with silver, china, and a bowl of flowers; and at the table sat Clodagh. She was wearing a simple dress of black muslin, and her hair—which gleamed almost bronze in the clear, strong sunshine—was twisted into one thick coil. But it was neither her dress nor appearance that attracted her visitor; it was something vaguely disturbing—something subtly suggestive—in her attitude, as she sat close to the table, an array of letters and papers spread before her, a gold pencil held thoughtfully against her lips.

Thinking it was a servant who had entered the room, she did not change her position with the opening of the door; and Lady Frances Hope had a full minute in which to observe her; then, having made her deductions, she allowed her presence to be known.

"Can you tolerate such an early visitor?" she asked.

Clodagh started almost guiltily, and drew the array of papers into a confused heap; then she rose hastily, laughing to cover her momentary confusion.

"How you frightened me!" she said. "I must be developing nerves. But come in! I am delighted!"

She went forward with apparent cordiality, and, taking her visitor's hand, kissed her.

"How nice and energetic you look! You make me feel very lazy. I wasn't in the mood for a ride this morning. Come in! Sit down!"

Lady Frances responded to the suggestion by moving across the room. Pausing by the breakfast-table, she bent forward and buried her face for a moment in the flowers, at the same time stealing a swift glance at the scattered letters beside Clodagh's plate. Then, straightening herself again with apparent nonchalance, she moved to the open window and stood looking down upon the park.

"Clodagh!" she said suddenly. "Are you busy? Can we talk?"

Clodagh turned sharply, and almost with a gesture of surprise. The whole round of her intercourse with Lady Frances Hope had been of so easy, of so superficial a nature—the whole tone of their friendship had been pitched in so unemotional a key—since the one night in the Paris hotel, when they had touched upon things vital to them both—that the suggestion of reality, or even gravity, brought a sudden uneasiness to her mind.

"Oh, of course!" she said uncertainly—"of course! Let us sit down."

She returned to her own seat and indicated another to her visitor with a slightly hurried movement.

But Lady Frances did not respond to the invitation. Instead, she wandered back to the table, and again bent over the bowl of flowers.

"Why are we always climbing—only to slip back again?" she asked irrelevantly.

Again a faint uneasiness touched Clodagh's face.

"I thought you enjoyed climbing."

"Not to-day. Clodagh, you'll think me a horrid nuisance, but it's about that money— —"

She paused as she said the word, and involuntarily her quick glance passed once more over the papers on the table.

For a second Clodagh remained silent; then she spoke, a little slowly—a little haltingly.

"Oh yes—the money," she said.

Lady Frances looked at her shrewdly.

"Yes, you remember on Tuesday—when you borrowed that sixty pounds to pay old Lady Shrawle—I said I could wait for everything till August."

"Yes—oh yes!"

"Well, I've had a horrid drop since then—yesterday, in fact."

For a moment longer, Clodagh sat staring aimlessly at the papers in front of her; then she raised her head and looked at her companion. Her face was a little pale, but her eyes and lips looked almost scornfully unconcerned.

"Poor you!" she said easily. "What a bore! You must let me settle up our differences at once—to-day."

She rose and pushed back her chair.

A look of surprise crossed the older woman's face—this time it was surprise tempered with bewilderment.

"To-day! But can you? I know how many little expenses— —" She waved her hand expressively towards the breakfast-table, with its many costly adjuncts.

Clodagh made a lofty gesture of denial; and, walking across the room, paused beside her bureau.

For a minute there was no sound in the room save the abrupt opening and shutting of one or two small drawers; then Clodagh turned round again, a cheque-book in her hand.

"Now tell me what I owe you," she said. "I'll write you a cheque and post-date it to July the first. Will that do? I draw my money then, you know."

"Perfectly. But, my dear Clodagh— —"

But again Clodagh made a gesture that seemed to relegate the matter to a region of obscure—if not of absolutely contemptible—things.

"Don't trouble!" she said. "Money is never worth an argument. What do I owe?"

The Gambler | 239

During her words, her companion had sat silent—speculative and suspicious. To her worldly mind, Clodagh's grand manner—Clodagh's extraordinary behaviour—indicated but one possibility. She had found means of augmenting her income!

Any knowledge of the false pride, the empty magnificence that will, metaphorically speaking, fling its last coin to a beggar, while passing on to penury, had never come within her experience. It needs the environments of such places as Orristown to bring them to maturity. She looked now at her companion, and her eyes narrowed in a sudden, triumphant satisfaction. Something that she had anticipated had come to pass! At the imagined discovery, she gave a quick laugh.

"If you insist on being so scrupulous——"

Clodagh looked round from the bureau at which she had seated herself.

"How much?" she said laconically.

Lady Frances pretended to knit her brows.

"Well, there was the eight hundred pounds at Nice—and the forty pounds the night of your return to town—the night we played bridge with Val and Deerehurst——"

She looked very quickly at Clodagh.

But Clodagh gave no sign. "And the fifty pounds a fortnight ago—besides the sixty for Lady Shrawle," she interrupted.

"Yes—oh yes! Let me see, that makes——"

"Nine hundred and fifty pounds," Clodagh interjected in a very quiet voice; and picking up a pen, she wrote out the cheque, signing it with her usual bold signature. A moment later she rose, blotted it, and held it out.

As the flimsy slip of paper passed from one to the other, the elder woman permitted a gleam of curiosity to show in her eyes.

"A thousand thanks!" she exclaimed. "And don't think me a wretch if I run away now that I've got it. You know how fidgety my bay mare is. Well, good-bye! I shall see you at Ranelagh?"

But Clodagh was absently studying her cheque-book.

"I don't think so," she said. "Lord Deerehurst offered to take me down, but I shan't go. I—I have some business to attend to."

Lady Frances laughed; picked up her riding whip, which she had laid aside, and, coming forward, kissed Clodagh.

"Then I expect I shall see you. Deerehurst is much more insistent than any business." Once again her shrewd glance travelled over Clodagh's face. "Good-bye! In any case, you'll be at the Ord's for bridge to-night? We can arrange then about going down to Tuffnell."

"Yes"—Clodagh returned the pressure of her hand—"yes; I suppose I shall go to the Ord's. Yes; I shall—good-bye!"

She walked with her visitor to the door of the bedroom, and stood waiting on the threshold until the hall door had closed. Then, almost mechanically, she turned, walked back to the table, and with a sharp, nervous movement gathered up the heap of papers still lying beside her plate.

As she stood there, in the flood of June sunshine, beside the attractive disarray of the pretty breakfast-table, she was aware of a horrible sense of helplessness, of alarm and impotence. For the papers she held between her hands were bills—a sheaf of bills—all unpaid and all pressing.

As she stood there, a swift review of the past months sped before her mind, carrying something like dismay in its train.

In April she had entered upon the tenancy of her furnished flat, having already borrowed eight hundred pounds from her friend and counsellor, Lady Frances Hope; and under the auspices of this same counsellor, had began her career as a woman of fashion.

In social circles the period and the conditions of mourning become more slender every season. And nowadays, although a widow may not attend dances or large dinner-parties, there are a hundred smaller, more exclusive—and possibly more expensive—forms of entertainment at which she may appear in her own intimate set. Very quiet dinners—very small luncheon parties—even friendly bridge parties—are quite permissible, when it is a tacitly accepted fact that the mourner is, by a natural law, barely entering upon her life—that the one mourned has departed from it by an equally natural dispensation.

Under these conditions Clodagh had begun her London career; and for more than a month she had lived—in the most costly sense of the word. Her mourning had been the most distinguished that a famous dressmaker could devise; her electric brougham had possessed all the newest improvements; the flowers that filled her room had been supplied by a fashionable florist at an exorbitant cost. In a word, she had behaved like a child who has been given a pocketful of bright new pennies—and believes them to be golden coins.

Once or twice in the course of those extravagant weeks, a pang of misgiving had crossed her soul; but it had only been a pang of the moment.

The phantom of tradesmen's bills is one so easily dismissed from the Irish mind that, unless it materialises very forcibly, it may almost be considered non-existent.

On July the first she was to receive her half-yearly allowance; and towards July the first she looked with an almost superstitious confidence. A thousand pounds! It was sufficient to settle a planetful of debts; and if any remained as satellites to the planet, well—there was the first of January.

But now her confidence had been rudely shaken. In a sudden moment of pride—of bravado—she had signed away almost the whole of the anticipated half-yearly income. She stood possessed of fifty pounds, with which to dress, to eat, to exist from July to January; and in her hands was the sheaf of unpaid bills!

There is no race of people that undertakes liabilities so lightly, and that is so overwhelmed when retribution falls upon it, as the Irish race. As Clodagh gradually faced her position, panic seized upon her. For weeks she had lived upon the credit that the London tradesman gives to customers who come provided with good references; and now suddenly she had realised—first by the arrival of certain bills couched in a new and imperative strain; later by Lady Frances Hope's unexpected demand for her money—that English credit is not the lax, indefinite credit of such places as Muskeere and Carrigmore: that it is a credit demanding—insisting upon—timely payment.

And where was she to turn—where look—for the necessary funds?

In a dazed way she thought of David Barnard, who had returned a month previously from a holiday in Spain; but her pride made her shrink sensitively from the thought of the suave indulgence with which he would listen to her confession of folly. Once the thought of recalling Lady Frances Hope, and explaining the position to her, sped through her mind; but she dismissed it as swiftly as it came. In restless perturbation she turned and walked across the room, pausing once more beside the bureau, which stood in a recess between the windows.

Where could she turn, where look, for the money that would tide over her difficulties? In her mental distraction, she laid aside the bills she was still holding, and aimlessly picked up a half-dozen opened letters that lay awaiting answers. A couple of invitations to lunch; an invitation to play bridge; the offer of a box at the opera; Laurence Asshlin's monthly report from Orristown; Nance's last letter from America.

With a vague preoccupation she raised the last of these and looked at it.

How free and unhampered Nance seemed in her inexperience of life! She looked unseeingly at the closely written lines, her mind in a harassed way contrasting her own and her sister's fate. Then quite suddenly she dropped the letter and lifted her head.

A thought had struck her. As a flash of lightning might rend a night sky, an inspiration had illuminated the darkness of her mind. The thousand pounds which was to be Nance's property when she came of age, or upon her engagement, still lay to her own credit—in her own name—in the bank with which Milbanke had done business.

It is extraordinary how rapidly a thought can mature in a receptive mind. In one moment, as Clodagh stood beside the bureau, all the possibilities comprised in that thousand pounds broke upon her understanding.

How if she withdrew it as a loan? No one—not even Nance herself—need know; and she could refund it within six months, or within a year—long before the thought of marriage could enter the child's mind.

Then suddenly she paused in her mental calculations; and a new expression passed over her face. Was it right, was it honourable, to make use of this money left in her safe-keeping?

Uneasy and distressed, she turned to the open window, as though a study of the life beyond her own might help her in her dilemma. The scene she looked upon was interesting and even beautiful. The grass of the park still retained something of its first greenness; in the distance the clustering bower of chestnuts and copper beeches suggested something far removed from the traffic and toil of the great town; while below the window, under a canopy of leaves, the morning procession of horses and carriages passed incessantly to and fro.

What a curious world it was! How conventional and obvious, and yet in reality how inscrutable! What would it say of her, did it know her true position? What comfort—what aid—would it offer? Involuntarily, almost curiously, she laid her finger-tips upon the window-sill and bent slightly forward. Then, very suddenly, she drew back into the room, her face flushing.

Lord Deerehurst, mounted upon a high black horse, had passed the window at the moment that she had looked out; and raising his head, had seen and bowed to her.

The incident was slight; but at certain moments the Celtic nature is extraordinarily—even mysteriously—open to suggestion. Clodagh could not have defined her thought; but the thought was there, a vague, half-fearful, wholly instinctive thought that suddenly prompted her to shield herself, to ward off the nearer approach to this world that she had leant from her window to study impersonally; and from which she had received so peculiarly personal a response.

She continued to stand for a moment longer in an attitude of doubt; then, swiftly, almost abruptly, she turned round to the bureau and, kneeling down before it, reopened her cheque-book with tremulous hands and wrote out a cheque for one thousand pounds, payable to herself.

# CHAPTER VI

The habit of self-deception had become as a cloak in which Clodagh wrapped herself. She desired happiness: therefore she told herself that she was happy; she instinctively wished to live honourably: therefore, through her own persuasion, she believed her actions to be honourable. And under this insidiously sheltering garment, her appropriation of her sister's money was securely hidden away. To her own thinking—once the first misgiving had been buried—there was no real wrong, no real dishonour, in the taking of the thousand pounds. She needed it temporarily, and would, in due time, repay it with interest. The fact that she did not think it necessary to inform Nance of what she had done, certainly weakens the case for her defence; but had she come to be judged from some impersonal source, it is quite possible she would have made as subtle and specious a justification of her conduct as that which she offered to herself. In this light, the act stood recorded in her own conscience. She needed the money; she took the money; and having taken it, she set about banishing the recollection of it from her mind.

For three days after she had signed the cheque, she retired into semi-privacy. She was at home to no one; and although she continued to ride each morning and drive each afternoon in the park, she did so with so cold a demeanour that none of her friends had dared to accost her! For three nights she stayed indoors alone; but on the fourth, the insurmountable restlessness that settles so frequently upon the high-spirited woman devoid of home ties, seized on her remorselessly. The thought of further solitude became unendurable—the idea of another lonely evening something not to be borne. At eight o'clock she rose from her solitary dinner, tingling in every nerve for some companionship; and telephoning to Curzon Street, ascertained that Lady Frances Hope was at home and willing to see her. And a quarter of an hour later she stepped from her brougham at the door of the familiar house.

She was informed that Lady Frances was in her own room, preparing to go out, but would be glad to see her if she would come upstairs. She acquiesced quickly; and before the servant could conduct her down the hall, had brushed past him and begun to run up the stairs.

Opening the door of her friend's bedroom, she paused on the threshold, and gave a little exclamation of admiration. Lady Frances Hope was standing before a long mirror, while the maid Rees knelt upon the ground beside her, giving the finishing touches to the skirt of a strikingly beautiful dress.

Clodagh clasped her hands in a gesture of delight; then ran forward into the room.

"How splendid you look!" she cried. "Where are you going? What a heavenly dress!"

Lady Frances smiled.

"At last!" she exclaimed, holding out her cheek to be kissed. "What have you been doing with yourself? I have been persecuted with inquiries for you."

Clodagh laughed excitedly.

"I have been paying bills!" she said in a high, light voice.

"So that you may begin to run up new ones?"

"Quite possibly! But where are you going? All this magnificence makes me curious." She sank into a low chair and glanced with bright, interested eyes at her stately companion.

But Lady Frances ignored her question.

"We shall soon be finished with all vain glories!" she said. "The season is dying—even if it's dying hard. Do you pine for the country, now that the heat has come? I shall expect you to love Tuffnell, you know. It really is quaint! Even I am fond of it."

Clodagh looked up eagerly.

"Of course I shall love Tuffnell. It has been sweet of your sister to ask me there—but it has been sweeter still of her to ask Nance. You don't know what it will be for me to meet Nance down there—away from everything." Her voice fell a little.

Lady Frances laughed pleasantly.

"I am so glad you have arranged that she should come right on from Liverpool, instead of staying in town for a night," she said easily. "It will be much the simpler plan. By the way, what day will we arrange to go down? You and I, I mean? Diana's big dance is on the fifth. Suppose we go down a day or two before?"

Clodagh responded instantly.

"Yes," she said—"yes, certainly. But talking of the dance reminds me of my curiosity. Where *are* you going to-night?"

This time evasion was impossible. Lady Frances turned to the dressing-table and picked up a diamond ornament.

"You can fix this in, Rees," she said, "and then go. I am going to the Tamperleighs'," she added carelessly, without looking at Clodagh.

"The Tamperleighs'?"

"In Grosvenor Place. Dull people."

Clodagh picked up a fan that was lying on a table near her, and examined it thoughtfully.

"Isn't Lady Tamperleigh an aunt of Sir Walter Gore's?"

"Yes; and old Lord Tamperleigh is a cousin of my mother's—which connects Walter and me in a roundabout way."

There was a slight silence, while Rees hovered about her mistress with one or two last attentions and then quietly left the room. As she closed the door, Clodagh looked up from the fan she had been studying so attentively.

"Lady Frances," she said quickly, "you know Lady Tamperleigh very well?"

Lady Frances' eyes became vigilant.

"Yes," she said vaguely—"oh, yes!"

"Then take me with you to her party—as you took me to the Hensleys' and the Vibrants' last week? I'm wild to go somewhere—to go anywhere to-night." She paused excitedly; then, as her eyes scanned Lady Frances's face, her expression fell.

"Of course if there's the least—the very least—difficulty——"

With a swift, tactful movement, Lady Frances came towards her.

"My dear Clodagh! Don't! You *know* how proud I am of you. My hesitation was merely——"

"Merely what?"

Lady Frances laid her hand upon Clodagh's shoulder.

"Walter came back from Russia a week ago. He will be there to-night; and I think—I think"—she seemed to hesitate—"I think that perhaps, in view of his narrow ideas, it might be pleasanter for you——" She left the sentence expressively unfinished.

Clodagh rose rather hastily, her face red.

"Of course!" she said—"of course! Sir Walter Gore is the last man in London I should wish to meet."

Lady Frances said nothing, but moving calmly across the room, took her cloak from a chair.

"Where can I drop you?" she asked. "At the club?"

For a second Clodagh stood, staring with very bright eyes at an open window, across which a lace curtain hung motionless in the still, hot air; then she lifted her head and, in her own turn, crossed the room.

"Yes," she said quietly—"yes, at the club."

Not many days later, Clodagh—in company with Lady Frances Hope— left London for Buckinghamshire, on her promised visit to the latter's sister—Lady Diana Tuffnell.

The house party at Tuffnell Place was to include—beside one or two men and women of personal distinction—a small section of Lady Frances Hope's coterie from the merely fashionable world, comprising Lord Deerehurst, Serracauld, and Mrs. Bathurst. For although Lady Diana Tuffnell was very uncompromising in the choice of her own friends, she had always been a complacent sister; and Tuffnell Place generally opened its doors during the month of July to Lady Frances Hope and her intimates.

It was late in the evening when Clodagh arrived; and the old Elizabethan house, with its many windows of thick, small-paned glass and its fine oak-raftered hall, filled her with delight. After she had been greeted by Lady Diana, and introduced to Mr. Tuffnell—a typical, kindly English squire, who invariably went his own way straightly and was content to assume that others did the same—she passed up the shallow staircase and entered the room that had been allotted to her, with a sense of something nearer to happiness than she had known for months. In the whole air of the house and its inmates there was a suggestion of restfulness, of friendliness, of sincerity to which she had been long a stranger. Unconsciously she warmed and softened under the homelike atmosphere. And when, a quarter of an hour later, Simonetta came softly into the bright, chintz-hung bedroom, she found her mistress busily unpacking her writing-case and sorting her letters at an old-fashioned oak writing-table.

That night the two visitors—who had preceded the other members of the house party by a day—dined alone with their host and hostess.

They were a very small party for the great dining-hall; but Clodagh was conscious that at many a crowded restaurant she would have been less well amused. There was a feeling of sincerity in the atmosphere, an honest desire on the part of the entertainers to put their guest at her ease, that precluded dulness and artificiality.

After dinner, Lady Frances wandered off to the billiard-room with her brother-in-law, and Clodagh followed her hostess into the drawing-room—a long, tapestried room full of the scent of roses.

The lamps were lighting when they entered; but the windows were set wide open, admitting the fragrance of the garden. Involuntarily Clodagh crossed the room, and paused beside one of these broad windows.

A moment later her hostess followed her.

"Well, Mrs. Milbanke," she said, "what do you think of England? Isn't it a place to be happy in?" She spoke with something of the strength and domination of her sister; but it was a softened strength, as her face, although possessing the same bold outline as Lady Frances's, was softer, gentler, more sympathetic.

Clodagh turned and looked at her.

"I think it is a place to be *content* in," she said after a moment's pause.

Lady Diana Tuirnell's glance rested upon her interestedly. And, as the thought of her youth and her mourning rose to her mind, something like pity touched her face.

"You are very right!" she said. "We women make a great mistake in dissociating happiness and contentment. There is too much struggle in many of our lives, and too little peace. Frances, for instance! Her life is one restless race after something that is unattainable!"

"But Lady Frances is happy! She likes struggling!"

Lady Diana smiled.

"She thinks she does. But the truly contented woman does not need to persuade herself that she is satisfied. Happiness is a fact, not an attainment." With a quiet, kindly movement she turned aside and picked up two photographs that stood upon a side-table.

"Mrs. Milbanke, this is the happiness that comes—and stays. The happiness that needs no expounding." She held out the photographs.

Clodagh took them and looked at them. One was the picture of her host; the other the photograph of three plain-looking, honest-eyed boys, who each possessed in an almost ridiculous degree their mother's outline of feature. She looked at them intently for a long time; then she handed them back.

"Thank you!" she said almost inaudibly. Then, moved by a sudden thought, she looked up into Lady Diana's face.

"Lady Diana," she said, "I want you to like my little sister! Will you like her? I don't want her to be one of the struggling women— —" Then she paused suddenly, as the drawing-room door opened and Lady Frances Hope entered, followed by her brother-in-law.

At the sound of the opening door, Lady Diana gave her a quick smile of sympathy and understanding; and turned to greet the new-comers.

"What, Frances!" she exclaimed laughingly, as she caught sight of her sister's face. "Has George been beating you?"

Lady Frances came forward frowning.

"How ridiculous you are, Di! Your mind never soars above George." Then, realising that her annoyance had carried her away, she gave a short laugh and suddenly recovered her composure.

"I am angry because our game was spoiled. I was making a really excellent break, when we were interrupted by a stupid telegram from Walter Gore."

Almost abruptly, Clodagh turned back to the open window, conscious that her face and ears were suddenly burning and that her heart had given a great unsteady throb.

Lady Diana looked quickly from her sister to her husband.

"From Walter?" she said in surprise.

"Yes, from Walter." George Tuffnell came forward with an open telegram in his hand. "Listen to this! 'Back from Russia. Town insufferably hot. Gore Bridges in tradesmen's hands. No plans for immediate week. Can you put me up from to-morrow?—Walter Gore.' Luck, isn't it! Why, we haven't seen him for a year. Dear old Walter!" Tuffnell's good-natured face beamed with hospitable enthusiasm. "What do you say, Di?" he added. "Of course we can manage it?"

"Of course! Why, it will make our party complete." Lady Diana glanced at her sister. But, to her surprise, there was no response in Lady Frances's expression.

With a movement of sudden decision, she had stepped forward.

"Di, wait a moment!" she said. "You know Walter and Val Serracauld never hit it off—and Walter and Deerehurst detest each other. Do you think it would be wise?"

Lady Diana looked perplexed.

"It is a little difficult," she said. "But we cannot refuse Walter." She looked at her husband.

George Tuffnell responded with a laugh.

"Refuse Walter! Why, I'd as soon refuse to have the boys home for the holidays! The house is big enough for everybody! What do you say, Mrs. Milbanke?"

Clodagh turned from the open window. From being red, her face was now very pale.

"I," she stammered—"I——"

Again Tuffnell laughed good-naturedly.

"Certainly! Don't you think, Di, that Mrs. Milbanke could give us an expert opinion on the management of man?"

Clodagh laughed unsteadily. Then, all at once, her mental balance was shaken by a wave of feeling. The thought of Gore—the remembrance of Gore—rose like tangible things, blotting out all else. She lifted her eyes to her host's.

"I agree with you," she swiftly said. "I should say that—that the house is big enough."

# CHAPTER VII

The remaining hours of that night passed like a dream for Clodagh. Condemn herself as she might for the weakness, there was no subduing the tumultuous excitement kindled by the thought that she was to see Gore again.

It was not to be denied that time, intervening incidents, and a sub-conscious personal desire had blunted the first resentment that Lady Frances Hope's disclosures had engendered. In the reckless pursuit of excitement that had marked the past three months, she had imagined him banished from her mind; but now, at the knowledge of his promised advent, she realised that it had only been an imagination; that, despite everything, his place in her mind had never been usurped.

When at last she fell asleep, long after midnight, her thoughts were strange, exciting, almost happy; and when next morning the entrance of Simonetta roused her to consciousness, it was with something like hopefulness and anticipation that she turned her eyes to the open window, through which the clear country sunlight was breaking between the gay chintz curtains.

With a quick, eager wakefulness she sat up in bed and pushed back her loosened hair. A feeling, long forgotten, was stirring in her heart—the vague, delicious hope of future things that had been wont to thrill her long ago, when she rode her father's horses along the strand at Orristown in the untarnished dawn of an Irish day.

During the process of dressing, this sense of anticipation grew; and with it came a spontaneous wish for action. She became imbued with the same desire for light and air and freedom that had possessed her on the day in Florence when she had gazed out upon the distant hills from the window of the villa.

Something of her eager energy was shining in her eyes, as she descended the stairs and entered the sunny morning-room, where breakfast was always served when the party at Tufnell was small.

Lady Diana and her husband were already in the room, glancing through their morning letters, the former wearing a plain linen dress, the latter an old shooting suit that had seen much service. At the moment that she opened the door, Lady Diana was reading aloud from the letter in her hand, while George Tuffnell was laughing with enormous amusement. They made a very homely, pleasant picture of contented, successful married life.

Seeing their guest, they both came forward cordially, and George Tuffnell smiled warm-heartedly as he took her hand.

"Well, Mrs. Milbanke, and what is Tuffnell like in daylight? Isn't it worth a hundred Londons? Haven't you got an appetite for breakfast?"

Lady Diana laughed, as she led Clodagh to the table.

"George is a horrible egoist," she said cheerfully. "He thinks the only things in the world worthy of consideration are Tuffnell—and the Tuffnells."

Clodagh smiled as she took her seat.

"He is very much justified," she said softly. Then she glanced round the table. "But where's Lady Frances?"

Her hostess smiled.

"Breakfasting in bed. I knocked at her door at seven to ask whether she would care for a canter before breakfast, or whether she would like to walk over to the home farm with George, but she literally drove me away. She's out of sorts to-day. Poor Frances!"

"Oh, I am sorry!" Clodagh looked distressed. "Just to-day, when everybody's coming!"

George Tuffnell turned to her with his habitual bluff kindliness.

"Don't trouble, Mrs. Milbanke!" he said. "She'll be all right by the afternoon. It's the mornings that Society plays the deuce with. Look at Di! Look what a country life has done for her!"

Clodagh looked almost shyly at her hostess's straight shoulders and healthy, happy face.

"Don't make me more envious than I am!" she said gently. "Lady Diana has everything."

With a sympathetic gesture, Lady Diana extended her hand, and touched hers lightly.

"My dear," she said, "you have no reason to repine. And Tuffnell is to bring you enjoyment, not regret. What amusement can we plan for the morning, George?"

George Tuffnell looked up from the omelette to which he was helping himself.

"What would Mrs. Milbanke like? You may do anything you like here, Mrs. Milbanke—except be unhappy."

Clodagh smiled brightly.

"Anything?"

"Anything—in wisdom."

She hesitated for a moment, looking down at her plate; then, with a quick, winning movement, she lifted her head, glancing from one of her entertainers to the other.

"Then give me a horse," she said quickly, "and let me ride by myself till lunch time."

Lady Diana looked distressed.

"What, alone?" she asked.

But her husband laughed cheerily.

"Why not—if she wishes? Tuffnell is Liberty Hall, Mrs. Milbanke. You shall have the best horse in the stables."

Lady Diana smiled indulgently.

"I hope we are doing right! Four hours by oneself in the saddle is rather a lonely thing."

"Oh, but I won't be alone!" Clodagh cried. "A good horse is the best company in the world."

At the conclusion of breakfast, she rose to go upstairs and change into her habit. As she passed her hostess, she paused.

"Shall I run in and see Lady Frances?" she asked.

Lady Diana looked up at her.

"I think not. Frances called through the door this morning that no one was to go near her before twelve o'clock. I'd wait till then, if I were you."

And Clodagh nodded comprehendingly and left the room.

Half an hour later, she rode down a long avenue of chestnuts, mounted on a splendid bay horse of Lady Diana's, and emerged upon the road that skirted the park wall.

Tuffnell Place was situated in one of the richest corners of Buckinghamshire; and as she drew rein for a moment outside the large gates and surveyed the surrounding country, it seemed to her that, as far as the eye could reach, the land stretched away in one great tract of prosperous, well-tilled fields and sweeping meadow-land, broken by high hedges and low wooded hills.

The day was one to revel in; the scene one to bring complete repose. And as she gathered up her reins and allowed the bay horse to sweep down the gently sloping road into this land of plenty, she permitted the atmosphere to take full possession of her. For the moment, the thought of London, of her fellow-beings, even of herself, fell away from her conscious consideration; and she dreamed—as an Irishwoman can always dream—with her eyes open and her senses alert to her horse's slightest movement; yet wrapped in a world of her own, created from the warm blue haze of summer that lay over the rich country—from the summer sun that warmed her blood—from the close, instinctive comprehension of nature, that no artificiality has power to eradicate.

It was more than three hours later when she rode back to the gates of Tuffnell, having covered many miles of country, and revelled for a long delicious stretch of time in her own musings. The air and the hot sun had warmed her face to a splendid healthy colour, her lips were parted eagerly, and across her saddle she was carrying a spray of honeysuckle, plucked from the tall hedgerows. Her mood was generous, pliable, brimming with high impulses; if, in that moment, one loving hand had been stretched forth to hers—one honest soul come out of the sunlight to meet her own, many things might have been different. But the moment came—and the moment passed.

Riding quickly up the avenue, she drew rein at the hall door; and at the same instant Lady Frances Hope crossed the wide sunny hall.

Clodagh saw her at once, and a shade of disappointment touched her face. Lady Frances was so intensely suggestive of the world she had been trying to forget. Her impulses of a minute ago shrank instinctively; the habit of indifference came back to her by suggestion. She suddenly felt ashamed of her sunburned face and of the spray of honeysuckle.

But Lady Frances came forward to the hall door, and at the same moment a groom hurried round from the stables.

Clodagh slipped easily from her horse; took her flowers from the saddle; and then turned to greet her friend.

"How are you?" she said. "I was so sorry not to have seen you this morning. I have had a glorious ride."

Lady Frances did not respond to the words with her habitual smile. And, on closer scrutiny, Clodagh observed that, despite a very careful toilet, she looked tired and annoyed.

"You've been away an age," she said irritably. "It's after twelve."

"Then perhaps I'd better change. The coach is to be back from the station at half-past twelve."

"No. Never mind! Diana isn't conventional. You can meet the people—and lunch too—in your habit. I want to talk to you."

Clodagh's eyes opened. It was new to find Lady Frances's manner either hasty or perturbed.

"To me? What about?"

The other hesitated for a moment, then looked straight at her companion.

"About Walter Gore."

The onslaught was so sudden that Clodagh had no time to guard her feelings. She flushed—a deep, painful flush, that spread over her cheeks, her ears, her forehead.

Lady Frances looked at her mercilessly.

"I have been worrying so about his coming—worrying so about you."

"About me?"

Clodagh said the words consciously and uncomfortably.

"Yes. I feel so much for you—you, who are so sensitive. Clodagh!"—she laid her fingers lightly on Clodagh's arm—"Clodagh! I am your best friend. You believe that?"

"You—you have always been very good to me."

"And always *shall* be good to you. Look here!" Her voice suddenly took on the tone of seeming frankness that is the clever woman's best weapon. "I'm enormously fond of you—enormously fond of you. I should hate to see you hurt or—or——"

She paused judiciously.

"But who would hurt me? Why should I be hurt?"

"You *shouldn't* be, of course. But sometimes circumstances—chances—people—hurt one. Oh, my dear girl, I'm unhappy at this unlucky coming of Walter's. It's hard—it's really hard—on you."

As the words were uttered, it seemed to Clodagh that a faint cold wind blew from some unseen quarter, chilling the summer warmth—chilling her own happiness.

"Why—why hard on me?" she asked.

"Dear child!" Lady Frances's tone was deep and kind. "Do you remember the night in town when you asked me to take you to the Tamperleigh's party?"

"Yes. I remember."

"You remember why I refused?"

"Yes, I remember."

"But you did not know my full reason for refusing. I had met Walter a day or two before. We had discussed you."

"And what had Sir Walter Gore to say of me?"

"He said—oh, dear child, don't ask me to be too literal."

"But I do."

Clodagh freed her arm.

"Is it worth while? I tried to keep you two apart while I could. Now that it has become impossible——"

"But why should we be kept apart? What have I done?"

"Dear Clodagh! you know Walter—you know how entirely he disapproves——"

"Disapproves!—disapproves! What right has Sir Walter Gore to disapprove of me?—to criticise—to speak of me?"

Her voice shook, not—as she herself imagined—with outraged pride, but with uncontrollable disappointment and pain.

"Oh, I resent it!" she cried—"I resent it!"

Then suddenly she paused, turning to her companion with an almost frightened gesture. Up the long avenue came the sound of wheels and the rapid clatter of many hoofs.

Lady Frances put out her hand again, and touched Clodagh's wrist.

"Here they are!" she said. "I am glad to see your courage. I admire it."

As she had intended, the sharp concise words braced her companion. She stood for an instant longer in an attitude of nervous panic; then suddenly she threw up her head with a touch of the boyish spirit that had marked her long ago.

"I—I am not a coward, Lady Frances!" she said.

Side by side they waited, while the big yellow coach, piloted by George Tuffnell, swung round the bend of the drive. And as Clodagh stood there, watching the great vehicle sweep round to the hall door, her face became pale and her fingers closed tightly round the handle of her riding crop. It was her world—her world in miniature—that swayed towards her, while she impotently waited its approach!

On the box, beside George Tuffnell, sat Mrs. Bathurst, radiant in summer garments; behind were Deerehurst, Serracauld, Gore, and a middle-aged man who was unknown to her. As her eyes passed from one face to another, Tuffnell drew the horses up with great dexterity; the servants sprang to the ground; and Lady Diana came hospitably forward from the recesses of the hall.

The first guest to descend from the coach was Serracauld. Reaching the ground, he paused for a second to brush some dust from his light flannel suit; then he came forward to his hostess.

"How d'you do, Lady Diana!—and Lady Frances!"

He shook hands with both; then he turned to Clodagh with rather more impressiveness.

"How tremendously fit you look!" he said.

Before she could answer, Deerehurst joined them, calmly taking her hand as though it were his right.

"Well,—Circe!" he said below his breath. "We have followed!"

Clodagh turned her eyes hastily, almost nervously, from Serracauld's attentive face to the cold features of the older man.

"I—I should feel very flattered," she said lightly.

Her eyes were on Deerehurst's, her hand was in his, but her mind was poignantly conscious of Gore's figure standing close behind her—of Gore's voice exchanging grettings with Lady Diana Tuffnell.

A moment later, she knew that he had turned and had seen the tableau made by the old peer, Serracauld, and herself.

"How d'you do, Mrs. Milbanke? It is a long time since we have met."

It was not until he had directly addressed her, not until she had turned and met his glance, that Clodagh realised how deeply, how peculiarly he had influenced her. She drew her fingers sharply from Deerehurst's.

"It is a long time," she said very softly.

Gore took her hand.

At the same moment Deerehurst laughed—his laugh of unfathomable cynical wisdom.

"Mrs. Milbanke was the chrysalis in those old days, Gore!" he said lightly. "Now you see the butterfly!"

At the laugh and the tone, Gore's expression became cold, and he released Clodagh's hand.

"So I have been told," he said a little stiffly. "I must congratulate Mrs. Milbanke on her development." He gave a slightly constrained laugh and moved back to Lady Diana's side.

Deerehurst looked after him—a malicious, humorous look.

"Isn't it too lenient of the prettiest lady in London to allow a young puritan to take her to task in public?" he asked in his satirical voice.

Clodagh flushed; and turning, as if to answer, let the spray of honeysuckle slip inadvertently from between her fingers.

Instantly both Deerehurst and Serracauld stooped to recover it. The younger man was successful; and, straightening himself quickly, wheeled round to return it. Then his face fell; and again Deerehurst laughed.

Without a word, Clodagh had left the little group and disappeared into the house.

# CHAPTER VIII

At lunch time Clodagh sent word to Lady Diana Tuffnell that the long ride in the morning sun had given her a headache, and that she would be glad of a few hours' rest.

On receipt of the message, her hostess was much concerned, and came herself to Clodagh's bedroom door to inquire whether she could be of any use to the sufferer; but there, she was met by Simonetta, who conveyed the intelligence that her mistress was asleep.

But in reality Clodagh was not sleeping—was not even lying down; she was sitting in a low chair in the shadow of the drawn chintz curtains, striving to solve the question of her future conduct. Would she remain at Tuffnell and face the difficulties of her position? Would she turn coward— and run away?

She passed in review the incidents of the morning, until, by persistent contemplation of them, her humiliation kindled to anger. First, anger against herself; then, anger against the world at large; lastly, anger against Gore.

By the time afternoon tea was brought to her, the headache she had feigned had become a reality; and before dinner time arrived she had fallen into a state of miserable despondency. But scarcely had this black mood taken possession of her, than a new and more intolerable distress assailed her. She suddenly realised the gossip to which her abrupt retirement might give rise. What would the house party think of her disappearance? Would not Lady Frances Hope—if no one else—presume that she was suffering from wounded vanity? The thought was unendurable. No sooner did it present itself, than she sprang from her chair in a fever of apprehension, and rang hastily for Simonetta.

Ten minutes before the dinner hour, she emerged from her room and passed downstairs. Faint daylight was still filling the house, but everywhere the lamps had been lighted, and the mellow double illumination gave a curious softening effect to the old raftered ceilings and panelled walls.

In the hall she was met by Lady Frances Hope, who paused and looked at her scrutinisingly.

"What is the matter with you?" she asked, with unusual brusqueness. "You almost look as if you had a fever. Your eyes are glittering."

Clodagh laughed nervously, and put one hand to her cheek.

"Nothing is the matter."

Lady Frances's lip curled slightly.

"You should go to bed early."

"Yes. Early in the morning! I feel I could sit up all night."

"Playing bridge?"

Again Clodagh laughed, this time a little recklessly.

"Why not?" she asked. "Will you play to-night?"

"Not here. George is rather a stickler—where his relations are concerned."

"And his guests?"

Clodagh's question was quick and a little anxious.

"Oh, his guests can amuse themselves as they like, of course."

"Then I shall play to-night—if I can find any one to play with."

Lady Frances looked over her shoulder, attracted by the sound of voices.

"Well, here comes Rose!" she said. "Press her into your service! She won't refuse, if you give her Mr. Mansfeldt as a partner. The set she has made on that man the whole afternoon is perfectly disgraceful."

She turned with a smile to Mrs. Bathurst.

"Ah, Rose! How nice to see you! And you are just in time. We have been taking your name in vain."

Clodagh became the centre of a noisy party until dinner was announced. And during the meal itself, the same air of inconsequent gaiety was maintained in her regard, for she sat between Serracauld and his uncle.

A dozen topics were touched upon during the course of the meal—the latest sporting gossip, the latest social scandal, the latest Parisian play, all were discussed, and all laughed over the triviality of the world that has few prejudices, few responsibilities, fewer ideals.

From time to time, during the easy flow of this light talk, she found herself stealing surreptitious glances down the long table to where Gore was seated between Lady Diana Tuffnell and her sister; but not once did she surprise a glance from him. It seemed that he had very successfully banished her from his mind.

After dinner the whole party left the dining-room together, as was the custom at Tuffnell, some to play billiards, some to stroll in the gardens, others to find their way to the music-room, where Lady Diana usually gathered a little audience to listen to her singing. On this evening Clodagh was amongst the first to pass out of the dining-room; and moving into the centre of the hall, she paused and looked expectantly over her shoulder.

As she had anticipated, Deerehurst appeared almost at once, and came directly to her side.

"What is your pleasure?" he said. "Bridge?"

She looked up swiftly.

"Yes, bridge," she said quickly. "I feel I must have excitement to-night."

He looked at her immovably.

"As you wish," he said calmly. "I shall ask Rose Bathurst and Mansfeldt to play."

He turned away, and at the same moment Lady Diana came forward from a little group that included her husband and Gore. Coming close to Clodagh, she laid her hand kindly on her arm.

"Well, Mrs. Milbanke," she said pleasantly, "how shall we amuse you this evening?"

Clodagh turned swiftly. Her nerves felt so tense and strained that even her hostess's quiet voice set them tingling.

"Oh, I have chosen my amusement," she said. "I want a game of bridge, and Lord Deerehurst has gone to make up a four."

Lady Diana's expression changed, betraying a leaven of disappointment.

"Bridge?" she repeated. "Do you think you are quite wise? Remember your headache!"

Clodagh gave a short, excited laugh.

"Ah, you are not a bridge-player, Lady Diana! If you were, you would know that bridge is a cure for all the ills of humanity. Here comes Lord Deerehurst with two accomplices! Fancy, it is the first time I have met the rich Mr. Mansfeldt!"

Lady Diana was silent. She looked once more at Clodagh—a rapid, penetrating look that might have belonged to her sister. Then she compelled herself to smile.

"I hope your game will be a good one," she said graciously; and moving quietly away, she rejoined her husband.

Almost at the same moment Deerehurst approached, followed at some little distance by Mrs. Bathurst and Mansfeldt—a South African millionaire, who had recently found his way into society.

"Rose is making the running," he remarked in a maliciously amused whisper. "She asked me before dinner exactly what Mansfeldt is worth. Ah, here you are, Mansfeldt!" he added aloud. "Allow me to present you to Mrs. Milbanke! Mrs. Milbanke, will you show us the way to the card-room? I hear you are the spoiled child of the house!"

Clodagh bowed to Mansfeldt; and responding at once to Deerehurst's suggestion, led the way across the hall.

The card-room at Tuffnell was the only room in the big, rambling house that had not preserved an air of old-world repose; here alone, the artistic decorator had been allowed to encroach upon the handiwork of time; and the result, although comfortable and even luxurious, was modern and slightly bizarre. An Oriental carpet, a few divans and coffee stools, half a dozen chairs, and three or four baize-covered tables comprised the somewhat conventional furniture; while the walls were covered in fabric of bright scarlet and decorated with a peculiar and extravagant frieze representing the fifty-two cards of the pack. As Clodagh entered, an irrepressible recollection of London—of the clubs—the card-rooms—the smoking-rooms of London—where men and women idle away their lives and their money, rose to her mind, banishing the pictures of country peace that the last twelve hours had conjured.

Pausing by one of the tables, she looked back at her three companions.

"Let's cut for partners!" she cried quickly, picking up an unused pack of cards. "See! I've cut a ten!"

Mrs. Bathurst came languidly forward and raised a portion of the pack.

"A three!" she said. "Now Mr. Mansfeldt, and Lord Deerehurst!" She looked with graceful interest towards the men.

Deerehurst cut a four; then the millionaire followed with a two.

Her face flushed with pleasure.

"How strange!" she murmured. "Do you mind having a very stupid partner, Mr. Mansfeldt?" Her large brown eyes rested on the rich man's face, exactly as they had rested upon Deerehurst's in the days at Venice.

Observing and comprehending this, by the light of recent knowledge, Clodagh gave a sharp, amused laugh.

"I think every one is satisfied, Rose," she said. "Now, about points! Lord Deerehurst, what points?"

Deerehurst bowed complacently.

"What you like, partner! Our usual forty shillings a hundred?"

"Or twenty shillings a hundred?" suggested Mrs. Bathurst with a deprecating smile at Mansfeldt.

Again Clodagh laughed.

"You are getting very modest, Rose! Do you remember the last time we were opponents at bridge? But I won't tell tales out of school!"

Mrs. Bathurst looked annoyed.

"Would it be quite wise— —?" she asked sharply.

But Deerehurst intervened.

"Well," he said, "shall we decide on forty-shilling points? Mr. Mansfeldt, do you agree?"

Mansfeldt, who was an intensely reserved and silent man, looked up unemotionally.

"I am in your hands," he said; and following the example already set by Clodagh and Mrs. Bathurst, he seated himself at the card-table.

"Very well! Forty-shilling points." Deerehurst also seated himself, and began to collect the scattered cards.

But with a swift gesture, Clodagh leant across the table and placed a detaining hand over his.

"Wait!" she said. "Let's make it eighty shillings a hundred!"

Deerehurst raised his eyebrows, and the millionaire glanced at her curiously; while Mrs. Bathurst made a little affected exclamation of dismay.

"Clodagh, I couldn't! I'm horribly hard up!"

Once again Clodagh laughed shortly.

"Then trust to luck! You're more lucky than I am." Her voice was high, and charged with excitement; her eyes looked hard and very bright.

Deerehurst's cold glance rested for a moment on her face.

"You really want excitement to-night?" he asked in a low voice.

She threw up her head with a reckless movement.

"Yes; I do want excitement. Rose, will you agree to eighty-shilling points?"

Mrs. Bathurst allowed her gaze to flutter prettily from one face to another, until it finally rested upon Mansfeldt's.

"Will you decide, partner!" she said in a confiding whisper.

Mansfeldt looked at her for an instant in slight embarrassment; then he appeared to regain his stolidity of bearing.

"You may play," he said decisively. And a faint, indescribable smile flitted across Mrs. Bathurst's lips, as she sank back into her chair.

It was nearly two hours before the steady progress of their play was interrupted by any remark not directly connected with the game; then, at the conclusion of the second rubber, Clodagh looked across at Deerehurst, as if obeying a sudden impulse.

"I bring you bad luck, partner!" she said quickly.

Mrs. Bathurst laughed.

"Unlucky at cards, lucky in love! He won't complain, Clodagh."

Deerehurst smiled calmly.

"Is it well to aver that?" he said. "Look at your own score!"

She laughed again—a laugh of complete satisfaction.

"Ah, but I owe that to my partner's play, not to luck! Shall we lower the points, Clodagh? You are a horrible loser."

Clodagh's hot cheeks flushed a deeper red.

"Lower the points! I would rather raise them. But aren't we losing time? Deal, Mr. Mansfeldt, please!" Her excitement was obvious. Her lips were obstinately set; and her fingers tapped the table in nervous impatience.

A third rubber was begun and finished; then a fourth, and a fifth; and very gradually, as the play continued, the sounds throughout the house became fainter and fewer. At first, the tones of Lady Diana's voice had floated up from the music-room, and the usual hum of applause had succeeded, to be followed in its own turn by more music. Song after song had been sung; then had come the sound of talk and laughter, as the party from the music-room had adjourned to the garden. But slowly these sounds had lessened. The laughter had ceased; and the entertainment out-of-doors had died down to the murmuring of two men's voices and the slow pacing of a couple of pairs of feet up and down the terrace beneath the card-room window. At last even this had ended with the heavy shutting of a door; and, save for the occasional distant sound of a closing window, silence reigned in the house.

The sixth rubber was drawing to its close, when the door of the card-room opened quietly and Lady Diana entered, looking slightly tired and pale.

The Gambler | 265

She came forward to the table and stood looking at the players.

"Don't stir!" she said. "I only came to see that you are all right. Who has been lucky?"

Mrs. Bathurst looked up self-confidently.

"We have—enormously," she said. "Mrs. Milbanke was most daring, and doubled our ordinary stakes. The results have been wonderful—for us."

"Indeed!" Lady Diana's voice sounded unusually cold; and Clodagh was conscious that her observant eyes had turned upon her.

But she played on, without looking up.

At last the final trick was won, the score reckoned up, and the players rose.

Deerehurst pushed back his chair, and looked about him speculatively.

"It feels late!" he said. "What is the time, Lady Diana? My conscience begins to trouble me!"

Lady Diana smiled a little conventionally.

"I think it is about half-past two," she answered.

"Oh, Lady Diana, how wicked of us!" Mrs. Bathurst affected a charming penitence.

Mansfeldt looked genuinely uncomfortable and distressed.

"We owe you an apology!" he said. "We have kept you from your rest."

But Lady Diana graciously waived all apologies aside.

"It is nothing!—nothing!" she assured them. "We are not so rustic as all that. Lord Deerehurst, you and Mr. Mansfeldt will find George in the smoking-room." She gave the suggestion with her usual hospitable warmth; but the smile that accompanied the words was not the smile she had given to Clodagh the evening before—or that morning at breakfast.

And Clodagh, keenly sensitive to this altered bearing, stood silent, offering no apology. At last, as though the tension of the position compelled her to action, she held out her hand in a half-diffident, half-defiant gesture.

"Good-night, Lady Diana! Good-night, Rose! Good-night, Mr. Mansfeldt. Good-night!" Last of all, her fingers touched Deerehurst's, and as his cold hand closed over hers, he bent his head deferentially.

"Good-night, partner! Sleep well! We will be more fortunate in the future."

But Clodagh gave no sign that she had even heard. Almost ungraciously, she freed her hand; and, without glancing at any of the occupants of the room, moved quickly to the door, and passed out into the corridor.

Her brain seemed to burn, as she mounted the long flight of shallow stairs that led to the bedrooms; her head ached; her senses felt confused. She had lost money to a far greater extent than she could possibly afford; she had alienated the friend she had so ardently desired to make; she had acted wilfully—absurdly—wrongly.

She opened the door of her bedroom with hasty, unsteady fingers. The lamp on the writing-table was lighted, but the rest of the room was dim; through the open windows came a slight breeze that stirred the chintz curtains; in a chair by the dressing-table sat Simonetta in an attitude of weariness.

The sight of the woman's tired figure jarred on Clodagh's over-strained nerves.

"You can go, Simonetta!" she said sharply. "I'll put myself to bed."

Simonetta started up remorsefully.

"Pardon, signora——" she exclaimed.

But Clodagh cut her short.

"You can go!" she said. "Good-night!"

The woman looked at her for a moment in doubt and reluctance; then, instinctively realising that argument was useless, moved softly to the door.

"Good-night, signora!" she ventured; but as Clodagh made no response, she departed, silently closing the door.

Left alone, Clodagh moved aimlessly to the centre of the room, and stood there as if seeking some object which might distract her mind. Her glance passed vaguely over the dressing-table, laden with familiar personal objects; then strayed to a couch, on which lay an open book that she had made a fruitless attempt to read during the hot hours of the afternoon; at last, attracted by the light of the lamp, it turned to the writing-table, on which was placed the heavy leather writing-case that had belonged to her mother, and that had remained with her through all her wanderings since the time of her marriage. It lay unlocked, as she had left it the evening before, the contents protruding untidily from under the thick leather flap. Something intimate and friendly in the shabby object appealed to and attracted her. Without considering the action, she went slowly forward and laid her fingers hesitatingly upon it. All the small records that constituted memory lay side by side in this worn leather case: her cheque-books—her letters—the few souvenirs her life had provided.

She raised the flap lingeringly and lifted out the topmost papers. First to her hand, came a bundle of Laurence Asshlin's monthly reports from Orristown—boyish, spirited records of trivial doings, ill-constructed from a literary point of view, shrewdly humorous in their own peculiar way. These she tossed aside, as things of small account, and turned almost hurriedly to the papers that lay immediately beneath. They proved to be her sister's letters, dating from the time of their parting in London, when Nance had been sent to school. For a space she held them in her hand, while a curious expression, half antagonistic, half tender, touched her face; then, with a little sigh, she laid them down again, without having turned a page.

The next object that she drew forth was the faded telegram that, years ago, at the time of Denis Asshlin's accident, had brought the longed-for news that Milbanke was on his way to Orristown. She opened it, read it, then folded it and replaced it with something of uneasy haste; and again burying her hand in the recesses of the case, brought to light another link with the past—a large envelope into which were crushed a number of things, amongst them the first invitation from Lady Frances Hope in Venice; a ribbon that had tied a bouquet of flowers on the dinner-table at the "Abbati" Restaurant; a Venetian theatre programme; a couple of dry roses that she had worn on the night when Gore had taken her home from the Palazzo Ugochini. Very slowly she drew these trophies forth. Each breathed the romance of things gone by; yet each possessed the poison of present regret. As she lifted up the roses, her expression became suddenly pained and resentful, and with a fierce impulse she crushed the dry, brown leaves between her fingers, flung them from her across the room, and hurriedly lifted the next object from the writing-case. This last was a large bundle of papers, tied together with a black ribbon.

Lifting it into the light, she looked at it for a long time, without attempting to untie the string. It was the collection of her father's scanty correspondence and ill-assorted business letters, which she had bound together the night before her marriage—and had never since opened.

A curious feeling assailed her now, as she looked at these yellowing papers, eloquent of dead days; and at the mourning ribbon, significant of emotions keen and bitter in the living, but buried now under the weight of newer things. How strange, how distant and impersonal, the pages seemed! And yet the time had been when every written line had played its part in some human, personal endeavour! Each document had represented loss or gain to some individual; each letter had conveyed its fragment of earthly sentiment. Moved suddenly by the suggestions of the moment, she untied the string.

A faint, dry odour rose from the loosened papers—the intangible scent that indicates the past. It seemed that some world, distant and forgotten, had suddenly put forth a shadowy hand, pointing she knew not whither. Over her brain, fevered from the night's excitement, fell a stillness—an arresting calm; across her thoughts, distorted by mistaken struggles, glided a memory—a picture. She saw herself as she had been before her marriage, in the far-off isolated days when life had been a simple thing, when the world outside Orristown had been a golden realm lying beyond the sunset.

How young she had been then! How extraordinarily, indescribably young! How untrammelled in her actions and sweeping in her judgments! As the old existence pressed about her in a cloud of images, she opened the first letter. But so unsteadily, so agitatedly, that, in the opening, five or six of the pages slipped from the packet and fluttered to the writing-table, bringing with them a small unframed ivory miniature that had been wrapped within the sheets.

The thin, fragile picture dropped with a faint tinkling sound; Clodagh bent forward to recover it; then paused, leaning over the table in an attitude of attention. The miniature lay face upwards; and, in the strong light of the lamp, its outline and colours shone forth distinctly. It represented the head and shoulders of a man in a scarlet coat and hunting-stock—a man of thirty, with a handsome, defiant face, fine eyes, and an obstinate, unreliable mouth.

It lay, looking up into her face, while she stared back at it, as though a ghost had risen from the faded letters. On the night before her marriage she had come upon this miniature of Denis Asshlin; and in a frenzy of renewed grief had thrust it out of sight amongst the papers she had collected. Then, the picture had seemed pitifully sad in its presentment of the dead man in the days of his strength; now, as she looked upon it in the light of subsequent knowledge, it seemed a thing instinct with portent and dread.

Sharply and cruelly, the glamour cast by death receded from her memory. She saw Asshlin as she had seen him in life—selfish, obstinate, and yet weak. And, quick as the vision came, another followed. The vision of her-self—of her own attitude towards her existence and her responsibilities.

In silent, intent concentration she gazed upon the picture, until at last, seized by an ungovernable impulse, half-instinctive realisation, half-superstitious dread, she caught up the lamp and walked to the dressing-table. There, removing the coloured shade, she laid it upon the table; and, lifting the mirror, looked fixedly at her own reflection, intensified by the crude, strong light.

For several minutes she stood quite motionless, her questioning eyes searching the eyes in the glass, her pale face confronting its own reflection. And as she looked, expressions of doubt, of fear, of conviction chased each other across her features.

The image that confronted her was her father's image, softened by differences of age and sex, but fundamentally the same. The image of one who had wasted his life—ignored his duties—squandered the substance of those who were dependent upon him! One whom even his children had learned to despise!

With a sudden sensation of physical faintness she turned from the table. For every folly of Denis Asshlin's, there sprang to her mind some corresponding folly in her own more brilliant life. How inefficiently she had worked out her own destiny—she who long ago had been so rigid in her condemnation of him!

In sudden terror she moved unsteadily across the room, and stood leaning against the foot of the oak bedstead; then, all at once, she made a swift, passionate gesture, and dropped to her knees.

"O God!" she whispered wildly—"God, who made me!—I am afraid!"

# CHAPTER IX

At eleven o'clock on July the fourth, Nance was to arrive at Tuffnell. Her boat reached Liverpool on the third; but it had been arranged that she was to spend the night on board, and take an early train to Buckinghamshire on the following morning.

At ten o' clock Clodagh, wearing a hat and veil, and drawing on her gloves, left her bedroom and descended the stairs. Taking advantage of Lady Diana's arrangement that all the guests were at liberty to breakfast in their own rooms, she had elected to avoid the family meal, at which her instinct told her Gore would be present. After last night's mental crisis, the idea of encountering his polite avoidance had seemed to her intolerable.

As she passed downstairs now, with slow and sobered steps, she half paused as the burly figure of George Tuffnell appeared at the open hall door; but her hesitation was not permitted to last, for instantly her host caught sight of her, he came forward hospitably. And a new shame woke in her, as she realised that Lady Diana Tuffnell had preserved silence even to her husband upon the subject of last night's incident—or at least upon her share in it.

"Hallo, Mrs. Milbanke!" he cried cheerfully. "Has the London atmosphere got imported with our guests? These are London hours, you know!"

He strode up to her, followed closely by a couple of dogs, and seized her hand cordially.

Clodagh gave a little embarrassed laugh; and instantly stooped to caress the dogs.

"I feel ashamed of myself," she said hurriedly. "You and Lady Diana must forgive me. But I was very tired last night."

Tuffnell waived the matter good-naturedly.

"Don't apologise! Don't mention it! But you should be thinking about the train. I was just coming to tell you that the trap is ready, whenever you are. It was Di's idea to give you the trap; she said you'd hate a big conveyance that would tempt people to offer themselves as escorts!" He laughed in his hearty, untroubled way. "One of the men will drive you over, but you can get rid of him at the station. He'll come back in the dog-cart with Miss Asshlin's luggage."

Again Clodagh bent to pat the dogs.

"How kind of Lady Diana!" she murmured. "I haven't seen my little sister for years and years, you know."

"You'll find her changed, I'll guarantee. Children do spring up!" He gave a loud, contented sigh. "But shall I order the trap round? Or do you want to see Di first?"

"I think I'll—I'll see Lady Diana later—if it will not seem ungracious."

"Ungracious! Not a bit! I'll get the trap." He turned and swung across the sunny hall, whistling to his dogs. And Clodagh, still quiet and subdued, walked slowly after him to the door.

No one was about when the small trap was brought round from the stables, followed by Tuffnell and the dogs. And as Clodagh came down the steps the two animals pressed forward with upturned, eager faces; and the friendly appeal in their faithful eyes touched her to remembrance of many grey and misty mornings, when Denis Asshlin's high, old-fashioned trap would sweep round from the Orristown stable-yard, and dogs such as these would plead passionately for a share in the impending journey. A dry, painful sensation seemed to catch her throat.

"May they come with me?" she asked softly. "I love animals. I had to send my own Irish terrier home to Ireland when I gave up my house in Italy—and nothing has ever quite taken his place. Do let them come! They would be so good."

The two dogs looked swiftly from her face to their master's.

But George Tuffnell pretended to be stern.

"No!" he said loudly—"no! Dick and Tom can't go to the station to-day!"

Instantly the two tails dropped.

"Come, Myers!" he called to the groom. "Mrs. Milbanke has no time to spare. Dick! Tom! To heel!" He winked humorously at Clodagh, as she stepped into the trap; and a moment later the groom took his seat and picked up the reins.

Then suddenly he broke into a shout of genial laughter.

"You villains!" he cried. "Off with you! Away with you!" And with a yelp of wild delight, the dogs sped down the avenue.

Clodagh scarcely noticed the details of that swift drive, for a nervous sense of excitement and trepidation banished her powers of observation. And as she stepped from the little trap and entered the small country station, she could scarcely command a steady voice in which to ask whether the train was yet due.

The train proved to be over-due by three minutes, and the knowledge brought an added qualm of apprehension.

"What if little Nance were utterly changed? What if America had spoiled her?" But her thoughts and fears were alike broken in upon by a long, shrill whistle; the expected train loomed round a curve in the line, and a moment later roared its way into the station.

There was a second of uncertainty; then somewhere in the front of the train a door was flung open, a small slight figure in a muslin dress sped down the platform, and two warm arms were thrown about Clodagh's neck, bridging in one moment the gulf of years.

The sisters held and kissed each other, regardless of the one or two country passengers who had alighted from the train, and the two grooms from Tufmell who were waiting for Nance's luggage. Then at last the younger girl drew away; and, still holding Clodagh's hand, looked at her intently.

"Oh, Clo!" she cried, "how lovely you are!"

At the old name, the old candid admiration, tears rushed suddenly to Clodagh's eyes.

"I'm not, darling! I'm not! But you are sweet—and the same, oh, the *very same!*"

She laughed with a break in her voice; then, as two porters came down the platform rolling Nance's luggage, she remembered the necessities of the moment.

"Is this yours?"

"Yes; my American clothes. Do I look very American?"

"You look sweet! Myers," she added to the groom, who had come forward, "this is Miss Asshlin's luggage. And will you, please, go back in the dog-cart. I want to drive the pony home."

Myers touched his cap.

"Very good, ma'am!"

He turned, and passed out of the station.

Nance pressed her sister's hand with one of her old shy laughs, that sounded infinitely sweet from grown-up lips.

"Clo, I can never get used to your being called 'ma'am.' Do you remember the people at San Domenico, who would call you 'signorina,' when poor James— —?"

She stopped abruptly, colouring at her unconsidered mention of her brother-in-law.

"Clo, tell me all about Tuffnell Place!" she substituted, with another sympathetic pressure of her fingers. "Tell me about Lady Diana and Mr. Tuffnell! I think I should hate to be plain Mister, if my wife had a title! And all about Lady Frances Hope and Lord Deerehurst and Mr. Serracauld! I'm dying to see all the people you put in your letters. They're like characters in a book—and, of course, you are the heroine!

"Oh, I'm so happy, Clo!" she cried ecstatically—"I'm so happy! Do you care for me? Do you want me much—very much?"

Her dark blue eyes searched Clodagh's face, as they had been wont to search it long ago; for, beneath the pretty manner that time had taught her, her warm, loyal nature had remained unchanged.

And as Clodagh returned her glance, her heart suddenly sank. Until the moment of her meeting with Nance, she had been conscious of only one desire in her regard—the desire to fully confess to her appropriation of the thousand pounds. For, in the lull that had followed the previous night's crisis, she had seen this confession as the sole means of regaining self-respect. Her other follies—her gambling and her extravagances—offered no means of redress; but for this one personal act of weakness she could still do penance. And now, by her very faith, by her very love, Nance had shaken the desire.

This spontaneous, unsuspicious admiration was the sweetest experience that had come into her life. She involuntarily returned the pressure of the clinging fingers, as she drew her sister through the small gate of the station. She was glad to think that there was the drive home, the moments of arrival and of unpacking, before any mention of personal matters could break in upon the present calm.

Outside the station, Nance saw the two dogs for the first time, and insisted upon making friends with them before entering the trap.

"Did you miss Mick dreadfully, when you sent him back to Orristown?" she asked, when at last she took her seat.

"Dreadfully," Clodagh answered, taking the reins from the groom. "But I didn't know what to do with him when I left the villa. You see, I had no real plans."

"No; no, of course not. But you'll get him back soon?"

"Yes; I want to." Clodagh gathered up the reins, and the pony started forward at a swift trot. "But, do you know, Nance, I have thought of going to Orristown in a month or so. Would you like to come to Ireland?"

"Like to? Oh, Clo, I have dreamt and dreamt of our being at Orristown together—just you and me. Can you picture it? Wearing our oldest clothes—riding and walking and sailing all day long; and making Hannah cook us the most heavenly cakes for tea!"

She clasped her hands rapturously, regardless of her new white gloves.

Clodagh laughed softly and affectionately.

"Oh, you child!" she said, almost enviously.

How sweet and pretty and unaffected she was—this little sister who had suddenly stepped back into her life! An overwhelmingly tender feeling of protectiveness welled up within her—a sudden deep longing to shelter and guard her, to hedge her round with all that is sacred and fine.

"Nance!" she said impulsively, "have you ever thought that I behaved badly to you—behaved unfairly in any way?"

"Unfairly?"

"Yes."

Nance laughed.

"You're dreaming, Clo! How could *you* behave unfairly?"

"Suppose some one were to tell you that I had?"

"I shouldn't believe, that's all."

"If I were to tell you?" Clodagh's fingers tightened on the reins.

"If you were to tell me that," Nance said, very slowly, "I think it would spoil everything in the world. I believe so—so dreadfully in you. But why talk about it, when it's nonsense?" She shook off the momentary shadow that had fallen between them. "I hate 'ifs,' unless they're very happy ones."

So Clodagh struggled no more with her conscience during the drive along the shady Buckinghamshire roads. Yielding to the spell of Nance's voice, she lulled the knowledge of impending difficulties and opened her ears to the tale of her sister's experiences—of her friends, her acquaintances, her pleasures, her occupations—all poured forth with a perfectly ingenuous egotism that was a refreshment and delight.

Though they remained together all through the morning and afternoon, the sisters had no further opportunity of a *tête-à-tête*. Immediately on their arrival at Tuffnell, Lady Diana had made Nance welcome and had introduced her to her fellow-guests; and the remainder of the day had been spent, first in tennis and croquet, later in a long coach drive, which included a call upon some neighbours of the Tuffnells. Almost immediately after dinner, however, Clodagh had pleaded that Nance was tired, and had borne her off to her own room. There she dismissed Simonetta, and, closing the door, drew forward two chairs to the open window.

"Now!" she said—"at last! What do you think of Tuffnell—and of everybody?" She sank into one of the chairs with a little sigh.

But Nance, instead of answering, tip-toed across the room; and, bending over the back of her chair, gave her a long, impulsive kiss.

"Darling!" she cried. "Clo! You are so lovely. I am so proud of you."

Clodagh pressed her cheeks against the warm lips; then drew Nance round to the side of her chair.

"Talk to me!" she said. "Tell me whether you like Tuffnell?"

Nance gave a little laugh of inconsequent happiness, and nestled down at her sister's feet.

"Tuffnell is heavenly! But there are only four nice people here."

"Four nice people? What do you mean?"

"What I say. There are only four nice people here—you, of course"—she lifted one of Clodagh's hands, and pressed it against her lips—"and Lady Diana Tuffnell—and Mr. Tuffnell—and that nice, fair man with the sunburnt face."

Clodagh withdrew her hand from her sister's.

"Sir Walter Gore?"

"Yes. Don't you think him nice?"

"I——? Oh, I—I don't know."

"But why? He likes you."

Clodagh gave a quick, unsteady laugh, and sank back into her chair.

"Dear little Nance! What a baby you are! If there is one person in the world who does not like me, it is Sir Walter Gore!"

With a sudden movement of interest Nance sat up, and looked at her sister.

"But he does, Clo," she said. "I saw him looking at you over and over again, when you were talking to other people. He likes you. Oh, he *does* like you! And he doesn't care one bit for Lady Frances Hope, though she follows him everywhere he goes— —"

But Clodagh sat suddenly upright, and with an abrupt gesture put her hand on her sister's shoulder.

"Nance," she said sharply, "you are talking about things that you don't understand. Don't talk about them! It—it annoys me!"

"But, Clo— —"

For answer Clodagh stooped and kissed her almost nervously.

"When you are older, Nance, you will know that it is tactless to talk of certain things to certain people. Don't talk to me again of Sir Walter Gore. He and I have nothing to do with each other. We—we belong to different worlds."

Once more she bent and kissed Nance's startled, penitent face; and, putting her gently from her, rose and walked to the window.

For some minutes there was silence in the room; then Clodagh spoke in a completely different voice.

"Nance," she said, "there is something I want to tell you—something I should have written to you, and didn't— —"

Nance, in the swift relief of her sister's altered tone, sprang to her feet; and, running across the room, threw her arms about her.

"And, Clo, there's something I ought to have written to you, only I was too shy—and had to wait till I could say it like this, with my arms round you— —"

It was Clodagh's turn to look startled. She tried to hold Nance away from her, that she might see her face; but Nance only clung the closer.

"Clo, you love me? Oh, say you love me!"

"Of course I love you."

"And you won't be vexed?"

"Nance, what is it? You frighten me! What is it?"

"Oh, it's nothing frightening. It's—it's about Pierce—Pierce Estcoit— —"

The words came forth with a tremendous gasp.

"What is it?"

"He—Clo, he wants to marry me. You're not vexed? Oh, Clo, you're not vexed?"

At last Nance's arms relaxed, and she looked up beseechingly into her sister's face.

In sudden nervous relief and amusement, Clodagh laughed; then her face became grave again, and she drew her sister to her with deep, impulsive tenderness.

"Vexed, darling?" she said—"vexed?"

Nance kissed her ecstatically.

"Oh, the relief of having it said!" she cried. "I have felt like a criminal, keeping it to myself. But Pierce said I could do more with one word than a dozen letters."

Clodagh looked down into the pretty, eager face, and laughed again softly, though her eyes were full of tears.

"Pierce was right," she said. "I don't think any one could say more in one word than you could. But do you love him, Nance? Do you love him? That is the great, great thing. And you are so very young." A look of keen anxiety crossed her face, and she gazed into Nance's eyes, as if striving to read her heart.

Nance returned her look with a steadfast gravity, curious in one so young.

"Next to you, Clo, he's the best person in all the world," she said.

The tears in Clodagh's eyes brimmed over.

"You put me first? Really, Nance? Really?"

Nance nodded seriously.

"And next to you, he's the very best! But, Clo"—she blushed deeply—"he wants me to marry him soon—fearfully soon—in the autumn. He's coming over with Mrs. Estcoit and Daisy in three weeks' time, to try to persuade you. Clo, you're not vexed? He has promised that we shall be together more than half every year, if you wish."

Clodagh, touched by a pang of loneliness, turned away and gazed through the open window across the sleeping country.

"And you love him? You are certain that you love him?" She turned again and laid her hands on her sister's shoulders.

Nance's gaze, wise in its very youthfulness, met hers unflinchingly.

"I care for him like I care for you, Clo. And I've cared for you always."

Clodagh drew a long breath.

"Then I am satisfied. I shall not keep you from happiness." With a quiet movement she bent forward and kissed the soft hair above Nance's forehead.

After this seal of love, both were silent for a minute or two; then Nance spoke again, her lashes lowered, her fingers twisted tightly about her sister's.

"Clo, doesn't it seem wonderful that he should care for me—he, who is so bright and clever and rich? But I've been lucky in everything, haven't I? I haven't liked to say it before, but wasn't it awfully kind—awfully good of James——?"

Clodagh half withdrew her hand. In the surprising news that Nance had given her, she had forgotten the confession she had still to make.

"Clo, wasn't it awfully kind of him?"

Clodagh did not answer at once; and when she did so, her voice was strained.

"—To leave you that money? That thousand pounds?"

"Yes; the thousand pounds. Clo, you don't know the dozens and dozens of times it has made me happy to think of that since—since Pierce has cared for me. It isn't that I like money for itself; but, when one is horribly poor, one is sensitive about marrying a millionaire. I mean, you know——" Again her fingers clung to her sister's.

"Yes?"

"One feels that one would like to come to him with everything that—well—that his sister would have, if she married. It's very silly, of course. Clodagh, do I seem very silly?"

At any other time, Clodagh would have smiled at the ingenuousness of the words; but now some feeling within herself banished amusement.

"What is it, darling?" she asked. "There's something you are trying to say."

Nance looked up into her face.

"Clo, it's all this stupid pride. Of course Pierce and Daisy and Mrs. Estcoit know that I have nothing, except my share in Orristown—which, of course, *is* nothing. And I know that for all the rest of my life I shall be dependent on Pierce for everything. But it's just because of that, that I want to come to him with all the things—the clothes and things—that other girls have. Oh, I know it's hateful of me—it's weak and vain."

Clodagh pressed her hand suddenly.

"No, darling! I understand."

"You do? Oh, Clo! dear Clo! Then you know what the thousand pounds seems like. A thousand pounds all my own! Money of my own to buy beautiful things with—things like Daisy's—things like yours! I, who have never had a penny that really belonged to me! And Clodagh, may I have it soon? That's what I want to say. May I have it soon? I won't spend it all, of course—not half—nor quarter——" She laughed. "But may I have it soon? It—it would be heaven!"

With a swift, involuntary movement, Clodagh freed her hand.

"Clo, I have said too much! I have asked too much!"

"No, darling! No! No!"

"Then I've tired you? Clo, you're tired!" She caught Clodagh's hand again. "And *you* wanted to tell *me* something. Oh, I've been selfish! Won't you forgive me, and say it now?"

But Clodagh turned from her and walked to the writing-table—the table on which her father's miniature had rested the night before.

"No, I won't talk to-night, darling," she said, without looking round. "I—I think I have forgotten what I was going to say."

# CHAPTER X

The key-note of Clodagh's character was impulse. She loved, she hated, she was generous, she was foolish, with a wide impulsiveness.

When Nance had spoken of her engagement, her unselfish joy and relief in the security it promised had aroused a renewed desire for self-sacrifice, as represented by confession of her weakness; but a moment later, when Nance had spoken of Milbanke's legacy—of her innocent joy in its existence—of her innocent desire for its possession—the wish had faltered. She had given her tacit agreement that the thousand pounds should be placed in Nance's hands—the thousand pounds, of which the greater portion had already gone to swell the coffers of London tradesmen or fill the pockets of her friends!

That was her position on the night of Nance's confidence; and on the following morning she woke with an oppressive sense that action must be taken in some direction.

The whole house party, with the exception of Deerehurst, put in an appearance at the early breakfast. And as Clodagh entered the breakfast-room, her spirits rallied a little at the sight of the crowded table; and she took her place between George Tuffnell and Serracauld with a sense of respite.

Lady Diana, who was occupying her usual place at the head of the table, had borne Nance off to sit beside her; while Lady Frances, looking a little worn in the searching morning light, was keeping Mrs. Bathurst, Mansfeldt, and Gore amused.

The breakfast was not a long meal; and at its conclusion Lady Diana looked round the table.

"Now, people!" she said amiably, "what are the morning's plans? You know, you are none of you to forget my dance to-night, and tire yourselves!"

Mrs. Bathurst turned to her with her pretty, languid smile.

"I'm going to play croquet with Mr. Mansfeldt," she announced. "Nice, lazy, old-fashioned croquet. We shall turn up at lunch time."

"And you, Walter?" Lady Diana asked. "Will you drive over with me to Wynchley? We might take Frances and"—again she looked round the party—"and Miss Asshlin."

But Nance glanced quickly down the table to where her sister sat.

Clodagh caught the questioning look, and bent her head.

"Yes. Go with Lady Diana," she said affectionately. "It's very sweet of her to take you."

Nance smiled shyly.

"I know," she said, looking from Clodagh to her hostess.

Lady Diana returned the smile.

"It's sweet of your sister to spare you to me."

While she was speaking, Serracauld turned to Clodagh.

"Will you give *me* the morning?" he said in an undertone.

She drew back and laughed a little.

"What a conceited suggestion! Fancy throwing my little sister over, to spend the morning with you!"

He looked at her unabashed. And, as Tuffnell turned to address his neighbour, he bent close to her again.

"You're very hard on me! When will you be really, properly kind?"

"Oh, sometime—perhaps!" Clodagh's tone was careless and light.

"This morning, then? Come for a ride with me."

She laughed once more, and shook her head.

"I have a letter—a terrible business letter—that must be written—a letter to Mr. Barnard."

Serracauld raised his eyebrows a trifle satirically.

"To Barny? Ah, then I shan't press the point. But how many dances am I to have to-night?"

"Dances? You know I shan't dance." She glanced down at her black linen dress.

He smiled a little.

"Am I a schoolboy, that I should want to dance? How many dances are we to sit out?"

"To sit out? Oh, I'll—I'll tell you that when we've sat out one." Without looking at him, she pushed back her chair, as Lady Diana rose.

"Then let that be the first dance?"

She nodded inconsequently.

"Perhaps! The first dance!" She stood up, and joining the rest of the company, moved down the room.

As she gained the door, Nance ran to her.

"Clo, darling! Can't I stay with you?"

Clodagh smiled down into the eager upturned face.

"Not this morning. I have a business letter to write."

"Then I *must* go?" Nance's face fell.

"Must, darling."

"But, Clo, you'll think of me—and love me—all the time you're writing the horrid thing?"

Clodagh laughed; then all at once her face looked grave.

"Dearest," she said suddenly, "you don't know how much!" And without explaining her words, or waiting for Nance to speak again, she passed quickly across the hall and up the stairs.

Four different times Clodagh began her letter to Barnard. Sitting by the writing-table close to the open window of her bedroom, she watched the various members of the house party depart on their different ways; but the quieter and more deserted the house became, the more impossible it seemed to her to accomplish the task she had in hand. At last, with a gesture of despair, she tore up the half-written letters that lay strewn about her; and, rising from the table with a sigh of vexation, left the room, closing the door softly.

With a frown of unhappiness and perplexity still upon her forehead, she descended the stairs, crossed the hall, and passing round the back of the house, made her way to the rose garden.

The rose garden at Tuffnell was always a place of beauty; but in the month of July it was a paradise of scent and colour. Down its centre ran a long strip of close-cut lawn, flanked on either side by stone seats and stone nymphs and satyrs, brought from an old Italian garden; on the high wall, that preserved to the place an absolute seclusion, a dozen peacocks sunned themselves gorgeously; while over the entire enclosure grew—and climbed—and drooped—roses; roses of every shade and of every size; roses that filled the air with a warm scent that seemed at once to mingle with and to hold the summer sun.

She paused for an instant upon entering this enchanted garden, and drew a deep breath of involuntary delight; then, walking slowly, as though haste might desecrate such beauty, she passed down the long smooth lawn that formed an alley of greenness amid the pink and crimson of the flowers.

Pausing at the farther end, she stood, soothed by the sights and scents about her, until suddenly a harsh, disturbed cry from one of the peacocks broke the spell. She turned sharply, and saw Deerehurst standing close behind her.

"I saw you from my dressing-room window," he said, in answer to her look of surprise. "Was it very presumptuous of me to follow you?"

The cold, familiar voice banished the thought of the roses. Her vexations and perplexities came back upon her abruptly, causing her face to cloud over.

"No!" she said hastily—"no! I—I think I am glad to see you. I am in a hopeless mood to-day. Things won't go right!"

He took her hand and bent over it, with even more than his usual deference, although his cold eyes shot a swift glance at her distressed face.

"But you must not say that," he said softly. "Things can always be compelled to go right."

She shook her head despondently.

"Not for me."

He freed her hand gently, and pointed to one of the stone seats that stood under the shadow of the rose bushes.

"Shall we sit down?" he said. "There is a great deal of repose to be found in this garden of Lady Diana's. She had it copied many years ago from my rose garden at Ambleigh."

Clodagh looked up at him, as they moved together across the grass.

"Indeed!" she said—"from your rose garden?"

"Yes; she and Tuffnell stayed with me at Ambleigh shortly after they were married—when my sister was alive. And Lady Diana fell in love with my rose garden. I remember I sent a couple of my gardeners down here to plant this one for her. It is an exact reproduction, on a smaller scale."

There was silence while they seated themselves; then Clodagh, looking meditatively in front of her at the evil face of one of the stone satyrs, spoke suddenly and impulsively.

"I envy you!" she said.

"You envy me?" There was a curious, almost an eager tone in Deerehurst's voice; but she was too preoccupied to hear it.

"All people are to be envied who have power—and freedom. I get so tired of myself sometimes—so rebellious against myself! I am always doing the things I should not do, and failing to do the things I should. I am hopeless!"

For a space he made no attempt to break in upon her mood; then, very quietly, he bent forward and looked up into her face.

"What is worrying you?" he asked in a whisper. "Confession really *is* very good for the soul!"

For a moment she answered nothing; then, yielding to an impulse, she met his scrutinising eyes.

"Oh, it's only a letter that won't let itself be written—one of those abominable letters that one has to write. Talking of it does no good!"

"No good? I am not so sure of that. I believe in talking. Tell me about it!"

Clodagh laid her hand nervously on the arm of the seat.

"I have been stupid!" she said almost defiantly. "I have overstepped my allowance, and must ask Mr. Barnard to advance me some money. And—and I, somehow, hate to do it. Am I not a fool?" She laughed unsteadily, and turned to look at her companion; but he had drawn back into the shadow of the seat. "Oh, it's childish! Ridiculous! I am disgusted with myself!" Her glance again crossed the strip of green lawn to where the stone satyr stood.

Quite silently Deerehurst bent forward again.

"What is the amount?" he asked softly.

"A thousand pounds."

"And is Barnard such a very great friend?"

Clodagh started.

"No! Oh no! Why?" She turned quickly and looked at him.

"Because I wish to know why it should be Barnard."

There was a long silence, in which she felt her heart beat uncomfortably fast. A sudden surprise—a sudden confusion—filled her. Then, through the confusion, she was conscious that Deerehurst was speaking again.

"Why should you think of Barnard?" he murmured. "Barnard is not a rich man. To advance you a thousand pounds may possibly inconvenience him; whereas a man who need not consider ways and means——"

Clodagh sat very still.

"Yes. But I think——"

"And why think?" he spoke calmly, considerately, without a tinge of disturbing emotion. "Why think? Why write that troublesome letter? Why ask a favour when, by granting one——"

"Granting one——?"

"Yes. When, by granting a favour, you can make everything smooth. Think what it would be to me, for instance, if some of the money I am saddled with were used to bring you happiness—or peace! Think of the favour *you* would be doing *me*!"

She half rose, then sank back again.

"Oh, but I couldn't! How could I?"

"And why not? Look! I have only to open my cheque-book"—he very quietly drew a cheque-book from his breast-pocket—"find the all-powerful pen"—he searched for, and produced, a gold pen—"and—look!"

He wrote rapidly for a moment; then held a fluttering white paper in front of Clodagh's eyes.

"Look!"

With a little start, a little cry of deprecation, she rose from her seat. In a flash of memory she recalled the night on the balcony at Venice, when he had kissed her hand; she recalled the letter she had found awaiting her in her room at the hotel. In sudden fear, she glanced at him. Then her fear faltered. To her searching eyes, he presented the same aspect that he had assumed since their first meeting in London—the aspect of a tried, deferential friend.

"How could I?" she asked again; but unconsciously her tone had weakened.

For answer, Deerehurst folded up the cheque and held it out to her with a respectful—almost a formal bow.

"By extending to me the merest act of friendship."

She sat very still, not attempting to take the cheque.

"I—I could not repay it before January—perhaps not entirely even then."

"January, or any time. I understand the art of patience."

For one moment longer her uncertain glance wandered from the slip of paper to the glowing rose bushes; from the roses to the cold malignant face of the satyr that confronted her across the strip of grass.

"You—you are very kind. In—in January, then."

Deerehurst bowed again. And in complete silence the cheque passed from his hand to hers.

# CHAPTER XI

Action—decisive action—always brings relief. An hour after it had come into her possession, Clodagh had dispatched Deerehurst's cheque to her bankers in London; and when, at seven o'clock, she entered Nance's room with the intention of dressing for the night's festivities, she was carrying a cheque from her own book.

As she came into the room, Nance was kneeling before her trunk; but at the sound of the closing door she looked round, and sprang to her feet with a cry of delight.

"Clo!" she cried, running forward—"Clo, how lovely of you to come! Shall we dress together, like long ago?" Then her eyes fell to the folded slip of paper in Clodagh's hand. "What is that?" she asked curiously.

Clodagh looked down at the cheque.

"I have come to do my duty!" she said, with a faint laugh. "Here is your thousand pounds, darling. May it be enough to buy everything in life worth having!"

Her voice faltered on the last words; but the touch of emotion was lost in a sudden embrace from Nance.

"Oh, you darling!—you love!" she cried. "A thousand pounds! I feel a queen!" She drew back a little, flushing with excitement and pleasure; and opened the cheque almost reverently. "And can I really, really get a thousand pounds by signing my name on the back of this? I can't believe it, you know—I simply *can't*."

She raised her shining eyes to Clodagh's.

Clodagh's face softened.

"Oh, you child!" she said—"you child! It makes me remember our weekly pennies, just to listen to you. How poor—and how very happy—we were long ago! Do you remember?"

Nance gave a little cry of recollection.

"Remember, Clo! *Could* I forget?"

Then followed another impulsive embrace, a kiss, and a whole torrent of reminiscence. And a quarter of an hour had slipped away before the entrance of Simonetta with Clodagh's dress recalled them to the knowledge of present things.

Five minutes before the dinner hour had struck, the sisters entered the hall. At the foot of the stairs Nance was detained by George Tuffnell; while Clodagh, left alone for the moment, was at once claimed by Serracauld.

He came forward from one of the windows, moving with his usual graceful indolence, and, pausing beside her, looked intently into her face.

"You look radiant to-night," he said.

She laughed.

"Can one ever look radiant in black?"

Serracauld's eyes passed slowly from her face to her slim white neck.

"Yes," he said, in his cool, deliberate voice.

She gave another laugh, slightly shorter and more conscious than the last. But before she could speak again, he moved a trifle nearer, and laid his fingers lightly on her fan.

"And how many dances am I to have?"

"I told you I must not dance—yet."

"And I told you that I would not make you dance. How many may I have?"

He bent very close to her; then frowned a little, and drew away again, as Lady Frances Hope, followed by Mrs. Bathurst and Mansfeldt, came towards them across the hall.

"You'll give me the dances?" he asked quickly.

Clodagh glanced at the approaching party; then bent her head in assent.

"And which?"

His tone was eager.

"The first—at least," she said.

With a faint satisfied smile he turned and moved away.

Dinner that night was a very lively meal. Everybody seemed imbued with the spirit of the coming ball, and anxious to display a personal sense of anticipation. After the company had risen from table, Clodagh and Nance met again in the hall by previous arrangement and retired to their rooms, that Simonetta might put some finishing touches to their hair and dresses, and that they might get the bouquets they were to carry at the dance.

As they mounted the staircase side by side, Nance, after the custom of old days, slipped her arm through her sister's.

"Clo!" she said softly, "you are excited too! I can feel it!"

Clodagh smile a little.

"Well, it is my first dance!"

Nance halted and looked at her.

"Why, of course it is! And you must feel like I did the night of Mrs. Estcoit's ball—the night——" She stopped, blushing.

"Oh, darling," she added, "fancy my not realising that you had never been to a dance? It must feel lovely and strange to you!"

Clodagh drew her onward up the stairs.

"Yes; it does feel different from anything else. Of course, I shan't dance; but then people may ask me to—to sit out."

"*May?* I wonder who *won't* ask you!"

Nance's eyes spoke volumes, as they travelled from her sister's face to the long lines of her soft black dress.

Arrested by the look, Clodagh spoke again, abruptly and a little anxiously.

"Nance, why do you say that?"

"Say what?"

"That people would ask me for dances—that people would care?"

Again Nance paused and looked at her.

"I am nearly angry with you, for asking anything so silly," she said after a second's pause. "But I won't be. I'll forgive you. Though you know perfectly well that there isn't a man here who wouldn't sit out—or dance—or do anything in the world with you, from now till Doomsday."

She looked up laughingly; but, as she did so, her expression fell.

"Clo, you're angry?"

Clodagh patted the hand that lay upon her wrist.

"Angry, darling? No! Only thinking how wrong you are."

"Wrong?"

"Yes; I know one man who would not dance with me, even if—if I were to offer him a dance——"

She made the confession swiftly, in obedience to a sudden impulse.

The Gambler | 289

Nance looked at her afresh in involuntary curiosity.

"Clo——"

But Clodagh raised her head, in a half-defiant return to reticence.

"Don't mind me!" she said. "After all, no one man should fill anybody's world, should he? Come along! It's half-past nine, and I hear the first carriages."

And without waiting for Nance to reply, she swept her down the corridor to the door of her bedroom.

The presence of Simonetta precluded the possibility of further confidences; and ten minutes later, as the sisters again emerged upon the corridor, the appearance of Lady Frances Hope from the door of her own room deprived Nance of the moment for which she had been waiting.

Seeing them, Lady Frances came forward smilingly.

"How charming!" she said. "A study in black and white! Where did those wonderful roses come from, Clodagh? They are nearly as dark as your dress."

Clodagh looked down at the damask roses in her hand.

"Yes. Aren't they nearly black?" she said easily. "I was saying to Lord Deerehurst the other day that there were no flowers one could wear in mourning. And to-day I found these in my room. He had wired for them to Ambleigh. It was very thoughtful of him."

Lady Frances gave an odd little smile.

"Very," she said. "I wonder if he meant them to be mourning. I believe there was a language of flowers when he was young."

She gave a short amused laugh and turned to Nance.

"And this is your first English dance, Miss Asshlin?"

Nance, whose eyes had been flashing from one face to the other, gave a little start at being so suddenly addressed.

"Yes—yes; it is. I came out in America."

"Then you can tell us in the morning which men make the nicest partners, English or American."

Nance laughed. And Clodagh, with the new, protective instinct, put out her hand and drew her close to her.

"Nance has made her choice," she said impulsively. "The field is not open to Englishmen, But let us go downstairs! We are barely in time."

At the foot of the stairs, the three turned to the left and made their way to the ballroom through the throng of arriving guests.

Entering the long room, they moved slowly forward to where Lady Diana and her husband were receiving their guests.

Reaching Lady Diana's side, Clodagh felt her heart beat quicker, as she caught side of Gore's fair head and tall, straight figure. And a strange sense of repeated sensation surged about her. It might almost have been the night at the Palazzo Ugochini, when Lady Frances Hope had held her reception. Her hand felt a little unsteady as she laid it over Nance's; her voice sounded low and uncertain as she spoke her hostess's name.

"Lady Diana!" she said, "here is Nance! You told me to bring her to you before the first dance."

At her tone, so very soft and pleading, Lady Diana turned; and a smile— the first real smile she had given her since the episode of two nights ago— broke over her face.

"Yes," she said, with sudden geniality—"yes; that is quite right! Leave her with me; I will find her the nicest men." She paused, and her eyes travelled kindly from Clodagh's face to her black dress.

"And you? Won't you have some partners?" Her glance swept the little group about her. "Walter, Mrs. Milbanke won't dance, but— —"

At the moment that she spoke, Serracauld's light voice sounded from behind them, and his slim figure emerged from the surrounding crowd.

"Ah, here you are, Mrs. Milbanke! I have a strong suspicion that I am only just in time. Where shall we go? Into the music-room? Or out into the garden?" Supremely ignoring the rest of the group, he offered Clodagh his arm and led her out into the throng, at the moment that the swaying notes of the first waltz floated down from the musicians' gallery.

With a faint disappointment, warring with a faint elation, Clodagh suffered him to guide her down the long ballroom. Life seemed suddenly a brighter thing than it had seemed for days. Nance was with her; Lady Diana had smiled on her again; and only a moment ago she had met Gore's eyes in almost the first direct glance they had exchanged since his coming to Tuffnell. She lifted her head in response to a sudden excited happiness, as the dancers flashed past her over the polished floor, and the deep, long notes of the violins vibrated on the air.

Unconsciously her fingers tightened on Serracauld's arm; and in instant response, he paused.

"Can you resist?" he said.

She looked up at him. The colour had rushed into her face with the emotion of the moment. An inordinate longing to be young—to enjoy—to be as the crowd about her—swept her mind imperiously.

A peculiar look crossed Serracauld's eyes.

"Just for two minutes?" he whispered. "No one will see you in the first crush. There is no waltz like this!" Almost before she was aware of it, he had slipped his arm round her waist.

For an instant a gleam of surprise—of alarm—showed in her face; then the long, persuasive notes of the stringed instruments dropped to a lower, more enticing key. She yielded to the pressure of his arm, and the two glided in amongst the dancers.

They made the half-circuit of the room, escaping the observation of the house party at its further end; and as they reached the door, Clodagh pressed her hand detainingly on Serracauld's arm.

He paused.

"Tired?" he asked, looking down into her flushed face and brilliant eyes.

She shook her head faintly. Her heart was still beating too fast—her brain still felt too elated—to notice the ardour and the intentness of his glance.

"We must stop," she said softly. "You know, even the two minutes were stolen."

He slowly withdrew his arm from her waist, but still kept his eyes on hers.

"I suppose all the things in life worth having are come by dishonestly," he said lightly. Then, in a lower tone, he added, "Do you know that you dance—gloriously?"

Clodagh made no answer. Her mind was more occupied with the dance just gone through than with the partner who had shared it. And for the moment Serracauld was content with her silence.

Leaving the ballroom, they passed together down a long corridor that ended in a short flight of stairs, leading to the card-room.

At the foot of these stairs he paused, struck by a new idea.

"Suppose we look into the card-room?" he said. "I believe it will be deserted at this early hour."

Clodagh assented.

"If you like," she said. "It *would* be rather nice to find a quiet spot." And, leading the way with careless unconcern, she began to mount the stairs.

The door of the card-room was open. The baize-covered tables were arranged for play; but only one small, green-shaded lamp had been lighted; and the window was uncurtained and open to the still summer night.

She paused on the threshold, and Serracauld stepped quickly to her side.

"It might almost have been arranged for us," he said. "Won't you go in?"

She waited for a moment longer; then she walked slowly forward and halted beside one of the tables.

Very quietly her companion closed the door, and, crossing the room softly, paused close behind her.

"Do you know that you dance—gloriously?" he said again. "But I always knew you would. A waltz with you is one of the things I promised myself a long time ago."

As he spoke, she was conscious that his shoulder almost brushed hers. With a faintly uneasy movement she raised her head.

"What do you mean?" she asked, turning and meeting his eyes.

In the dim light of the room there was something curious, new, and alarming in the glance she encountered. He was standing exceedingly near; his face looked very pale; the pupils of his eyes were dilated, giving them a peculiar, unfamiliar look.

Embarrassed, and yet doubtful that her embarrassment was justified, she turned away, and, nervously taking a pack of cards from the table, began to pass them through her fingers.

"I don't know what you mean," she said again. "I don't understand."

Quite suddenly Serracauld laughed; and, passing his arms over hers, caught her hands, so that the cards fluttered to the table.

"Nonsense!" he said in a sharp, whispering voice—"nonsense! The prettiest woman of the season not understand!"

He laughed again, and with a swift movement freed her hands; and, clasping her suddenly and closely, forced her head backwards and bent his face to hers.

The action was not so much a kiss, as a vehement, almost painful pressure of his lips upon her mouth—something that stung her to resentment rather than to fear.

For one instant she remained passive; the next, she had freed herself with the muscular activity that had always belonged to her slight, supple frame.

As she drew away from him, she was trembling and her face was white; but there was a look he had never imagined in her eyes and on her lips. For one moment it seemed that she meant to speak; and then her lips closed. She turned away from him and walked out of the room without a word.

# CHAPTER XII

Hardly conscious of her movements, Clodagh left the card-room and passed down the corridor.

Her only tangible sensations were anger and self-contempt. The thought that Serracauld, who had seemed less than nothing in the scheme of her life—Serracauld, with whom she had laughed and jested and flirted because he was a boy and of no account—should have treated her lightly; should have presumed to kiss her, to seize her violently in his arms, was something shameful and intolerable. The simplicity of her upbringing—the uncontaminated childhood that her country had given her—rose to confront her in this newest crisis. Vain, frivolous, foolish she might be, but beneath the vanity, the frivolity, the folly, she was—and always had been—good, in the primitive, fundamental sense of the word.

She hurried down the corridor, and down the staircase that she had ascended so short a time before; but, reaching the ground floor, she did not turn towards the ballroom, from which the sound of the violins still floated. Instinctively, she moved in the opposite direction, towards the quieter portion of the house in which stood the music-room.

The door of the room was closed when she reached it, and no sound came to her from within. For a space she stood hesitating outside; then the distant murmur of talk and laughter roused her to action. Her hesitancy fled before her distaste for companionship. She raised her hand and noiselessly opened the door.

To enter the music-room was to enter a region of romance. For, as the card-room upstairs suggested the world and the things of the world, this room seemed to embrace all the repose, all the dignity, all the peace that such places as Tuffnell gather unto themselves with the passage of time. It was a long, low-ceiled room with wainscoted walls and a polished oak floor; and the first object that met the visitor's eye, was an old harpsichord, mutely eloquent of bygone days; for, with rare good taste, Lady Diana had hidden her piano behind a tapestry screen, worked many centuries ago by another lady of the house. Even on this night of festivity, the place retained its peculiar quiet; only half a dozen candles burned in the sconces that hung upon the walls; and the scent of lavender and dried rose-leaves lingered upon the air.

It seemed what it was—a room in which, for numberless generations, women of refinement had made music, read poetry or sung songs, while they wove about them the indescribable atmosphere of home.

And into this room Clodagh stepped, her heart burning, her mind distressed, pained, and hurt.

For an instant she paused upon the threshold, overwhelmed by the contrast between the aloofness, the graceful repose of the place, and tumult of her own thoughts; then, yielding to the spirit of peace, she closed the door resolutely and went forward into the room.

But at sound of the closing door, at sound of her dress upon the polished floor, an answering sound came from behind the tapestry screen—the noise of a chair being quietly pushed back—of some one rising to his feet.

In sudden consternation, she stopped. For one instant she glanced behind her, contemplating flight; the next, a faint exclamation of surprise— the merest audible breath-escaped her; and her figure became motionless.

The occupant of the room came quietly round the screen; and in the uncertain light of the candles she recognised Gore.

The position was unusual; the moment was unusual. For the first time since the night at the Palazzo Ugochini, they were entirely alone—for the first time since the night at the Palazzo Ugochini they looked at each other without the commentary of other eyes—without the atmosphere of conventional things.

Involuntarily, inevitably, their eyes met. Clodagh looked into his; and in the contact of glances it seemed that a miracle came to pass. By power of that magnetism that indisputably exists—the magnetism that draws certain natures irrevocably together, although circumstance and time may delay their union—she saw the gleam of comprehension, of question, of acknowledgment spring from his eyes to hers; and she knew, without the need of words, that he stood within the circle of her power, that—whether with, or against his will—his personality claimed response from hers.

She did not move; for it seemed to her, in that instant of understanding, that her life and his were mysteriously suspended. Her heart beat extraordinarily fast, yet her mental vision was curiously clear. By the light of her recent misgivings, by the light of her sudden confidence she seemed to see and to read herself and him with a strange and vivid clearness.

Some power, tangible yet invincibly compelling, drew them together. In the personal scheme of things there were only two persons—he and she. Beyond the walls of the music-room life swept forward as relentlessly, as rapidly as before; but inside the walls of the music-room there were only he and she.

Almost unconsciously she took a step towards him.

"Do you remember that night in Venice?" she asked. "The night you said all the things that sounded so hard, and hurt so much, and—and were so true?"

She did not know why she had spoken. She did not know how she had framed her words. She only knew that, exalted by the consciousness of great good within her reach, she was moved to dare greatly.

It was the moment of her life. The moment when all social barriers of prejudice and of etiquette fell away before a tremendous self-knowledge. She realised in that space of time that her thoughts of Gore—her attraction towards him—her reluctant admiration—had been insensibly leading up to this instant of action; that on the evening when they stood together on the terrace of the hotel at Venice, and watched the night steal in from the lagoon, it had been irrevocably written in the book of fate that they should one day look into each other's hearts—for happiness or sorrow.

"Do you remember that night in Venice?" she said again, almost below her breath. And in the pause that followed the whispered words, the most wonderful—the most wholly perfect—incident of her life occurred. The voice that had power to chill or stir her, spoke her name; the hands she had believed closed to her for ever were held out towards her. Gore came slowly forward across the shadowed room.

"I do remember," he said. "I have never forgotten, I never shall forget."

# CHAPTER XIII

Nearly three weeks had passed since the night of Lady Diana Tuffnell's dance; and Clodagh was once more occupying her London flat.

The season was long since dead; the fashionable world had betaken itself to its customary haunts; London had, in the eyes of society, become intolerable; and yet it seemed to her, as she woke each morning and looked across the park, lying under a haze of heat, that she had never known the great city until now; that she had never experienced the exhilaration that can lie in its crowded, strenuous life until now, when her own existence—her own soul seemed lifted above it on the wings of happiness.

The hours, the days, the weeks that had followed the night of Lady Diana's dance had been a chain of golden dreams, linked one to the other. From the moment that Gore had made his confession, the face of the world had altered for her. One overwhelming fact had coloured the universe. The fact that he loved—that he needed her.

They had entered into no lucid explanations in the moments that had followed the confession; for men and women in love have no need of such mundane things. With the glorious egotism of nature, they are content with the primitive consciousness that each lives and is close to the other.

Clodagh had, it is true, made some faint and deprecating allusion to the past—to Gore's first disapproval, and subsequent avoidance of her. And he had paused in his flow of talk and looked at her with sudden seriousness.

"I have never disapproved of you," he had said. "I have never felt it was my place to disapprove."

"But you have avoided me?"

"Never intentionally. I have watched you; I have studied you, since we have been here together."

"And what have you seen?"

Clodagh had remembered the card-room and Serracauld—the rose garden and Deerehurst—with a quick, faint sense of fear.

But Gore had taken her hand and, with quiet courtesy, had raised it to his lips.

"I have seen—or believe I have seen—that though you may like these people, may be amused by them, may even court them, not one of them is more to you now than they were in Venice. That is what I believe. Am I right?"

And Clodagh—in sudden relief, in sudden gratitude for his faith—had caught his hand passionately between her own, and looked up confidently into his face.

"You are right!" she had cried. "Oh, you are right! They are nothing to me! Nothing!—nothing!"

And Gore, moved by her vehemence, had leant forward and looked deeply into the eyes that challenged his.

"Not one of them is anything to you—in any way?"

"Not one of them is anything to me—in any way."

That had been the only moment of personal doubt or question that had obtruded itself upon the first hours of mutual comprehension. Until more than half the programme had been danced through, and the older guests had begun to depart, they had walked together up and down the solitary paths of the old garden upon which the music-room opened—a garden where thyme and lavender and a hundred other sweet-smelling plants bordered the prim flower-beds and recalled by their scents the days when the harpsichord had tinkled out across the silence of the night. As they paced slowly to and fro, they had made many confessions, sweet in the confessing, of thoughts and desires and doubts felt by each—when each had believed the other out of reach; and quietly, hesitatingly, eagerly they had touched upon the future, upon the days when Clodagh's mourning should be over and they could permit the world to share their secret—upon the days, still later, when their lives should no longer be separate things, but one perfect whole.

Gore was an unusual, and a very delightful lover. The slight suggestion of reticence that marked him in ordinary life clung to him even in these intimate moments. He gave the impression that behind his extreme quiet, his almost gentle deference of manner, lay reserves of feeling, of dignity, of strength that he himself had, perhaps, never fathomed.

And for this very reserve—this courtliness—this indescribable fineness of bearing, Clodagh felt her own nature leap forth in renewed admiration.

At last, at one o'clock, they had parted, he to smoke and pace the garden paths until the early summer dawn broke over the woods; she to wait by the open window of Nance's bedroom, with her face buried in her hands, her whole being alive and tingling with the tumult, the excitement of the joy that had come to her.

At six o'clock next morning, before any member of the house party was awake, Gore had made his way to the stables; and a few minutes later had emerged, leading two saddled horses. In the drive he had been joined by Clodagh, dressed in her riding habit, and fresh and buoyant as on the first morning when she had ridden alone through the great gates, and had dreamed of his coming to Tuffnell.

No companionship can be more delightful than that of two people wholly occupied with each other, who ride together on a summer morning. To Clodagh, the frank happiness of that stolen ride—the intoxicating sense of reality conveyed by Gore's glance, as she met it in the searching sunlight, had been things that possessed no parallel. Her natural, spontaneous capacity for joy had wakened within her like a flood of light. The misgivings—the dark hours—the feverish artificiality of the past months had been dispersed as if by magic. She had become as a child who, by the fervour of its own delight, sheds delight upon all around.

And so it had been with the days that had elapsed before their departure from Buckinghamshire. They had met as often as chance would permit; but, with the exception of the first stolen ride, they had arranged no more secret meetings. And to Clodagh the half-furtive, ever-expectant existence had been fraught with new pleasure. To talk and laugh with others, to watch Gore do likewise, and all the while to know that, unseen by any eyes, unsuspected by those around them, their lives were linked together—their thoughts belonged to each other—was a source of intense excitement, of unending joy.

To Nance alone did she confide her secret; and here lay another source of happiness. For every night, when the house party had retired, when Simonetta had been dismissed, and the house given over to the great sheltering stillness of the country, the sisters had exchanged such confidences as all women love—talking of their hopes, their fears, their pasts, their futures, in the half-reluctant, half-eager confessions that the dark suggests.

Then at last these days of mystery and possibility had come to an end. Gore had received a letter from his mother asking him to join her in Scotland; and almost at the same hour had come a cablegram from Pierce Estcoit saying that he, with his mother and sister, had sailed for England a fortnight earlier than they had at first intended.

So bidding good-bye to the Tuffnells, to her fellow guests, and to Gore, Clodagh had returned to London. And now, a fortnight later, she and

Nance were driving homeward through the park in the warmth of an early afternoon.

The morning had been devoted to the preparation of Nance's trousseau—a matter which, in these days, claimed absorbed attention; and, later, the sisters had lunched together at one of the restaurants.

The day—or at least the earlier portion of it—had been a complete success. But now, as Clodagh's motor car sped along under the canopy of trees, already whitened with summer dust, a cloud seemed to have fallen upon the sisters' gaiety. Clodagh lay back in her corner, looking straight in front of her; Nance sat stiffly upright, her face flushed, her head held at an aggressive angle.

At last, unable to maintain the silence longer, she turned and looked at her sister.

"It—it seems to me so stupid!" she said.

Clodagh took up a parasol that lay beside her, and opened it with a little jerk.

"Was it my fault that he lunched at 'Prince's'? Was it my fault that he sat at the table next to ours? You know perfectly well that I don't care where he lunches—or whether he ever lunches——"

Nance maintained her rigid attitude.

"I wonder if he is of that opinion," she said dryly.

Clodagh flushed suddenly.

"It is you who are being stupid! Lord Deerehurst is one of my best friends. It's impossible to treat him rudely when we chance to meet."

Nance gave a little angry laugh.

"When you chance to meet!" she repeated with immense scorn. Then she turned afresh and looked at her sister. "Do you think engaged people ought to have best friends? I wonder what Pierce would say if I were to get flowers and books and things every day——"

Clodagh shut her parasol sharply.

"How can you, Nance! Books and flowers and things everyday! Four times Lord Deerehurst has sent me flowers since we came back to town."

"And how many times has he written to you? And how many times has he called? And why did he come back to town from Tuffnell, instead of going to France with Mr. Serracauld?"

Clodagh looked away across the park.

"He had business in town."

"Business! Was it business that brought him to the flat at nine o'clock the second day after we arrived—and that made you ride with him? Oh, Clo, I wonder, when you think of Walter, that you're—you're not ashamed!" She brought the last word forth with a little gasp.

For a moment Clodagh's face was suffused with red.

"I do not need anybody to tell me how I should care for Walter," she said, after a moment's pause.

At the low, hurt tone, Nance's antagonistic attitude suddenly deserted her. The expression of her face changed, her figure unbent.

"Clo! Clo! I was a wretch!—I was a wretch! Forgive me! It's only that, knowing Walter is coming back to-morrow, knowing that he hates Lord Deerehurst, and seeing you allow him to go everywhere that you go——Oh, Clo, I can't properly explain, but sometimes I have felt—afraid. Walter is so—so honourable himself."

Clodagh put out her hand and laid it for a moment upon her sister's.

"When one loves like I do, Nance," she said, "one simply doesn't *see* anybody but the person that one cares for. Other people don't count—other people don't exist!"

Nance looked down at the hand still resting upon her own.

"Perhaps not," she said wisely, "but the point is that the person one cares for may not be quite so blind."

Clodagh withdrew her hand.

"You mean that Walter might imagine—you mean that Walter might be *jealous* of Lord Deerehurst?"

"I do mean that."

With a sudden gesture of amusement, Clodagh threw up her head and laughed. Then almost as suddenly her face became grave.

"Nance!" she said in a new voice.

Very sharply Nance turned.

"Yes?"

But Clodagh's mood had veered once more.

"Nothing, darling!" she said—"nothing! Here we are at home! Aren't you longing for a nice, cool room and a cup of tea?"

# CHAPTER XIV

The fragmentary quarrel between the sisters was very suggestive. Nance's anger, and Clodagh's irritable repudiation of her advice, had each been fraught with its own significance. For, much as the former might busy herself in the happiness of her own engagement and the preparations for her marriage, she could not blind herself to the fact that Clodagh was acting, if not with genuine folly, at least with something that might readily be mistaken for it; and much as the latter might resent a criticism of her action, she could not mentally deny that possibly the criticism was justified.

Yet, when the matter came to be sifted, it was hard to say exactly the point to which exception could reasonably be taken.

Undoubtedly Deerehurst did obtrude himself with curious—with almost intimate—frequency into the plans of each day; but then the intrusion was so natural—so simple—so subtle, if one might use so extreme a word. If London is large in one sense, it is socially as small as any other capital; and the man who wishes to seek the society of a member of his own set finds his way rendered very easy.

And in all matters of tact and subtlety Deerehurst was an adept. If, in Nance's eyes, his comings and goings were things to cavil at, he knew exactly how to arrange them for Clodagh's consideration, so that the gift of a bunch of flowers—the offer of seats at a theatre—the loan of a horse—or the retailing of an amusing bit of gossip seemed the merest courtesies from one friend to another. For in one fact lay his advantage—the fact of a really great favour, secretly given and secretly accepted, in comparison with which all trivial civilities became as nothing.

Not that he ever pressed this advantage home. He was far too wise to allude to it by look or word. But the very passivity of his attitude served to fix the consciousness of his generosity deeper in Clodagh's mind. Not that the knowledge of it galled her; she was too exultantly happy in her own life to be hampered by any debt. But the knowledge of its existence was there—unconsciously bearing upon her ideas and her actions.

On the morning following her return from Tufinell, a faint thrill of surprise and uneasiness had touched her when her eyes had fallen upon a big square envelope, bearing a black coronet, that lay amongst her letters on the breakfast table. And another remembrance of Venice had caused her fingers to tremble slightly as she tore the letter open.

But at the first line her face had cleared—her confidence in life and in herself had flowed back in full tide. There was not a word in the letter that Gore himself might not have read.

So great had been her relief, that a new wave of kindly feeling for Deerehurst had awakened in her mind; and when, on the following morning, he had joined her in her early ride, she had received him with friendly warmth.

And from that, things had drifted, until Deerehurst's presence— Deerehurst's discreet, deferential, amusing personality—had become a factor in the day's routine. The Estcoits had arrived from America, and, with their advent, she had been compelled to see less of Nance; the majority of her friends had already left town, so that even had she desired the old existence, amusements and occupations were less easy to find than they had been a month ago. There was, of course, her daily letter from Gore—the most precious thing in her existence—and there was also her daily letter to him. But even a woman in love cannot read and write—or even dream—all day; and in the intervals of idleness there invariably seemed to be—Deerehurst.

But now at last the day had arrived upon which Gore was to return to London. It was four o'clock in the afternoon; the hot summer air was beating upon the green-and-white sunblinds of the flat; and Nance was standing at a table in the window, arranging a bowl of heliotrope, when Clodagh opened the door of the drawing-room.

She was dressed in her riding habit; her riding crop was under one arm; and as she came forward into the room she was drawing off a pair of chamois gloves.

"He hasn't come?" she asked quickly. "Oh, I'm so glad! I was terrified that that last gallop might have made me late! How lovely life is!" She came quickly across the room; and, linking her arm in Nance's, buried her face in the heliotrope.

"How lovely life is! And summer! And flowers! Do you know, the sun to-day made me long for Orristown. Think of it all, Nance! Burke and Hannah, and Polly and the dogs! Oh, we must all go there together—you and I, and Pierce and Walter——" She paused suddenly and looked at her sister.

"Nance! You're cross!"

Nance refused to look up.

"Nance, you're cross!" Her voice was less sure—less confident.

Nance caught the tone of hesitancy, and turned quickly round.

"I wish Walter had driven through the park ten minutes ago," she said. "I do—I really, really do."

Clodagh's face flamed, and she drew away from her sister.

"And I wish——" she began hotly. Then she paused.

The door of the drawing-room was thrown open; and Gore was announced.

For one instant, Clodagh stood hesitating with a new and charming diffidence; the next, all thoughts of self were blotted out by the consciousness of his presence—his bright, strong presence, typified by his frank eyes, his clear, healthy skin, his close-cropped fair hair. With a little exclamation of greeting, she hurried towards him.

In quick, warm response, he took both her hands.

"Well!" he said—"well! It's good to see you! How splendid you look! And Nance, too!" He turned to the window with quiet cordiality.

"Can Nance find time to shake hands with a mere Englishman?"

Nance laid down the bunch of heliotrope she was still holding.

And at the same moment, Clodagh looked round impulsively.

"Nance and I were quarrelling," she said.

"Quarrelling! What on earth about?" Gore looked amusedly from one to the other.

"Oh, about——"

But Nance interrupted by stepping quickly forward.

"About nothing!" she said hastily. "How are you, Walter? I'm so glad to see you! But I must wash my hands before I even try to talk. Heliotrope is much stickier than you'd think." She looked down at her fingers, then laughed and moved across the room. But as Gore hurried forward to open the door for her, she glanced up into his face with an almost serious look.

"I'm so glad you have come back!" she whispered. "Make up to her for the time you've been away!"

Gore's feelings were very pleasant, very protective, as he closed the door and turned back into the room. He was too essentially an Englishman to be very demonstrative; but the leaven of sentiment that so often lies in the English character had always held a place in his nature. In confessing his love to Clodagh—in acknowledging that love to himself—he had indisputably swept aside some difficulties—difficulties born of inherent prejudice, of a certain stiff-necked distrust of what he had begun by criticising. But they had been thrust aside. He had acknowledged himself stirred to the depths of nature by something brilliant and vivid in her personality. He had made his choice.

His whole expression, his whole bearing, was attractive as he came towards her; he seemed to carry about him a breath of the country—the clean, open spaces of the country. And her heart gave a throb of pride and satisfaction, of complete, ungrudging admiration, as he took her hands again and drew her to him.

"Well!" he said fondly—"well! Have you really missed me as much as your letters said?"

For a moment she remained silent, drinking in the joy of his presence.

"Won't you tell me?"

"In a moment—in one moment. Oh, Walter, the heavenly rest of knowing that you care!"

Then suddenly shaking off her seriousness, she drew away from him, looking up into his face with eyes that shone strangely.

"I'm not crying, Walter!" she exclaimed. "I'm only—frantically happy!" She gave a little gasp, followed by a little laugh.

And Gore, carried away by her charm, by the unconscious flattery of her words, caught her suddenly in his arms, and, bending his face to hers, kissed her passionately.

At last they drew apart, laughing; and Clodagh moved across the room to the open window, and sat down upon the low sill.

A second or two later, he followed her.

"Well! And so the fiancé is perfection?" he said smilingly. "Little Nance looks very happy." He seated himself on the edge of the table, strewn with the *débris* of the heliotrope.

Clodagh glanced up, pleased and interested.

"Yes, Pierce is charming," she said eagerly. "And so are his mother and sister. I told you, didn't I?"

"Yes."

"We dined with them at the Carlton last night. And they're coming here to tea this afternoon. I know you'll love them. Mrs. Estcoit has the most fascinating——"

But Gore made a rueful face.

"To-day!" he said. "Oh, you might have given me the first day!"

Clodagh laughed happily.

"How greedy of you! This is to be a family party."

Gore smiled.

"And Nance was decorating the room for the sacrifice?" He idly gathered the stalks and leaves of the heliotrope into a little heap.

The action was purely mechanical, purely inadvertent. But as he drew the broken stems together, a small object, hitherto hidden under the scattered leaves, was suddenly brought to light.

It was very trivial, very uninteresting—merely a man's visiting-card. Without consideration he picked it up and looked at it. Then, with an extremely quiet gesture, he laid it down again.

It bore the name of the Earl of Deerehurst; and across it Clodagh's name and address had been scribbled in pencil.

"So you owe the decorations to Deerehurst?" he said in a low voice.

There was a short silence. Then suddenly he rose and stepped to Clodagh's side.

"Dear, forgive me!" he said.

At the unexpected words, Clodagh's heart swelled. With a sudden impulse she caught the hand he had laid upon her shoulder and pressed it against her face.

"No, Walter!" she said. "Say all that was in your mind! Be angry, if you like!"

For answer, Gore seated himself beside her on the window-sill.

"I don't think I should ever be angry with you," he said gently. "Anger seems to belong to lesser things than—love. I should either believe in you or disbelieve in you."

He said the somewhat curious words gravely.

Clodagh turned to him swiftly.

"Walter, there was no doubt of me in your mind then?"

He met her searching eyes quietly.

"Not one doubt. Do you think I have forgotten that night at Tuffnell?"

He spoke almost gently; but at his words, the remembrance of the night at Tuffnell rushed back upon Clodagh with an almost exaggerated vividness. On that night love had shone upon her—love, with its coveted accompaniments of trust and protection. She remembered the dimly-lit music-room, the dark garden with its old-fashioned scents; she remembered Gore's quiet, distinct question. "Not one of these people is anything to you—in any way?"

She remembered this; and she remembered also the infinitesimal pause that had divided his question from her answer, when the images of Lady Frances Hope, of Serracauld, of Deerehurst, had flitted across her imagination. Then, last of all, she recalled her own answer—

"Not one of them is anything to me—in any way."

The moment that had brought forth that answer had been crucial—had been, psychologically, intensely interesting. It had been the triumph of love—the triumph of the egotism that is, and ever must be, a component part of love.

And now, as she reviewed the incident in the colder light of day—as she turned involuntarily and looked at Gore—she was suddenly mastered by the certain knowledge that, were the circumstance to be repeated, her action would be the same.

With a swift movement, she held out her hand.

"Walter," she said impulsively, "you are the only person in the world! No one else exists!"

It was an hour later, and the outward aspect of Clodagh's drawing-room had been changed. The sunblinds had been drawn up, and a full flood of light allowed to pour in across the table in the window; the *débris* of leaves and stalks upon the table—and with them Deerehurst's card—had been removed to give place to a tea-tray; while through the room itself rang the gay talk and laughter of people who have enjoyed a genuinely pleasant meal.

The tea had been disposed of some little time ago; but Nance still lingered beside the tea-table; and at her side stood Gore and a young man of five-and-twenty, with a tall, slight figure, a pale face, and intensely shrewd and penetrating eyes.

Clodagh, still wearing her riding habit, sat in the centre of the room in radiantly high spirits, talking animatedly to a distinguished-looking woman with beautiful white hair, and to a slim, graceful girl of about Nance's age, who sat one on either side of her.

"Isn't it unkind of Mrs. Estcoit, Pierce?" she said, suddenly turning towards the tea-table. "She says you must go!"

Estcoit laughed—and when he laughed a very agreeable gleam of humour showed in his shrewd eyes.

"But it takes my mother ten minutes to go from anywhere," he said. "Ask Nance if it doesn't!"

Clodagh laughed gaily.

"Good! Then I can ask ten more questions about Boston. Mrs. Estcoit, please tell me——"

But she paused before her sentence was finished. For the handle of the door had turned; and, looking up quickly, she saw the tall figure of Deerehurst.

Had any member of the party looked at her in that moment, he or she would have seen a wave of colour sweep across her face, then die out, leaving her almost white. But beyond this, she betrayed no emotion; and, a moment later, when Deerehurst came towards her across the room with his habitual slow, silent step, she raised her head, smiling a conventional welcome, and held out her hand.

He took it silently, and with a slightly ostentatious impressiveness.

"A thousand apologies if I intrude on a social gathering," he murmured. "But on returning home, I chanced upon the book we were discussing to-day, and remembering how interested you were——" With a very quiet movement he laid a small and costly little book of verses on the arm of Clodagh's chair, and turned with his usual dignity to where Nance was standing.

"How d'you do, Miss Asshlin! Is it too late to beg for a cup of tea?"

Nance held out her hand.

"I'm afraid 'twill be rather cold," she said a little ungraciously. "But if you don't mind that, will you please ring the bell? We shall want another cup."

Estcoit glanced at her, a humorous look hovering about his thin lips; and at the same instant Gore was conscious of a sudden wave of brotherly affection.

But Deerehurst showed no embarrassment. He turned to the fireplace, pressed the bell, then looked round again upon the little group.

"Hallo, Gore!" he said carelessly. "I thought you were killing salmon at the home of the ancestors. How d'you do, Mr. Estcoit?"

He nodded to the young American; then moved away again to where Clodagh sat.

"What a dreadful afternoon!" he said. "Why haven't you changed into something lighter?" He glanced at her riding habit.

She blushed and looked up hastily.

"We have just been saying what a glorious afternoon! But I don't think you have met Mrs. and Miss Estcoit. Let me introduce you! Lord Deerehurst, Mrs. Estcoit!"

Both ladies bowed, and Mrs. Estcoit broke at once into an unaffected flow of talk, to which Deerehurst listened with polite interest, smiling now and then, and occasionally raising his eyeglass.

At last, as she paused, he looked at her in faint curiosity.

"And you really find an interest in England?" he asked.

She gave a bright, cordial laugh—a laugh that seemed to testify to the perennial youth of her countrywomen.

"This is the twenty-first visit I've paid to England," she said, "and I love it more every time. When my son turns me out of my home in Boston, I shall buy one of your country places—as a dower-house!" Again she laughed, casting an affectionate glance towards Nance and Estcoit! "But, Clodagh, we really must fly. Good-bye, Lord Deerehurst! Delighted to have met you!" She rose gracefully, shook hands with the old peer, and turning to Clodagh, took both her hands and kissed her warmly.

"Good-bye!" she said—"good-bye! It has been perfectly charming!"

Clodagh smiled a quick response.

"Indeed it has—for me. Don't forget to-morrow night!"

"Forget! Why, I'm existing to see that play! Come, Daisy!" She turned to her daughter, who had joined the group at the tea-table. "Pierce, are you ready? Good-bye, Nance! Come with us to the elevator?"

Nance crossed the room readily, while Estcoit shook hands with Clodagh.

"Good-bye!" he said. "I shall see you to-morrow night—if not sooner."

She pressed his hand warmly. "Make it sooner!" she said. And they both laughed, after the manner of people who understand and like each other.

The momentary departure of Nance, left Clodagh, Gore, and Deerehurst the sole occupants of the room. After Estcoit had closed the door there was a faint pause; and in that pause Clodagh was a prey to conflicting feelings—passionate hope that Deerehurst might see fit to go, passionate fear that Gore might leave before they could have a word in private.

And while her mind swayed between hope and fear, Deerehurst drew forward a chair, and seated himself beside her.

"I shall be interested to know what you think of this!" he said, leaning forward and lifting the book from the arm of her chair, where she had allowed it to lie untouched.

She smiled mechanically, though her senses were strained to observe Gore's attitude.

"It is very good of you! I am sure—I am sure I shall like it."

For an instant his cold glance rested curiously on her face; the next, it fell again to the book.

"I shall expect you to like it," he said enigmatically.

"What is the book?" Gore came quietly forward and stood looking down at them.

Deerehurst raised his eyes with an expression in which amusement and a faint contempt were to be read by a close observer.

"The book?" he said. "Oh, something, I am afraid, that wouldn't interest you! I don't believe the writer knew anything of far countries—or even of fishing." He paused, and deliberately turned half a dozen pages. "He only understood one thing, but that he understood perfectly."

Gore laughed.

"And may a philistine ask what it was?"

"Oh, certainly! It was love."

The door opened as he said the word in his high, expressive voice, and to Clodagh's indescribable relief, Nance entered.

In the second that she stepped across the threshold her bright eyes passed from one face to the other, and a rapid process of deduction took place in her mind.

"Walter," she said pleasantly, "Pierce says there's one question he forgot to ask you about Japan. Do you mind if I ask it now?" She walked to the open window.

Gore followed her; and Clodagh drew a breath of deep relief.

Ten minutes passed—ten interminable minutes, in which she strove to attend to Deerehurst's words, while her ears were strained to follow the conversation in the window. Then at last relief came. He rose to go.

"I must say good-bye!" he said, taking her hand. "I shall await your verdict on the verses. There is one I want you specially to read—the last one. Good-bye!"

She smiled, scarcely hearing what he said; and a moment later he had bowed to the two in the window, and passed out of the room.

As the outer door closed, Nance came across to her sister.

"Do you mind if I run down to Sloane Street, Clo?" she asked. "I never remembered those lozenges for Aunt Fan, and I can just catch the Irish mail."

Without waiting for an answer, she stooped and kissed Clodagh's forehead; and, turning, passed out of the room.

After she had left, there was a silence, in which neither Clodagh nor Gore made any attempt to speak.

Filled with a nervous sense of something inevitably impending, Clodagh sat very still. She dreaded to look at Gore, lest she might precipitate what he was going to say; yet, to her strained mind, suspense appeared intolerable. She clasped her hands suddenly, with a little catching of the breath.

At the faint, yet significant sound, he turned from the window; and coming quietly across the room, paused behind her chair.

"Clodagh!" He bent over her, laying his hands gently on her shoulders. "Clodagh, we talked to-day of the night at Tuffnell—of what you said that night."

"Yes."

Clodagh's throat felt dry.

"And it was all true—perfectly true?"

"Yes. Oh, Walter, yes!"

Gore stood upright, still keeping his hands upon her shoulders.

"Then I am going to ask a great favour of you. I am going to ask you to break your friendship—to break your acquaintance—with Deerehurst. I want you never to have him in your house after to-day. Dearest, believe me, I know what I am saying!"

As Clodagh remained silent, he bent over her again.

"It isn't jealousy, Clodagh. It isn't pique. It is just that I cannot bear to see the man in your presence, knowing what I know of him."

"What do you know of him?" Clodagh asked faintly.

"Nothing that I care to tell you! Be satisfied that I know what I ask and that I do ask. Give him up! Cease to know him! Cease to have him here!" In the intensity of his feelings, his fingers pressed her shoulders.

"Clodagh, am I asking too much?"

Quite suddenly, almost hysterically, Clodagh rose; and, turning to him, caught his hand.

"No, Walter!" she cried—"no! no! Nothing you could ask would be too great to grant. I will do what you wish. I will give him up—*utterly*—entirely—from to-day!"

# CHAPTER XV

The next morning Clodagh rose imbued with new decision. During Gore's absence, things had worn a vague, even an impersonal aspect; for, like all her countrywomen, she possessed a fatally pleasant capacity for shelving the disagreeable. While Gore was absent, it had seemed so easy to meet Deerehurst on the footing he elected to maintain—the footing of calm, reassuring friendship. But now, with Gore's return, the aspect of affairs had altered. She was forced to look circumstances in the face—forced to consider her position. She might be a shelver of difficulties; but, before all things, she was a woman in love; and with the instinct that such a condition of mind engenders she had interpreted the look in Gore's eyes when the name of Deerehurst had been mentioned between them—and had recognised that it was not to be ignored.

As she dressed that morning, she mentally surveyed the courses of action that lay open to her; and with each moment of reflection, it became plainer to her understanding that only one was worthy of consideration. However difficult the task, she must make known her position to Deerehurst, and trust to his generosity to find means of helping her.

Her mind was full of this new and somewhat optimistic scheme when she came into the dining-room, where Nance was already reading her morning letters. With a slightly absorbed manner she kissed her sister and, passing round the breakfast-table, picked up her own correspondence.

In a perfunctory way she turned the envelopes over until one arrested her attention, as being intimately connected with her thoughts.

It was a letter from Deerehurst, and she tore it open hastily, skimming the contents with an eager glance.

"Dear little Lady," it began,

"Yesterday the fates who watch over my affairs were unkind. The afternoon was frankly a failure. But I shall claim recompense; I shall look in upon you in your box at the Apollo at nine to-night. A vexatious business matter calls me out of town to-day, or I should strive to see you earlier. But at nine make me welcome.

"Always devotedly,

"Deerehurst."

She finished reading the note, then laid it down and hurriedly picked up another letter. How annoying it was! How malicious of Chance!

The second letter proved to be from Lady Frances Hope; it was from Brittany, and reproached her extravagantly for not having written since they parted at Tuffnell. Imploring for news of her movements, it informed her that the writer, with Mrs. Bathurst and Valentine Serracauld, was on her way back to London. She followed the lines mechanically, but her mind was elsewhere. At last she threw the letter down.

"Nance!" she said suddenly.

"Darling?"

"Nance, I'm in a horrid difficulty."

Nance's high, arched eyebrows drew together in a frown of concern.

"Nothing bad?" she said. "Nothing about Walter?"

"No. Yes—yes it is. You know Walter dislikes Lord Deerehurst. Well, he was vexed at finding him here yesterday; and after he had gone I—I promised not to see him any more—I promised to break off my friendship with him."

Nance nodded, tactfully refraining from any joy in the proving of her theories.

"Yes?" she prompted softly.

"And now Lord Deerehurst writes that he will be at the Apollo to-night, and is coming round to our box at nine."

Nance pursed up her lips.

"Oh!" she said. "And you'll have to put him off?"

"That's the annoying thing. I can't. At least, not easily."

"Why?"

"Because he's going into the country to-day, and won't be back till evening."

"Send him a note. He must go home to dress before going to the theatre."

"He might dress and dine at his club."

"Write to his club as well."

Clodagh's perplexity showed itself in annoyance.

"How absurd you are, Nance! Fancy writing a man two letters asking him not to see you, and giving no explanation! It would simply bring him round here at ten to-morrow morning."

She poured herself out a cup of tea and drank it hastily.

"Life is a hateful tangle!" she said.

"No it isn't, darling, if you only had a little patience."

Clodagh made a very impatient gesture.

"You don't understand!"

"I understand one thing—that you care for Walter."

Clodagh looked up, her mutable face lit by a sudden change of expression—a sudden look of almost passionate seriousness.

"Yes, I do care for Walter," she said suddenly; "I care so much that I honestly and truly believe it would kill me if anything came between us. I have had lots of things in my life—pleasure, excitement, admiration—but I have never had happiness until now. And I won't lose it!—I can't lose it!"

The words poured forth in vehement sincerity; then, as she saw the expression on Nance's face, she gave a little laugh and put out her hand across the table.

"Dearest! I frightened you! Of course everything comes right, if one has a little patience. Let's begin breakfast properly! My head aches."

With another laugh, she pressed Nance's fingers, gathered up her scattered correspondence, and poured herself out another cup of tea.

Nance spent a long morning with her future mother-in-law, lunching with her afterwards at her hotel. Clodagh, left to herself, ordered her horse for eleven o'clock; and after two hours of recklessly swift riding in the Row, lunched alone at her club. After lunch she wrote two telegrams—one addressed to Deerehurst's London house, the other to the club he most frequented; these she handed in herself at a telegraph office, and having despatched them, drove straight home.

At four o'clock Nance returned to the flat, to be met by the announcement that her sister had a bad headache and had gone to her own room. Full of concern, she flew along the corridor and knocked on Clodagh's door.

In a very low voice Clodagh gave her leave to enter.

She opened the door swiftly; then paused, alarmed. The blinds were drawn, and by the subdued light she saw Clodagh lying on a couch near one of the windows.

"Why, Clo! What's the matter?"

She ran forward and dropped on her knees by the couch.

Clodagh extended two rather cold hands, and took possession of Nance's warm ones.

"Nothing but a wretched headache! It will go, if I lie down all the afternoon and keep quiet to-night."

Nance looked up.

"But how can you—at the play?"

"I'm not going to the play."

"Not going?"

Clodagh drew her sister closer.

"Now, darling, don't make a fuss! If you say one word of objection, my head will get ten times worse than it is. You are just to listen, and do as I tell you. You are to telephone to Mrs. Estcoit and explain what has happened. She will do the chaperoning instead of me."

"But Walter——"

"Walter is to go with you. You are to be as nice to him as you possibly can be. Everything is to be exactly as we arranged—*exactly* as we arranged."

She raised herself on her elbow to enforce the words.

"And what about Lord Deerehurst?"

Clodagh did not answer immediately; then, sinking back among her pillows, she spoke in a somewhat hurried voice.

"That will be all right; I—I took your advice and sent him two messages, one to Carlton House Terrace and one to his club. He won't be at the theatre."

"But if he doesn't get the message? If he comes all the same?"

"Then be polite to him. And now go, like a good child. Don't ask any more questions. Don't say anything. Let me see you when you're dressed, and I'll give you a letter for Walter. I'm afraid I can't dine with you; I'll just have something sent in here." Then, as if in sudden remorse, she put her arms about Nance's neck and drew her close to her.

"Darling, forgive me, if I seem impossible!"

At half-past eight Nance left the house, having shown herself to her sister, made a last loving inquiry as to her health, and taken possession of the note for Gore.

As she passed out of the bedroom, Clodagh threw off the fur rug that lay across her feet, and sat up with an expression of sharp attention. As the sound of the closing hall door reached her ears, she drew a little breath of excitement and rose from the couch with no appearance of her recent indisposition.

Without calling in Simonetta, she changed from the white silk wrapper she was wearing into a black walking-dress, and crossing to one of the wardrobes took out a black hat and veil.

She scarcely looked at herself, as she smoothed her hair and fastened on her hat. Beneath the enforced repression of the afternoon, there burned in her mind a certain sense of adventure—of enterprise—that turned her hot and cold. For though the Irish nature may procrastinate, it takes action with a very keen zest when once circumstance has compelled a decisive step.

Having finished her dressing, she picked up a pair of gloves, switched off the electric light, and left the room. In the corridor outside she met one of the maids; but without giving the woman time to show any surprise, she made haste to offer an explanation.

"I have forgotten to tell Miss Asshlin something of importance," she said. "I shall have to drive to the theatre and see her. Please ring for the lift. The porter will find me a cab." And without waiting to observe the effect of the somewhat disjointed statement, she passed to the hall door.

A few minutes later the hall porter had put her into a hansom, telling the cabman to drive to the Apollo Theatre.

While the cab doors were being closed, and the order given, Clodagh sat very still; and for a few minutes after they had started, she lay back in her seat, watching the familiar succession of lights and trees and indistinct massed faces that form the nightly picture between Knightsbridge and Piccadilly; but at last, as Hyde Park Corner loomed into view, she sat upright, and raising her hand, shook the roof trap.

The cabman checked the pace of his horse and, opening the little door, looked down.

"Don't mind the Apollo," she said. "Drive to Carlton House Terrace instead."

The man muttered an assent, and, wheeling his horse to the right, cut across the traffic.

Five or six minutes passed while the cab threaded its way across the Green Park, past Buckingham Palace into St. James's Park; then Clodagh gained her first close view of Deerehurst's town house. For one moment she felt daunted by the unfamiliarity of its aspect; but the next, she rallied her determination, and, stepping from the cab, paid her fare and walked resolutely across the pavement to the imposing door.

It was opened at once by a servant in very sombre and decorous livery; who, having thrown the door wide, looked at her, then looked at the cab, just wheeling away from the kerb. There was nothing uncivil in the man's glance—nothing that one could reasonably complain of—yet, to her intense annoyance, Clodagh coloured.

"Is Lord Deerehurst at home?" she asked.

The servant's eyes left the retreating cab.

"Have you an appointment with his lordship?"

"If he is in, Lord Deerehurst will see me. I am Mrs. Milbanke."

At the coldness of her tone, and her ready mention of her name, his manner changed, though a flicker of curiosity passed across his face.

"Are you the lady his lordship is expecting?" he said, in a different voice.

"Yes, Lord Deerehurst is expecting me."

There was a slight pause; then, with the air of one who admits a novice into inner mysteries, he stepped back, ushering her up into the spacious hall.

"Will you kindly step this way?" he said. "His lordship is in his study."

Glad that the ordeal of entering the house was over, Clodagh readily followed the man across the hall, up a wide stairs, and along a softly carpeted corridor. At the end of the passage he paused in front of a curtained door, and, pushing the curtain back, entered an unseen room.

"The lady your lordship is expecting!" she heard him say.

Then he turned quickly and threw the door open for her. An instant later, she had entered Deerehurst's room.

At the moment, her thoughts were too confused to permit of detailed observation of the room; although afterwards, when the interview had taken place, and she had time to sift reality from imagination, the scene and its central figure were destined to stand out with the accuracy of a picture that has made an indelible, if an unconscious, impression upon the observer's mind.

The room was an anomaly, viewed from a studious point of view; but the merely artistic eye would have found nothing to cavil at. It was not large,

The Gambler | 319

as one counts rooms in a great London house, though elsewhere it would have seemed spacious. Numberless books in costly bindings were strewn about on tables and in cases, but they were not the books of the thinker. They were the romances, the memoirs, the poems of the last half-century, but not one volume dealt with science, or even with philosophy. The walls were panelled in dark red; some beautiful lamps hung from the ceiling; and in a distant corner a large silver bowl full of crimson roses was set up, as if in homage to beauty, before an exquisitely modelled statue of Venus.

In a quick, half-comprehended flash of instinct, it came to Clodagh that she had never really seen Deerehurst until now, as he stood backgrounded by the atmosphere he himself had created. He was dressed as he had been on the night in Venice when she had first seen him. He wore the curiously cut evening clothes that he always affected, and which gave to his appearance the peculiar distinction that set him apart from other men; the diamond ring that she had noticed on that first night glittered on his hand; and, as then, the black ribbon of his eyeglass showed across his shirt front. But more clearly than in the dusk of the Venetian night she saw the long outline of his face, the peculiar artificial pallor of his skin, the cold vigilance of his eyes. And in that moment of entry a faint, indescribable hesitancy chilled her resolution. Involuntarily she halted on the threshold of the room.

But Deerehurst gave no time for her indecision to mature. As the door closed upon the servant, he came quickly forward and took the hand she mechanically offered him.

For one moment he held her fingers closely; then he lifted them and, before she could anticipate the action, pressed them to his lips.

That a man should kiss a woman's hand by way of greeting is not necessarily a significant thing. It may be a slightly ostentatious act—but it may be nothing more. Uncertain how to construe the movement, Clodagh gave a faint laugh and withdrew her fingers.

"Were you very much surprised to get my wire?"

She moved away from him into the middle of the room. Now that she put it to the test, the interview seemed infinitely more difficult than when contemplated from a distance. She felt nervous and ill at ease.

Watching her with his close, attentive look, Deerehurst drew forward a chair.

"Sit down, little lady!" he said in his thin, impassive voice.

Reassured by the formality of the action, she took the proffered seat.

"Now take off your gloves. We shall feel more at home."

Again she gave a little laugh.

"My gloves! But I must go in five minutes."

"In five minutes? When the night is so young?" He drew forward another chair, and sat down beside her.

"Do you know how glad and proud I feel?"

She looked up quickly. His tone had subtly changed.

"Lord Deerehurst," she said, "I must explain that the reason I came— the reason I came, instead of sending for you or writing— —"

Deerehurst leant forward and laid his cold hands over hers.

"Let me take these off! It feels so very formal and unlike ourselves."

He began softly to open the buttons of her glove and draw it deftly from her hand.

"But you haven't listened to what I said," she objected. "I want to explain at once, so that you can understand at once— —"

Before answering, he drew off the second glove and laid the two upon the table.

"Why should you explain? Have I ever been lacking in imagination?"

"No—oh no; I did not mean that!"

"Then why explain anything? Don't you think we have fenced with each other long enough?" He picked up the gloves quickly, and again laid them down. "Don't you think I can understand without explanation?"

"Understand?"

"Why you came to me to-night."

"Understand—why I came to-night?"

"I think so."

He turned and looked straight into her eyes.

At the look and the movement the blood leaped to her face; she drew back into her chair.

"And why do you think I came to-night?"

Very swiftly Deerehurst bent forward.

"I think, little lady, that you came because you know that a man cannot be played with for ever. And because, being a very proud woman, you will not say in so many words, 'I give you leave to love me!' Dear little Clodagh!" He suddenly put out his hand towards hers. "It has all been very delightful—your reticence and your innocence. But we both know that such pretty things are perishable."

Clodagh sat perfectly still. She did not attempt to withdraw her hand; she did not attempt to rise. She sat watching him as if fascinated, while a hundred recollections of looks, of words, of insinuations directed against her and him by Lady Frances Hope—by Rose Bathurst—by other women of their set—strayed in nightmare fashion across her mind.

Deerehurst sat watching her, his hand holding hers, his eyes steadily reading her face. Then suddenly he gave a short laugh and leant back in his chair.

"Little actress!" he said.

The words, but more than the words the tone in which they were spoken, roused her. She rose incontinently to her feet, a sudden memory of Serracauld and the card-room at Tuffnell sweeping across her mind.

"Lord Deerehurst," she said breathlessly, "there is some terrible mistake. You utterly, utterly misunderstand."

It was Deerehurst's turn to show emotion. For the first time in her knowledge of him, the mask of impassivity dropped from his face; his cold eyes gleamed unpleasantly.

"And how, little lady? I am not often accused of misreading men—and women."

"You think——" She paused, unable to find the words she needed. She felt like one who has inadvertently stepped upon shifting sands, where the ground had seemed most secure.

"You think——" she began again.

But she got no further. With a silent movement, Deerehurst laid his hand upon her arm.

"Don't you think we have fenced long enough? Don't you think I have been extraordinarily patient?"

Clodagh turned very cold.

"Patient?" she said indistinctly.

He drew her suddenly closer to him; and before she could resist, he had kissed her hair, her lips, her neck.

"Yes, patient, because I have never before asked for this. Because I have been content to kiss your hand, when I might long ago——" He bent over her again. But something in the white face and wild eyes that confronted him arrested him. He drew back and looked at her.

"Come!" he said. "The play is over! Give me a kiss of your own accord."

Clodagh said nothing. Terror mastered her.

"Come! Give me a kiss!"

She lay almost passive in his embrace, her lips parted, her eyes fixed on his.

He gave another short laugh, half indulgent, half triumphant.

"What a little saint! Come! Show me why you came to me to-night! Be human! Be what you know you are!"

Clodagh made no answer; but he felt her sway a little in his arms.

"What is it?" he asked sharply. Selfish annoyance was written on his face, though he asked the question solicitously.

"I feel faint," she said—"a little faint."

"Faint? Nonsense! It will pass. Rest for a moment." Without ceremony, he half lifted her across the room to a couch that stood between the fireplace and the door.

"Poor little girl! Don't be frightened! It will pass in a minute. Is there anything you would like?"

Clodagh opened her eyes.

"A little water, I think," she said in a tremulous voice.

His face cleared.

"Or some champagne! Nothing would pick you up like a glass of champagne. Why did I not think of it before? Lie perfectly still! We will have some champagne in one moment."

With the possibilities held out by the idea he turned eagerly from the couch, and crossed the room to the electric bell that was placed beside his desk.

But, quick as lightning, the instant his back was turned, Clodagh was on her feet. With a movement so swift and silent that only fear could have inspired it, she slipped to the door, opened it, and was speeding down the long corridor to the stairs.

The house was silent. The upper portion seemed darker than when she had arrived. The hall alone lay brightly lighted—a place of hope and promise, figuring the world outside—the good wholesome world lying suddenly within her reach.

She ran down the broad stairs, indifferent to the fact that the servant who had admitted her had risen from a seat near the door, and was looking at her in frank surprise. Her ears were strained to catch any sound from upstairs, her eyes were on the door.

As she hurried across the hall, the man came forward.

"Do you require a cab, madam?" he asked a little doubtfully.

"No. Just open the door!"

Still with a shade of uncertainty he obeyed, and at the same instant Deerehurst's voice sounded from the head of the stairs.

What he said—whether he addressed her or the servant—Clodagh never knew. At the mere sound of his high, thin tones she went blindly forward through the open door.

As she passed down the steps, a cab wheeled round the corner of Carlton House Terrace. Instinctively she looked towards it, still animated by the desire for flight. But the next instant she looked away again, realising that it already held a fare, and that there was luggage on the roof.

In the perturbation of the moment she failed to see, what was infinitely more material, that the occupant of the cab was Valentine Serracauld; that he had leant forward in sudden, eager curiosity as she passed down the steps of the house to which he was driving; and that, as she turned her head in his direction, he had drawn quickly back into the shadow of his seat.

# CHAPTER XVI

Almost immediately a second cab appeared, and, finding it at her disposal, Clodagh hailed it eagerly and gave the address of the flat.

As the horse sped away in the direction of her home, she sat almost motionless, her only gesture being to lift her hands to her eyes from time to time, as if to shut out some near and unpleasant vision. Life in its crudest, its most repulsive aspect stared at her out of the darkness. She sat crushed by the disillusionment of the last hour.

And a new furtiveness—born of the new realisation—assailed her when at last she stepped from the cab at her own door. With an instinctive lessening of her natural fearlessness, she hurried through the vestibule and passed straight to the lift. Gaining her own door, she let herself in by her latch-key, and then paused, looking fearfully and eagerly about, in expectation of some unwished-for sound. But everything in the flat was still; and crossing the hall, she entered her own room. The electric light had been switched on and the place set in order, and Simonetta sat at the dressing-table, mending a piece of lace.

"No one has come back?" Clodagh asked.

"No one, signora." Simonetta arose and turned to her mistress.

Seeing the expression on her face, Clodagh nervously anticipated her words.

"My head still aches," she said. "I think you may go. I should like to be alone."

From previous knowledge of her moods, the woman made no protestations, but folded up her work and went quietly towards the door.

As she gained it, Clodagh turned.

"Simonetta!"

"Yes, signora?"

"Tell the servants they are to say nothing to any one of my having gone out to-night. You understand."

"I understand, signora."

"That is all—good-night!"

"Good-night, signora!"

It would be futile to relate the thoughts that passed through Clodagh's mind in the hour that followed Simonetta's departure; but when, at half-past eleven, Nance returned from the theatre, and, hurrying to the bedroom, opened the door swiftly and anxiously, she was standing by one of the open windows, her hat and veil still on, her gaze fixed resolutely on the shadowy trees of the park.

Crossing the threshold softly, Nance tip-toed into the room.

"Clo," she whispered, "'how are you? Better?" Then she paused in pleased surprise.

"What? You've been out? Then you *are* better. How glad Walter will be! He insisted on coming back to know how you were."

At Gore's name, Clodagh started and looked round.

"Walter here?" she said.

"Yes; but, Clo! what's the matter? You've been crying."

Clodagh stepped to her side and laid her hand imperatively on her arm.

"Hush!" she whispered. "Go back at once and tell Walter that I'm—that I'm asleep. Tell him that Simonetta said I was better and fell asleep. Tell him anything you can think of that will make him happy and get him away. He must be got away. I can't see him. Do you understand, Nance? He must be got away."

For one surprised moment Nance looked at her sister; then conquering her curiosity, she turned quietly and moved to the door.

"All right, darling!" she said reassuringly; "I'll send him away happy."

Clodagh put her hand across her eyes.

"Thank God!" she said. "If you had asked me one more question I couldn't have borne it. Send him away, and then come back."

In silence Nance left the room. Five minutes passed—ten minutes; then Clodagh's straining ears caught the closing of the outer door, and her hand dropped to her side in a gesture of excessive relief.

"Thank God!" she said again.

When Nance re-entered, she was still standing in the middle of the room, her face white and tear-stained, her figure braced.

"Nance," she said, almost before the door had closed upon her sister, "I am going to tell you things I have never told you before. I feel I shall go mad to-night, if I don't tell some one. Don't ask me any questions. Just listen and—if you can—love me!"

Nance paused just inside the door. Her own face looked pale above the shimmering blue and silver of her evening dress; her dark blue eyes were full of a peculiarly tender light.

"I don't love you, Clo," she said below her breath. "I adore you. Tell me whatever you like."

Clodagh threw out her hands despairingly.

"I'm not worth love like that," she cried. "You'll know it when I've finished. Do you remember long ago, Nance, when James and I went to Venice? Do you remember my letters from Venice?"

Nance showed no surprise at the sudden irrelevant questions.

"All of them," she answered—"I have them all."

"Then you remember how I met Frances Hope and Val Serracauld—and Lord Deerehurst?"

"I remember."

"I was very much alone at that time, Nance. James was only a shadow in my life; and they—they seemed like sunshine, and I wanted the sunshine. I have always been like a child, turning to bright tawdry things."

"Clo! you're upset to-night!—you're ill!"

"No, I'm not. I've been seeing myself and seeing my life to-night. I liked these people—I liked these men who talked to and flattered me, and ignored the fact that I had a husband—I liked them and encouraged them. And one night, on the balcony of the Palazza Ugochini——" She stopped, then made a sudden gesture, as if to sweep unnecessary things aside. "But I won't talk of that!" she cried. "It is the later time I want to come to—the time after James's death, when I met Frances Hope again." She paused to regain her breath; but the look of determination did not leave her face. Her dark eyes seemed; almost to challenge Nance's. "When I went to Monte Carlo with Frances," she went on, "I did not go to forget poor James's death, as you believed; I went to forget something else that had made me much more unhappy; and the way I set about forgetting was to gamble. Yes, I know what you feel!—I know what you think! But it cannot alter anything. I gambled. I lost large sums of money that Frances advanced me. I *had* to borrow, because there were formalities to be gone through about James's will, before I could draw my income. Then I came back to London; I met Val Serracauld and Lord Deerehurst again; I took an expensive flat; I lived like people six times as well off as myself; I gambled again——"

"Clodagh!"

Clodagh put up her hand.

"Wait! It's all leading up to something. I was utterly foolish, utterly mad. I borrowed again to pay my debts at bridge. Then one day Frances asked me for her money. It seemed like the end of the world; but it was a debt of honour—it couldn't be shirked. I wrote her out a cheque that left me beggared of the half-year's income I had been counting on to put me straight."

"Oh, Clo, Clo! Why wasn't I here?"

"Yes, why wasn't somebody here? But the worst is to come. I did not know where to look, I did not know where to turn, when suddenly—quite suddenly—I thought of your thousand pounds——"

Nance gave a little gasp.

"I remembered that. And, Nance—Nance, can you guess what happened?"

Nance did not attempt to answer.

"I took that thousand pounds. I stole it. Don't say anything! Don't try to excuse me! I want to face things. I told myself I would write and tell you; then I told myself I would say it when you came back. But when you did come"—she halted for a second—"when you did come, Nance, you loved me, you admired me, you *respected* me, and—and I couldn't. When you asked me for the money that night at Tuffnell, I knew I would have to find it and pay it back without making any confession to you."

A sound that was almost a moan escaped Nance's lips.

"Yes!" Clodagh cried—"yes! I know exactly how great a fool I was. But what is done is done. The day you drove to Wynchley with Lady Diana and Walter, I stayed behind to write to Mr. Barnard and ask him to advance me the money. But somehow I couldn't do that, either; and then—hate me, Nance! hate me, if you like!—Lord Deerehurst came to me when I was most disheartened, most depressed, and offered to lend me the money."

"And you took it?" Nance said almost quietly.

"I took it—yes, I took it. I have always been like that—always—always; grasping at the easy things, letting the hard ones slip by. And now!—now!"

"Now?"

"Nance, listen!" She took a swift step forward. "It was because of that loan that I couldn't slight him since we came back to town. You were right— you were quite right in all you advised; but I couldn't do it. He had lent me the money. He had seemed my best friend. I felt I couldn't do it—until yesterday.

"But yesterday, when he left, and Walter spoke of him, I knew there was no choice. It was my own happiness or his friendship. And I—I decided for my own happiness."

She stopped, and drew a quick, deep breath.

Nance clasped her hands, fearfully conscious that more was still to come.

"When I have a difficult thing to do," Clodagh went on, "I must do it quickly. I can't wait, I can't prepare and plan, I can't brood over things. After Walter left yesterday I decided that what must be done must be done at once. I made up my mind that I would see Lord Deerehurst to-night; that I would be quite candid with him, explain my position—and appeal to his generosity to let our friendship end."

"Then to-night——?"

"To-night was all a deception. I had no headache—I wasn't ill. I shammed it all, that I might be alone."

"And while we were at the theatre you sent for him——?"

"No! I went to Carlton House Terrace to see him."

"Went to see him! Clo!"

"I said you could hate me! Do hate me! Despise me! Think anything you like! I went to see him; I went to his house—at night, alone—thinking, believing—— Oh!" She made a gesture of acute self-disgust. "Nance, need I say it all? Need I?—need I? Can't you understand without my saying? All that I had imagined about his friendship was untrue. Such people don't understand friendship. All along he had been waiting, quietly and silently, like one of those horrible hawks we used to watch at Orristown—waiting to swoop down when the right moment came." With an almost hysterical gesture she put her hand to her throat.

Nance's face had become very white; but in the intensity of her pity and love, she did not dare to approach her sister.

"Clo," she whispered, "you must tell Walter."

Clodagh's face suddenly flamed.

"Tell Walter! Tell Walter that I owe Deerehurst a thousand pounds—that I lied to him and to you all to-night, that I might go alone to Deerehurst's house! You don't know Walter! There is only one thing in the world that I can do—that I must do, and that is to go to Ireland and arrange about raising money on my share of Orristown. It can be done somehow. Father did it. I shall not eat or sleep or think until that thousand pounds is paid."

Prompted by a swift and eager impulse, Nance's face flushed, and she ran forward. Then almost as she reached her sister's side, her expression changed. She suddenly curbed her impetuosity.

"Perhaps it *would* be a good idea," she said slowly. "When would you like to go?"

"To-night if I could! I feel—oh, I feel——!" Clodagh put her hands over her face.

Nance stood watching her for a moment longer. Then she slipped softly to her side, and put one arm about her neck.

"Don't be sad, darling," she murmured—"don't be sad! You shall go to Ireland to-morrow, if you like; and all the planning—all the explaining to Walter and to everybody—will be done by me."

And so it came to pass, in the extraordinary way with which events sometimes precipitate themselves, that at four o'clock on the following afternoon Clodagh was borne swiftly out of Paddington Station on the first stage of her journey to Ireland.

The chain of incidents that had been forged by Nance to make this departure feasible, as well as possible, had been too minute and complex to make any impression upon Clodagh's mind. Her confession the night before had been more a confession to herself than a conscious unburdening of her soul to other ears; and having made it, she was satisfied to resign herself into any hands that were willing and capable of guiding her actions.

The first incident of the morning had been a visit from Gore. But it had been Nance who had interviewed him first; and a quarter of an hour later, when Clodagh had come into the drawing-room, nervous and guilty, she had found him full of sympathy and solicitude for what he believed to be her sudden recall to Ireland. Then had come the Estcoits; and with their advent, more solicitude and more sympathy. Lunch time had crept upon them almost unawares; and—again on Nance's initiative—the whole party had adjourned to the Hyde Park Hotel, and had partaken of a meal in company.

More than once during the crowded hours of the morning, Clodagh had striven to draw her sister aside; but Nance, animated by an unusual excitement, had evaded every possibility of a *tête-à-tête*.

It was only at the door of the railway carriage, when Gore and Estcoit were superintending the labelling of her luggage, and Mrs. Estcoit and Daisy were buying books and papers for her amusement, that at last they had a word in private. Clodagh was standing in the open doorway of the carriage, and Nance was on the step, when quite suddenly the latter put up her hand and pressed a letter between her sister's fingers.

"My proper good-bye is in this letter, darling," she said. "I couldn't say it before everybody. Kiss me, will you?"

Impulsively Clodagh bent forward, and the sisters exchanged a long kiss.

"You have been an angel, Nance! I will thank you when—when——"

"No!—no! There can never be thanks between you and me. We are one. Remember that always! Always, Clo—always!"

She drew back quickly, as the rest of the party came hurrying to the carriage.

And so the good-byes had all been said, and the train had steamed out of the station; she had watched the platform melt into obscurity, and then had dropped into her seat with that sense of quiet—of flatness—that follows the moments of parting.

The long railway journey and the night crossing to Ireland still lay between her and action. She looked impatiently at her travelling companions, an uninteresting brother and sister who had already buried themselves behind newspapers in their respective corners of the carriage, and almost angrily she turned to the heap of magazines lying beside her; but as she did so, her glance brightened. Nance's letter was still to be read!

In the midst of her perplexities, a tender thought flashed over her mind as she opened the envelope, and her face softened instinctively as she began to read. But gradually, as her glance passed from one line to another, her expression changed, she sat upright in her seat, her bearing altered in a sudden, inexplicable manner.

"Darling, darling Clo!" the letter began,

> "I must have seemed a wretch last night and to-day! I mean I
> must have seemed very strange, showing hardly any surprise
> or sympathy at anything you told me, and taking your going

to Ireland as though it were a thing that happened every day. But, Clo, it wasn't because I didn't love and worship you, and feel for you in every tiny thing, but because I was afraid you would guess what was really in my mind—what I was plotting and planning all the time.

"Clo, I wanted you to go to Ireland because—oh, do forgive me for even writing it!—I wanted to get you away.

"Dearest, you are to do no more silly things. At the risk of hurting you, I am saying this. You used to say long ago that I saw more than you, because I looked on instead of doing things myself. Clo, you are *not* to raise money on Orristown, because you have no need to do it. Lord Deerehurst has been paid his thousand pounds and you are free—quite free.

"My little sister, imagine that my arms are round your neck so tight that you can't be vexed! When you told me last night that my thousand pounds really belonged to him, my first thought was to say—'Well, let's give him back as much of it as we have left!' But I stopped in time. You were not in the mood last night to take the most loving favour in the world. You wanted to sacrifice yourself; so instead of saying what was in my heart, I locked it up closely and thought about it all night; and before you were awake this morning, I sent for Pierce and asked him to lend me three hundred pounds— the three hundred we had spent out of the thousand.

"Don't say anything, darling! Don't be angry! Don't even think! Pierce was perfectly sweet; he never asked one question, and at three o'clock to-day, just after we came back from lunch, I sent the thousand pounds in notes to Carlton House Terrace, with a card of yours enclosed.

"Darling, *don't* be vexed! Don't question it! It is right, I know. It was a debt of honour, in the fullest sense.

"And now, Clo, it's all finished, all done with, all passed, and you can repay me the money slowly in years and years. Be happy! Oh, darling, be happy! Go back to Orristown, as I would have you to go back, with your heart full of all the great, good, true love that Walter and I have for you.

"Ride and walk and swim, and be without one care; and in a week or two, when the hateful thought of last night has been swept away by the splendid strong sea winds, come back to us, a newer, wiser, happier Clodagh.

"Darling, I am, now and always,

"Your true sister,

"Nance."

Clodagh closed the letter; then suddenly she rose from her seat and stepped from the carriage into the narrow corridor.

The engine was swinging forward at great speed; the train itself was swaying to the swift motion; outside, the pleasant English country seemed to fly past the long line of windows. For a second, she stood by the carriage door; then she stepped forward to the open window and, leaning out, let the strong current of air play upon her face, blowing back the hair from her temples.

How good God was! How good the world was! The great machinery of the train—the great wheels of life—ground out the same sudden song. She was free! By the unlimited power of love, she had been made free!

# CHAPTER XVII

It was eleven o'clock on the day following when Clodagh's train steamed into the little station of Muskeere. Her boat had arrived in Cork in the early hours of the morning; but she had only given herself time to take a hurried breakfast at one of the hotels, before driving to the railway station. Now that she had set foot in Ireland, the racial love of home had awakened in her, making the hours leaden until she found herself at Orristown.

The great lifting of the spirit that Nance's letter had brought into being, had not subsided since the moment she had arisen from her seat in the train, filled with the knowledge that an insupportable burden had been lifted from her. At Reading she had despatched an answering telegram to her sister; and for nearly an hour afterwards, she had sat in the corner of her carriage, covering sheet after sheet of note-paper with hasty pencilling. Two letters were the result,—one to Nance, all love, all spontaneous gratitude; the other to Gore, full of tenderness, of promise, of almost vehement reassurance.

Thus the long and usually monotonous train journey ran itself out; and in the confused darkness of the crowded landing-stage, she went on board the boat at New Milford.

The crossing of the sea had ever been a delight to Clodagh. The love of the sea—the almost mystical knowledge of it—was in her blood. And that night for many hours she had paced the deck, rejoicing after a fashion understood by few in each forward plunge of the vessel—in the sense of exhilaration and action conveyed each time the prow dipped to cut the waves and send the spray flying.

She was going home! There had seemed a curious, thrilling sensation in the knowledge. She was going home! After many experiences, she was returning to the spot where her life had first separated its thread from the great tapestry of existence—the spot where happiness and unhappiness had first presented themselves as differentiated things—where the elemental facts of pain and pleasure had been first demonstrated to her unformed mind. The memory of Orristown had materialised, as she had walked to and fro under the summer sky powdered with faint stars; and she had closed her eyes until the salt sting of the sea had conjured up the square, white house, the green fields, and the long, shelving rocks.

The picture had remained with her long after she retired to her cabin, and had been still before her mind when the first low line of Irish land had broken across her vision in the silvery morning. Then it had been dispersed by more immediate things,—the arrival at Cork—the breakfast—the drive across the town to the Muskeere train; until at last the shrill whistle of the small engine, announcing that her destination was reached, swept everything but the incidents of the moment from her consideration.

As the train stopped, she sprang to her feet and leaned out of the window. How intensely familiar it was!—the narrow platform; the wooden paling, behind which the incursion of summer visitors to Muskeere congregated each day to watch the Cork trains arrive; the slovenly, good-natured porter, absolutely unaltered by the passage of time!

Her thoughts swam, as she tried vainly to reconcile her own many experiences with this amazing changelessness. Then all need for such comparison was brushed aside, as a tall figure came striding down the platform, followed by a couple of dogs; and she recognised Laurence Asshlin.

Her first conscious thought was, "How fine-looking he has grown!" her second, "How badly his clothes are made!" Then she laughed to herself from happiness, and from that sense of comradeship and clannishness to which the Irish nature is so susceptible.

"Larry!" she cried a moment later, as she threw the carriage door open.

But her dog Mick was the first to gain her side. Leaping forward at sound of her voice, he sprang into the carriage, whimpering with joy.

"Mick!—darling Mick! Oh, you bad thing!" She laughed again delightedly; then she turned, flushed and radiant, to greet her cousin.

"Hold him, Larry! That's better! Now, how are you?" She held out her hand and laid it in Asshlin's disengaged one.

Larry flushed with excitement and embarrassment.

"How are you, Clo? You're awfully unchanged! Let me help you out! The trap is waiting!"

As in a dream, she passed through the little station that had seemed so large and imposing to her childish eyes in the time when a day's shopping in Cork had represented the acme of adventure and enterprise; but half-way down the narrow platform she paused.

"Oh, the sea, Larry!" she exclaimed, drawing in a long, deep breath—"the heavenly smell of the sea!" Then she suddenly caught sight of Burke, waiting, as he might have waited six years ago, beside the high, old-fashioned trap.

"The same trap!" she said, with a little gasp.

Asshlin laughed.

"The same, only for a coat of varnish. But won't you speak to Tim?" He added the last a trifle diffidently, with a shy glance at her costly clothes and her general air of refinement and distinction.

Without a word she went forward.

"Tim!" she said very softly.

The old man turned quickly; then drew back.

But Clodagh held out her hand, regardless of the staring summer visitors.

"Tim! I'm not so changed that you don't know me?"

The old man remained motionless.

"I'd know you if I was under the sod, and the sound of your voice come anear me," he said almost solemnly.

Clodagh felt her throat tighten, as the old horny hand was slowly extended to clasp her own.

"I'm glad to be home, Tim!" she said impulsively—"I'm glad to be home!"

There was a delay of several minutes while the porter extricated her luggage from the van; and during this interval, she found time to admire the young horse, which had been bred at Orristown, and to make friends with the Irish terrier that had been Mick's companion on the run to Muskeere, besides asking a dozen questions concerning people and things at Carrigmore. Then at last, the trunk was deposited under the roomy seat of the trap; and Asshlin stepped forward to help her into her place.

"Larry," she said, pausing with her foot on the step, "may I drive? I'd love to drive."

Asshlin gave a ready assent, and, taking his own seat, handed her the reins, while Burke mounted to the back of the trap.

It was wonderful to Clodagh, that first gathering up of reins rendered hard by long service and Irish rain—that first forward start into the strong, sea-scented air. A sudden joy filled her. She was young; the world was a goodly place, when one studied it in this untainted atmosphere; above all, she was possessor of the great prize—love. Far away, in the tumult and press of the greatest city in the world, the man she set above all others thought of her—waited for her—trusted her.

Out of her own bright confidence, she made the sunny morning brighter, as she drove along the well-remembered roads, halting every mile or so to gaze at some thrice-familiar object that stood now as it had stood in the days of her babyhood.

At last Carrigmore was reached. She saw the clustering pink-and-white cottages of the village; the sleeping ruins guarded by the Round Tower; the long, yellow strand and the glassy bay, on whose farther headland stood the house of Orristown—-a square white patch, to be seen for many miles. She looked at it all long and closely.

"Oh, Larry," she said, below her breath, "how wonderfully the same it is! Nance told me, but I couldn't imagine it. Why, there's scarcely a weed changed!"

Asshlin laughed a little.

"We didn't think you'd care much about it, after Italy and places," he said, with a slight touch of shy awkwardness that seemed more than ever to link the present with the past.

"Not care about it? Larry!" Her voice quivered; then she laughed quickly and touched the horse with the whip.

"Shall we go straight to Orristown? or shall I run in and see Aunt Fan?"

Asshlin looked slightly distressed.

"You're tired after the journey," he said. "And, anyway, it's one of her bad days. They come oftener than ever now. To-morrow she'll enjoy seeing you more."

A quick recollection of her aunt on her bad days swept over Clodagh's mind; and she looked up suddenly into Larry's handsome, spirited face.

"Is she often cross now, Larry?" she asked, as she might have asked when they were children.

Asshlin turned at the sound of her voice; his diffidence forsook him; the old comradeship, the old sense of sympathy and understanding, came rushing back.

"She is harder than ever to get on with," he said. "And every day seems worse than the last. Sometimes——" He stopped; but a shadow of discontent, of depression, had darkened his face.

"Poor Larry!" Clodagh said very softly. And without further comment, she turned the horse's head in the direction of Orristown.

The cousins spoke rather less during the drive along the low, flat road lying parallel to the strand; but, despite the silence, each was conscious of an awakened fellowship; and as they descended the sharp hill that led to the gates of Orristown, Clodagh pointed with her whip to where the sky hung low and brooding over the glassy line of the horizon.

"This heat will break in a storm, Larry," she said, aware of having spoken the same words a hundred times in almost the same spot.

Asshlin scanned the sea thoughtfully.

"I believe you're right!" he answered. "But a puff of wind would do no harm. You'd like a scud across the bay, wouldn't you?"

Clodagh's eyes danced.

"Love it!" she substituted enthusiastically. "Come for me at ten to-morrow, Larry, and we'll sail back together to Carrigmore. We'll have a long day there and see everything; and then you'll come back with me to dinner." She flashed a quick smile at him, as she piloted the trap through the rusty gates.

As they swept up the long, narrow drive, she looked eagerly to right and left; then suddenly she gave a little laugh of pleasure, and waved her whip towards a field that skirted the avenue, in which a very old man had paused in the act of digging potatoes, and now stood in an attitude of rigid salutation, a broken felt hat held above his head.

"Look, Larry! It's Pat Foley! Poor old Pat! Isn't it lovely the way every one remembers?"

Her eyes filled with sudden tears, as they passed the last clump of trees and came full upon the old white house; then, as the horse drew up sharply under the well-remembered iron balcony, she gave a little cry and threw the reins to Asshlin.

Hannah had opened the hall door, and stood broad-faced, honest, beaming as of old.

"My darlin'!" she cried—"my darlin'!"

And in an instant, regardless of her dress and of the eyes of Asshlin and Burke, Clodagh sprang to the ground and rushed into the arms that had so often sheltered her.

At eight o'clock on the same evening, Clodagh, with Mick at her feet, sat in a shabby leather arm-chair by the open window of the bedroom that she had shared with Nance for so many years. Outside, the soft beating of the sea against the rocks came to her ears with strange familiarity; by her side stood a small table set out with a homely tea; while in front of her, jealously watchful that she did justice to the meal, stood Hannah.

"An' 'tis a millonaire they tells me the child is goin' to marry?" she asked in one of her tentative, round-about questions. "Glory be to God! an' she only out of the school!"

Clodagh glanced through the window at the golden evening sky.

"You married me before I had been to school, Hannah," she said, below her breath.

The old shrewd light gleamed in Hannah's eyes. She moved awkwardly and yet softly round the tea-table, and laid her broad hand on Clodagh's shoulder.

"Many's the day I do be ponderin' on that match, Miss Clodagh," she said earnestly. "The ways of God are dark; and what I done, I done for the best."

Clodagh, touched by the deep solicitude of the voice, put her own smooth hand over the old rough one.

"I'm sure God did everything as it should be done, Hannah,—because it—it has all come right in the end."

Hannah's hand dropped from her shoulder in sudden excitement.

"Miss Clodagh!" she said breathlessly—"Miss Clodagh, is it a husband you'll be thinkin' to take?"

Again Clodagh's gaze wandered across the sky, melting now from gold to orange.

"There is a man who wants to take me for his wife, Hannah," she corrected, very gently.

"An' you do be puttin' him before everythin' in the world?"

Clodagh turned swiftly and met the small, anxious eyes.

"So much before everything, that if I were to lose him now I should lose"—she paused for an instant, then added—"myself."

Hannah's eyes narrowed in the intensity of her concern.

"An' he do be carin' for you, Miss Clodagh?"

Clodagh learnt forward; and the warm light from the sunset touched and transfigured her face.

"Yes—he cares," she said very slowly.

# CHAPTER XVIII

Late on the afternoon that followed her arrival, Clodagh—with Larry in attendance—climbed up the uneven path that led from the Orristown boat-cove to the house. A considerable change had taken place in the weather since the previous evening. The sky no longer hung low and motionless above the horizon line; the sea no longer shone white and polished as a mirror. A gale had sprung up, breaking the clouds and whipping the sea into small green waves; and more than once, as the cousins clambered up the rugged track, Asshlin paused to look back at his small boat, lying with furled sail and shipped oars on the shingle.

"I hope I've beached her high enough," he said. "There will be a big sea to-night."

Clodagh laughed. The prospect of a storm stirred her. She felt boundlessly happy, boundlessly confident in this free, open life.

The night before, after Larry had left her, and the first tinge of twilight had fallen across the old house, there had been a moment in which the ghosts of memory had threatened to assail her—to come trooping up the gaunt staircase, and through the great, bare rooms. But her will had conquered; she had dispelled the phantoms, and had slept dreamlessly in the big four-post bed.

In the morning she had awakened, as James Milbanke had awakened long ago, to a world of light and joy. But with this difference, that to him the world had been a thing to speculate upon and study, while to her it was a thing familiar—understood—possessed. While she partook of breakfast and while she visited the stables, she kept Hannah by her side, learning from her the vicissitudes of the many humble lives around Orristown that had been known to her since childhood; then, before the tales had been half recounted, Larry had arrived in his boat; and the two cousins, like children playing at a long-loved game, had gone down together to the boat-cove to where the little craft flashed its white sail like a seagull in the sun, and danced with impatience to be off across the crisp green waves.

Clodagh's first act on landing, at Carrigmore, had been to visit the little ivy-covered post-office, in the hope that the Orristown letters might possibly be intercepted. But the postman had already left the village, and she had no choice but to wait patiently for Gore's first letter until her return in the evening. But the postponement had not been sufficient to damp her spirits; and she had started on her various expeditions with a very light heart. Last of all, had come the visit to Mrs. Asshlin, who now rarely left her room, but lay all day in the semi-light made by drawn blinds, drinking numerous cups of strong tea and keeping up a fitful murmur of complaint.

With senses that rebelled against the depressing atmosphere, Clodagh had entered the bedroom and had sat for nearly an hour beside her aunt's couch, listening with all the patience she could muster to the oft-repeated tale of discontent and ill-health. Then at last, feeling that duty could demand no more, she had risen and kissed Mrs. Asshlin's worn cheek.

"We must have you over in London, Aunt Fan," she said cheerfully. "We must take you to a really good doctor, and have you made quite well."

But Mrs. Asshlin had shaken her head dubiously.

"I never had faith in really good doctors since Molyneaux came down to see your poor father."

To this, there seemed no possible response; so Clodagh had kissed her aunt once more, and, with a promise that she would return the next day, had slipped silently out of the gloomy room followed by Larry. Outside, in the vivid daylight, the cousins had looked at each other involuntarily.

"Sometimes life seems awful, Clo!" Asshlin had said, in a despondent voice. And with a momentary shock, Clodagh had caught a gleam of the restlessness, the brooding gloom, that used long ago to settle on the face of her father.

"Why don't you leave Carrigmore, Larry?" she had said quickly. "It's a wonderful place to rest in, but it's not the place for the whole of a man's life."

Asshlin had made a descriptive gesture, indicating the house behind him; then, with a sudden impulse of confidence, he had thrust his hand into his pocket, and had drawn out six five-pound notes.

"When this represents the whole exchequer of the next three months, there isn't much question of foreign travel—or fortune-seeking," he had said. "Come along! The gale is freshening!"

And Clodagh had obeyed, depressed for the moment by contact with that hidden poverty of the proud and well-born, that is one of the most pathetic factors in the scheme of Irish social life. She had longed ardently to make some suggestion, some offer of help, to this bright, spirited boy, who was wasting the best years God had given him in coping with an estate that could never be made to pay, and attending upon an invalid who hovered perpetually on the borderland of shadows; but a native comprehension of the position held her dumb. An offer of help made on the moment of his confidence would set an irrevocable barrier between them in the very dawning of their renewed friendship.

So she had talked to him of the crops, of the fishing, of the Orristown live-stock, while the boat carried them back across the bay. And the sail homeward under the scudding clouds, while the little boat danced and dipped to the buffeting of the waves, had erased the passing gloom; and now, as they climbed the steep pathway and passed across the fields to the house, Clodagh's heart was beating high in her own egotistical joy at the mere fact of life.

She laughed out of sheer pleasure, as they passed round the house and four or five dogs rushed forth from the hall to greet them; and stooping impulsively, she drew Mick close to her and kissed his rough head.

"Larry, do you remember how you won him from me long ago, and how nobly you gave him back? I have never forgotten it." She smiled affectionately at her tall young cousin; and, freeing Mick, led the way into the house.

On the shabby hall table, where the silver sconces stood as of old, lay a small heap of letters; and with an exclamation of pleasure, Clodagh ran forward and picked them up, passing them hastily in review.

There was a thick, important-looking one from Nance. And—yes! the first letter from Gore—the letter she had been waiting for!

For an instant her face fell. It felt thin and disappointing, as she held the envelope between her fingers. But almost at once her face cleared. After all, men had not as much time as women for the writing of letters! And this had been written on the day of her departure! She looked at the postmark: "London—10.30." Of course he had only had time to scribble a line. How good and thoughtful of him even to have sent that line! She turned and looked at Larry, her face radiant once more.

"Larry," she said, "will you tell Burke that we'll dine in half an hour, if Hannah has everything ready? And tell them to have candles in all the sconces. It is to be a dinner party, you know!" She gave a pleasant little laugh and turned towards the stairs, closing her fingers over her letters in a delightful, secret sense of anticipation and possession.

Her own room was filled with a cold grey light as she entered it—a peculiar light drawn from the wind-swept sky and the pale, agitated waters; and she noticed, as she crossed the threshold, that the wind roared draughtily down the wide chimney, in a way that suggested autumn and autumnal gales. But the circumstance made little impression; she carried her own world in her heart—and here, in the letter Gore had written.

In a second impulse of love, she laid the others aside, and opened Gore's envelope. Drawing out the letter, she held it for a moment against her face. On this paper his hand had rested when he wrote to her! There was a sense of personal contact in the mere thought. Then, at last, with a smile at her own sentiment, she opened it slowly and smoothed out the pages.

The written lines—scarcely more than a dozen in number—danced for an instant before her eyes; then focused themselves with terrible distinctness.

There was no formal beginning to the letter; it was merely a statement made in sharp, uneven characters, as though the sender had written under great stress—great emotion or resolve.

> "I find," it began, "that you have treated me with an unpardonable want of honour and want of truth on a matter that concerned me very deeply—the matter of Deerehurst; and it seems to me, under the circumstances, only just and right that our engagement should come to an end. A marriage built upon such a basis could only have one termination. If this seems hard or abrupt, I can only say that the knowledge of my mistake has come hardly to me. I shall go abroad again as soon as I can make my plans. I am glad to think that, as no one but your sister knew of our engagement, my action can cause no public comment or unpleasantness for you.

> "Walter Gore."

Clodagh read the lines—read and re-read them. For the first time in her life, her quick brain failed to respond to a first suggestion; then, at last, as though the cloud that obscured her mind had been rent asunder, conception of all that the letter conveyed sprang to her understanding.

Walter had written this letter! Walter had given her up! Her face became very white; she swayed a little, looking about her vaguely, as if for some physical aid; then suddenly revolt took the place of panic. It was all some horrible mistake. She must go to him—rend the web of doubt that had divided them—if need be, humble herself, show him the greatness of her love, until he must condone—must forgive—must reinstate her in his heart!

Moving swiftly, she crossed the room to the fireplace, drawing out her watch as she went. With a good horse, she might still catch the last train from Muskeere—take the night mail from Cork to Dublin—cross to Holyhead in the morning, and be back in London to-morrow!

She lifted her hand to the frayed and tasselled bell-rope that hung from the ceiling: then, by a strange impulse, her arm dropped to her side.

When her journey was accomplished—when she met Gore, what had she to explain? what had she to confess? The tassel of the bell-rope slipped from between her fingers.

The vision of herself pleading with him rose vividly before her,—she, with her passionate impulsiveness; he, with his grave dignity, his uncompromising integrity. She recalled the peculiar words he had made use of on the day he had discovered Deerehurst's gift of flowers. "I should either believe in you—or disbelieve in you!" His critical attitude in their first acquaintance started to life at the remembrance of the words. He, who expected of others what he himself performed—he who, as Nance had said, was "so honourable himself"—how would he receive the poor, lame story she had to offer? A horrible, confusing dread closed in about her. A week ago, she would have gone forth confidently, to make her confession; but now her faith was less. On the night in Deerehurst's study she had tasted of the tree of knowledge—had seen things as men see them; and her fearlessness had been shaken.

She looked helplessly round the bare room filled with cold grey light.

No; Walter would never believe!—Walter would never believe! The knowledge that she had lied to him even once would stand between them, condemning her hopelessly. An appalling weight seemed to press her to the earth. She was cut adrift. She was separated for ever from all safe, sheltering human things; somewhere in the dim, far regions where the decrees of fate are made, a knell had been sounded!

She glanced once more round the bare, familiar room, from the great four-post bedstead to the long window, beyond which lay the green fields, the wind-swept sky, and the livid line of the sea; then suddenly she turned, and fled through the open door and out into the empty corridor.

Asshlin was still standing in the hall, as she came downstairs; at the sound of her approach he looked up, but in the falling twilight he noticed nothing unusual in her appearance.

"We've made a great illumination!" he said—"quite a blaze of light!"

Clodagh made no answer; but descending the stairs quickly, passed into the dining-room.

As on the night years ago, when Milbanke had come to Orristown, the old room was prepared to do honour to a guest. The tablecloth was laid, places were set for two, and the great silver sconces were filled with candles that glowed so brightly that even the dark portraits on the walls were thrown into relief. But no fire blazed in the wide grate as on the former occasion, and the curtains of the three long windows were drawn back, admitting the light from the stormy evening sky.

Clodagh's first glance, as she entered the room, was for these windows, and her first words concerned them.

"Larry, draw the curtains!" she said.

To her own ears, her voice seemed to come from some distant place—to sound infinitely thin and far away; but Asshlin seemed to observe nothing. He went forward obediently and drew the six long curtains.

As the last was pulled into place Burke entered, and carefully laid two dishes upon the table. A moment later Clodagh took her seat.

"What will you eat, Larry?" she said hurriedly. "Chicken? Ham?"

Asshlin turned to her, as he in his turn took his place.

"What will *you* have?" he said.

"I? Oh—anything! But talk, Larry! Tell me things! Let's—let's be gay!"

Asshlin was busy cutting up the chicken. He did not hear the faintly hysterical note that underran her voice—the note of warning from a mind trying with panic-stricken haste to evade itself.

He helped her to some chicken; and Burke, laying the plate before her, went in search of wine.

She toyed for a moment or two with the food, making pretence to eat.

At last Larry looked at her.

"You're eating nothing. Aren't you hungry?"

She started nervously.

"No; I'm not hungry. I—I had a glass of milk in my room. I couldn't wait for dinner." She tried to laugh, as she told the falsehood.

He accepted the explanation.

"Then you must have a glass of wine now!" he said genially, as Burke re-entered with a dusty bottle of port. "Give me the bottle, Burke!"

He took it from the old man's hands, and poured some wine into Clodagh's glass; and as he leant forward, he suddenly saw by the light of the candles that her eyes were wide and black, her face very white.

"Clo, you're not feeling ill?" he asked, in quick concern.

Clodagh put her hand to her face with a startled gesture.

"No! Do I look ill? It's the storm. The storm has got on my nerves. We develop nerves in London, you know!" Again she attempted to laugh.

Once more Asshlin accepted her explanation, as something he had no authority to question.

"I want you to talk, Larry!" she added hurriedly. "I want you to talk. Say anything! Take me out of myself!"

She raised her glass to her lips and drank some of the wine. It brought a faint tinge of colour to her cheeks, but only increased the bright darkness of her eyes.

While Asshlin consumed his dinner, she sat very upright in her chair, sipping her wine from time to time or breaking small mouthfuls from her bread.

At last, having hovered anxiously about her, Burke made bold to speak his thoughts.

"Is it the way the chicken isn't nice, ma'am?" he ventured.

She started, as she had started each time she had been directly addressed.

"No, Burke! Oh no!" she said hastily. "The chicken is very nice. It's only that the storm has—has given me a headache."

Burke shook his head sympathetically, as a sudden gale swept round the house.

"'Tis lookin' for a bad night, sure enough!" he said, as he passed round the table with the next course.

When the pudding had been served and partaken of by Asshlin, Clodagh at last pushed back her chair, and with a curiously unstrung movement walked across the room to the fireplace.

"Larry," she said suddenly, "will you play cards with me when Burke takes the things away?"

Asshlin looked up with interest.

"By Jove!" he said, "what a good idea!"

When Burke reappeared, solemnly carrying some cheese, Clodagh turned to him quickly.

"Is there a pack of cards in the house, Tim?" she asked.

He glanced at her white face and upright figure, but his expression betrayed nothing.

"I do be thinkin' there's a deck some place, if I could lay me mind on it."

Asshlin leant across the table.

"There's a pack in the drawer of the side-board."

Burke crossed the room, but not over-eagerly; and, opening the drawer, produced the cards.

"'Tis the deck poor Misther Dinis got from Cork the self-same day — —" he began. Then he stopped consideratedly; and added under his breath, "The Almighty God be good to us all!"

Clodagh took the cards from him, and stood very still, fingering them nervously. At any other time, the thought of playing with cards that belonged to the dead would have filled her with repugnance; but to-night all ordinary standards had been lost—all the world was chaos. She was like one who is slipping down into a bottomless abyss, and stretches desperate hands towards any straw that might offer respite.

She never changed her position while the table was being cleared; her only sign of emotion still being shown by the spasmodic way in which she passed the cards between her fingers. When at last the cloth had been removed and the candles replaced, she came quickly across the room and stood looking down upon her cousin.

She still mechanically shuffled the cards; but her glance, as it rested on Asshlin, was unconscious and absorbed, seeing only its own mental pictures.

"What shall we play, Larry? What game can two people play?"

Asshlin looked up.

"Piquet," he said, "or euchre."

She nodded.

"Euchre! Yes, euchre!" She drew a chair up to the table and sat down. "What stakes?"

Asshlin looked uncertain.

"You say!" he suggested a little diffidently.

She gave a nervous start, as a fresh gale shook the windows.

"Thirty shillings a game? Twenty shillings a game?"

For an instant he looked at her amazed; but seeing the unconsciousness of her expression, his breeding forbade him to offer any objection. With a reckless excitement he had never before had opportunity to feel, he leant back in his chair, and taking up the glass Burke had set beside him, poured out some port and drank it.

"Thirty shillings a game!" he said magnificently.

Clodagh did not seem to hear; certainly she saw nothing of his scruple and his yielding. Her own thoughts rode and spurred her, pressing her forward in a wild, panic-stricken search for oblivion.

"Come, Larry! Play!—play! I feel"—she paused and laughed hysterically—"I feel that, if I were a man to-night, I should drink all the port in that bottle! I want to forget everything. Play!—play!"

Asshlin picked up the cards that she had laid upon the table. He could not understand her in this new mood; but he was satisfied not to understand her. He felt stimulated—lifted above himself—as he had never been before.

For two hours they played, with luck evenly balanced; then Asshlin made a reluctant attempt to draw out his watch.

"Did you hear that?" he said, as the wind roared up from the sea like an invading army. "I ought to be getting home. She'll be worrying about me."

He spoke firmly enough, but his eyes wandered back to the cards.

Clodagh rose, and, crossing to the sideboard, poured some water into a glass and drank it.

"No! no!" she said eagerly. "It's quite early. It's only eleven. She won't expect you yet."

He put his watch back into his pocket; Clodagh returned to her place at the table; and the play went on.

By twelve o'clock a change had come in their positions. Fortune was no longer impartial; and Clodagh stood the winner by several games. Again Asshlin made a movement towards departure. His face was flushed now, and a look of alarm had begun to mingle with his excitement.

"I—I ought to be going now, Clo," he said a little huskily.

Clodagh gave a sharp laugh. At last it seemed to her that she was drowning thought—holding at bay the black sense of loss and agony that threatened to inundate her soul. She threw up her head, and her eyes challenged her cousin's.

"You are a coward if you go now, Larry! You are afraid to take your revenge!"

He coloured like a girl, and gave a half-angry, half-embarrassed laugh.

"Don't say that, Clo!"

"Then will you play?"

"I—I oughtn't to."

Again Clodagh laughed—a laugh so nervous and high-pitched that it rang almost harshly across the room.

"Then you're not an Asshlin!"

"Am I not?" He tilted his chair forward, and leaned upon the table. "Let's see! Come along! I'm game for anything after that!"

There was a new note in his voice—a fiery note, that seemed to challenge fate and throw reason to the winds.

It stirred some latent power in Clodagh's brain. A faint colour crossed the pallor of her face; she half rose from her seat.

"Shall we 'play like the devil,' as father used to say?"

Asshlin threw up his head. It was as if flint and steel had struck—the spark followed inevitably.

"Yes!" he cried; "we'll play like the devil!"

At one o'clock they rose from the table. Clodagh's face was white again; but Asshlin's was deeply flushed; and as he stood up, confronting his cousin, it almost seemed that he had drunk more than the two glasses of port to which the bottle testified.

"I must go now, Clo," he said. "May I ring for Burke to get me a lantern?"

Clodagh took a step forward.

"Stay the night, Larry? You can have father's room."

He shook his head and crossed to the fireplace.

"I owe you forty pounds," he said in an unsteady voice. "I'll leave thirty here"—he drew out the notes he had shown her at Carrigmore, and laid them under the clock on the mantelpiece—"the other ten I'll—I'll give you to-morrow."

But Clodagh scarcely heard.

"Do stay! Oh, do stay!"

Again he shook his head, and pulled the bell-rope.

"I've put the notes here—under the clock."

"All right!—all right! But, Larry, can't you stay? It's a horrible night."

"I can't!" Then, as the door opened and Burke appeared, he turned to him hastily: "Burke, bring me a lantern. I want to get the boat out."

At last Clodagh's mind was torn from its own concerns.

"The boat! You're not going to cross the bay on a night like this?"

Old Burke came forward, looking from one to the other.

"Wisha, Masther Larry, is it crazy you are?"

Asshlin turned his flushed face on the old servant.

"We're all a bit crazy now and then, Tim. But I was never afraid of the sea. Get me the lantern!"

Still Burke hesitated. But suddenly Asshlin stepped forward, with a look so full of pride and domination, that by instinct he succumbed.

"As quick as you can, Burke!"

And the old man hobbled off.

There was silence between the cousins after he had gone. Asshlin leaned upon the mantelpiece, with his face averted; Clodagh walked nervously about the room, changing the arrangement of the silver on the sideboard, snuffing the candles that had begun to gutter, doing any aimless and unnecessary thing that could blur her sense of impending solitude. At last she paused in the middle of the room.

"Larry——" she began desperately.

But at the same instant Burke's step sounded in the hall, and his voice came to them through the open door.

"The lanthern is here, Masther Larry!"

Asshlin started.

"All right! I'm coming!" he called. "Good-night, Clo!" He walked forward almost awkwardly, and took her cold hand.

She looked up into his face, her own misery blotting out all other things.

"Larry! can't you stay?"

Asshlin passed his hand across his forehead.

"Don't ask me, Clo! Good-night!"

An instant later he was gone.

She ran out into the hall on the moment that she realised her desertion.

"Larry!" she called—"Larry!"

But her voice was drowned in the gale, as Burke opened the hall door and the wind rushed in, filling the wide black hall. There was a confused suggestion of storm and lantern-light; a vague silhouetted vision of Burke, bent and small, and of Asshlin, straight, lithe, and tall. Then the door closed with a thud. Lantern, figures, and storm were alike shut out from her knowledge. She was alone in the great house.

# CHAPTER XIX

Almost at the same hour that Clodagh sat down to play cards with Laurence Asshlin at Orristown, Nance was seated with Daisy Estcoit in the lounge of the Carlton. After her sister's departure, Mrs. Estcoit had borne her off to be her guest at the hotel; and now, the little party of four having dined in the restaurant, she had gone to her room to discuss a business letter with her son, leaving the two girls ensconced under one of the big palm-trees.

It was very pleasant and interesting to sit there, and watch the groups seated on the low couches beside the little coffee-tables, or to study the throng of people that moved constantly through the large glass doors of the vestibule, and up the flight of shallow steps to the restaurant itself, with its shaded lights and pretty artificial garden. The crowd was unusually large for the time of year: the band was playing a waltz: the whole atmosphere seemed gay and happy to one who only that morning had performed a great act of love.

"How lovely life is, Daisy!" Nance said suddenly, unconsciously echoing Clodagh's words on the day of Gore's return to London.

Daisy Estcoit laughed.

"Of course it is—with a trousseau like yours! But look over there—by the big palm!"

Nance had bent to rearrange some roses in her belt.

"Where? What?" she said, glancing up.

"Don't you see?"

"No. What?"

"Sir Walter Gore. He just rushed through and into the restaurant. He seems in tremendous haste."

"Walter! Where?" Nance looked round eagerly.

"I've just told you. In the restaurant. But here he is back again! He must have been looking for some one."

Nance rose from the quiet corner in which they were sitting, and stepped forward to greet Gore; but, as he came towards her down the flight of shallow steps, her smile of welcome died, and a look of surprise and concern crossed her eyes.

"Walter," she said softly.

He looked round at sound of his name.

"Oh! Nance!" he said. His manner was as quiet as usual, but he looked like a man who has undergone some great fatigue and has not yet found time to rest.

They shook hands in silence, Nance's dark blue eyes scanning his face.

"Have you heard from Clo?" she said, at last. "I have. Such a dear letter—written in the train."

He flushed.

"Yes," he said laconically, "I have heard. But I can't wait to talk about the letter now. I only came here hoping to find a man I know; they told me at his rooms that he was dining here, but 'twas evidently a mistake. I must say good-night!"

He held out his hand, and Nance took it mechanically; but as their fingers fell apart, she stepped forward and walked with him resolutely across the lounge.

In the vestibule she paused, and compelled him to meet her eyes.

"Walter," she said, "something is wrong!"

Gore's face hardened.

"Nothing is wrong."

She tightened her fingers round the fan she was carrying.

"That is untrue, Walter."

Something in the entire candour of the words touched him. He looked at her with new eyes.

"You are right," he said quietly. "It was untrue."

"Then something has happened? Something about Clo?"

"Yes. Something—something that will break our engagement."

Nance turned very pale.

"Walter!" she said faintly, after a moment's pause. Then, before he could speak again, she looked up at him. "Wait for a minute!" she said sharply—

"wait for a minute!" And turning, she hurried back to where Daisy Estcoit was still sitting.

"Daisy," she said, "tell Pierce that I have gone out with Walter, and that I'll be back in half an hour. Tell him that it's something most—most important." She spoke hastily; and, without waiting to see the effect of her words, turned again, and threaded her way between the groups of people back to where Gore was standing.

"Call a cab, Waiter!" she said. "We *must* talk."

"But, Nance——"

"A hansom, please!"

She turned without embarrassment to one of the attendants.

"But Nance——"

"You cannot refuse me, Walter. Clo is everything in the world to me."

The jingle of harness sounded, as the hansom drew up; and, walking deliberately forward, she got into the vehicle.

"Tell him to drive anywhere that will take half an hour," she said to Gore, as he reluctantly followed.

"Out Holland Park way!" he said, pausing on the step. "I'll tell you when to stop."

He took his seat and closed the doors of the cab.

"Won't you be cold without a wrap?"

Nance ignored the question.

"Now," she said, "what is it? Is it about Deerehurst?"

At the sudden onslaught, Gore started, and turning round, looked at her.

"I don't intend to discuss this matter," he said in his coldest voice.

"But I mean to discuss it." She met his glance with a resolution that was not to be denied. "Is it about Deerehurst?"

"If you wish to know, it is about Deerehurst."

In his voice there was all the reserve, all the coldness of the Englishman who has been very sorely wounded.

"And what about him?"

Quite suddenly Gore's reserve flamed to anger.

"Do you think I am going to talk of such things with a child like you?"

Nance clasped her hands on the closed doors of the cab, formulating a sudden prayer that help might be vouchsafed her; then she spoke, with eyes fixed steadily in front of her.

"I am not a child, Walter," she said in a very low voice. "And you *must* speak to me—for Clo's sake. And if you won't, then I must tell you that I know all about her staying away from the theatre the other night—about her having no headache, but wanting to see Deerehurst—about her going to Carlton House Terrace at nine o'clock—I know it all, because she told me——"

Gore drew a quick, amazed breath.

"She told you?"

She nodded. Her throat felt very dry.

"Clodagh told you that?"

"Yes. Who told *you*?"

He made no answer.

"Walter, was it Lady Frances Hope?"

"What does that matter?"

"It was Lady Frances?"

He put his hand wearily over his eyes.

"If you wish to know, it was."

"I guessed so. I always hated her. The other day, as we drove from Paddington after seeing Clodagh off, we passed her in the Park with Valentine Serracauld. He must have seen or guessed, or heard from Deerehurst—and told her. He is an enemy of Clo's, too, since the time at Tuffnell."

"Oh, Walter!" She turned suddenly, and looked at him—"Walter, have you ever really known Clodagh?"

The pain and question in her voice broke through his wounded self-esteem.

"Clodagh has made a fool of me, Nance," he said harshly. "She has never been straight with me—never from the very first."

"And do you know why?"

"No; I can't pretend that I know why."

His tone was very bitter.

"Because she cares too much. She idealises too much."

Gore made a sound that might have been meant for a laugh.

"I think it is I who have idealised."

Nance straightened her small figure.

"Then you have always treated her wrongly. What Clo needs is not to be idealised, but to be taken care of; not to be praised or blamed, but to be taken care of." Her brown fingers were tightly clasped, as they rested on the cab doors. "All her life she has wanted to be taken care of—and all her life she has been thrown back upon herself. When I was little, I had her; but when she was little, she had no one. Our mother died when I was born."

Something in the simple pathos of this statement stirred Gore's ever-present sense of the sacredness of home ties.

"I never knew that," he said very quietly.

"Yes, our mother died when I was born; and Clo grew up in our father's care. Did she ever tell you about our father?"

"No. At least——"

"Then I shall. I've told Pierce. People ought to know. It helps them to understand.

"Our father was a spendthrift—a gambler—a man without any principles. If somebody stronger than himself had taken him in hand when he was young, things might have been different. But he began by ruling everybody who came in contact with him, until at last nobody dared to rule him.

"Can you imagine how a man like that would bring up a daughter—you who had a mother to help you in every year of your life?"

Her blue eyes darkened with intensity.

"Our home in Ireland is a big lonely house on the sea-coast. Imagine growing up in a house like that, without care or money or friends—for father drove all his friends away. Imagine Clo's life! Her only learning was what she got with our cousin from the schoolmaster of the nearest village; her only amusements were sailing and riding and fishing. She never had the love or friendship of a woman of her own class; she never knew what it was to be without the dread of debt or disgrace; and then, at eighteen, she married the first man who came into her life—not because she liked him—not because she wanted to marry, or knew what marrying was—but because he had saved our father's honour by paying his debt!"

She paused to take breath; but before Gore could speak, she went on again:

"Do you know what I always wonder, Walter, when I think of Clodagh?"

Gore made a low murmur.

"I wonder, considering everything, that she hasn't done really wrong things, instead of just terribly foolish ones! It doesn't seem strange to me that she should have behaved like a child, when she first felt what it was to be free and flattered and admired. Listen, Walter! There have been too many clouds between you and Clodagh. Neither of you has understood. You have been too proud; and she has been too much afraid. But I am not afraid!"

And in the prosaic London cab, with her eyes fixed resolutely on the heavy copper-coloured sky that hung above the housetops, Nance performed her second act of love. While Gore sat silent, she poured forth the whole mistaken tale of Clodagh's life, from the days in Venice to the hour of her departure for Ireland. She omitted nothing; she extenuated nothing. With a strange instinct towards choice of the right weapons, she fought for her sister's future. Everything was told—Lady Frances Hope's poisoning of Clodagh's mind against Gore himself—the scene with Serracauld in the card-room—all the temptations, all the follies, confessed in the darkness of the nights at Tuffnell, and in Clodagh's own bedroom on the night she visited Deerehurst. It was the moment for speech; and she spoke. Her own shyness, her own natural reticence, were swept aside by the great need of one who was infinitely dear. The scene at Carlton House Terrace she described without flinching; for candour and innocence move boldly where lesser virtues fail and falter. She told the story with a simple truth that was more dignified than any hesitancy.

When at last she had finished, Gore sat for a space, very silent and with bent head; then abruptly, as if inspired by a sudden resolution, he put up his hand to the trap in the roof.

"The nearest telegraph office!" he called, as the cabman looked down.

The man whipped up his horse. But Nance turned sharply.

"What are you going to do?"

"To wire to Clodagh."

"To Clodagh?"

"Yes."

"But Clodagh doesn't know? Walter, you haven't told Clodagh! Walter!"

Gore bent his head. "I wrote to her the night I saw Frances Hope," he said. "She had my letter this morning."

"This morning?" It was impossible to fathom the pain and alarm in Nance's voice. "What did you write?"

"Very little. Just that I knew about Deerehurst—that I thought it better we should not marry."

"And she got that letter this morning? She has been hours and hours alone, believing that you don't love her—that she is left utterly by herself? Oh!"

"Nance, don't! I'm sufficiently ashamed."

Nance put her hands over her eyes.

"I'm not thinking of you!" she said cruelly.

"I know. But remember, there's the wire. We can still wire. I shall tell her that you and I are coming for her to Ireland—that she will never be alone again."

Nance's hand dropped.

"But you don't understand!" she cried. "No telegram can reach her to-night. It will only get to Carrigmore to-morrow morning—and from there to Orristown. If we were to give everything we have in the world—if we were to die for it—we could not save her from the blackness, the loneliness and horror of to-night!"

# CHAPTER XX

Early on the morning that followed the storm, Clodagh stepped from the hall door of Orristown. As she stood on the gravelled pathway in the clear, strong daylight, she looked like one who has fought some terrible battle in the watches of the night, and who has been worsted in the encounter. She was pale and fragile, with a frightened query in her eyes, as though she had propounded some enormous question, to which Fate had as yet made no answer. For a time she stood in a helpless attitude, looking toward the green hill, crowned with sparsely foliaged trees, that fronted the house; then, seeming to take some vague resolution, she walked slowly forward towards the avenue, pausing where the gravelled pathway joined the fields.

There was a curious look upon the land and sea that morning, as though both were lying exhausted by the tumult of the night. All around beneath the avenue trees lay twigs and short splintered branches, to which the limp leaves, whipped to untimely death by the vehemence of the storm, still hung. Across the bay, as far as Carrigmore, the sea lay like a sleeping tiger that has prowled and harried through the dark hours of night, and now lies at rest. A wonderful pearly blue was upon the waters—long, rippling lines spread from headland to headland, like faintly pencilled shadows; but massed in a dark fringe along the curve of yellow strand was a ridge of packed seaweed, that held within its meshes a thousand evidences of the strife that had been, in twists of straw, pieces of broken cork, and long black chunks of driftwood.

She stood for an indefinite space, looking at this significant dark line standing out against the smoothness of the sand, until, half unconsciously, her attention was attracted by a sound that made itself audible from the direction of the gate, growing in volume as it advanced—the swish, swish of bare feet on soft ground. She turned from the vision of the sleeping sea, to behold a small peasant child in torn dress and dirty apron speeding up the drive.

The child neared her; then swerved away as if in fear, and continued her flight towards the house.

A sudden impulse seized Clodagh.

"Come here!" she called. "Where are you going?"

For an instant the child looked too frightened to speak; then her lips parted.

"Misther Asshlin—beyant at Carrigmore!" she said inarticulately; and, turning, she fled onward to the house.

Clodagh stood still for a moment; then she also turned, and recrossed the gravelled pathway.

She walked forward, scarcely feeling the ground beneath her feet. Her heart beat fast; a cold premonition ran through her, chilling her blood. Something was about to happen! The inertia that lay upon her mind was to be shattered! Something was about to happen!

As she reached the hall door, she saw the child vanish into the stable-yard by the small latched door in the great wooden gate; and saw Mick, escaped from confinement, come careering towards her. But for once she took no heed of his manifestations. Scarcely even noticing that he followed her, she passed into the hall, and from thence to the dining-room. There she stood for a long time listening—listening intently. At last the sound she instinctively waited for reached her—the sound of a sharp, wailing cry. With a frightened gesture she put her hands over her face; then let them drop to the back of a chair that stood beside the centre table.

She stood holding weakly to this chair, her limbs trembling, her face white, while the wailing sound drew nearer, growing more spasmodic as it approached. At last the door was thrust wide open, and Hannah burst into the room, her face blanched, tears streaming from her eyes, her whole air demoralised.

"Miss Clodagh, Masther Larry!" she muttered inarticulately—"Masther Larry!"

Clodagh held to the back of the chair.

"What is it?"

"Gone! Drownded!"

Clodagh swayed a little.

"Drowned!" she echoed in a faint voice.

"He nivver went home at all last night. And to-day mornin' they found the little boat capsized beyant at the head. O God, help the poor mother! What'll the poor woman do at all?"

"Drowned!" Clodagh said again—"drowned! Larry drowned!"

Hannah stepped forward, as though she expected her to fall; but she motioned her away.

"How did it happen?" she asked in a vague, thin voice.

"'Twas the storm! Sure, 'twas the storm!"

"But Larry was the best sailor in Carrigmore!"

She said the words involuntarily; but as they left her lips, they brought into being a new thought. She stood upright, and by a strange, slow process of suggestion, her eyes travelled to the mantelpiece, where the bundle of notes still protruded from under the clock.

What if Larry had quailed before the thought of confessing his losses to the querulous mother, who could so ill spare the money he had squandered? What if Larry had not fought the storm last night as it might have been fought? She suddenly contemplated last night's play from Larry's point of view—contemplated Larry's losses by light of the hard monetary straits that Ireland breeds.

Her blood seemed to turn to water; she felt like one beyond the pale of human emotion or superhuman help.

"Leave me to myself, Hannah!" she said faintly. "I want to be alone."

"Lave you? But, my darlin' ——"

"I must be alone."

Hannah looked at her in agonised concern.

"Miss Clodagh——" she began. But something in Clodagh's stony quiet daunted her. She gave a muffled sob, and moved slowly across the room.

Clodagh was conscious of the wailing sounds of grief for several minutes after she had disappeared; then gradually they faded, as she descended into the lower regions, to share the appalling and yet grimly fascinating news with Burke and the farm-labourers; and silence reigned in the lonely room.

When full consciousness that she was alone came to Clodagh, she let her hands drop from the back of the chair; and, moving stiffly, crossed the room to the fireplace.

She made no attempt to touch the notes that lay as Asshlin had placed them; but she looked at them for long with a species of horror. And at last, as though the thought of them had begotten other thoughts, she raised her eyes to the picture hanging above them—the picture of Anthony Asshlin in his lace ruffles and black satin coat, with his powdered hair, his gallant bearing, and dark eager face.

The eyes of the picture seemed to look into hers with an almost human smile of satire. Time had passed since that gay, reckless presence had filled the old room; dice and duelling were gone out of fashion; but human nature was unchanged—there were still Asshlins of Orristown!

"O God——" she said aloud; then she stopped. "There is no God!" she added wildly—"there is no God!"

At the sudden sound of her voice, Mick rose from the corner where he had been crouching. The sight of him calmed her; she passed her hand once or twice across her eyes, then walked quite steadily across the room.

The dog followed her closely; but at the door she stopped and looked at him.

"No, Mick! You cannot come!"

By some extraordinary sagacity the animal whimpered, and pressed closer to her skirt.

With an almost fierce impulse she stooped, kissed him once; then, holding him back, slipped through the door and closed it.

He gave a frantic bark of misery, but she did not pause, she did not even look back. Walking rapidly, she passed across the hall and out into the open.

Turning to the right, she skirted the stable-yard and the orchard, and, hurrying past the spot where years ago Milbanke had asked her to be his wife, took the path to the Orristown cliffs.

Her thoughts trooped up like living things as she stumbled forward along the uneven track. She was conscious of no fear, only of a desolating loneliness—an enormous sense of futility, of finality. Last night she had looked into the eyes of Fate, propounding the question of how she was to carry on her life, and to-day she had read the answer in the face of the portrait.

She hurried on unseeingly, covering the same track that her father had covered on the night he had ridden out and met death on the dark headland.

From time to time she stopped and looked at the sea—looked at the long curve of shining beach with its margin of dark wreckage—looked at the clustering cottages of Carrigmore, and marvelled in a dumb way at the tragedy that could underlie so calm a scene.

She had none of the nervous panic that had assailed her the night before. She was conscious of nothing but a black despair—a despair such as Denis Asshlin had been wont to drown in drink and cards. She had lived her life;

she had had her chance; and the end was failure. She had tangled the thread of her existence; and the one hand that could have unravelled the tangle was closed against her.

One thought alone she rigorously refused to harbour—the thought of Nance. Nance would have her husband—Nance would have her home, she assured herself. Nance would forget. In vain the remembrance of her faithful loyalty rose to make the assurance doubtful. As she had closed the door upon Mick, so she closed her heart to the knowledge.

There were certain hours in every life, she told herself, when the soul judged the body—judged and forgave, or judged and condemned! Her shaken mind drove her feet faster along the rugged track—faster—faster, as though Nemesis pursued her. Terrible visions rose from the sea, creeping over the cliff's edge—visions of Larry, stiff and dead, as she had seen her father, as she had seen Milbanke—visions of the cottage at Carrigmore, of her aunt's dark room, filled with the sound of lamentation.

Before she was aware of it, she turned a bend in the path, and came full upon the scene of her father's accident. She paused, gave a faint gasp, and involuntarily put her hand to her throat. Her destination was nearer than she had thought.

In a vague, startled way her eyes scanned the place, roving from the chasm in the cliff to the sweep of short grass, with its tufting of hardy flowers that throve in the strong, salt air. It was also still—so extraordinarily still! Fifty yards away a goat browsed on the cliff, and the quiet, cropping sound of its eating came to her distinctly; overhead in the pale blue sky a hawk was poised, seemingly motionless; down below her, three hundred feet away, the sea made a curious sucking noise, as it filled and receded from some invisible fissure in the rocks.

Still with her hand to her throat, she tip-toed forward to the edge of the chasm. Then suddenly she drew back, trembling and giddy. Beneath her, at what looked an incredible distance, the clear green waters formed a narrow estuary, shadowed by the towering rocks. They were like a grave, those waters—so secret, so full of mystery! Again she forced herself to look, compelling her unwilling eyes to travel up and down the great sweep of red sandstone, from the grass at the edge of the abyss to the dark water, from the water back again to the grass.

She could not be a coward in this last moment! She had never been a physical coward!

She stepped back; she took one dazed look at the world that, until yesterday, had been so very fair; she drew one long, tense, shuddering breath, closed her eyes, and went forward.

But at her first step something or some one came rushing down the cliff behind her. She gave a terrified cry, opened her eyes, and recoiled from the chasm. A moment later she had turned, trembling, crying, utterly unnerved, to find Mick leaping round her.

"Mick!" she said tremulously—"Mick!" Then a voice called to her; and, looking up, she saw Hannah, her hair dishevelled, her eyes still streaming, the yellow envelope of a telegram held in the corner of her apron.

"The fright you gave me, Miss Clodagh!" she began. "Sure, I'd nivver find you at all, only for the dog!"

Then she stopped, looking sharply at her mistress.

"Miss Clodagh, what is it all? Come home!—come home, my lamb!" Her voice, husky from tears, dropped suddenly.

But Clodagh still stood white and shaking. She had been too near the verge to be easily recalled.

"Sure, God's ways are quare, but 'tisn't for us to be judgin'; maybe He's saved worse, Miss Clodagh! Keep thinkin' that! Maybe He's saved worse!"

Clodagh covered her eyes.

"But here's somethin' for you. God help us! I was forgettin'! Will you be seein' what is in it?" She came slowly forward, extending her arm.

Clodagh took the telegram. Without thought or interest she tore it open, and her eyes passed mechanically over the written words. Then suddenly it slipped from between her fingers, blew a little way across the close grass, and fluttered down over the edge of the chasm.

As it disappeared, she turned. Her face was entirely without colour; her eyes had the dazed look of one who is confronted with a great light.

"Hannah!" she cried—"Hannah! there is a God after all!—there is a God!" She swayed suddenly; and the old servant, rushing forward, caught her in her arms.